ARCHON'S GATE

A novel by

Scott Gamboe

Published by Scott Gamboe at Createspace.com

Copyright 2011, Scott Gamboe

This book is licensed for your personal enjoyment only.

Thank you for respecting the hard work of this author.

Acknowledgements

First, I'd like to thank Mariah Donner for her hard work on the excellent cover for this novel. From the beginning, I resolved to make sure this book had a high quality image for the cover, and Mariah truly exceeded my expectations.

I'd also like to thank all the hard-working authors in the "Novel Ideas" office at zoetrope.com. Their suggestions and ideas regarding this work have helped me to shape this project into the novel you now have. I'd especially like to mention Rick Taubold, administrator for the office, and a close personal friend.

And finally, I'd like to thank my wife, Jill, and my daughter, Erica, for their continued support in my writing efforts. Without that kind of support at home, this could never have happened for me.

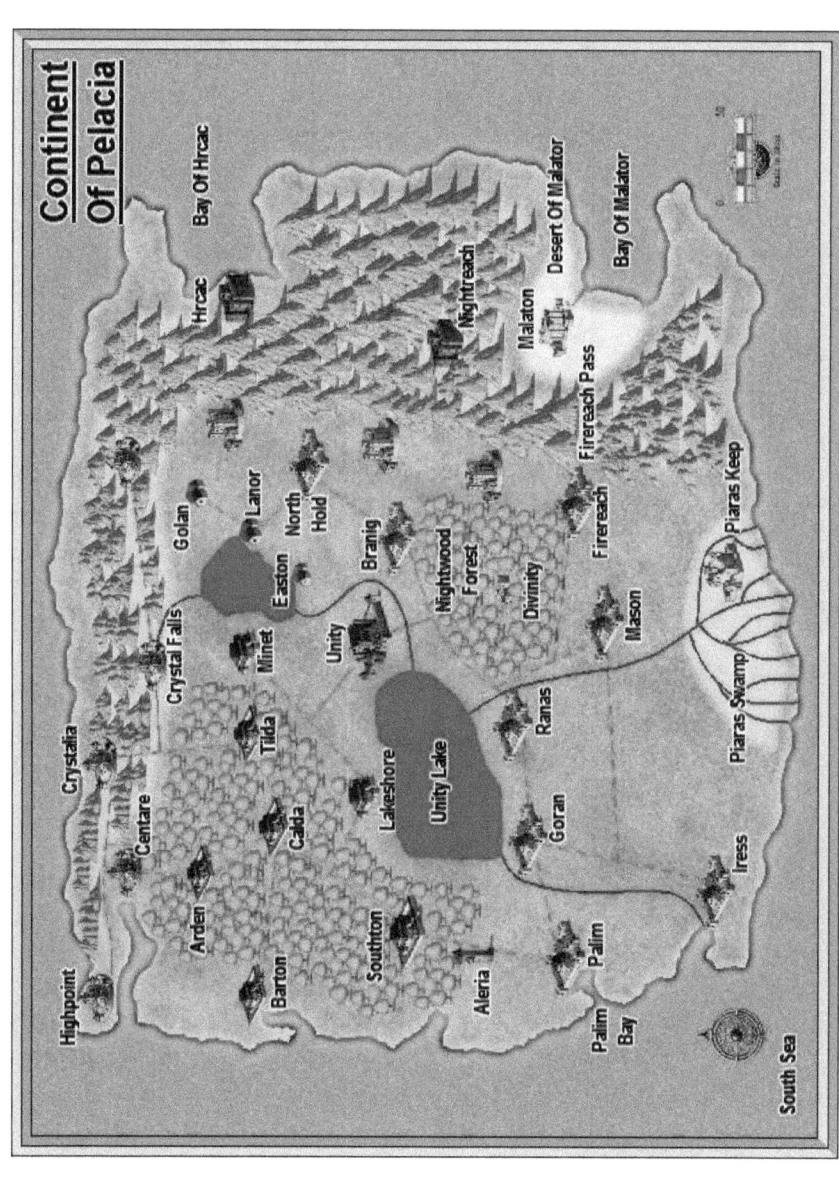

Continent Of Pelacia

Wyborn Island

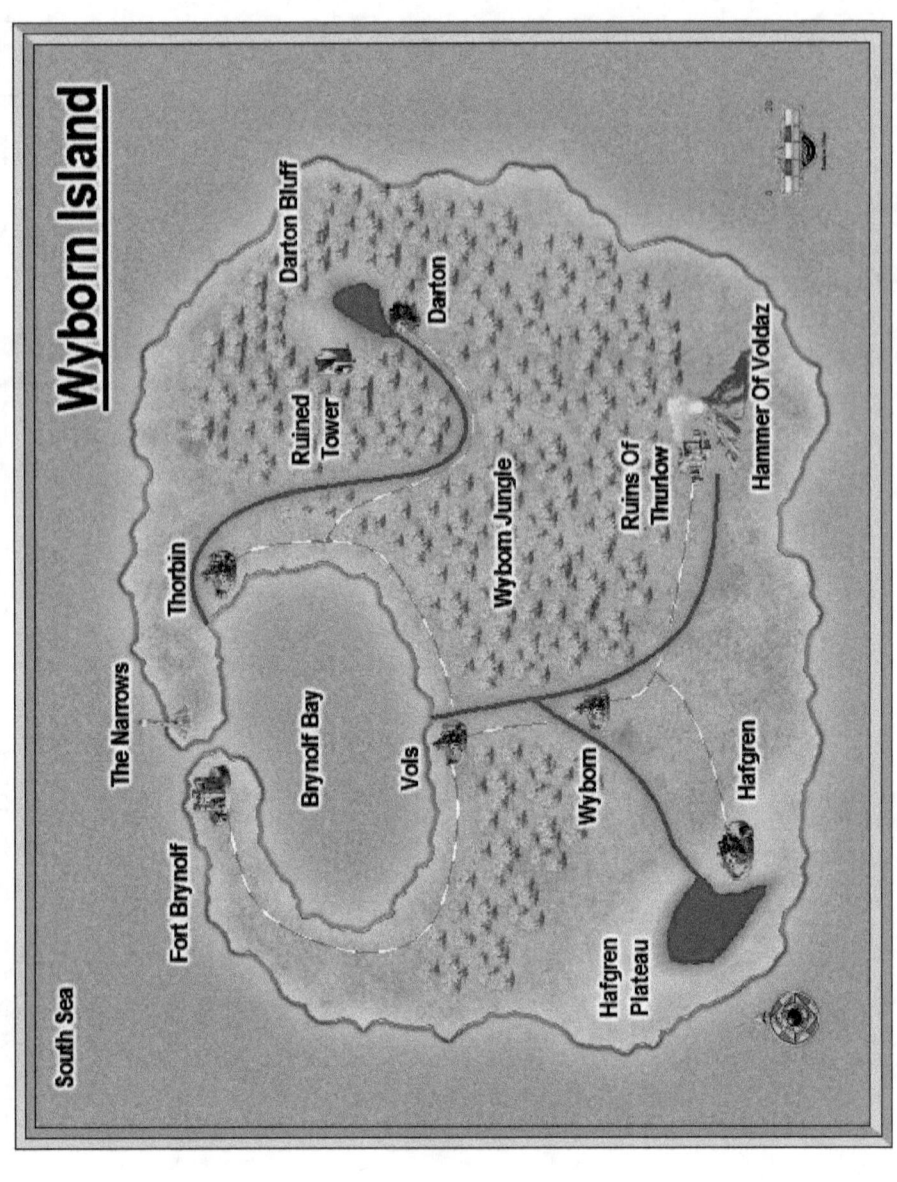

ARCHON'S GATE

CHAPTER 1

Elac shifted in his saddle as he pushed the enchanted Sword of Sir Draygen into a more comfortable position. Jayrne sat astride her own horse beside him, framed by the soaring bulk of the Paheny Mountains to the East. She wore her hair pulled tightly behind her head in a ponytail, revealing that, unlike her Elven husband, she was a Human. Elac's wife of five years gazed out at the rolling grasslands while he and Rilen discussed their tactical situation. Rilen, the only Elf to attend the War College at Fort Julan, had an uncanny grasp of military tactics. Adalyn, Rilen's wife, studied a map she held in her hands. The Elven mage pushed a lock of hair behind her ear.

Verond, their guide from the nearby farming village of Fieldstone, indicated a spot on the map. "Our village has been here for over five hundred years. It stands halfway between Fort Philand and Fort Nightwood in order to provide food for both castles. We are relatively near Nightwood Forest, but we've been protected by mounted patrols from the outposts. With the defeat of the Necromancers, the undead have all but disappeared from Palindom, so Nightwood Forest is no longer a real threat. Even the Kobolds have been only a minimal problem. Until recently, they'd hardly been seen since they retreated into their mountain stronghold following the slaughter at the end of the Third Necromancer War."

Rilen, a veteran of countless skirmishes with the Kobolds, removed his helmet. "When did the problem start?"

"We lived in peace for the first five years after the war. But about a year ago, they began attacking some of our caravans. At first, it happened rarely. But now, any caravan not heavily guarded gets hit. The few survivors brought with them tales of Kobold involvement. The village elders appealed for help, first to Duke Lonn of the Duchy of Nightwood, and finally to King Aldaris himself. Duke Lonn was too busy plotting against the neighboring duchies, and the king's army was committed to protecting the capital."

Rilen tucked his map back into a pouch. "That's why the Unity Council sent us. I have a little experience fighting Kobold raiders. After we eliminate a few of their raiding parties, they'll find another way to spend their afternoons."

Elac toyed with the golden medallion dangling from his neck. It was circular, with a curved triangular shield embedded in the center. A precious stone stood at each corner of the shield, representing the three nations of the Unity pact: jade for the Elves, sapphire for the Humans, and onyx for the Dwarves. The pendant identified him and his friends as Knights of the Council. The rank had only existed for a year. The Unity Council had promoted Elac and his companions a year prior, during festivities marking the fifth anniversary of the end of the war. Although none of them were present for the actual ceremony, they were all given the new rank. Even Prince Cassius had been given the honor, albeit posthumously.

He looked back to Verond. "How can we be certain they will attack today's caravan?"

"We haven't sent any wagons out for over a week. And this one won't be heavily guarded. We believe they watch the village and wait for an opportunity like this."

Rilen chewed on his lip. "When should they pass this way?"

"Within the next hour."

Jayrne edged her horse closer to Elac. "I don't like this. I'm going to check out the village." Without waiting for a response, she galloped away.

"She's right," Rilen said. "Something about this doesn't feel right. Let's marshal our forces and be ready to move."

"You mean, cancel the ambush?" asked Verond. "I think it's a bit premature."

"Trust him." Elac slung his shield across the saddlebow. "When Rilen's instincts speak, they're usually right."

Adalyn passed the word to the various leaders of their force of Elven militia. Within minutes they had mobilized.

"Let's keep the horses at a walk," Rilen advised. "I want to save their strength, in case we need it."

For fifteen minutes, they rode in silence. A light breeze blew, setting the grass to waving. The sun burned hot overhead in the azure sky. Elac's armor grew warm, but after years of wearing chainmail he had grown accustomed to it. Although winter had almost arrived, on this day the temperature soared. With a rueful smile, he realized that he fully expected snow within the week.

He studied the undulating foothills to their left as they meandered south. He worried that a force of kobolds might lay in wait among the crags and boulders. These days, ambushes were not uncommon. But Rilen had taken the militia far enough onto the plain that, should the Kobolds attack, they would be met with a wave of arrows from the Elven longbows. Rilen would settle for nothing less. Although the war had been over for six years, his hatred of the Kobolds had not lessened in the slightest.

Elac took a long drink from his waterskin and mopped the sweat from his brow. He reached down to stroke his horse's neck, but a flash of light to his left caught his attention. He looked up and saw a flaming arrow streak into the air.

"Rilen! Jayrne's signal!"

Rilen's face went taut. He rose in his stirrups.

"The village is under attack! Let's move!"

The horses thundered away, Rilen in the lead, with Elac and Adalyn right behind him. Elac's mount ran smoothly beneath him, matching Rilen's charger stride for stride. To their rear, fifty Elves fanned out in a wedge formation. Some loosened their swords in their scabbards, but most readied the deadly longbows that had become the signature of the Elven militia. The force roared eastward, leaving a trail of crushed grass in their wake.

They rose up from a deep swale to see the village of Fieldstone laid out before them. A force of Kobolds, at least a hundred by Elac's reckoning, had engaged in hand-to-hand combat with a score of Elves. The defenders had rallied behind an earthen berm. Jayrne charged over a nearby hill to rejoin Rilen's troops.

Rilen turned and signaled to his troops. They split into two groups. Adalyn and Jayrne led twenty Elves, longbows in hand, to flank the Kobold lines and harass them from behind. The rest, swords drawn, charged directly at the heart of the enemy formation. Elac's horse drew even with Rilen, and the two comrades led the vanguard. Elac drew the Sword of Sir Draygen. The enchanted blade, hundreds of years old, had been the gift of Sir Draygen's ghost. Although the magic within the weapon affected only the undead, the sword would still serve him well in the coming battle.

Too late, the Kobolds tried to react to the new attackers. Some of the soldiers on their left flank turned to meet the charge. With most of their numbers engaged in fighting the Fieldstone warriors and the rest trying to silence the new longbows, there were not enough Kobolds to do more than slow Rilen's assault. The crash as the two sides met left a ringing in Elac's ears. His horse pounded into one Kobold, who fell beneath the animal's hooves. Elac slashed to his left and right, sending Kobolds tumbling away. They passed through the fight, turned, and charged back in.

The Kobolds retreated into a tight defensive perimeter. Jayrne ordered her archers to cease fire and enter the fray. Even with the Elven lines closing on them from every direction, the Kobolds refused to surrender. Elven swords rose and fell, and Kobold blood stained the grass. Rilen, now on foot, slashed his way into the center of their defensive ring. He brought the dull edge of his sword down across the unprotected head of the Kobold leader. The Kobold grunted as he fell.

But even without their leader, the remaining Kobolds refused to stop the fight. With a final charge, the Elven militia swarmed all over the raiders. The battle soon ended.

Rilen issued orders to his lieutenants. While some soldiers burned the Kobold dead, others gave the Elves lost in the fight a proper battlefield burial. Rilen and Elac tied the Kobold leader's hands behind his back and set two Elves to watch him. Rilen sent squads out in different directions to scout for further enemy patrols.

Rilen and Elac returned to their prisoner. Elac knelt beside him, raising one furry eyelid to check the Kobold's pupils. "I wish Gillen was here. He could wake up this Kobold in a heartbeat."

Rilen snorted. "That's if Zantar would allow it. Personally, I don't know why the Unity Council wanted us to try and take one of them alive in the first place."

"We need to know what they're up to."

"Isn't it obvious?" Rilen stood and gestured all around. "The king of Palindom is dying, and the dukes are more interested in putting themselves on the throne than they are in protecting their own. We'll have civil war by year's end. Palindom is about to go up in flames, and the Kobolds know it. They see this place as ripe for conquest." He kicked the unconscious Kobold's booted foot. "I don't need a murdering Kobold to tell me that."

Elac sighed. "The Council just wants to get some answers. We need to trust their leadership."

Jayrne joined them, a shiny longsword in her hands. "Look at this. I think this sword belonged to your prisoner."

Elac glanced up at the well-polished blade. "It's nice. A little long for a Kobold, perhaps, but I don't see the point."

Rilen frowned as he hefted the sword. "This is a new kind of steel. Much lighter than anything I've ever seen before." Stepping away from the others, he brought the sword up to an *en garde* position. The weapon hissed and whistled as he swung it through an intricate display of swordsmanship. He looked around, found a discarded Kobold helmet, and slammed the blade against it. "Incredible. The balance is perfect, and hitting that helmet didn't even nick the blade. I'd like to know where he came by it."

Adalyn hung her helmet and shield on her horse. "Did they all have these swords?"

"No." Jayrne shook her head. "Only five, that I've seen. Maybe they have a limited supply, so only certain people get them."

The sun hung just above the horizon when the group finally took a break for dinner. The funeral pyre consuming the Kobold bodies cast an eerie glow on Elac's plate. His appetite was subdued, and he ate more out of necessity than hunger. Rilen, seemingly unaffected by the day's events, flopped to the ground beside Elac with his second plate. Jayrne and Adalyn had gone further upwind to escape the stench.

An Elven soldier approached and knelt beside Rilen. "Shantos wanted me to tell you your prisoner is awake."

Elac shoved the last few bites into his mouth and handed his plate to the soldier. He and Rilen crossed the encampment to where an Elven healer tended to their prisoner.

Rilen folded his arms. "How is he, Shantos?"

She rose to her feet, packing her medical supplies into a leather bag. "I'd say he has a concussion at the very least. It's too early to be certain, but I don't think you fractured his skull. He'll live."

"Pity." Rilen moved closer to stand over the Kobold. "You. What's your name?"

He hesitated for a few moments. "Rhun."

"What was the purpose behind this raid?"

Rhun glared at his captor, then turned away. "Go to Hell."

Rilen drew his sword. "I guess that's the end of this conversation."

Elac stepped between the two antagonists, his hands on Rilen's shoulders. "Will you let me deal with this?" He winked.

Rilen gave a barely perceptible nod, then glared at their prisoner. "You can try. I can always kill him later."

As Rilen stalked away, Elac eased himself into the grass beside the Kobold. "Are you hungry?"

Rhun nodded. "I could eat."

At Elac's request, two Elves repositioned Rhun's bindings to put his hands in front. Another brought him a steaming plate of stew. Rhun wolfed his food down, pausing to drink from a waterskin.

"If you're waiting for me to thank you, don't hold your breath," he said.

Elac shook his head. "I just want to save you some unnecessary trouble. Rilen has difficulty handling these matters in a civilized way."

"He's right, you know." Rhun set his plate aside. "Taking prisoners is a sign of weakness. If our situations were reversed, I would have killed you."

Elac motioned to where two Elves sat and studied one of the new blades. "Where did you get such a magnificent weapon?"

"From a friend."

"You're not being very helpful."

"Never said I would be. Mark my words. You had better take your comrade's advice and kill me now. The first chance I get, I'll escape, but not before I kill as many of you as I can."

Elac rose to his feet. "You know what will happen to you now? We're to turn you over to the Duke of Branig for trial. I don't think there's any doubt as to how the trial will end."

"So?"

"So, I'm trying to save your life! Help me, and I can help you."

Rhun snarled and bared his teeth. "Run along back to your gardens, little Elfling. Let's put it this way. If you had been captured, and your soldiers slaughtered, would you answer any questions put to you? I think not."

Elac gave a casual shrug to cover the bitter disappointment he felt. "Suit yourself. We'll be on our way in about an hour."

\#

The Elven patrol, positioned both in front of and behind the wagon, passed under the raised portcullis and into the city of

Branig. While not as heavily fortified as a castle, Branig nonetheless was well-protected. Thick walls of stone towered above the plains, surmounted by battlements and protected by ballista towers at each corner. Steel portcullises warded both entrances. Piles of stone completely blocked the southern entrance, which Elac took as a sign of the times. The northern gate, open only during the hours of daylight, had a strong military presence.

The caged wagon bearing Rhun rattled and wobbled on the cobblestone streets. A squad of city militia, aware of the Elves' prisoner, met them just inside the city walls. After a brief exchange, the city troops led the way into the heart of the city.

They passed through the city market, which appeared quite subdued compared to Elac's last trip. Those few merchants present spoke in hushed tones, and many shops were closed. A number of citizens filled the streets, but all walked at a brisk pace, heads down, not speaking to their neighbors. The populace stood on edge.

The wagon rattled to a stop in front of the city armory. Four men dressed in leather armor emerged, one of them carrying shackles, and they stood before the cage. Rilen unlocked the door. The guards dragged their captive onto the street. They shackled and tied their prisoner, then dragged him into the building. The captain of the guard offered the Elves the hospitality of the barracks across the street before he slipped inside to follow the guards.

After seeing that their soldiers had been taken care of, Elac and his friends went to a small pub down the street for dinner. The Happy Harpy, a clean establishment with attentive barmaids and a skilled cook, had few patrons. They chose a booth near the back of the room and huddled down over their drinks.

Elac stared into his ale mug. "Do you think they'll execute him?"

Rilen laughed. "What else? Duke Norseth is struggling to maintain order among his subjects. Palindom is on the brink of civil war. With the public execution of a Kobold raider, he can show his people that he's doing all he can."

"Or at least provide that illusion," Jayrne said.

"How bad is the friction here between duchies?" Adalyn asked.

Rilen raised his hands slightly. "Hard to say. Some of the dukes have aligned against others. Some are trying to stay out of the fighting for now and hope to be the strongest faction when the king dies. Others are simply too weak to be any real threat. But there's plenty of trouble to go around. Most of the duchies are on the verge of open warfare."

Elac tapped a finger lightly on his lips. "I think we could use the Kobolds to our advantage. If we sent neutral emissaries, maybe Elves or Dwarves, to the various dukes, we might get them to work together. They could declare a truce and work together to eliminate the Kobolds. That should make it more difficult to go back later and fight one another."

Jayrne gave Elac a sympathetic smile. "Elac, dear, sometimes you are still a bit naïve. If you could somehow convince the dukes that your plan wasn't some elaborate scheme to defeat their armies and seize power yourself, they would turn on each other in a heartbeat as soon as they defeated the Kobolds. They all have their eyes locked on one target: the crown."

"Exactly." Rilen moved his enchanted longbow to give himself more room. "The Kobolds are actually little more than a nuisance to them. In fact, their presence provides the dukes with a legitimate reason for having their troops in the field. The Unity Council could never make them call their soldiers back, at this point."

Jayrne waved to the barmaid and ordered four more mugs of ale. "What of the stories about the strange creatures attacking small settlements and convoys on the Ranset Plains?"

"I've heard the tales from several travelers, myself," Elac said.

Rilen shook his head. "I think the people are still jittery. It's only been six years since the end of the last Necromancer War. All manner of nasty beasts had been summoned up back then. It's no wonder the peasants are jumping at shadows. All the Kobold activity of late is probably driving some of the larger animals down from their homes in the Paheny Mountains. There are things living up there that not even the Kobolds have seen."

"And don't forget," Adalyn said, "there is still a connection to the Plane of Mist near Trackers Keep. Anyone passing through there could be attacked by the denizens of Ardea. And the mist demons aren't the only things living there. I'm sure that's the source of at least some of the stories."

Elac frowned. "Maybe in the mountains, but not out on the plains. I'm not ready to write this off just yet."

Rilen smiled, his eyes brighter. "I'll tell you what I am ready for. Dinner."

The barmaid stood before them with steaming plates of beef and potatoes. The ale flowed freely, and all talk of Kobolds, wars, and strange new monsters faded away.

#

Seven uneventful days passed. Elac emerged from the tent he shared with Jayrne. He clambered to his feet and stretched as he admired the red ball of the rising sun. Their patrol had seen no further action. For some reason Elac could not fathom, the Kobold raids had come to at least a temporary halt. If the peace lasted for three more days, Rilen's militia would head home to Golen, and another militia would take their turn.

Rilen knelt by the fire, brewing a hot drink. Elac moved to his side. "Good morning."

"Elac."

"What's on the agenda today?"

"We'll move our sweep a little closer to the Paheny Mountains. I don't want to allow Kobold scouts to roam freely out there and report our troop movements. If we haven't seen anything by tomorrow night, we'll make our final pass right up into the foothills."

"Rilen!" The shout came from a sentry. "Several horsemen are approaching from the north, riding hard."

"Make ready!"

At Rilen's shouted command, the camp came to life. Elves spilled from their tents, some still sliding into their mail shirts and groping for their weapons. Elac joined the archers. He nocked an arrow and waited for the riders to draw closer.

But their preparations were unnecessary. The red and white banner of the Unity Council fluttered from the lead rider's lance. At a gesture from Rilen, the soldiers galloped into the center of the camp.

A man dressed in outrageous, bright finery climbed shakily from his saddle. "Are you Rilen?"

"I am."

"By order of the Unity Council, you and the other Knights of the Council are to leave your troops in place and proceed forthwith to the Duchy of Nightwood. Word has reached the Council that Duke Lonn is about to make open warfare upon the Duchy of Firereach. You will take whatever steps are necessary to prevent this."

Elac exchanged a look with Rilen. "What do we do?"

"We have no choice in the matter." Rilen kicked dirt on the fire. "We go to Nightwood." He looked back at the courier. "What about my militia? Their time is almost done. I don't want them being left out here any longer than necessary."

"That is up to you. You may either assign them to continue their patrol under a new leader, or send them home early. The Lanor militia is already in this region, so you stand relieved."

Rilen turned and strode away from the group. Elac nodded to the messenger. "We'll send our troops home. You may inform the Council that we will look into this matter and report back to them."

With a stiff bow, the man remounted his horse and led his retinue away at a trot. Elac returned to his tent to pack what he needed for the journey.

An hour later, the four Knights of the Council rode north to Fort Nightwood, the seat of power for the duchy. Rilen seethed in a silent fury, his jaw muscles twitching. His scowl warned his companions that he would not engage in conversation. Elac rode beside Jayrne. As usual, she seemed nonplussed. Adalyn rode on the other side of Elac, her expression unreadable.

Elac could bear the silence no longer. "Don't you think it would have been prudent to at least bring a few troops with us? After all, we don't know what Duke Lonn's reaction to our arrival will be. Besides, we've moved into areas of the Ranset Plains that our troops haven't been regularly patrolling. I'd hate for the four of us to run into a company of Kobolds."

Jayrne smiled and nodded to their reticent leader. "Yeah. I'd feel sorry for the Kobolds."

Rilen turned and glared at the riders behind him. The three remained silent as long as they could, then one by one started laughing. Rilen looked away, but not quickly enough to hide the traces of a smile.

"Seriously, though," Elac said, "I would have been more comfortable with an escort."

"Me too," Adalyn said. "But if we rode into Duke Lonn's territory with a small army at our backs, his reaction would have been less than cordial."

Jayrne chewed her lip. "Do you think he'll respect our banner from the Unity Council? We could order him to back down."

Rilen did not bother to turn in his saddle. "Hah."

"I doubt it," Adalyn said. "He will probably grant us safe passage. He may even deign to meet with us. But if these dukes won't respond to orders from their own king, I seriously doubt they'll listen to the Council."

"Then I'm not sure what the Council expects us to do," Elac said.

"They expect us to fail," Rilen said. "That way, they can place the blame on us when the whole country breaks out into civil war."

Elac thought about that as they rode along. His own cynicism regarding the Unity Council had faded somewhat following the end of the Third Necromancer War. The old, corrupt Council had been replaced with a young, idealistic group who seemed to have the best interests of the people at heart. For a time, Elac's faith in the governing body had been restored.

The trouble in Palindom had showed him how wrong he may have been. First one dispute and then another had arisen, but the Council had done nothing. Certainly, they had issued their share of proclamations that certain hostilities had been resolved, but the fighting never stopped. Even threats of intervention had not helped. Of course, the Council had been issuing such threats for over two years but had never acted on them. Such empty promises lose their luster over time. He sighed. He and Jayrne had fought and defeated Volnor, the most powerful Necromancer in history. The undead army, on the verge of defeating the allied army, had been routed. Now, just six years later, petty differences and power-hungry leaders pushed the continent toward open warfare once more.

"What was that?" The sharp cry came from Jayrne.

All four stopped their horses, peering into the darkened grassland. Jayrne squinted and pointed west. Elac's hand hovered over the hilt of his sword. He swept his gaze back and forth through the rolling terrain, but found nothing.

"What did you see?" he asked in a quiet voice.

"I'm not sure. It all happened so quickly. There was something out there, about three feet tall. I think it was brown in color, but it's too dark out to be certain. Right after I saw it, it disappeared."

Rilen relaxed in his saddle and turned his horse once more. "I think we've been on the road too long. We're all exhausted, and that can make you see things that aren't there."

Jayrne gave a slow nod, her eyes still fixed on a point somewhere in the darkness. "Rilen may be right. Nothing could move that fast. It just vanished."

Adalyn shook her head. "I'm not ready to dismiss it. I trust your senses, Jayrne. And I'm not ready to dismiss the rumors of strange creatures as a falsehood. It's not beyond the realm of possibility for some of the stories to be true."

They set out once more, but without the light banter they enjoyed earlier. All four wanted nothing more than to reach Fort Nightwood and get a night of rest before the negotiations began. They rode for another hour before Rilen called a halt. He suggested they eat dinner and rest the horses before they went any further. If they should encounter a large force of Kobolds, he wanted their horses to be ready to run. They ate a cold dinner and washed it down with water. Elac kept a nervous watch while they ate.

It began as a movement in the corner of his eye. He spun quickly and faced to their rear. Something dark and narrow, standing upright and walking on two spindly legs, darted around the perimeter of their camp. He thought he saw two short arms protruding from the front.

"Rilen!" he hissed between clenched teeth. "Over there!"

At the sound of his voice, the shape stopped, turned . . .

And disappeared. One moment it was there, and the next, it was just gone. Elac rose to one knee and drew his sword. He spun and faced different directions to try and catch another glimpse of the creature stalking them.

"Rilen, did you see it?"

Rilen shook his head. "No. When I looked where you were pointing, there was nothing."

"I saw something." Adalyn grasped her bow in her free hand. "I happened to look that way right before Elac called out. There's something out there."

Rilen swept his gear together and tucked it into a saddlebag. "Okay, people. Let's ride. We need to get to Fort Nightwood as quickly as possible."

CHAPTER 2

They chose not to risk injury to their horses, so they kept the pace at an easy trot. Besides, Rilen had cautioned them that they still had no idea what followed them, or if it posed an immediate threat. Kobold patrols, on the other hand, were a more likely danger, especially if they galloped around in the dark. Even on the darkest of nights, Elac's Elven eyesight allowed him to see for a short distance. He rode close to Jayrne. As the only Human in the group, she would be the most vulnerable to an attack out of the murky night.

Elac caught sight of something ducking into a tall stand of grass, but with just a fleeting glimpse he had no way of knowing what he had seen. He spun in his saddle and watched the spot where it disappeared. Nothing emerged to threaten or follow them. He felt jumpy, and wondered if his edginess had caused him to see things. He rubbed his eyes and rode on.

Twice in the next hour, Rilen spotted something moving along their right flank. Each time, as soon as he pointed, whatever he had seen disappeared. Elac wondered if there was just the one creature, or if there was a whole pack of them. He found the prospect of fighting a bunch of creatures in the dark, strange beasts that could vanish at will, daunting. He wiped the sweat from his palms and focused on keeping watch.

They were still a league from the fort when the creature finally struck. Elac heard a low grunting, snuffling noise. The grass to his left ruffled violently. His horse lurched to the right, then bolted in a panic. Elac yanked on the reins, but the horse refused to slow. With a shrill whinny, it pounded across the plains. He finally managed to stop the beast. He dismounted as his friends charged up.

Blood flowed down his horse's left rear leg. He dabbed at the wound with his tunic to clean it up. A shallow, wedge-shaped incision marked the chestnut coat. Rilen slipped out of his saddle to examine the wound.

"I've never seen anything like this, Elac."

"Nor have I. I think we'd better be moving. If that thing returns . . ."

Jayrne's eyes darted about. "Or if it brings friends."

The two Elves swung back into their saddles and resumed their journey. Elac thought he heard the grunting sound behind them again. Before he could warn the others, a group of torch-bearing footsoldiers appeared over a distant hill. Adalyn bowed her head in concentration, spoke in the language of magic, and gestured. After a few moments, she looked up, a half-smile on her face.

"Human soldiers, on patrol. I think we can pick up the pace a bit."

Elac slapped his horse's reins, and the beast leapt ahead. They galloped over the uneven ground, somehow managing to stay in the saddle. Rilen lit a torch and held it high to illuminate their Unity Council banner. The soldiers formed up and awaited their arrival.

Rilen reined in, but his prancing horse refused to stand still. The gleaming golden medallion announcing him as a Knight of the Council hung over his burnished chain mail. The soldiers' captain recognized it immediately.

"Good Sir Knight! What brings you into these dangerous lands this late?"

"We've been ordered to speak with Duke Lonn regarding the matter of the conflict with the Duchy of Firereach," Rilen said. "We would like to discuss the matter with him behind the safety of your walls."

"Sir Knight, I am afraid that is impossible. You see, Fort Nightwood has but one hundred soldiers manning the walls. His Grace and the rest of his army have marched south to engage the enemy. We shall escort you there at once."

"Do you have any medical supplies with you? One of our horses was injured during our journey. I would see his wounds tended before we move on."

The captain called to his soldiers, and a short, thin man in leather armor emerged from the formation, a cloth bag slung over one shoulder. He glanced at the Knight of the Council medallions and bowed. "My name is Heloss. Who is injured?"

"My horse." Elac swung down from his saddle and touched his horse's leg. The horse quivered and stomped as Heloss brought his torch closer to examine the wound.

He gasped. "Captain Lohosh! They were attacked by the Cassibellanaus!"

A nervous mutter rippled through the assembled soldiers. Several of them broke formation to face out into the night. They lit more torches and carried them to the perimeter. Several sergeants barked orders, and the cohort reformed to place the travelers within their ranks. The soldiers stood shoulder to shoulder, shields locked to form a solid barrier.

Heloss cleaned the blood from the wound on the horse's leg. He applied an herbal salve, which he said would prevent infection, before he bandaged the leg. Another group of soldiers erected a series of tents in the center of the periphery.

Elac exchanged a look with Rilen, then placed a hand on Lohosh's shoulder. "Captain! It's imperative that we meet with the duke as soon as possible! Surely we're not stopping for the night?"

"I'm sorry, good Sir Knight. When the Cassibellanaus is about, it's too dangerous to travel. We have to form a shield wall and wait for daytime. Once the sun is fully up, the beast will rest for the day."

Rilen folded his arms across the chest and sighed. "Captain, you and I both know that the battle will likely be joined at first light. We cannot afford to—"

"As I said, Sir Knight, it's too dangerous. I have already lost too many men to that evil creature. Come. Sit by the fire with me, and I'll tell you the story."

#

The fire crackled and popped. The dancing light added an eerie effect to the tale Lohosh revealed to them. "It's a creature straight out of ancient mythology, really. Of course, I can't say for certain it is the actual Cassibellanaus mentioned in the old tales. But for all intents and purposes, we treat it as such.

"According to legend, the Cassibellanaus was created by the evil elder god, Telandos. He had planned to make hordes of them. A Human demi-god named Lomor penetrated Telandos's sanctuary and did battle with him. At the time, the Cassibellanaus was but a drawing.

Lomor defeated Telandos in battle. With his dying breath, Telandos breathed life into the image of the Cassibellanaus. It came alive just as it was. From the side, it appears as a brown, short-haired creature with thin legs, short arms, and sharp claws and teeth. But from the front, it is so thin that it cannot be seen. That's what makes it so dangerous. How can you fight something you can't see?"

"Is there just the one creature?" Jayrne asked.

"In our mythos, yes, it was unique. But in reality, who's to say? There might have been just the one tonight, or there might've been a dozen. When you can't always see it, there's no way to be certain. We've learned some hard lessons in the last six months. We no longer send out small patrols at night. Just six weeks ago, a twelve-man patrol disappeared two leagues from here. We found their bodies the next day, with wedge-shaped bite marks on them. The creature is dangerous."

Rilen eyed the defenses the soldiers had erected. "Now I see the reason for the circular line. No matter which way the Cassibellanaus faces, someone will be able to see it."

Lohosh rose to his feet and gave a respectful bow. "I must take my leave and tend to my soldiers. We'll leave as soon as the sun is high enough."

#

They left at first light and rode hard across the plains. By the time they arrived, it was too late. Elac placed a hand on Jayrne's shoulder. The two stared across the plain at the abhorrent sight before them. The armies of Nightwood and Firereach had locked in battle. Infantry soldiers from the two sides had fully engaged. The screams of the dying carried on the light breeze. Archers from both sides fired indiscriminately into the melee, killing friend and foe alike. Elac swore and kicked a small rock.

At that point in the battle, Duke Delan of Firereach appeared to have the advantage. His forces had the superior position of higher terrain. Not only did this give his archers greater range, but the thought of a downhill charge from Delan's heavy cavalry made Elac shudder. The battle lines formed by the purple- and black-clad soldiers of Nightwood began to crumble. Delan's archers increased their barrage.

Duke Lonn's forces rolled a pair of catapults into place. They loaded the weapons with pots of burning pitch while engineers waved batons to direct the crews in the aiming of the siege engines. With a deep thrum, they fired their deadly fusillade into the air. The twin fireballs arced across the morning sky to land with devastating effect among the ranks of Duke Delan's archers. Flames erupted and spread in earnest, consuming the whole of the hillside in a wall of fire and black smoke. The catapult crew scrambled to reload their weapons.

Without the support of their archers, the Firereach soldiers' assault faltered. Duke Delan, situated further up the slope, signaled for a full cavalry charge. The target was clear: he had to take out the catapults. In response, Duke Lonn committed his reserve of heavy spearmen. They formed a bristling wall between the reloading catapults and the charging cavalry.

Rilen threw his hands in the air. "For the love of . . . someone please tell me this isn't happening."

"What?" Adalyn asked.

"A cavalry charge against spears? Head-on? Downhill or not, it's suicide! To stop these Kobold raids, we need as many of these men as we can muster. They're going to slaughter each other while we stand here and watch."

Rilen's words proved prophetic. The horsemen flanked the battle lines and, at a full gallop, lowered their lances as they charged the line of spearmen. The two forces met with a titanic crash. The agonized squeals of the horses mingled with those of the warriors. Elac, sickened by what he saw, turned away to contemplate the distant horizon. When he looked back several minutes later, the tide of the battle had turned. Lonn's forces had punched through Delan's defensive lines. All along the front, Firereach soldiers fell back singly, then in groups. Soon, it became a rout. The victorious soldiers of Nightwood pursued their foes across the grasslands and slaughtered those they caught. The battle had ended.

Duke Lonn's forces had emerged victorious, but at a steep price. The dead from both sides carpeted the battlefield. Elac guessed Lonn's casualties to be well over half of his force, and

Delan's were even worse. Many of those who lived would be unable to fight for weeks, or even months. Both sides had been severely weakened by the conflict. Elac wondered what the battle had accomplished.

Rilen took up his horse's reins and swung into the saddle. "Come on. Let's go round up the two dukes and get to the bottom of this mess."

With their escort formed up around them, they rode at a trot onto the battlefield. Elac held their banner high so there would be no confusion as to what they were about. One of the soldiers with them led the group to the brightly colored tents marking Duke Lonn's headquarters. They dismounted and left their horses to be tended by Duke Lonn's grooms. The group slipped between two of the tents into a circular amphitheater. Their escort guided them across the open area to the entrance of an enormous, solitary white tent. A pair of hulking soldiers, dressed in gold burnished ceremonial armor, guarded the opening. Each bore a long, highly polished silver pike. At the group's approach, the soldiers crossed their pikes, barring entrance.

"Who comes before his grace, Duke Lonn, Lord of Nightreach?" one shouted with a great, booming voice.

One of the men escorting them dropped to one knee, his head bowed deeply. "Noble Sir, I am but a humble servant of his Grace, bringing before him a messenger, who—"

With a wide sweep of his arm, Rilen brushed the obsequious soldier aside. "We are Knights of the Council. Now step aside and let us through before I gut you where you stand."

The two guards stood immobile, their jaws hanging slack, shocked into inaction by the outburst. They reminded Elac of a pair of bookends, and the thought brought a brief chuckle to his lips. When the guards still didn't move, Rilen grabbed one of the pikes from its owner and snapped the shaft across his knee. He glared at the other guard, who hastily yanked the tent flap aside to allow them entrance.

Duke Lonn stood at a low, wooden table in the center of the pavilion, surrounded by four of his military advisors. A detailed map lay unrolled across the table, with hand-drawn symbols denoting the locations of the forces of the two armies. While the duke looked on, his aides redrew the symbols based upon the latest information supplied by his scouts. Their discussion of the battle broke off as the group entered.

The duke's gaze fell on the newcomers, then dropped to the golden pendants around their necks. Hands on hips, he stepped around the table. "Ah. Messengers from the Council. And to what do I owe the honor of this visit? Come to congratulate me on my victory, no doubt."

"Hardly." Elac answered the challenge. Rilen had suggested earlier that Elac, the most diplomatic of the group, would perform their duty with more tact. "The Council wants to know why you have gone to war."

"Bah! When I am king, we will dissolve that worthless body. I owe them no allegiance!"

"You have sworn fealty to your king, and he has pledged his loyalty to the Council. You violate the king's trust by waging this war."

"Are you ordering us to stop the fighting?"

"Not yet. But I must insist you tell me what led to the conflict."

"We march to war because of atrocities committed by that foul pretender to the lands of Firereach. His soldiers have been raiding our outlying villages. They raze our lands, kill our men, and take our women and children. Delan's armies are responsible for more heinous crimes against my people than even those committed by the Kobolds six years ago." His eyes narrowed and he clenched a fist in the air. "I will not rest until his entire duchy lies in ashes!"

Adalyn took a step forward. "Your Grace, how can you be certain it was the armies of Firereach who are responsible? We've seen a resurgence in raids by Kobolds, all along the border of the Paheny Mountains. It could just as easily have been—"

"Do not question my word!" he shouted. "But if you must take proof back to that petty excuse for a council, I have it. I sent my new domestic policy advisor, Penallo, to investigate several sites that were burned to the ground. He found ample evidence. Some of the villagers defended their homes. Although these brave people fell in battle, they cast down some few of their attackers. Penallo found bodies of men in full Firereach military uniform, buried in the rubble of three different villages. And in one case, he found a witness who yet lived. Before the man died, he told of the atrocities committed by the soldiers of Delan."

Jayrne shook her head slowly. "Your Grace, surely you have something more than this. Any man may imitate the crest of another. Perhaps one of your rivals dressed his soldiers in the uniforms of Firereach, in an effort to start a war that would weaken both of your duchies? That's how I would do it. I could sit back and watch you two slug it out. After you've sufficiently weakened each other, I could invade both territories almost unimpeded."

"And besides," Rilen said, "this isn't exactly what I would call a victory. Yes, you drove Delan's forces from the field, but look at your own army. You took heavy casualties in every division except your archers. And Duke Delan's ridiculous head-on charge into the formation of spearmen decimated his heavy cavalry. Between both duchies, you don't have enough of an army left to take over an unarmed caravan."

The duke's face turned red, and the veins bulged in his neck. "Do not try to minimize what my army has accomplished here today! We routed a numerically superior foe and decimated

Delan's ability to make war! He barely has enough men left to hold his castle. I'll muster another army and lay siege to what remains of his domain.

"And as for further proof, I have it here in my camp. I shall instruct someone to take you to the tent where we are holding Duke Delan's top general, captured this day as the coward fled the field of battle."

His plate mail armor rattled as he stomped across the tent and shouted few orders to the men outside. Another soldier led Elac and his friends back out of the command area and through several rows of tents. They stopped at a rickety wooden building, which may have been a barn at one time. The entire building leaned to one side, and gaps in the seams where the walls met allowed torchlight inside the building to be seen from without. The door hung from hinges coated with rust. It screeched when one of the leather-clad guards opened it to allow the Knights of the Council to enter.

No more than a dozen prisoners sat inside. All of them were bloodied and battered, and some were not even conscious. The guard indicated an area at the rear of the building, cordoned off by a canvas flap. Rilen led the way, sweeping the flap aside as he stepped through the opening.

The general lay strapped to a table. His uniform clung to his body in tatters. Sticky trails of blood ran from numerous wounds up and down his body. Two men stood at his side, one in a leather smock, and the other in blue finery.

The man in leather spoke first, his voice low and rough. "What do you want? No one is allowed in here."

The other waved him to silence. "It's okay, Hamor. These people are Knights of the Council. I am Penallo, king's advisor. Have you come to hear the story of how this devil led his men to attack our lands? General Halton has issued a full confession."

The general stirred, trying unsuccessfully to raise his head. "Knights of the Unity Council? Have you come to participate in this, too?"

"General," Elac said, "we have come to learn what has caused the two duchies to go to war. Can you help us? Have your troops been conducting raids into Nightreach?"

General Halton slowly licked his cracked and bloodied lips. "No. Not once, at least not before we came over the border in retaliation for—"

Hamor struck a stunning blow across the general's temple. Penallo crossed his arms and stepped closer. "My dear general. We were doing so well just moments ago. Things will go much easier for you if you just cooperate."

With a feral growl, Rilen crossed the room. He seized Hamor by the smock and threw him into the wall. Bloody knives and white-hot pincers tumbled to the floor. Hamor rolled to his feet, dagger in hand. Rilen left his weapons sheathed and took a step closer. Hamor lunged with his blade, but Rilen caught his wrist in a vise-like grip. He slammed Hamor's arm across his knee, snapping the bone and sending the knife skittering away. He seized Hamor by the shoulders, slammed his face into a wooden pillar, and allowed the limp body to slide to the floor.

Penallo backed away a step at a time, his wide eyes locked on the unconscious man on the floor. Jayrne stepped between him and the door, her hand on the hilt of her shortsword. "Going somewhere?"

Adalyn pulled a chair away from the wall and slid it over to Penallo. "Have a seat. It looks like we have a lot to discuss."

Penallo eased himself onto the chair as he looked back and forth between the four Knights. "What do you want? Are you with Delan?"

"We told you what we want," Elac said. "We're here at the behest of the Unity Council. All we want to know is why your two duchies are at war."

"But . . . but this general has already confessed to unspeakable acts of warfare! Surely the word of such an officer is proof enough."

"I place no faith in any confession obtained by torture. This man would have confessed to being a Kobold, if you wanted him to." He jabbed a finger at Penallo's face. "Don't move, and don't speak. We'll deal with you shortly."

While Adalyn severed the prisoner's bonds, Elac found a clean towel and a bucket of water. He used them to clean the blood from the general's face. Adalyn tended to his wounds, and Jayrne stood behind Penallo, in case he decided to try to leave.

"General Halton? My name is Elac. My friends and I are Knights of the Council. We are here to determine the cause of this war. What do you know of the events leading up to the conflict?"

The general groaned as he pulled himself into a sitting position. "I believe it started about six months ago. We lost several wagonloads of food supplies along the border with Nightwood. At first, we assumed it was Kobolds. But then some of our border villages were attacked. Our mounted patrols roamed the lands between the sites of the attacks and the passes in and out of the mountains, but to no avail. It wasn't until one of our cavalry units stumbled upon a dozen infantrymen from Nightwood, leaving the scene of another caravan attack, that we learned the truth of the matter."

Rilen's expression never changed. "So you deny the allegations made by the Duke of Nightwood?"

"Absolutely. The only time my soldiers have crossed the border into his realm is in pursuit of the bandits who have attacked us."

Elac tossed his medical supplies onto a table. "General, for your sake, you had better not be lying to us. The penalties for lying to investigators acting on behalf of the Unity Council can be quite severe."

"I swear it upon my life."

Rilen stood motionless for several moments. He stepped around the prisoner and grabbed Hamor by his apron, hauling him to his feet. Hamor groaned. Rilen shoved him across the room, where he fell beside Penallo. At a gesture from Adalyn, the two remaining guards sat down beside the duke's advisor.

"Listen to me." Rilen took a few steps closer and glared down at them. "This man is still your prisoner, until such time as the hostilities cease. But there will be no more torture. Not of him, nor anyone else. There will also be no accidents. All of your prisoners will still be alive and unharmed when we return. If I find out you have violated this command, I will order your executions. And I will carry them out, personally. Do I make myself clear?"

Silence greeted his harsh pronouncement. The four men before him managed over-exaggerated nods in response. Rilen stomped from the room, pausing to knock a brace of knives from their stand near the entry. The others followed him outside. They were a safe distance from the prison before Elac spoke.

"Do you think they believed you?"

Rilen smiled. "I think my point was clear."

"Do we actually have the authority to execute those men?" Jayrne asked.

"I have no idea. But if I don't know, I can promise you they don't know, either. They won't take a chance."

"What now?" Adalyn asked. "Each side has accused the other of atrocities. We all know this is just part of their posturing for the throne, but we still need to put an end to it."

"Actually," Elac said, "I think we've learned a great deal here today. We know both sides firmly believe the other has made forays into their territory. I had the impression that they truly believe the accusations."

"So, where does that leave us?" Jayrne asked.

"We need a little more information," Elac said, "but I believe someone external to the conflict is playing both sides against each other. Someone who could benefit from a weakened army in both duchies."

Rilen grabbed an apple from a food cart and took a bite. "My first supposition would be another duchy. It wouldn't even have to be a neighboring duchy. Any duke with aspirations for the throne might be involved."

"Could there be more than one duke involved?" Adalyn asked.

"I doubt it," Jayrne told her. "One thing all conspiracies have in common is that the fewer people who know about it, the better. Each additional duke involved in the plot doubles the number of people who are aware of it. That also doubles the chances of someone either defecting or releasing the information in an interrogation."

"We're leaving out two very viable suspects," Rilen said. "The Kobolds and the Unity Council."

"Rilen." Adalyn looked to the sky. "The Kobolds are a definite possibility. But the Unity Council? I think you're going a bit far with that one. Why would they send us here if they were the ones stirring up trouble? And why would they want turmoil within Palindom anyway? It makes them look like impotent fools."

"The Council is a long shot, I'll grant you," Rilen said. "But think about it this way. What happens when we come back and haven't resolved this conflict? Troops under the banner of the Council will march into both duchies to put an end to the fighting. The Council will declare the fighting to be over. Anyone who defies the declaration will be subject to Council sanction. Or attack by Council forces. Either way, the Council wins."

"We need to find a neutral observer," Jayrne said. "There has to be someone who knows what's going on but isn't involved in the fighting and has no aspirations of gaining power."

"How about Duke Marac of Ranset?" Adalyn asked. "I've heard that he has no desire to become king. And being this close to the fighting, he is bound to have some observers in the area."

Rilen nodded. "Marac is a good man. I'll trust what he tells me. I would guess that he has some of his forces arrayed along the border with the Duchy of Firereach." He glanced up, squinting into the late afternoon sun. "Let's rest our horses for tonight. That'll give Elac's mount a chance to heal a bit more before we ride out again. Besides, I'd rather not risk running into that Cassi-whatever tonight."

"Cassibellanaus," Jayrne said with a laugh.

"Do you want to take any troops with us?" Elac asked.

"Let's take a few," Rilen said. "We'll take a dozen of Duke Lonn's heavy cavalry for our escort. We can keep our numbers low, so we don't worry Duke Marac. At the same time, we'll be weakening Lonn's offensive capability. I imagine both he and Delan will have to return home, at least for a while, to recover from the day's festivities. Maybe by then, we can come up with an answer."

CHAPTER 3

A strong, cool breeze kept the air comfortable despite the bright sun overhead. Cuts and draws overlaid the seemingly endless plains especially the further south they rode. A young knight named Kilbourn, the commander of Duke Lonn's cavalry unit, rode at the head of the column with Rilen. Kilbourn's squire rode to his left and slightly behind him, bearing the standard of the Knights of the Council. Kilbourn had wanted to travel under his own banner, but Rilen had refused. Elac agreed with him. Keeping to the symbols of the Unity Council assured that their intentions would not be misconstrued. Elac did not want another battle.

They passed the indeterminate border between duchies and continued riding south. Kilbourn, his visor raised, swiveled about in his saddle.

Elac nudged his horse closer. "What's the matter, Sir Kilbourn?"

"I had expected to find Duke Marac's soldiers at the border. His realm appears undefended."

"They're out there," Rilen told him. "His scouts picked us up over an hour ago. I'm sure at least one has ridden back to let the duke know we are here."

Kilbourn's eyes flew open wide. "I've seen nothing. Are you sure?"

Rilen frowned at him, an eyebrow raised, then shook his head and looked away. For the next hour, Duke Marac's forces remained hidden. Rilen halted his column to rest the horses.

While Kilbourn's soldiers watered their mounts, Rilen faced south, one hand raised to shield his eyes from the sun.

A lone rider appeared from a draw two hundred yards in front of the group. Kilbourn shouted to his men, but Rilen ordered them to stand fast. The rider carried a flag of truce in one hand. He approached at a casual walk. Rilen and Elac stepped forward to meet him. The man stopped his horse, plunged the staff of his banner into the ground, and dismounted.

"I am Kuminol, advisor to Duke Marac. What business do the Knights of the Council have in these lands?"

Elac removed his riding gloves. "We have come, under the authority and order of the Council, to determine the root causes of the conflict taking place north of your borders. To that end, we need to speak to Duke Marac."

"My scouts mentioned four Knights of the Council. Who are these others?"

"They provide our escort," Elac said. "We have been set upon by a strange beast. A creature so thin, it can only be seen from the side."

Kuminol's easy manner changed immediately. His face drew into a scowl, and his hands balled into fists. "We, too, have encountered this creature. A demon from the netherworlds, it is."

"The soldiers accompanying us are here for our protection, in case we see this beast again."

"A wise precaution. I will take the lot of you to see the duke."

Elac nodded. "You have our thanks."

After gathering their group once more, they followed Kuminol southwest across the grasslands. A stretch of woodlands in the distance drew nearer. Without delay, Kuminol led them into the woods along a well-worn path. Five minutes later, they entered the encampment of Duke Marac.

The duke greeted them as they dismounted. He wore a simple blue robe, his only weapon an unadorned shortsword. He wore a neatly trimmed gray beard, and kept his hair cut just below the shoulders. He extended a calloused hand in greeting.

"Welcome, Knights! What brings you to Ranset?"

Rilen cast a glimpse over his shoulder at Duke Lonn's heavy cavalry. "Your Grace, might we meet somewhere in private?"

Marac's expression never changed. Elac's merchant's instincts told him the duke had immediately understood the caution implicit in Rilen's request. "By all means. Follow me."

Marac brought the four Knights to a small wooden structure. He held the door open while the others stepped inside. Elac explained the nature of their quest, as well as the events that had befallen them. Marac sat in stoic silence while he listened to the tale.

"My friends, these are indeed sad tidings you bring. I'm afraid I can only offer you scant assistance in your quest. I can confirm what you already suspect about outside interference in the conflict. About a year ago, a man came to my court. He claimed to have information about a neighboring duke's plans to invade the Duchy of Ranset. He seemed believable, at least at first. Had he come to town freely offering the story, I would never have listened. But he only gave vague hints of what he knew, then refused to tell us anything further without being paid.

"He told us that Duke Delan of Firereach planned to invade my lands. He gave me a broad overview of how the duke's scheme would work. He said it would start with border raids. Delan would capture some of my caravans and harass my people. As he grew bolder, he would strike at my villages. Eventually, he would have enough power to confront me directly. The man showed us an intercepted letter, written by Delan himself, attesting to this claim.

"I consulted my council of advisors on the matter. While we agreed that his story sounded, at the least, plausible, we were hesitant to accept it. The letter he brought could easily have been forged. I would not drag my army into battle unless I knew it was unavoidable.

"I sent my spies and scouts all along the border with Firereach, day after day, but nothing materialized. At last, I decided the man was either mistaken or lying. I ordered that he be brought in for further questioning, but word must have gotten back to him. When my men went after him, he had disappeared.

"I heard nothing further on the matter until today. From the way you described the situation, I'd say the plot that failed here has succeeded elsewhere."

Jayrne set her wine cup down. "I wonder why the other dukes were so inclined to believe him."

Marac shrugged. "It's fairly simple, really. Many of our dukes, Delan and Lonn included, have their eyes set on the throne. They simply had to act as if they believed the stories of atrocities in order to justify their rush to war. Each feels he can eliminate the competition for the crown of Palindom. The current dynasty is ending, and with it, I'm afraid, our national stability."

"We appreciate your help, your Grace," Jayrne said. "I think we had better be going."

"Where?" Elac asked.

"Back to where Duke Lonn's forces are encamped. The man who attempted subversion here is likely in league with those who caused the war between Firereach and Nightwood. Lonn said Penallo was his new advisor. He might be the link we are seeking. If he is, he won't be sticking around much longer."

Elac smiled. "You're pretty good at this, dear."

She arched her eyebrows. "I've had practice. Not to mention all the time I spend with some pretty unscrupulous Elves."

They led their horses to the edge of the trees and mounted up. Over the objections voiced by Sir Kilbourn, Rilen led the group away at a fast trot. They had little chance of completing their return journey before sunset. The knight voiced his displeasure with the thought of being caught in the open after dark, especially with so small a force.

Sir Kilbourn rode between Elac and Rilen. "I'm not worried about the Kobolds, you understand. It's these various creatures spotted on the plains the past few months. Some of them have decimated cavalry units twice our size. Just last week, a platoon of fifty horsemen was set upon by two of these beasts. Only one man made it back alive."

"Regardless," Elac told him, "the urgency for us to return is too great. Even if we were certain to be attacked, we would still need to ride tonight. Penallo could be a full day ahead of us if we wait."

They ate dinner in the saddle. Rilen allowed short, infrequent breaks to rest the horses. As the sun slowly faded to a red ball of fire, he allowed them to rest their mounts one final time. By Elac's reckoning, they still had over five leagues to go before they returned to Duke Lonn's army. Until they did, they were vulnerable.

Rilen gave a sharp command, and they picked up the pace once more. Elac made certain he kept the Sword of Draygen clear of his cloak, ready to be drawn at a moment's notice. He removed his longbow from his pack, strung it, and slipped his quiver over one shoulder. They rode past a grove of trees to their right. The green and brown boughs faded to gray in the dying light.

At the rear of the column, a horse shrieked in pain. Elac wheeled his mount about. An armored knight tumbled away and tried to rise to his feet. His horse lay on its side, ravaged by a nightmare. The creature had dark, leathery skin coated with a viscous slime. It stood on four short, powerful legs, and a long, narrow tail thrashed about behind it. A red tongue snaked out from between enormous teeth as it raised its head to study the rest of the group.

Kilbourn raised his sword. "Cingesta! Poisonous bite!"

Elac nocked an arrow, aimed, and fired. The arrow streaked across the grassland to bury itself in the thick hide. Rilen fired several arrows in rapid succession. The Elf's uncanny accuracy, coupled with the enchantments in Sir Aleron's longbow, made every shot strike true. He put the bow aside as he closed with the cingesta. Adalyn and Jayrne drew their own bows, while Elac discarded his and joined Rilen in the assault. All about the group, swords rang free of their scabbards.

Two knights closed with the cingesta, one from each side. It leaped to the rear, teeth gnashing at the closest knight as it moved. The substantial jaws clamped down on the knight's leg. The dagger-like teeth punched through the steel armor. Blood gushed through the ruptures in the greaves. The knight swung his sword at the leathery neck, but the blow barely managed to cut the cingesta's hide. The creature drove at him again. The long white fangs punctured steel once more, and this time it dragged the knight from his horse.

Rilen jumped from his saddle onto the creature's back. He drove the point of his sword home as he landed. His blade bit deeply, and the cingesta roared in pain. It rose on its hind legs as it thrashed about. The tail snapped sideways like a whip. It knocked two more knights from their saddles and sent their horses sprawling in the grass. Rilen, his legs wrapped about the cingesta's midsection, held onto his sword with both hands to keep from being thrown. Several knights swung their weapons at its legs, but the damage they inflicted was minimal.

Elac charged the cingesta, head-on. Sir Draygen's sword slashed at a front leg and drove deep into the limb. The cingesta backed away and turned its full attention on Elac. He held Sir Draygen's ancient blade before him and followed the creature's darting head movements with the tip of the sword. The cingesta became so focused on him that it failed to see the danger creeping up on it from behind.

Encased in the near-invisibility of Sir Draygen's cloak, Jayrne fired an arrow point-blank into the cingesta's hindquarters. With a deafening bellow, it whipped its head about to face the new assailant. Elac took advantage of the distraction to deliver another crippling blow. His stroke completely severed the undamaged front leg. Rilen, one hand still firmly on his sword, drew a dagger. As the head whipped about one more time, he plunged the short blade into one glowing eye.

This time, he could not stay on the cingesta's back. It rose on its hind legs to stand nearly vertical. He fell to the ground and rolled to his feet, dagger in hand. The cingesta roared once more, then began to back away.

Elac stabbed at the remaining eye, but the cingesta jumped out of his reach. The muscular tail snapped sideways and lashed across a knight's armored torso. He spat blood as he fell to one knee, the side of his armor caved in. The cingesta moved in to finish him off, but Adalyn intervened. The Sword of Salenas, its enchanted length glowing slightly in the near-darkness, swung in a swift arc at the creature's neck. The blade, which could penetrate even the strongest armor, clove through skin, flesh, and bone to sever the neck. With a gush of blood and a final thrash of the tail, the cingesta fell silent.

Elac panted as he stared at the fallen creature. For a few moments, he was entranced. Where had this powerful beast come from? Why had it attacked them? Then he remembered the wounded. All about him, human and cingesta blood dappled the trampled grass. Five knights lay on the ground, and three of their horses had been critically wounded. Elac cleaned and sheathed his sword, then set about checking the fallen knights.

He knelt beside a man whose breath came in short gasps. The side of his armor had been caved in during the fight. Blood flowed from his mouth and nose. Elac feared he might have internal injuries, wounds which were too grave to be treated in the field. He reached for a buckle to remove the breastplate.

Kilbourn grabbed him by the shoulder and spun him around. "You fools! This is why I didn't want to travel at night! Your foolishness has cost us dearly!"

"As we told you, this matter was urgent." Elac brushed the gauntleted hand from his shoulder and stood. "It's still urgent. We must treat the wounded and see about making some litters to carry the fallen. We can still reach the encampment safely."

"No. My men will go no further. We make our stand here. If you and your friends choose to ride further this night, then begone. You carry the devil's luck with you. I don't doubt you'll be killed before you go another league. If you have half a brain, you'll wait here with us."

Rilen wrenched his shortsword free from the cingesta's back, wiped it, and slid it into his scabbard. "We don't have that option, and neither do you. Tell your men to make ready. As soon as the wounded can be moved, we'll be riding out once more."

"As I said, we will go nowhere this night."

Rilen reached for his sword, but Adalyn placed a restraining hand on his arm. "Sir Kilbourn, you have been ordered by your duke to escort us and to obey our orders as his own. We also carry the authority of the Unity Council. You must finish your task and escort us back to the encampment."

"No." He looked around at his troops. "Men, I would not deign to speak on your behalf in this matter. If any of you would choose to obey the command to continue with these Knights of the Council, do so now." Only a few even bothered to look up, and those immediately returned to their tasks. "The matter is resolved. Stay or go. I care not. We'll be here until the dawn."

"As you wish," Adalyn said. She placed a foot in her stirrup and swung into her saddle. "This will be brought to the attention of Duke Lonn upon our return."

They rode into the night, leaving the armored soldiers to their own defenses. After an hour of hard riding, the faint, distant glow of torches appeared. At one point, Elac thought he heard screams on the plains behind them, but he had no way to be certain.

They slowed their mounts to a walk as they neared the perimeter of Duke Lonn's forces. After a brief delay, the guards escorted them to the central amphitheater. Duke Lonn sat in his tent. On one side sat a young, raven-haired woman, and on the other he had a barrel of ale. He looked up at their approach.

His laugh faded to a frown. "I hadn't expected you back so soon. Where is Sir Kilbourn?"

"Sir Kilbourn chose to abandon his duty," Rilen said through clenched teeth. He recounted the battle with the cingesta. "He said his knights would stay in a defensive posture until morning, and he refused the order to come with us."

Lonn dropped his head against the cushions and closed his eyes. "Larina, get out. Now." The young woman rose to her feet and scampered out through a rear entrance. "Where are they?"

"We left them about four leagues southwest of here," Rilen said. "Several of them were pretty badly wounded."

"The ones who were bitten won't live through the night. The bite of a cingesta is almost always fatal."

Elac's eyes opened wide. "You mean there are more than one of those things?"

"Yes. We've seen as many as three cingestas at one time. The Cassibellanaus is unique, as far as we can tell." He raised his voice. "Wenol! Get it in here!"

The tent door parted, and a short man with gray hair, dressed in silver robes, stepped inside. "Yes, your grace?"

"At first light, I want you to send one hundred men southwest from here. Sir Kilbourn and his men have disgraced their positions. They are to be arrested and brought to me at once." Wenol bowed and backed out of the tent.

Lonn's voice dropped to a more subdued tone. "What will you do now?"

Elac eased himself into a chair. "We need to speak to Penallo. Where is he?"

"He rode to Fort Nightwood immediately after you left. Why?"

"A man recently approached Duke Marac of Ranset. His story of looming border raids mirrored the one you told. Except in his version, you were the aggressor. Luckily, rather than rush to war, Marac investigated the matter further and found the story to be false. He tried to locate the man to clarify the matter, but he had disappeared.

"That would have been probably a month or two before you started hearing those same stories. Based upon what General Halton told us, someone gave an identical story to Duke Lonn at about the same time. It looks like the three events are connected."

"Bah! General Halton confessed his crimes. He has admitted to participation in those very raids."

"He was tortured into that confession, your Grace," Adalyn said. "Tortured at the direction of the very man we need to talk to. Penallo, your advisor."

Duke Lonn gnawed at a fingernail. "I won't risk a small detachment of my troops at night. Tomorrow morning, I'll send a group of light cavalry to track him down. They should be able to catch up to him. I'll wring the truth from Penallo myself."

Elac nodded. "Keep us posted. We'll be leaving for Duke Delan's castle at Firereach in the morning. Hopefully, we can arrive while his advisor is still there. Maybe we'll get some answers."

Lonn swirled the ale in his glass as he stared at the contents. He remained silent for several long moments before he spoke. "My friends, I would like to accompany you. I fear my war here may have been in error. My rush to judgment may have cost hundreds of lives on both sides. I would like to speak to Delan personally. We need to hammer out a peace accord as soon as possible."

#

At dawn, Elac and his friends left for Firereach Castle, accompanied by Duke Lonn and ten of his personal bodyguards. Rilen did not rush their pace. They had only about a four hour ride ahead of them, so there was no need to push the horses. The overcast cast a chill on them, and the rains came almost immediately. Elac drew his cloak about his armored frame. One thing he had not missed from the quest six years prior was bad weather. Near the halfway point of their trek, their journey was delayed by the slow, painstaking crossing of a rain-swollen creek.

Elac judged the time at near noon when the castle guarding the entrance to Firereach Pass appeared in the distant gloom. One of the duke's bodyguards raised the standard of the Knights of the Council, while the duke himself held up his banner of truce. Rilen slowed their pace even more to allow the defenders in the castle time to assemble a group that would ride out to meet them.

The two parties came together about a half-mile from the gates of the castle. Duke Delan sent out a contingent of heavily-armored cavalry to parlay on his behalf. Duke Lonn planted his banner of truce in the ground and dismounted. One of Delan's soldiers snarled and reached for his sword, but a companion stayed his hand with a gesture.

"Hold. You will not violate the banner of truce."

"But my brother—"

"Your brother was killed in battle. There is nothing dishonorable about that." He dropped to the ground and bowed to the duke and the Knights of the Council. "I am Sir Droliss. What is the purpose of this visit, my Lords?"

Elac returned the bow and extended a hand in greeting. "We have come in peace. We bring only the soldiers you see here. Someone has been manipulating the forces of both duchies to cause this war. We are here to undo the problem before things get any worse."

Duke Lonn stepped forward. "And I have come, virtually alone, to show the sincerity of my desire for peace. My bodyguards will come inside your gates, for their own safety, but will go no further. I will travel alone to speak with Duke Delan. We must end this conflict as quickly as possible."

Droliss's eyes shifted between the men standing before him as he considered their statements. "Okay. Come with me."

He led them to the gates of the ancient castle. Vines climbed the outside of the walls. The mortar holding the bricks together had crumbled in places, but the walls still seemed sturdy enough to withstand an assault. Soldiers dressed in red livery leaned out over the battlements to peer at the group passing through their gates. As he had promised, Duke Lonn ordered his troops to remain just inside the castle walls. He proceeded deeper into the castle without them.

The entourage stopped in a central square. Elac recognized what he remembered as a thriving marketplace, filled with villagers selling their wares. Now, the shops were closed. The streets were piled high with supplies in anticipation of the coming siege by the forces of the Duchy of Nightreach. Two men entered the square from the far side and stood before them.

One of them, an elderly man in blue robes who walked with a cane, Elac recognized as the duke's chief advisor, Rastec. Elac had met him several times over the past few years while negotiating trade agreements between the duchy and Golen. The other wore battered chain mail armor surmounted by a dirty black cloak. A silver medallion hung from his neck.

Rilen stepped forward and grasped forearms with the armored man. "General Kasowen, it's good to see you."

"Rilen. How did you end up in this mess?"

"All in good time, General. We need to speak with Duke Delan immediately. We have Duke Lonn with us, and he seeks peace between your duchies."

Kasowen studied Duke Lonn for a few moments. He gave a curt nod before he whirled about, his cloak flitting behind him. He led them along a wide thoroughfare to an ornate stone building. Twin statues of lions flanked the stone walkway, and a pair of guards stood on the porch. They banged their fists to their chests as the general passed. They kept their gazes locked straight ahead and never even glanced at the general's guests.

Kasowen traversed a long, wide hallway. Red carpet interwoven with complicated patterns in a variety of colors covered the floor. Various portraits of Duke Delan and his family adorned the walls. The door at the end opened into a study. Duke Delan sat on a plain wooden bench, his head against the wall and his eyes closed. He opened one eye, nodded at the general, then rose slowly to his feet as the others entered.

He crossed his arms when he saw the man who accompanied the Knights of the Council. "Duke Lonn. What are you doing here?"

Before Lonn could answer, Elac stepped between them. "We brought him here under a banner of truce, your Grace. We learned of a plot against the entire nation of Palindom. The instigation of war between the various duchies is a part of it. To that end, men posing as advisors worked their way into your trust and convinced you that the other side was making raids into your territory. Duke Lonn is here to negotiate a cease-fire between your duchies."

Delan glanced back and forth between Lonn and Elac. His narrowed eyes betrayed his suspicion. "You have proof of this, I take it?"

"We do. They first approached Duke Marac in this manner. He investigated too deeply and learned of the deception, so the perpetrators moved on. They succeeded here and in Nightwood. We tried to question Lonn's advisor, but he fled the castle as soon as we left for Ranset.

"We learned from one of your generals that you were given stories of villages being burned to the ground by Nightreach forces. Is this true?"

"A man named Hedgrel approached me several months ago about these attacks. I was skeptical at first, but as the attacks mounted, his warnings became harder to ignore. But it was more than just stories. I would not send my troops to war based upon the word of someone I hardly knew. He brought word of a planned assault against a border village. He warned us that Nightreach soldiers would conduct the raid.

"I hid a company of soldiers among the villagers. Just as he had predicted, a group of bandits attacked the village. We easily drove them off after killing half of their numbers. At first, they seemed to be a bunch of rogues out to loot the village. But beneath their shabby equipment, we found the markings of the soldiers of Duke Lonn. And those who ran away escaped by returning north, across the border and into Nightreach. There was no doubt in my mind at that point."

"Where is Hedgrel now?" Rilen asked. "We need to speak with him."

"A man rode into camp yesterday as sunset. He spoke to Hedgrel immediately, and the two left at first light. Hedgrel said he had a family emergency, and . . ." Delan froze in mid-sentence. He took a few halting steps to his desk. With a bellow of rage, he swiped a stack of papers and books onto the floor. "I have been deceived! When I learn who was responsible for this, he will pay with a thousand deaths!"

"The first step, your Grace, is to end the fighting," Adalyn said. "Duke Lonn is here. Summon a scribe and draw up the peace proclamation."

"And I would like to look at any documents he left behind," Jayrne said. "In fact, I want to see everything he didn't take with him. I might be able to find a clue as to who is behind this."

"And then we march to war, once again," Lonn said. "This time, side-by-side."

Delan strolled forward to stand in front of Lonn. They grasped forearms in the warrior's salute. "So be it."

CHAPTER 4

Elac and Rilen sat at a long table, eating a breakfast of roasted mutton. The low murmur of the conversations of Delan's soldiers filled the room. Mainly, Delan's men discussed the end of the war. Elac decided that for the most part, they were happy the war had ended, as they had dreaded the possibility of a protracted siege. But he sensed an underlying regret over their lost opportunity to seek retribution against the army which had just driven them from the field so effectively.

Jayrne dropped down beside Elac and tossed her plate onto the table. She slammed her mug next to the plate, sloshing a small amount of ale onto her hand. After a moment's consideration, she lifted the mug and drained its contents.

"Good morning, Jayrne." She grunted in response. He decided to try once more. "You were gone when I woke up. I take it you didn't find what you wanted in Hedgrel's possessions."

She exhaled sharply. "I just dug through everything in his room. There wasn't one scrap of parchment to be found. Nothing to show where he came from. Nothing to tell me who is paying him. What a colossal waste of three hours." She rose slightly from her seat, then dropped back once more. "Maybe you guys can help with one little mystery." She reached into a deep pouch at her waist and pulled out a silver medallion. "This means nothing to me. I was hoping you could shed some light on it."

Elac held it up to the light. The medallion was highly polished and fit comfortably into the palm of his hand. The outer edge was engraved with the image of interwoven branches. The likeness of a wild boar adorned the center. It had an exquisite design, down to the boar's sharp tusks.

"Nice. Where did you get it?"

Jayrne's dimples betrayed her attempt at maintaining a scowl. She smiled. "Just keeping in practice. It was the only item Hedgrel left behind that was worth anything. But seriously, since it stood out, I thought it might be important."

"I don't recognize it. Rilen?"

He handed the medallion to his companion. Rilen examined both sides, shrugged, and handed it back. "I've never seen anything like it. Adalyn should be here soon. We can ask her."

"Ask me what?" Adalyn surprised Rilen with a kiss as she sat down beside him.

Elac slid the medallion across the table. "Jayrne . . . recovered this from Hedgrel's possessions. We were hoping you might know if it has any significance."

"You found this in Hedgrel's room?"

"I did. Everything else in there was old clothing and boots."

Adalyn laid the medallion on the table and tapped the engraving with a slender forefinger. "This is the family crest for the Dukes of Ranset. Or rather, it used to be. I was at his castle about five years ago, doing some research for Silvayn, when Duke Marac changed the emblem. Most of these were melted down, but he kept a few of them around as keepsakes."

Jayrne's jaw dropped wide open. "You mean . . . he stole it!"

Elac smiled. "He stole it . . . from Duke Marac. He stole it a year ago, when he was there trying to stir up trouble."

Rilen pursed his lips. "It's pretty thin evidence."

"It's the best we've got."

They were silent for several moments, until Rilen took the medallion once more. "Okay. Let's return to Unity. We'll make the journey in stages to avoid any more night encounters on the plains, if at all possible. We can escort Duke Lonn back to Nightreach, then swing north around the forest and make our way to Unity."

"Maybe once we deliver our report, we can return to Golen," Elac said. "I'm ready to go back home."

Rilen rubbed his eyes. "Elac. I thought I had cured you of your grand visions of the Unity Council. You know as well as I do that after we tell them what we know, they'll find another task for us. We'll have to find out who is behind the conspiracy. Or maybe there's another brushfire somewhere else, and they'll want us to put it out. I wouldn't make any long-term plans, if I were you."

#

Elac dozed in his saddle, lulled to sleep by the constant rolling motion of his horse. The overcast sky obscured the morning sun. The clouds were heavy with the threat of rain. A chill wind blew from the north, a harbinger of the cooler late-autumn weather on the way. Elac opened one eye to check their progress, then resumed his nap.

Rilen's voice woke him. "Riders are coming."

Elac followed Rilen's gaze to see a formation of about fifty soldiers on horseback, riding over the hill to their west. Even from a distance, the jingling of their armor was faintly audible. Rilen cast his scrying spell, but Elac knew the answer before Rilen announced it. The riders were Elves.

Elac and his friends waited as the Elven force crossed an open field and joined them. Rilen shook hands with the Elven commander, a veteran warrior named Jarok. Elac recognized the banner, a maple tree on a red background, as belonging to the militia from the rebuilt village of Lanor.

"Rilen," Jarok said. "The Council said you would be in the area. They were vague about the purpose of your mission. I assumed you were trying to find another way to annoy Silvayn." He winked at Adalyn. "Besides having your wife teach you magic outside of Aleria."

"It's been a little busy around here. I hope you can handle it after your last task."

"You mean the trip to the Desert of Malator?" Jarok rolled his eyes. "Someone reported seeing strange people in the ruins of the temple of Malator, so we had the distinct pleasure of wandering the ruins for a week. At least here, we might see a little rain." He glanced at the gray skies. "Or snow."

"I figured you would be the one to replace my militia on patrol, Jarok. Have you had any encounters with Kobolds yet?"

"Just one, and they ran off as soon as they saw us."

Elac nudged his horse closer. "Have you seen any unusual creatures?"

Jarok looked askance. "Now that you mention it, the last two nights my sentries have reported seeing something. It's short and thin, and it's very fast. It hasn't actually attacked us, but it has been stalking us. My soldiers have tried to get a better look at it, but as soon as they approach, it disappears."

"We've seen it," Elac said. "The local armies are terrified of it. It's so thin, it can only be seen from the side. It hunts at night and is afraid of nothing. And it has waylaid small armed patrols, so don't count on your numbers to protect you."

Jarok nodded slowly. "We'll keep that in mind. So, Rilen, what brings you here?"

"We had to shut down the conflict between Firereach and Nightwood."

"What did you do, kill everyone?"

"Hah. Hah, hah. It looks like a foreign power may be involved. Someone misled each duke into thinking the other had been making border raids. The two men responsible have escaped. After we escort Duke Lonn to Nightwood, we'll take this news to Unity."

"That's a long side-trip. How about if we take the duke to Nightwood? You would save several days if you ride directly to Unity from here. You could skirt Nightwood Forest along the southern edge."

Rilen glanced back to the duke, who nodded. "That would be very helpful, Jarok. I owe you one."

"Yes, you do. And I'm one to collect on my . . . what's that?"

To their north, a column of black smoke drifted into the air, leaning slightly toward them as the wind dragged it southward. Rilen drove his heels into his horse's flanks. Elac, Adalyn, and Jayrne followed right behind him. The combined armies joined the race northward across the plains.

They topped a small rise. Less than a quarter mile distant, a caravan of wagons lay in smoking ruins. All along the line, Kobolds scurried about. Some, swords in hand, chopped at the soldiers who remained to oppose them. Others dashed from place to place, lighting new fires and rounding up the caravan's horses. Rilen urged his force to run faster. Elac glanced to his rear where the heavily armored Human cavalry fell behind the fleet horses of the Elven patrol.

Rilen took aim with Sir Aleron's Longbow. Even from over two hundred yards, Elac knew the enchanted weapon would enable Rilen to hit his target. The bow string snapped, and an arrow streaked away. Rilen nocked another arrow and fired again. The others prudently waited until they were closer to release their first volley. Elac checked on the cavalry again, but they were nowhere to be seen.

The Kobolds, under a wave of incoming arrows, located the source. Most of them charged in chaotic fashion to meet the onrushing Elves. The two sides collided with a resounding crash. Many of the combatants were hurled from their saddles. Adalyn parried a sword blow with her shield, then countered with a swing of the Sword of Sir Salenas. It cut through her opponent's shield and severed the arm at the elbow. She thrust the sword home, and the Kobold tumbled from his horse. Rilen drove his horse into the midst of the enemy. He swung his sword from side to side, and the Kobolds gave way before him. Those who opposed him lay piled in his wake.

Elac guided his horse into the trail of carnage behind Rilen. As Kobolds tried to close on Rilen from behind, they met Elac and his magical blade. Once, three Kobolds closed on Elac, intent on eliminating Rilen's protector. Jayrne appeared suddenly off to one side. She cast off her near-invisibility and dragged one Kobold to the ground. A slash of her dagger ended his struggle.

The tide of battle turned against the Kobolds. First singly and in pairs, then finally all at once, they tried to flee the scene of the battle. Some gained riderless horses and raced away from the encroaching Elves. Jarok's troops encircled the remaining Kobolds, but they refused to surrender. Elac and his friends had no choice but to kill them all.

Elac rode a short distance in pursuit of the fleeing Kobolds, but his fear that they would escape proved unfounded. Duke Lonn had led the heavy cavalry in a flanking maneuver. The Kobolds rode their horses right into a waiting trap. The armored horsemen fell upon them like a pack of dogs. None escaped.

Detached and lightheaded, Elac surveyed the damage to the caravan. Had it been just six years prior that a group of

Kobolds had attacked a caravan Elac had been part of? He was but a merchant then, and had required Rilen's help to live through those hectic weeks and months. Now, he was the rescuer. He felt somehow redeemed.

While many of the Elves and Dwarves in the caravan were dead, many more yet lived. There were a number of grave injuries to tend, and the fires had to be put out. But it could have been much worse. Elac dismounted, Adalyn and Jayrne at his side. They inspected the bodies of three fallen Kobolds piled together near a burning wagon.

One Kobold opened his eyes. Blood poured from an ugly wound in his side. His eyes wobbled about uncertainly, and a trickle of blood came from his ears. Elac thought he did not have long to live. He knelt beside the dying man.

"What's your name?"

"I am called Enecs. Fifth Phalanx. I am sorry, Overseer. The filthy Elves snuck up on us, and there were too many. We fought hard . . ." He broke off in a fit of coughing.

Adalyn murmured in the language of magic, then released her spell with a gesture. She leaned close to whisper in Elac's ear. "He thinks you're a Kobold. I've cast a spell to encourage it."

Elac nodded. "You fought very well, brave soldier. This defeat was not your fault. Someone should have warned you about the Elven patrols in the area. Who gave you the order to come here without proper information about enemy troop movements?"

"The orders came from my phalanx leader. He said Solone had assured him the military forces of these duchies would be too busy fighting each other to worry about us." Another coughing fit wracked his body. He grasped Elac's cloak, leaving a trail of blood on the cloth. "What happened? Solone was never wrong before. He is guided by the hands of the gods. He—"

The kobold exhaled slowly, and his entire body went limp. Elac stood up. "I guess we better burn the bodies or we'll have plague out here."

The gruesome cleanup took several hours to complete. During dinner, the leaders of the two groups met in council. Between mouthfuls of bread and salted ham, Elac related the words of the dying Kobold soldier.

"Why would he tell you this?" asked Lonn.

"I believe he thought I was a Kobold. He was dying, and I don't think he could see. He was probably delirious. Adalyn reinforced his belief with a spell."

"As far as it goes," Rilen said, "I think the Kobold was telling the truth. I've seen this sort of thing before. Often, a man dying in battle will believe he is speaking to members of his unit, or even his family. His information may not turn out to be accurate, but I believe it will be as accurate as he knows it to be."

Duke Lonn poked at the coals of their cooking fire with a long stick. "So where does that leave us? Does this information help?"

"Definitely," Jayrne said. "I think we can take a leap of logic and say the Kobolds are, at the very least, complicit in the situation here in Palindom. This Kobold knew the Human armies in this region were fighting each other. He even said his leaders promised him it would stay that way. I think this may be the link we needed."

"There is one problem, though," Jarok said. "Solone is not a Kobold name. Kobolds would never allow an outsider to order them around."

Adalyn squinted at her cup. "Now that you mention it, I remember some old stories about a group of Humans who broke away from the Kingdom of Palindom. One of their leaders was named Solone, or something close to it. If there is a 'Solone,' I'll bet you he's Human."

"How can you find out for sure?" Lonn asked. "The Kobolds have never been much for open borders, other than a few trading posts along the eastern edges of Verlak."

Rilen scowled. "We do have someone who can tell us. And he is being held in Branig's prison while awaiting trial. Rhun."

"Actually," Jarok said, "he's been moved. Branig has been trying to mend his fences with the Unity Council ever since his outburst during one of their sessions last year. He offered to let Rhun's trial be held in Unity. That way, the Council gets some of the credit for the vengeance exacted upon him."

Rilen brushed away the crumbs of his dinner and reached for a bottle of wine. "I think we need to stick with our plan. Jarok, I'd still like you to escort Duke Lonn to Nightwood. The four of us need to get to Unity as soon as possible. I'd hate for the Council to get anxious and cut Rhun's head off too soon."

"Sounds good," Jarok said. "How many of my men do you want for an escort? We do have the added help of the Human cavalry, so we can spare a few."

"Actually, I don't think you can. You have all of these wounded from the caravan to care for. Many of them will be unable to walk, and the wagons have all been destroyed. You'll have to put the wounded on horseback and your soldiers on foot. You need every warrior you can find."

"What about the creatures we've been seeing? What if you encounter them?"

"The only one I really worry about is the Cassibellanaus. We'll have to be especially careful at night. Hopefully, we can make it to Unity by the day after tomorrow."

"We'll need a good night's sleep," Elac said as he pulled his blankets from his pack. A crack of thunder echoed in the distance. With an exaggerated sigh, he reached for his tent canvas. Jayrne laughed, patted him on the cheek, and helped him in his search for someplace to build their tent.

#

The rain had not yet let up when Elac pushed open the flap to his shelter and stepped onto the damp grass. Briefly, he wondered why, with all the spell research taking place in the School of Magic at Aleria, no one had bothered to create a spell to waterproof clothing. His own limited skills with magic would certainly be no help. Jayrne slipped out behind him and helped pack their gear. A bitterly cold wind blew out of the north.

The steaming horses stood picketed along a line of heavy brush. The four Knights of the Council saddled their mounts in silence. Elac swung into the saddle. He pulled his cloak tightly about his body and followed Rilen into the swirling mist. Although the sun had risen some time before, Elac found it difficult to judge the time of day. The murky gray clouds overhead obscured the sun's position. He pulled up his hood and lowered his head against the weather.

They ate lunch in the saddle. Rilen wanted to get as far into their journey as possible before nightfall, to minimize the chance that they would have to spend a second night in the open. Periodically, Jayrne pushed her horse out into the fore. She would disappear for fifteen or twenty minutes, only to return without having seen anything. As the wind grew stronger, the temperature fell.

Once the heavy skies began to darken toward evening, the temperature dropped faster. Before the light faded completely, the rain had changed to a messy, wet snow. Rilen and Adalyn took the first watch. They had decided early on that they would have two people awake at all times. The chances of a dangerous encounter were too great for them to risk having only one person awake. Jayrne and Elac huddled together in their blankets. Rather than put up their tent, they stretched the canvas across two poles and used it as a lean-to.

He tossed and turned until Rilen woke him around midnight. He and Jayrne moved into the open, where they stood back-to-back. To stay warm, they kept their feet moving, stepping together in what was almost a dance. The snow continued to fall. He took solace in the fact that with the ground not yet frozen, it would be a long time before the snow would accumulate. He rubbed his hands together, then slipped them back inside the sleeves of his coat.

At first, he thought he was mistaken. An enormous shadow passed over a hill to his left, but quickly vanished. His heart leapt in his chest as the first thought came to him: the Cassibellanaus. But the shadow he saw was much too large for that diminutive creature. He stared hard into the snowy darkness, but nothing moved.

Jayrne grabbed his arm. "What is it?"

"I thought I saw something moving out that way," he whispered. "Just a flash of movement, then it was gone. Something huge."

"Are you certain? We should wake the others."

He pursed his chapped lips. "I really don't know what I saw. It's too dark out here to see much of anything."

Rilen sat up on one elbow. "If you two are whispering about what you're going to do when we get to Unity, I'm going to be really unhappy."

Elac gave him an easy smile. "I thought I saw something. It's gone now."

Rilen rolled over to peer out into the night. "Trust your instincts, Elac. I've told you that a hundred times. What was your first thought?"

"That something big was stalking us. That it was hunting."

Rilen nudged his wife. "Wake up, Adalyn. Elac saw something."

"How do you want to handle it?" Elac asked.

"What time do you think it is?"

"I'd say it's still at least an hour before first light."

Rilen stared first at the sky, then at the falling snow. "Let's chance it. Pack the gear, but do it quietly. We'll mount our horses here. We can walk them slowly until we reach the top of that hill, then run them for a mile or so. Once we have some distance behind us, let's ride easy until sunrise."

They worked as silently as they could. While Jayrne kept watch, the others stowed their gear in their packs. Elac strung his bow and hung the quiver from his saddle. Jayrne already had her bow ready. She wrapped herself in Aleron's cloak and boots. If not for her steaming breath, Elac would have had no idea where she was.

Rilen checked the campsite over once more for any remaining equipment. "I think we're ready. Let's go. Stay close to each other and watch our flanks. If whatever is out there is going to attack, it'll have to be soon."

A deep, guttural bellow broke the stillness of the night. A nightmare emerged from a cloud of churning snow. It stood at least eight feet tall and was covered in course, dark fur. The long, bulky arms reached past the creature's knees and ended in almost human-like fingers. The furry muzzle protruded from a leathery face surmounted by a set of protruding tusks. Its eyes glowed fiery red as it closed on them.

It reached for Rilen first, but he danced aside. His blade swung in a tight arc and struck an outreaching arm. The creature's tough hide deflected the blow. There was barely a scratch on the arm as it reached for him once more. Elac darted in low and slashed at the powerful legs. His magic blade bit more deeply. Its blood stained the snow as it whirled to face the new attacker.

Adalyn whipped her blade against the creature's back. The roar of pain rolled across the grasslands. Elac tried to strike again, but it was ready. With a speed that surprised Elac, it danced aside from the blade and brought a massive fist down on his shoulder. The arm went numb, and his sword tumbled away. Elac fell to the slushy ground and tried to rise. The monstrosity lifted a foot to stomp the life from him.

Jayrne appeared immediately behind it, dagger in hand as she charged into the fight. She drove her small blade into its broad back. Rilen stepped in behind her and used his shield as a hammer to drive the blade to its hilt. It swung a thick arm to the rear and caught Rilen with a chance blow, sending him tumbling.

Adalyn took advantage of the beast's momentary distraction. She darted in and slashed the Sword of Sir Salenas across the front of the creature's neck. A thick fan of blood sprayed out as the beast reached for its throat. It dropped first to its knees, then had to prop itself up with one hand. Adalyn stepped back and swung a two-handed blow. The enchanted shortsword cut cleanly through the stump of a neck. The head rolled away as the body dropped into the bloody snow.

Elac struggled to a sitting position. As the shock wore off, the pain came to agonizing life. Every breath seemed to fill his chest with fire. He stretched out his hand for Aleron's sword. Jayrne hefted the blade for him and slid into its sheath. She held him close.

Adalyn checked on Rilen, but he assured her he was okay. They gathered around Elac.

He cradled his right arm to brace the shoulder. "Sorry, Rilen. I didn't realize how quick that thing was."

"Adalyn, why don't you check his injuries? Jayrne and I can round up the horses. We need to leave as soon as possible."

Jayrne raised one eyebrow as she stood up. "Are you going to be able to ride?"

Elac groaned. "We'll find out soon enough."

Adalyn eased his cloak down his back. She wrapped him in a blanket as best she could to keep him warm. She gave him a brief examination. The frown on her face told Elac the prognosis she gave him would not be good. Rilen and Jayrne returned with their skittish mounts, packed the gear, and came over to stand behind Adalyn.

Elac forced himself to smile through his pain. "What do you suggest, doctor?"

"Bed rest. About a week of it. Unfortunately, that's not an option. None of us knows any healing magic, and the closest temple will be in Unity. The best I can do is to tie his arm to his body and minimize the motion."

He winced. "Is anything broken?"

"Possibly some ribs. Your shoulder is definitely dislocated. You also may have broken your collar bone. That's the best I can do while you're wearing your chainmail, but I don't think removing it right now is a good idea." She sighed. "I'd like to try and reset the shoulder. That should help you ride more easily."

Elac nodded his agreement. Jayrne handed him a bottle of rum she had pulled from somewhere in one of their packs. He took as long a drink as he could stand and shut his eyes. Adalyn gently took his arm, one hand above the elbow, and one below. Rilen braced him from behind. Adalyn gave a sudden, sharp pull, and he felt a pop in his shoulder. Excruciating pain shot through his chest.

He sat trembling for several moments before he spoke. "Next time, I'm finding another healer."

CHAPTER 5

The walls of Unity appeared on the horizon. Elac rode in a half-doze, partly due to extreme fatigue and partly because of the nearly-empty bottle of rum held loosely in his good hand. The snow had finally stopped, the temperature climbed, and the sun emerged. The warming rays came as a welcome relief to the chill wind that had blown all week. Elac swayed in the saddle as he took another drink.

They rode through the gates. The guards snapped to attention and stood aside as the four Knights of the Council passed. Rilen led them along the winding streets to Silvayn's sprawling residence. The others dismounted in the courtyard, and servants emerged to take their horses. Rilen and Jayrne eased Elac from his saddle. Adalyn left to make arrangements to have a litter brought for him. He assured them he could walk, but after his first faltering steps they guided him to a wooden bench to await Adalyn's return.

Two of Silvayn's servants carried him inside and eased him onto a comfortable bed. Adalyn stoked the small fire until it roared and crackled, filling the room with its heat. Jayrne helped him out of his armor and the remainder of his sodden clothing before she disappeared in search of the healer. Rilen pulled up a chair and sat next to Elac's bed.

The door opened, and Jayrne returned, followed by Silvayn and an older Elf with white hair. Silvayn came straight to Elac's side. "How are you, my friend?"

"A little sore, I guess." Elac slurred his words. He held up the nearly empty bottle. "I'm on my third bottle of pain medicine."

Silvayn slowly turned to his former pupil. Adalyn shrugged her shoulders and grinned. "Sorry, Silvayn. Best we had."

Silvayn rolled his eyes. "Everyone, this is Verana. She's a priest of Maya. She'll take care of Elac while you tell me what happened."

Elac directed his unfocused eyes at the woman who loomed over him. "A priest? But you're a woman. Doesn't that mean you're a priestess?" He laughed at his own attempt at humor, a drunken outburst that continued until she laid a hand on his brow. She muttered a short prayer, and he fell fast asleep.

#

He awoke with a headache to match the dull, fading pain in his chest and shoulder. His mouth felt cottony. A pitcher of water and a glass sat on the bedside table. He drank most of the water before he climbed out of bed to dress and go in search of his friends.

He found them in Silvayn's study. The conversation broke off as he entered. Jayrne patted the cushioned chair beside her, and he took a seat.

Rilen waved a mug in his direction, unable to conceal a smile. "Ale?"

"Water, thanks. For some reason, I don't feel like drinking right now. Or eating."

Jayrne slipped an arm about his waist. "I wonder why."

"I'm glad to see you're feeling better, Elac," Silvayn said. "That graemon broke five of your ribs. The worst of the damage to your body has been repaired, but it'll be a few days before the muscles are fully recovered."

"Graemon?" Elac asked.

"Another ancient mythological creature come to life," Adalyn said. "Silvayn figured out what it was, once we told him about the other beasts we saw."

"We've been discussing this all morning," Silvayn said, "but I'll give you the short of it. These strange creatures on the Ranset plains are not just creatures of legend. At one time, they walked the lands and were as real as you and I. For the last several thousand years, they have remained in Archon, the Plane of Chaos.

"So this graemon was another of those, just like the Cassibellanaus?"

"Yes, but I fear this is just the beginning. Someone very powerful has opened a Gate from Archon to Pelacia. This person has been releasing creatures from the realm of Chaos and doing so for a reason. We need to find out why."

Elac looked back to Rilen. "Do you think it's connected to the conspiracies against the duchies of Palindom?"

Rilen nodded. "That's our theory."

"It takes a very powerful mage to summon creatures from another plane," Silvayn said. "Also, the caster would need help from someone who has tremendous resources at his disposal. Unfortunately, this helper could be any number of people. There are at least three Human dukes who have the kind of connections that would be needed. And of course, there are always the Kobolds."

"I'm still a little uncertain on this whole 'Gate' issue," Jayrne said. "I've never heard of anyone using Life magic to summon creatures from another plane of existence."

Elac felt a cold shock in the pit of his stomach. "Are the Necromancers resurging already? I had hoped we put them out of business for several centuries."

Silvayn shook his head. "This is not the work of the Necromancers, although they may not be quite as weak as we hoped. No, this is something altogether different. For the past several centuries, many of our more powerful mages have reported sensing a use of magic in their vicinity, like nothing they had ever experienced. To date, no one has identified the source.

"But think of it this way. Users of Life magic obtain their power from this world. Necromancers, who use Death magic, draw their arcane energy from Aceros, the plane of death. Would it not make sense that there is a third form of magic, one that draws from Archon? And if this is the case, it would explain how they are able to summon creatures of Chaos. As for their powers, it's hard to say what they are capable of doing. Necromancers can do things I can't, and vice versa. Users of Chaos magic could be able to cast spells we've never dreamed of."

"What exactly is a Gate?" Elac asked.

"A doorway between our world and theirs. They only operate one way, so there can be no return trip. The creatures that have been sent here have no way back."

A knock at the door interrupted the discussion. A servant entered, apologized, and announced the arrival of the transportation to take the four Knights to their meeting with the Unity Council. Silvayn decided to accompany them. They filed through the door and followed Silvayn to the courtyard.

The ride to the Council chambers took ten minutes. Ceremonial guards stood watch outside. Upon the group's arrival, the guards made a show of escorting them into the Council meeting.

Jarm, the Human who had thwarted the old Council's purpose during the events leading up to the Necromancer invasion, held the position of Council Chair. She had put on a little weight since the war, and streaks of gray touched her hair. She and the Elf, Nasontas, were the only members of that body not summarily dismissed following the conclusion of the war. The new Councilors were more humble. In Elac's opinion, they had restored a measure of respect to the Council. Rilen remained skeptical.

Jarm held up her hand for silence. "Welcome, Knights of the Council. What news do you bring? Have you found the source of the struggle between the duchies of Nightwood and Firereach?"

"We have," Elac said. "Two unidentified individuals convinced the dukes of the two duchies that each was committing atrocities against the other. Their efforts to incite strife originally failed in Ranset, but succeeded in the other two lands. We have brought this matter to the attention of those involved. The hostilities are over."

"Excellent. The Council, and indeed the whole of Pelacia, owes you a debt of gratitude."

"There is more, your Honor," Rilen said. "We have found some truth to the rumors of strange beasts roaming the Ranset Plains. We were set upon several times by creatures I have never seen before." He described the graemon, the Cassibellanaus, and the cingesta. Elac noticed several raised eyebrows. The incredulous looks betrayed the disbelief of the Councilors.

"Sir Rilen," said Nasontas, "please do not take offense, but are you certain these were not creatures of our realm? After all, the mountains and southern marshes contain many varieties of animals most people have never seen."

Silvayn placed a hand on Rilen's shoulder to silence him. "Councilors, I believe most of you know me. I am Silvayn, from the Aleria School of Magic. I have walked these lands for almost a millennium. I have never seen creatures like these the Knights have described, save in my books. They are creatures of Chaos, summoned by a powerful mage to sow discord in our eastern lands."

The Human to Jarm's right wiped a fine layer of dust from the table, scarcely seeming to listen to the discussion. Elac squinted at the writing on his nameplate. His name was Dalan.

Dalan yawned and looked at the ceiling. "Summoned? By whom?"

"We don't know, at this time. We believe the summoner is affiliated with those who have tried to ignite a civil war in Palindom."

"And is there a way to find out?" Dalan asked.

"We can try," Elac said. "There is a prisoner in your dungeon, transferred here for trial following his capture a few days ago."

The Dwarf closest to Jarm stroked his long red beard. "Would that be the Kobold brought here by the Duchy of Branig? The one scheduled to be executed next week?"

"Yes. The Duke of Branig wanted to try him in his own citadel but brought his prisoner here at your request. We would like to interrogate him. Perhaps he knows who is behind all of this."

At Jarm's direction, the Council took a unanimous voice vote, which granted the Knights permission to interview the condemned prisoner. The scribe drew up the proclamation. On the way out, Elac grabbed a cask of ale and four glasses. The four weary travelers and their mage companion retired to their carriage for the ride across town to the prison. The horses leapt away, and the carriage lurched forward. Elac broached the cask and poured glasses for his friends. He decided to forego the beverage himself.

"You see?" Elac handed Rilen a cup. "The new Council is completely different from the old. Under Jarm's leadership, they are no longer corrupt."

"You're right, they're not. Now they're just incompetent."

They managed to finish their drinks before the carriage jolted to a stop. The driver held open the door while they clambered out to stand before the gates of the prison. Their status as Knights of the Council gained them immediate access, Silvayn included. The warden bade them to make themselves comfortable in a waiting area while he had the prisoner brought out.

Elac poured a glass from a pitcher of water. Although he had expected a long wait, he was only halfway through his drink when he heard the clink of chains. The door opened, and two leather-clad guards dragged Rhun into the room. His hands were chained to a leather belt at his waist, while his feet were clamped to a stiff, rusty iron bar. Rilen motioned to a chair. The guards dragged their prisoner across the room. They forced him to take a seat, bowed, and left the room.

Rilen paced across the floor at a deliberately slow pace. When he stood within an arm's reach of the Kobold, he stopped and bent closer. They stared at each other for several long moments.

Rilen broke the silence first. "You're a condemned man."

"It seems that way."

"We have some questions for you. If you help us, I'll see what I can do for you."

Rhun's furry muzzle curled back in undisguised hatred. "I'll die before I tell you anything, Elf." He spat at Rilen's feet.

Rilen stood erect and folded his arms across his chest. "I'm not talking about a pardon, Rhun. I would never go that far to help a Kobold. I could get your sentence commuted to life in prison."

"I'm already dead. How much time I spend here before the executioner or old age makes it official matters not."

"Then look at it this way. Help me out, and I'll make sure the execution is clean and quick. I can always convince the warden to make it a full purification by pain. It could take days, if they do it right."

Rhun threw back his head and laughed. "I don't fear your tortures. Do what you must."

Elac decided to try a different tactic. "Look, Rhun. We're trying to help everyone here. Learning what you know will not only help us, it could end up saving your people."

Rhun gave an expressionless stare and said nothing.

"Someone has been causing trouble in the Human lands. We believe there may have been Kobold involvement. We hoped you could tell us what you know. If King Aldaris believes your people are responsible for the conflicts in his lands, he'll issue a declaration of war. All three nations will rise up and march on your cities. We know where your tunnel entrances are. We could have your underground cities besieged in a week. And the human fleet would blockade the port at Hrcac. They could bring in troops by ship and burn your capital to the ground.

"Based on what we know of your casualties in the last Necromancer War, within a month we could depopulate the Paheny Mountains."

Some of Rhun's self-confidence melted away, evidenced by the droop of his shoulders and his wide eyes. Elac pressed his advantage. "If there is anything you know that could help us prevent this from happening, now is the time to tell us. When a dozen frigates are raining fire on Hrcac, it will be too late to stop the annihilation."

Rhun dropped his gaze to the floor and let out a long breath. "It started five years ago. A Human named Solone came to the docks at the Bay of Hrcac. He asked to see Overlord Hamedon. Ordinarily, had a non-Kobold come into our lands to provide counsel, he'd have been killed on the spot. Very few foreigners are allowed beyond the wharf.

"But he was granted an audience with Hamedon. I was suspicious from the start. Something supernatural had to be at work. The next morning, Overlord Hamedon announced that Solone would be his new military advisor. We immediately set about rebuilding our armies. The smithies worked night and day to turn out the weapons of war. Unfortunately, as you pointed out, our losses at the end of the Necromancer war were extreme. It will be decades before we fully recover.

"Solone recommended a new tactic. The first step was to sow discord in the Human lands. Several duchies were on the verge of open warfare anyway. To add to the confusion, we conducted border raids. I advised against it and was almost taken to the gallows."

"So we were right," Adalyn said. "The Kobolds are behind all of this."

"No. Solone is behind it. He has some kind of hold over Overlord Hamedon. Just six months before Solone came to us, my father spoke to Hamedon privately. They developed plans to open a dialogue with the Unity Council. They planned an increase in trade, maybe even a mutual defense treaty. Eventually, he wanted to have the Kobold nation join the Unity Pact." He snarled. "My father was one of the first to be executed under Solone's guidance."

"Did Solone bring anyone else with him?" Jayrne asked. "A mage of some kind? Or is he, perhaps, a mage himself?"

"He was alone. As for his own powers, I have never seen him use magic, but I suspect he has some ability in that area."

"Someone has been summoning powerful creatures to attack travelers in the eastern plains," Silvayn said. "This person has to have logistical support in order to maintain the gateway to draw these beasts from another world. Perhaps he convinced Hamedon to give him the help he needs, so that the new creatures could be used as a weapon against the Humans."

"I don't think so," Rhun said. "A number of our raiding parties have reported being attacked by strange beasts. At first, we thought them crazy. But as more reports came in, we began to believe them. Now, I have no doubt. Our tunnels around Tracker's Peak are no longer safe. The mist still surrounds the valley where the castle stands, even though the spell of banishment is broken. This mist extends into our tunnels, and demons haunt the mist. Tracker's Peak is worse. A dragon made of fog has made it his home, a fierce beast that eats anything that moves. Not even our finest warriors can stand up to it."

Rilen chewed on a fingernail. "Mist demons, Silvayn? Here? Is that possible?"

"Definitely possible. The rift between worlds will never fully be healed. Perhaps the rift between our world and the Plain of Mist is open wider than we thought."

"We have a dilemma," Jayrne said. "It sounds to me like Hamedon, while complicit in the scheme against Palindom, is completely unassociated with the creatures from Archon. Solone might be responsible for both, or he might not. I can only think of one way to be certain."

"We travel to Hrcac," Elac said. "We speak to Overlord Hamedon and explain the situation. If we can expose Solone for who and what he is, his whole scheme will fall apart."

Rhun's lip curled up in a sneer. "And just how do you propose to do that? One of Solone's suggestions was to stop all trade and seal the borders to outsiders. And even if you managed to sneak past the patrols and make it to Hrcac, what then? You'd be killed on sight."

"How about a truce?" said Adalyn. "We can take you with us. You get us entry to Hrcac and a parley with Hamedon. When we leave, you can stay behind."

Rhun laughed, a low, growling chortle. "Not on your life."

"I agree," Rilen said. "He must still pay for his crimes."

"What if we do this as part of a diplomatic mission?" Elac asked. "If both sides have had trouble with these creatures, we should use that as an angle. Tell Hamedon we want to discuss a temporary truce in order to address the mutual threat."

Although Rilen and Rhun continued to express their objections to the plan, the group eventually decided to try it. The guards took Rhun to his cell. The Knights returned to Silvayn's house to finalize their proposal to the Unity Council.

Silvayn assured them he could bully the new Council into going along with his idea. Elac remained skeptical, but the Council approved the measure on the first vote. Back at Silvayn's once more, Elac and Jayrne retired to their room for the night. Rilen had promised an early start. Based upon Rilen's dark mood, Elac knew better than to expect anything else.

#

The walls of Piaras Keep loomed ahead, barely visible in the shifting mist. Elac floated above the bog. His boots never touched the oily surface of the water. He drifted through the soundless night until his feet were planted firmly on dry land. When he passed through the gates, the great barriers shimmered and became whole. Everywhere he looked, the castle returned to life. The crumbling stone of the walls became impenetrable once again. In the distance, he heard the ringing echo of a blacksmith's hammer.

Seven armored knights on massive chargers rode through the courtyard and dismounted. They raised their visors and removed their gauntlets. Elac stepped away with a sharp intake of breath. Beneath their armor, the knights were nothing but bone. The undead walked the land once again.

Elac recognized the crests on their moss-covered shields. The seven knights before him were the spirits that haunted Piaras Keep. The same knights who had bestowed their artifacts upon Elac and his friends years before. Their armor showed deep rents, as if they had just fought in a mighty battle. At first, the dead knights ignored him. Finally, one bearing the crest of Sir Draygen removed his helmet and tucked it under his arm. He crossed the flagstone courtyard to stand in front of Elac. When he bowed, the sickening creak of his bones mingled with the rusty grind of his battered armor. The figure never spoke. He turned his sightless eye sockets on Elac, then pointed to a wooden structure in the center of the castle.

Elac drifted across the stones to the ancient building. The doors were closed and locked, but Elac passed through them as if they were but a curtain of mist. He entered a circular room, where maps covered the walls. A table in the center of the room held a model representing the entire nation of Palindom. An armored figure stood silhouetted against the flickering light of a fireplace on the far side of the room. Elac recognized him immediately.

"Prince Cassius?"

The specter rotated soundlessly. It raised hollow, haunted eyes to greet the Elf. "Hail, Elac." His words seemed distant. They echoed as if overlaid with others' voices. "I greet you in the castle of my forefathers. It was here that our fates were made known six years ago, so it is only fitting that history repeat itself."

"What . . . what has happened to you?"

"I am a victim of my own arrogance. I thought myself invincible when I led that charge from the gates of Unity. My self-serving deed caused the deaths of a great many men under my command. But we were worse than dead. Our souls were torn asunder. We were raised as the undead, forced to do battle against our own kind. For that, I am doomed to walk the afterlife until such time as my sins have been cleansed."

"And that is why I am here?"

"Possibly. If my absolution should come to pass, then so much the better. But my first concern in death is for the land of Palindom. A great evil has stretched out its hand to take what was to have been mine. I am permitted this time to give you certain insights to help you in your quest."

"Permitted? By whom?"

The shade of Cassius shook its ephemeral head. "It doesn't matter. What's important is that which lies before you. For you to succeed, you must have the same spiritual alignment about you as you did ten years ago. The original questors must come together once more to stand as one against an evil so powerful, it dwarfs the threat of the Necromancers."

"But how can that be? You're . . ."

"Dead? Yes. I cannot be there. My daughter, Noria, must take up the Shield of Sir Omonis and go in my stead. Each of you will have tasks to perform. All must go, or all will fail.

"Your first task is to slow the onslaught of chaos in eastern Palindom. To that end, you must travel to Hrcac, even as you have planned, and convince Overlord Hamedon to abandon his desperate plan to overthrow the West. The Kobold prisoner must accompany you, lest you perish before you reach Hrcac."

"He has refused to help us."

"He, too, will have a vision in his dreams. He shall assist you. The combined armies of the West and the Kobolds will be needed, lest all four nations will fall."

"And after that?"

"My vision is clouded and imperfect. I cannot even see if you will succeed in this first task. With the uncertainty surrounding this part of my vision, I cannot see beyond it. If you accomplish this first task, your next step shall be made plain."

Elac took a long, deep breath. His ghostly body shimmered with the effort. "It shall be as you say, my Lord. We will solve this riddle and free your soul from this eternal punishment, that you may rest in the House of the Dead."

"My fate is unimportant. You must first free the nations from the shadow that hangs over them. If it should be my destiny to spend eternity haunting these halls, then so be it."

With that, Prince Cassius, the room, and the entire castle shimmered and vanished.

CHAPTER 6

Elac sat bolt upright in bed, bathed in sweat, his heart racing. Jayrne pulled herself up beside him and placed a hand on his shoulder.

"Elac, are you all right?"

He took several gulping breaths while his disorientation passed. "I think so. What a vivid dream." He described for her the ghostly visit to Piaras Keep. Oddly, while most dreams tended to fade from memory almost immediately, every detail of this dream remained firmly embedded in his mind.

"Do you think it was a visitation?"

"I don't know. It all seemed so genuine, and yet, surreal. I don't know how to be certain about it."

"I do. Let's talk to Silvayn."

They dressed in silence. Elac lit a candle, and the two followed the hallways to Silvayn's room. Elac knocked, waited several moments, and knocked once more. Silvayn mumbled something from behind his door. Finally, the latch turned, and a sleepy-eyed Silvayn opened the door.

"What?"

"We have a problem."

Silvayn opened the door further and motioned with his head. He eased himself into a chair at his desk. "What is it?"

"I just had a dream. At least, it may have been a dream. I was at Piaras Keep. Prince Cassius spoke to me about what has been happening here on Pelacia."

"But you're not certain if it was a dream?"

"No. Can you use magic to tell the difference?"

"Maybe. But it would be more effective if I have Adalyn's help. Meet me in my study in fifteen minutes."

#

"And that was when he told me that we will need all four nations to stand together in order to defeat our enemy. Whoever that enemy may turn out to be."

"Adalyn, let's see what we can find out."

The two mages stood on opposite sides of Elac, hands outstretched, palms joined. They chanted in unison. Elac's vision blurred, and the room darkened. He tried to concentrate on what Silvayn and Adalyn were doing, but his mental focus wavered. He lost track of the passage of time. As if it was happening to someone else, he felt distant pressure on his hand. Vaguely, he realized someone's hand lay upon his own. He opened his eyes.

"What happened?"

Silvayn's face was drawn. "Elac, your dream was truly a vision. Prince Cassius has reached out from beyond the grave to help us."

Rilen slammed a glass down on the table. "So you're suggesting we go to a Kobold, who has been convicted of murder and is awaiting execution. We pull him out of prison and ask him to help us. Is that it?"

Silvayn squinted at the ceiling. "Well, let me think about it for a moment . . . yes, I think that pretty much covers it."

"Do you think we can convince the Unity Council to let us have him?" Jayrne asked.

"The Council won't be the problem," Adalyn said. "I think they'll listen to their Knights. Duke Norseth of Branig is the wildcard here."

"I don't think the duke's response will be that hard to figure out," Elac said. "He wanted to execute Rhun himself, but the Council convinced him to let them do it as a symbol of their authority. If the Council won't execute him, Norseth will certainly want to take him back to his stronghold and hang him there."

"Are we decided in this?" Rilen's frown was deeply etched in his face.

"Yes," Silvayn said.

"Then I have a suggestion. Cassius said we needed our original companions to travel with us. If we send messengers on fast horses, we can have Noria and the Dwarves here in less than a week. Let's gather our group together first, before we go to the Council. That way, if Norseth throws an obstacle in our way, we have the option to take direct action."

"Direct action?" Adalyn asked.

"We break him out of the prison and run for the Paheny Mountains. If we move before the others arrive, it would be almost impossible to find them after we leave Unity."

No one had any other suggestions. Silvayn summoned a servant and issued orders for a messenger to be sent to the Dwarven city of Centare, where Gillen and Hadwyn were overseeing the rebuilding of the Dwarf army. Another courier would be sent to the War College at Fort Julan, where Princess Noria was engaged in tactical training. In the meantime, at another of Rilen's suggestions, they made plans to gather what supplies they would need for the journey. Jayrne, however, had a different task.

Elac and Jayrne entered the prison. His eyes slowly adjusted to the dim interior. The Sergeant of the Guard checked their papers, decided they were valid, and allowed them access. They were taken to Rhun's cell this time, at Elac's request. Ostensibly, his reason was that he felt the Kobold would be more pliable deep in the dungeon, as opposed to in a relatively comfortable conference room. While the impetus was valid on its face, it covered the real intention of their visit.

The guard inserted his key into the lock and turned it. The rusty mechanism creaked and groaned but gave way. The cell door slowly swung open. Rhun stirred on his cot. When he saw who had come, he lay back down. He folded his hands across his chest and stared at the ceiling.

"What do you want now?"

"We've come to update you on our plans, since they include you."

"I'm not going anywhere with you."

"Only twelve days remain before your execution. If you don't come with us, you're facing the hangman's noose."

"Twelve days? I wish it was today. Or even now. I would rather die than come with you."

Elac glanced over at his wife, but she was preoccupied with studying the cell and surrounding corridors. "Rhun, we need your help. Without you, we can't do this."

"You'll have to take me out of here in chains. And even then, I'll escape at the first opportunity. Maybe I'll even kill one of you before I go."

"We'll see." Elac moved to Jayrne's side. "Get what you came for?"

"Yes." She smiled. "I could pull this off in my sleep."

Elac smiled at the Kobold prisoner. "Don't get too comfortable. We'll be back."

#

The next ten days were a blur. Rilen and Silvayn kept everyone busy securing what they needed for the trip. With the approach of winter, they would bring cold weather gear to protect them in the frigid mountain passes. There was always a need for food and water. Jayrne kept to herself as she gathered what she needed in case she had to use stealth to remove Rhun from Unity's prison.

On the evening of the tenth day, they gathered in Silvayn's study once more. They had just eaten dinner, and a chilled barrel of ale stood in one corner. Elac had already sampled it more than once. His head spun slightly as he lowered himself onto a couch. Off to his right, Jayrne and Adalyn were discussing the artist they had seen at the Unity museum that afternoon, while they were retrieving Prince Cassius's magically endowed shield. Apparently, her painting of the Temira, Unity's holiest artifact, was the most beautiful thing the two women had ever seen. He shrugged and took another drink.

Someone gave a soft knock at the door. It opened, and the two Dwarf princes, Hadwyn and Gillen, entered. Both wore red cloaks, held at the neck by a silver broach. Gillen gave Adalyn a dignified kiss on the cheek, but his brother was not so restrained. He roared his excitement as he gave Jayrne a crushing hug. He grabbed Elac's outstretched hand in both of his.

"Elac, my friend! Good to see you!"

They exchanged greetings, then everyone sat down. While Silvayn gave the two Dwarf princes a brief summary of current events, Hadwyn downed two tankards of ale. A young Elf woman arrived with steaming bowls of soup. Hadwyn swirled the contents of his mug while he eyed Silvayn's serving girl. Elac sighed. Some people would never change.

"When will we go before the Council, Silvayn?" Gillen asked. Elac was surprised at Gillen's lack of a response to his brother's drinking. Maybe over the years, he had resolved to accept Hadwyn the way he was.

"Tomorrow night. Princess Noria should arrive sometime today."

Hadwyn handed his mug to Elac and pointed at the ale barrel. "The daughter of Prince Cassius, huh? I hope she is a little more humble than her father."

"Noria is her own person. She's not perfect, mind you, but I think you'll find her very unassuming, especially in comparison to Cassius. She's been breaking the gender barriers down in Palindom, and that's no easy task. She was the first woman allowed to compete in the annual jousting contest. And she won. Now she's the first Human woman allowed to attend the War College at Fort Julan. Actually, she should hold the position of chief military advisor to the king, but Aldaris passed her over for the job."

A servant opened the door and stuck his head into the study. "Silvayn? Princess Noria of Palim is here and wishes to speak with you. She says she was invited."

"Ah. Send her in."

When Noria entered the room, Elac immediately saw the similarities between her and her father. She had the same proud bearing and the same penetrating blue eyes. While her body was decidedly feminine, her arms and legs carried a little of her father's muscular build. Her long, dark hair was pulled tightly together behind her head and held by a leather wrap. She wore a tight blue smock, with the silvery likeness of a panther woven into the material, wrapped at the waist by her sword belt. She acknowledged Silvayn with a nod of her head. Hadwyn froze in the act of taking a drink of ale and stared, his eyes wide.

"Silvayn," she said. "I have come as you asked. What is this matter of importance you spoke of?"

"Elac, perhaps it would be best coming from you."

Elac licked his lips, stood, and bowed to the princess. "Your Highness. What I'm about to tell you may sound incredible, but it is true."

Noria raised one eyebrow and looked to Silvayn. "What is this about?"

"Listen to Elac. I will vouch for everything he has to say."

"You are aware that the seven of us journeyed with your father six years past. I had a dream several nights ago. In it, your father came to me." Noria maintained her composure, but Elac noticed the trembling in her hands. "Your Highness, he told me that there is a great evil at work. He has tasked us with combating the evil. We need you, and the Shield of Omonis, if we are to succeed."

"My father . . . said this to you?"

"Yes. His spirit haunts the ruins of Piaras Keep, just as do the knights who gave us direction six years ago. Perhaps if this quest is successful, his soul will be free to move on to his final reward."

Elac held out his hand to Noria. "Your Highness, we can't do this without you. Will you join us?"

Noria never hesitated. She clasped forearms with Elac. "You have but to ask, and I will join you. Even had Silvayn not asked this of me, just knowing I can help my father would be reason enough."

Silvayn raised his mug in a salute. "And now, we are eight."

#

The solid oak doors to the Unity Council chambers swung open, and Silvayn led the group inside. All had dressed in formal attire. Noria wore her polished, blue-black suit of plate mail armor, surmounted by a blue cape with the panther crest embroidered across the back. Her face tightened when the Human members of the Unity Council muttered at her warlike appearance. Elac and Rilen wore chain mail armor with their best woodland cloaks and trousers. The Dwarves, Gillen in banded mail and Hadwyn in splint mail, had braided their hair and combed out their beards. To Elac's surprise, not only was Hadwyn completely sober, but he paid no attention to the attractive scribe sitting by the doorway. Jayrne and Adalyn wore gowns of the finest silk.

Silvayn, with a white robe and his lustrous wooden staff, stopped at the podium reserved for guest speakers. Since the topic of the evening's discussion involved the arcane, the group had decided Silvayn would be their most effective speaker.

"Honorable members of the Unity Council. We come before you this evening with the gravest of news. A warning has come to us from the spirit world. A powerful being of absolute evil has placed a conspiracy into motion. If left unchecked, this foul plot could enslave all three nations."

Jarm ran her fingers through her brown and silver hair. "What is this evil you speak of, Silvayn?"

"We don't know the source at this point. We have determined that this person is behind the unrest in eastern Palindom. We also have reason to believe the Kobolds have fallen under this foul influence. This is the reason for their raiding parties crossing into our territory.

"We had assumed the source of the conspiracy was either the Kobolds or one of the other duchies scrambling for the throne. But one of your Knights had a visitation in his sleep." Silvayn neglected to mention the almost two weeks that had passed since Elac's dream encounter, and Elac chose not to mention it. "The spirit of Prince Cassius of Palim came to Sir Elac in a dream. He warned of certain steps that must be taken if we are to thwart the plot standing against us."

"And what steps are those?" Jarm asked.

"We will need to travel to the Kobold city of Hrcac. There, we must discredit the man who has the Kobold overlord in his thrall. We have interrogated the Kobold prisoner, Rhun, and learned there is indeed a man who has, in recent years, become one of Overlord Hamedon's top advisors. The attacks by Kobold raiders are a direct result of this man's influence."

An Elf on the Council raised her hand. "How do you know this to have been a true message from the spirit world, Silvayn? It could just as easily have been a dream."

"Such was my concern, Falas. But Adalyn and I have used our own magic to determine the visit was a true commune with Cassius's spirit."

"What will be your next step?" Jarm asked.

"We need the Council's help in this matter. We must take the Kobold prisoner, Rhun, with us when we travel to Kobold territory. Without his help, we could never hope to reach Hrcac."

"Impossible!" The shouted protest came from the rear of the room. Duke Norseth of Branig, his face red and his fists clenched, stomped his way into the circle of torchlight. "He stands convicted of crimes against my realm, including murder. He is to be executed on the morrow."

"I think everyone in this room knows we would like to see Rhun hang for his crimes," Noria said. "But the greater good of the entire continent hangs in the balance. We must do as my father's shade advised us."

Norseth snarled and spoke through clenched teeth. "I do not have to stand here and listen to this . . . this . . . woman, addressing me this way!"

Hadwyn launched himself at the duke, and it took both Rilen and Gillen to restrain him. Elac placed himself between the duke and Noria, who had also taken a few steps toward her antagonist. Several minutes passed before order returned to the chamber.

Jarm sat back in her chair and rubbed her eyes. "I call for a vote on the matter. We have been asked for release the Kobold prisoner Rhun into the custody of these Knights of the Council. I vote for the prisoner's release."

The voice vote went around the table. The other two Human Council members voted against the measure, but the rest of the Council was in favor. Jarm rose to her feet.

"The measure carries. We will draw up the proclamation immediately."

"Hold!" Norseth stepped forward to the center of the horseshoe-shaped Council table. "When I brought this Kobold to Unity, it was with the understanding that he was to hang for his crimes. I granted the Council jurisdiction in this matter. However, if the Council is planning to renege on the deal, then I hereby revoke your jurisdiction, and I remand it to the criminal court in my castle at Branig." His eyes narrowed as he faced the Knights. "I will take custody of the prisoner immediately."

"I don't think it can happen so quickly," Jarm said. "Proper paperwork must be completed before he can be released from our prison."

"Then I shall station some of my own soldiers at the door to his cell. Certainly, the Council should have no objections to my providing extra security."

Jarm regarded him with an expressionless face. "So be it."

#

An hour later, they gathered once more in Silvayn's study. Judging by Hadwyn's proximity to the ale barrel, Elac surmised the Dwarf's extended bout with sobriety was coming to an end. Silvayn faced away from the group, hands clasped behind his back.

Elac could bear the silence no longer. "What now, Silvayn?"

"I'm thinking. As it stands, it looks like we'll still have to break Rhun out of prison. The problem is Norseth's extra men. With people actively guarding the one cell we need to access, it's going to be much more difficult, if not impossible."

The door opened, and a servant escorted Jarm into the room. "Hello, Silvayn."

"Jarm."

"I'm sorry about the way things turned out. I hadn't counted on Norseth's reaction."

"Nor had we. At worst, we figured he would put up a fight on the matter. I never thought he would take it as far as he did."

"It will make it much more difficult for you to break him out." She regarded Silvayn silently. A smile tugged at the corners of her mouth.

"Your Honor?"

"Oh, don't play coy with me, Silvayn. Once Norseth said he was refusing to allow you to take custody of Rhun, I knew you would try to remove him from the prison. Now, you're going to need my help."

"Your help? What can you do?"

"I have close ties with the commander of Unity's defense forces. Actually, he's my husband. I managed to talk him into helping. He has issued orders for all military forces in the city to be ready for a Kobold attack we'll be facing by morning."

Rilen rose to his feet. "Kobolds are coming here?"

"Of course not. But no one else knows that. We'll march soldiers around outside the walls all night. Toward morning, our scouts will return and report having seen no Kobold army. My husband will release the soldiers under his command, but after being on duty all night, they'll be in no condition to do anything but sleep. You can sneak out of the city in the confusion."

Jayrne raised her wine glass. "It's a nice plan, as far as it goes. But it still doesn't help us get Rhun out of his cell. I checked the prison out several days ago. Now that Norseth has men watching him, it will be fairly difficult."

"Ah, but those who are currently guarding Rhun will have been conscripted and sent out with the other troops. Norseth will be forced to assign untrained men from his entourage. I think you can take it from there."

"Only one problem," Gillen said. "Even an idiot like Norseth will know what happened if we and the prisoner all disappear at the same time. We'll have his soldiers dogging our steps from behind while we dodge the Kobold patrols in front of us."

"I'll see what I can do. I think I can find a way to keep his soldiers inside the city a while longer." She opened the door and stepped halfway through. "Good luck to all of you." Her gaze lingered on Noria's armored form as she left.

#

Rilen crossed the darkened street. His forest cloak rendered him nearly invisible, even to Elac's sharp Elven eyesight. He gave a low whistle, which Elac barely heard. He and Jayrne slipped from hiding and followed him up against the wall of the prison.

Jarm's promised ruse had been extremely effective. They had not encountered a single member of the night watch. Elac looked around one more time, but he saw no one. He glanced up and saw the open window on the second floor of the prison complex.

Rilen pulled a wooden box from a nearby alley and placed it against the building. He climbed atop the crate and braced himself against the wall, legs spread wide. Elac climbed onto his back, scampering up until he had planted his feet on Rilen's shoulders. He heard the Elf warrior grunt and felt him shake. He tensed his own body as Jayrne clambered up onto his shoulders. She stretched up on her tiptoes until her fingers found a purchase on the ledge of the window. The pressure on his shoulders eased, and she disappeared through the opening above. Elac dropped to the ground.

A slender rope descended from the window. Rilen tested it with two sharp tugs, then he ascended the line hand over hand. Elac's climb was more gradual. His right shoulder was still a little tender, but he made the ascent safely. Jayrne grabbed him under the armpits and hauled him inside. Rilen pulled the rope back through the window, coiled it, and set it aside. The three rogues crossed the room and stood motionless by the door for several moments.

Rilen eased the door open. Jayrne took the lead. Under ordinary circumstances, the guard presence in the prison would have been much more prominent. But the assistance provided by Jarm and her husband proved invaluable. While the soldiers watched for a non-existent Kobold army, the guards at the gates of the prison had been doubled, which reduced the chance of a random encounter inside the walls.

Jayrne took them down a long flight of stairs. Elac surmised that they had descended far enough to be on the second floor below ground level, which was where Rhun's cell was located. He scarcely recognized any landmarks, but Jayrne chose their path with confidence. She guided them down a winding hallway, then motioned them out of sight. Rhun's cell lay around the corner. The next few moments would tell if her plan would work or not.

#

Baren was not cut out for guard duty. Actually, he was not made for much physical labor at all. He preferred his routine task of planning Duke Norseth's social schedule. But with the general mobilization, the duke had pressed him into service guarding the Kobold prisoner.

It was not as if the prisoner needed to be watched. He was in a locked cell, and by the duke's order, he was manacled to the wall. The prison's only entrance was heavily fortified and manned by at least twenty guards. Unless some sinister supernatural force was at work, the Kobold criminal would go nowhere. Baren would rather be back in his quarters, enjoying cold ale and a warm maid.

He shifted his weight to his left leg. His right leg had long since gone numb. The palms of his hands were sweaty from continued contact with his spear, so he wiped them on his tunic. If only the duke had granted his request to have someone else stand the post with him. At least he would have someone to talk to and pass the time. The night promised to be long and boring.

A light step brought him about. He saw a petite young woman, her features hidden in her shawl, at the nearest hallway junction. It was odd, since he had seen no one in the area for over an hour. She lowered her hood to reveal her exquisitely beautiful features.

"What are you doing here, Miss? This area is restricted."

Her only answer was to slightly part her robe in the front, tantalizing him with what lay beneath. She winked, closed her robe, and backed away to duck around the corner. He stood frozen in place, not certain what to do. After several moments, her hand poked out around the way and gestured for him to come closer. He took a hesitant step.

"Miss, you need to come back out. It's not safe for you to be alone down here."

Her hand disappeared for a few moments, then came back into view dangling her robe. The mantle dropped softly to the floor. She leaned her head and bare shoulders around the corner and blew him a kiss.

His resistance crumbled. He leaned the spear against the cell door and scampered around the corner. A shadowy figure appeared next to the young woman. The cudgel in the figure's hand descended on Baren's head.

#

"Nice work." Jayrne's face was aflame as she scrambled back into her clothes.

"Same to you," Elac said. "It's a good thing you talked Hadwyn out of coming with us. He might have enjoyed the view a little too much. If he wasn't thinking about Noria, that is."

"Are you two finished?" Rilen asked.

Jayrne knelt before the cell and studied the lock. She pulled her lockpick set from her boot and went to work. Within moments, she defeated the lock and opened the door. Rhun sat against the far wall, asleep. His arms and legs were secured to the wall by lengths of rusty chain. Rilen knelt beside him. He placed a hand over the furry muzzle and roughly shook the Kobold's shoulder.

Rhun came awake in an instant. His eyes narrowed. "What do you want?"

"Keep your voice down," Rilen whispered as Jayrne unlocked his bindings. "Duke Norseth plans to take you with him tomorrow. You're to be hanged at his castle, after some suitable crowd entertainment, I'm sure. Another dead kobold won't cause me to lose any sleep, but as it turns out, we need you."

"And I told you already, Elf, I'm not going to help you."

"Look," Elac said. "We've learned of a threat that faces not only us, but the Kobold nation as well. You know what I speak of. You had a dream . . ."

Rhun's jaw dropped open. "How did you . . ." He took a shuddering breath and dropped his head to his chest. His face relaxed, and some of the rancor melted away from his voice. "I'm torn between loyalty to my fellow soldiers and loyalty to my country. I'm not sure what I want to do."

Rilen jabbed a finger at Rhun's face. "I don't give a damn about your wants. A lot of people are counting on us, including Kobolds. Are you such a coward that you would rather hide behind these walls than help to free your people from Solone's influence? His misguided advice is killing your countrymen by the score!"

Rhun's eyes narrowed. He climbed to his feet, and his chains fell away. "I'll come with you, Elf. I'll help you get rid of Solone. But mark my words. When we're finished, I'm going to kill you."

"You're welcome to try. Now, let's get out of here."

"Where are we going first?"

"Back to the home of a mage friend of mine. We're staging from there. We have a distraction in place, but we must leave at dawn. Until this is over, we need a truce. Agreed?" He held out his hand.

Rhun regarded him wordlessly, then accepted the hand. "Agreed."

CHAPTER 7

Silvayn sat on the bench of the wagon beside Adalyn, who was guiding the horses. Elac and Jayrne rode in front of them. The others followed close behind, Hadwyn deep in conversation with Noria. Elac had never seen the Dwarf so taken with a woman. To Hadwyn's credit, the attraction appeared mutual. Noria laughed as they rode, frequently reaching out to touch Hadwyn's arm.

Two more horses, burdened only with saddlebags, trailed behind the wagon. Crates and casks filled the bed of the wagon. Elac wore his traveling cloak, which hid the chainmail armor beneath it. Adalyn and Silvayn had acquired the Orion Stone from the Unity Museum, with the Council's blessings. The enchanted artifact dangled from a silver chain about Elac's neck. He took comfort in the legendary orb's ability to negate hostile magic.

They reached the gates of Unity, which were pushed almost completely to. The city's military still had its forces on alert for an encroaching Kobold army. The gap in the barrier was just wide enough for wagons to pass through, although each had to be inspected carefully before it left the city. They stood in a line of travelers. Elac had expected the line to be longer, but then most of the populace would not travel with the threat of a Kobold raid hanging over the city.

Their turn in line came. The guards motioned for Silvayn to stop his wagon. The old mage complied. He stood in the wagon and slammed the reins on the seat.

"What indignity is this? Don't you realize who I am? Who we are?"

"You are an old man, and they appear to be Knights of the Council. However, our orders are explicit. No one leaves or enters without an inspection of their belongings."

The other guards slipped forward to check the troop's packs. The saddlebags on the horses received only a cursory examination, but the cargo in the wagon drew special interest. They drew ale from each keg, pried open each crate, and untied each parcel to see what they contained. After several minutes, the guards backed away but left the wagon's cargo area a shambles. Silvayn crossed his arms and cleared his throat.

Two of the guards snickered but refused to respond. Noria slipped from her saddle and stood beside Gillen in front of the sergeant, Elac to one side and Hadwyn to the other. She placed a gauntleted hand on the hilt of her sword. "Sergeant, if you would be so kind, your men seem to have left their job half-finished. I think Silvayn would appreciate it if they cleaned up after themselves."

"Are you threatening me?"

Noria leaned closer until their noses touched. "Right now, it's a polite suggestion. I'll leave the rest up to you."

The sergeant could only bear the woman's intense gaze for a few brief seconds. He stepped back and waved his soldiers forward. It took several minutes to have the bed of the wagon back into a semblance of order. Elac and the others climbed back into their saddles, formed up, and trotted through the gates to the sound of Jayrne's ringing laughter.

Hadwyn leaned closer to Elac. "Isn't she glorious?"

Elac did not have an answer.

They rode at a steady pace for the first hour. Once they were out of sight of the city, Silvayn guided the wagon into a copse of trees. They unloaded the cargo, then pried up the boards in the wagon bed. Rhun sat up, his motions stiff, and rubbed his cramped muscles. While the Kobold recovered from his ordeal, the others broke down the cargo from the wagon into manageable portions, which they divided among the horses. Elac saved one particular crate for last. With Jayrne's help, he carried it through the trees to where Rhun sat rubbing his back.

"Rhun, I know you didn't want to come on this journey. I appreciate you being here. We need you with us if we're to succeed, but we need something else, as well. Trust."

Elac pried open the lid on the crate. He reached inside and retrieved a suit of chainmail. It was about the right size for an Elf, which meant it should fit the Kobold, if a little snugly. Rhun eyed him for several long moments before he took the proffered armor. While he shrugged the mail shirt into place, Elac placed the other items on a fallen tree. There was a round metal shield, a helmet, a shortsword, and a bow with a quiver of arrows.

Rhun donned his equipment before he drew and inspected the blade. Rilen checked the saddle straps on what would be Rhun's horse, then guided the animal closer to its rider. The Kobold watched him wordlessly, the still-drawn sword in his hand.

"This is your horse. We're putting a lot of trust in you, Kobold."

Rhun held his sword higher. "Remember this blade, Elf. When our task is done, it will taste your blood."

The two faced each other, only a few feet apart, and the challenge hung between them. Elac moved to head off the impending fight. "Silvayn, where will we go first?"

The old mage was also watching the heated exchange. "We will cut through Nightwood Forest. We can angle southeast once we're clear of the trees. Two of us will go into Firereach to replenish our supplies before we enter Firereach Pass. From there, we'll skirt the western edge of the desert until we find an entrance to the tunnels."

"Why not head straight to the mountains?" Noria asked. "We would save a few days."

"Because soon enough, Norseth will know of the escape and begin the search for us. The fastest way to the mountains would be by way of Fort Philand. That's where he'll concentrate his search."

Noria rubbed her fingertips on her temples. "I don't like the sneaking around. It seems dishonorable."

Rilen secured his mount to the wagon, where it stood beside the remaining extra horse. "Sorry, your Highness, but it's necessary sometimes. I'll take one of the wagons toward Fort Philand and leave a few leagues of false trail. Somewhere along the way, I'll dump the wagon and bring both horses back. I'll try to catch up to you before you get to Firereach."

"Do you want some company?" Elac asked.

Rilen shook his head and pointed at Rhun. "You need to stay here. He's your responsibility."

Rilen clambered onto the seat of the wagon. He slapped the reins, and the wagon lurched away. Elac watched him head northeast over the rolling grasslands. Silvayn announced it was time for them to go.

They reached the stifling trees of Nightwood forest and stopped for lunch. It was just as well that Rilen had taken the wagon. Elac saw no possible way for them to guide something so wide through the trees. Even the horses were cumbersome in the confined space beneath the boughs. Although ancient roads were still noticeable, they had long since returned to the forest. Since there was no danger of immediate pursuit, Silvayn suggested they walk and lead the horses.

Unbidden, memories of his first trip through Nightwood Forest came to mind. As clearly as if it was yesterday, Elac saw the undead skeleton warriors emerge from the fallen trees to attack the party. He could see the hand-to-hand battle, hear the crack of Silvayn's lightning spells, and smell the scent of the burnt remains. But this time was different. The undead had been defeated. Only rarely had anyone seen so much as a single thrall west of the Paheny Mountains since the final hours of the Battle of Unity.

He also remembered the strange ceremony in the tiny collection of huts known as Divinity. He wondered if they would see the village again. Would there even be anyone there? He doubted it. From what he had learned of the Diviners, he believed they would only show themselves to those who needed their guidance.

They reached the eastern edge of the forest. The sun was low in the sky, casting its ruddy glow over the yellowed grasses of the Ranset plains. In the distance, the jagged outline of the Paheny Mountains jutted up from behind the hills. Silvayn announced that they would stop for the night, then make the journey to Firereach at first light.

Rhun secured his horse to a tree. "Which shift should I take on the watch?"

"None." Hadwyn folded his arms across his chest. "If we left you alone, I don't think you'd still be here in the morning."

Rhun gave a short, harsh laugh. "You might be right, little Dwarf. In fact, had I not given my promise, I would have left already. Unfortunately, I am a man of my word. I have pledged to see you safely to Hrcac, and that is what I shall do. Regardless of whether I stand watch, I'll still be here in the morning."

"Then you take the first watch after dinner. I'm going to eat, have a drink and go to bed."

Elac joined Silvayn, Adalyn, and Jayrne beside the fire. His wife handed him a wineskin, and he took a sip. "Who will go into Firereach, Silvayn?"

"You and Jayrne can go. I'll give you a list of what we need."

"What about money?" Elac asked. "I didn't bring that much with me."

Jayrne smiled. The soft glow of the flames accented her dimples. "Don't worry. That sergeant from the gates of Unity is buying." She bounced a pouch of jingling coins in the palm of her hand.

Elac raised an eyebrow. "You stole his money?"

"Sure. I have to keep in practice. Besides, I didn't like his attitude. Perhaps this will teach him some humility."

Elac wrapped his arm around her shoulders. "You're right. A little hardship is good for the soul."

Rhun stepped into the circle of light, sword half-drawn and eyes darting around looking into the impenetrable forest night. "What was that?"

Elac whipped around to face out into the darkness. He heard a shuffling sound in the fallen leaves of the forest. He rose to one knee and drew his sword.

"I hear it, but I can't see it."

"Perhaps a little light," Silvayn said. He muttered in the language of magic and clapped his hands together. A glow arose in the trees, illuminating the forest for quite a distance. They stood motionless, all of them peering into the trees to see what approached.

A high-pitched shriek erupted from the trees, and Elac had to cover his ears. With a rustling of branches, dozens of short creatures burst from hiding to charge the group. Red leathery skin covered their bodies. Bat-like ears protruded from their heads. Stubby wings jutted out from their backs. They howled as they charged, exposing tiny sharp teeth. They were shorter than even the two Dwarves, but their astonishing agility gave them an advantage of speed, which easily offset their size. Elac spread his feet and awaited the charge.

"Imps!" shouted Silvayn. Once more, he spoke in the language of magic.

Rhun swung his blade in a tight arc. An imp tumbled away, bleeding profusely from the gaping wound in its side. Another leapt at him, but he impaled it on his sword. Two more lunged at him. They bore him to the ground in a tangle of claws and teeth.

Elac had no time to worry about the Kobold. He stood between the two Dwarves, a first line of defense to protect Silvayn. He heard the snap of twin bowstrings behind him as Adalyn and Jayrne opened fire. He slashed at the nearest imp, and its severed arm tumbled away. Hadwyn's hammer smashed open the head of one imp, while his brother's axe nearly cut one in half at the waist. Their weapons, more gifts from the Ghosts of Piaras Keep, were nearly weightless, enabling the Dwarves to wield them with lightning speed. An imp dropped from the trees above them and landed on Elac's back. The claws tore futilely at his armored torso. He slammed his body backward into a tree. The imp fell aside. He impaled it where it lay.

Noria stood in the midst of the imps' charge. She battered some away with her shield and struck at others with her sword. She howled her family's ancient battle cry and shouted challenges at their attackers. Although the imps pressed her hard, few were able to mark her. Elac had to admire her tenacity and skill in battle. She was definitely her father's daughter.

Hadwyn and Gillen had their side of the battle under control. Blood dripped from several scratches on Elac's neck, but he raced to Rhun's side. The Kobold fought their attackers with his bare hands. A few feet away, his sword jutted upward from the body of the last imp it felled. He bled from a dozen wounds, and it was all he could do to remain on his feet.

Elac threw himself into the fray. With a downward swipe of his sword, he killed the imp attached to Rhun's leg. He charged into a knot of imps to Rhun's left, and they gave way before him. Rhun took advantage of the distraction to kick the body off his discarded sword. Three more imps died by Elac's hand.

Rhun moved closer to his side. In a sudden rush, ten imps scampered directly at them. The first five died on the point of the defenders' swords, but the rest bowled them over. Elac lost his grip on his weapon. He rolled onto his stomach and whipped out his dagger. With a grunt, he drove the short blade into an imp's chest, up to the hilt. Teeth and claws ripped at the exposed flesh of his face and neck while he wrenched the blade loose. He jabbed all around with the dagger in an effort to break free. One by one, his attackers fell before him.

The last imp bit down on his hand, and the dagger tumbled away. He fell to his back with the creature on his chest. A blur of leathery arms and legs snapped and bit at every opening it found. Elac's bloody hands wrapped around his foe's muscular neck, but the imp wriggled free from his grasp. A slash of its clawed hand drew blood from his neck.

The forest shook with a titanic burst of thunder. A blue beam of light streaked across the ground to strike the imp full in the chest. It flew into the darkness, dead before it hit the ground. Elac scrambled to his knees and secured his sword once more.

Rhun was down on one knee. He held one hand to a deep cut on his side as he gasped for breath. The Dwarves, while battered and bruised, appeared to be in good shape. The last two imps fled into the depths of the forest. Elac heard the sound of their passage long after they had disappeared from his sight. The Dwarves came over to stand beside him. They all faced into the darkness, almost expecting the imps to return. Elac cleaned and sheathed his sword.

Gillen went to each injured member of the group and muttered a few prayers to Zantar. When his turn came, Elac felt the pain of his injuries fade. Rhun gave a fierce growl when Gillen offered to help him.

"I am a Kobold warrior. I do not need the help of your worthless gods."

"Look, Rhun." Gillen planted himself directly in front of the Kobold, hands on hips. "I really don't care what you think of me or my religion, but you're nearly incapacitated. If those imps should come back, we need you able to fight. Right now, I doubt you could fight off a cold. Now relax, and let me treat your wounds."

Rhun flopped to the ground and waited. Noria stood above him. "You dishonor yourself, Kobold. We are your companions. To refuse our help is to insult us."

Rhun stared at the ground. "I don't need advice from a woman."

"I'd be careful, Kobold," Hadwyn said. "That woman could kill you with her bare hands."

Noria glared at Rhun but said nothing.

While the Dwarf priest healed their compatriot, Elac turned his attention to Silvayn. "How did you know killing that imp wouldn't destroy you? I thought users of Life magic were not allowed to harm another living thing."

"Actually, the theory, while sound, is not entirely accurate. We can destroy the undead for the same reason I was able to kill that imp."

"You mean the imp was undead?"

"No. They are not of this world. Life magic exists to protect and nurture those who are of this plane of existence. When we say that we can destroy the undead because they are not alive, it's an oversimplification."

Elac raised an eyebrow. "So you knew ahead of time that it was safe to use your magic on them?"

Silvayn shrugged. "Not exactly, but I was fairly certain.

"That's quite a risk, Silvayn."

"It was the only way to find out."

Elac glanced at Noria to make sure she could not hear what he had to say next. "What's wrong with Noria? She seems awfully concerned with maintaining some sense of honor. She doesn't have her father's arrogance, which is refreshing, but this obsession of hers is getting on my nerves. Is she that worried that she won't be accepted, just because she's a woman?"

"Acceptance is a concern of hers, yes. Remember, the hierarchy in Palindom has never allowed a woman to rule. Until now, they had never allowed a woman to take up arms, for that matter. But things are changing. She isn't that far down the line of succession, both from the Duchy of Palim and even the throne of Palindom itself. She feels she has a lot to prove.

"Her father is the real reason for this obsession. In her opinion, her father dishonored himself by leading a wasted charge into the undead ranks during the Battle of Unity. He threw away his own life and that of most of his knights, all in a vain attempt at capturing glory for himself. Princess Noria is on this quest as much to restore her father's honor as she is to help us. Or herself."

The attack by the imps convinced Elac they needed two people awake at all times. For Rhun's benefit, Silvayn explained where the imps had come from and described some of the other creatures they had faced. Fortunately, Rhun had some experience with the peculiar beasts roaming the plains, so he was ready to accept what he was told, even the story of the Cassibellanaus. They set a double watch, ate dinner, and settled in for the evening. Elac had the midnight watch with Princess Noria. They sat with their backs together. The blazing fire warded off the chill night air. She wanted to know everything Elac could tell her about what they had encountered in the past few weeks. She seemed particularly interested in the creature so thin it could only be seen from the side.

At first light, they ate breakfast and struck camp. It took them two hours to cross the Ranset Plains and come within sight of the walls of Firereach. They had kept their pace easy in an effort to disturb the ground as little as possible. Jayrne scouted the area and found a deep draw, cut into a hillside by a noisy brook. The group hid themselves and their horses in the gulley. Elac and Jayrne kept their own mounts, with two extras to help carry the supplies, and headed to the gates of Firereach.

Although the city of Firereach was not actually a fortress, it was, like any major Human city, well-defended. The stone walls were high and thick. Siege engines stood at each wall juncture. Soldiers armed with pikes patrolled the tops of the walls behind the battlements. Although the portcullis warding the city was lifted to allow passage into and out of Firereach, at least thirty armored soldiers manned the entrance. Archers leaned out over the walls to watch the crowd below. Elac and Jayrne passed into the city without being questioned.

They used the money Jayrne had pilfered in Unity to buy dried beef, salted hams, and other non-perishable foodstuffs. Although they already had cold weather gear, Jayrne suggested they pick up several heavy blankets. The last few nights had been cold, and it would only be worse in the mountains. They gathered their new possessions together and set about packing them into the saddlebags.

Two uniformed soldiers emerged from a nearby tavern and stood near Elac and his wife. One of them looked as if he had recently seen combat. His face and neck were bandaged, along with one leg.

The injured man took a long drink from a wineskin held loosely in one hand. "Out with it, Mirtan. What word did the messenger bring? He nearly beat that horse to death getting here in such a hurry."

Mirtan gestured with his bottle. "Come on, Salor. You know I'm not supposed to . . . all right. It was a message from Duke Norseth of Branig. Apparently, some rogue Knights of the Council broke a Kobold out of prison. They think the group is somewhere north of here, but they want us to move some units up into the area and cut them off if they head south."

Salor cast an appraising eye at the sun, already past its zenith in the late autumn sky. "Surely we aren't planning to send troops out at night?"

Mirtan shook his head. "No. Not after what happened to your patrol. You had what, thirty men with you? That thing tore your group apart."

Salor shuddered. "I can't believe it either. Five of us returned out of thirty, and I'm the only one who can walk. I can't believe something so thin could be so deadly."

"How can you hurt what you can't see?"

"True." Salor looked back at the entrance to the tavern. "If we're heading back out in the morning, I think I need another drink."

"I'm with you, buddy."

Elac waited until the two returned to the establishment. "I think it's time to move along. As long as they're looking north from here, we'll be okay, but I'll be happier once we get through the pass and into the desert."

"I hope Rilen is okay."

"Yeah. Not much we can do, though. Let's get moving."

They rode back out of the city and rejoined their companions. Elac told them of the conversation they had overheard. They did not stop for dinner, but instead galloped straight out to the foothills of the Paheny Mountains. The sun had already dropped behind the peaks in the East by the time they stopped for the night. They lit no fire. They were as fearful it might draw the attention of any patrols in the area as that it might bring in something worse.

The extra blankets they bought at Jayrne's suggestion came in handy the first night. Even though thick clouds rolled in as the red sky faded to black, a north wind carried with it the smell of winter. The first flakes of snow fell before darkness completely overtook them.

Elac bundled his cloak tightly about his frame and sat down next to Silvayn. "How can Rilen find us in all this?"

Silvayn placed a comforting hand on Elac's shoulder. "Don't worry about Rilen. He's a very resourceful fellow. I believe he's only a few leagues away right now. Shortly after we set up camp, I detected a scrying spell, cast several leagues north of us. Adalyn thinks it's Rilen trying to find us, so she has cast a similar spell, which he can detect. She and I will take turns casting the spell. Rilen can follow the magic like a beacon."

Elac was surprised not to see any resentment in the old mage's eyes. The fact that Adalyn had taught Rilen some rudimentary magic skills had been a source of contention for years. Elac shrugged and returned to where Jayrne had pitched their tent. He crawled inside the heavy canvas into surprising warmth. Jayrne had dug a small pit and placed a burning candle inside. Although the fire was tiny, it had a tremendous effect on the temperature inside the tent.

She rubbed her hands together over the homuncular flame and gave him an impudent grin. "Cozy, no?"

"Very nice. I wondered why you picked up some candles. Won't we be warm enough with our blankets?"

"Who says I want to be under the blankets all night?"

#

It was late, and with the candle extinguished, the air in the tent was freezing. Elac awoke to a light scratching on the fabric of the tent. He thrust his head outside to see Gillen kneeling beside the flap.

"Elac, get up. It's out there."

He did not need to be told what *it* was. *It*. The Cassibellanaus. It had found them at last. He nudged Jayrne awake as he scrambled into his armor and grabbed his weapons. He slipped out of the tent to stand beside Hadwyn. His breath billowed out in silvery clouds. Behind him, Silvayn and Adalyn fed sticks and branches into a fire. The crackling conflagration cast eerie shadows onto the ground, which was covered with a layer of newly fallen snow. The fire roared higher when Gillen tossed parts of a fallen tree into its center.

A flash of movement caught Elac's eye. A short, brown figure appeared from behind a hillside, circling the group. It turned to face them and disappeared. Elac brought up the Sword of Sir Draygen into a defensive position. He stared hard into the snowy landscape but could not see their hunter.

"It's studying us," Hadwyn said in a soft voice. "This has been going on for several minutes. It doesn't even leave footprints in the snow. Can you believe that?"

Jayrne, bow in hand, emerged to stand at Elac's side. She nocked an arrow and half-drew the bowstring. "Where did you see it?"

He pointed to the hillside. "It disappeared just to the left of that big rock."

She hefted the bow, drew the string to her cheek, and fired. The arrow hissed through the air to bury itself in the hillside. An angry chittering filled the air. Several feet to the left of where she fired, the Cassibellanaus reappeared, running to the side before disappearing once more. She fired another arrow, but this time there was no reaction.

"I've had it!" she shouted. She pulled Sir Aleron's cloak about her body and disappeared, nearly as invisible as the creature stalking them. Elac faced this way and that, but he could not see it. Next to the fire, Silvayn and Adalyn readied their magic in case the creature should show itself. Rhun, Noria, the Dwarves, and Elac formed a wide circle and waited for it to appear. Except for a few fleeting glimpses, the Cassibellanaus defeated their efforts.

A horse squealed in pain. All along the picket line, their animals reared and pawed at the air, frightened into a near-panic. Elac and Noria rushed to their side. A blow struck Elac from behind, and he tumbled head-first into the snow. He rolled to his back and swung his sword at his attacker, but found only air. He climbed to his feet with Noria standing beside him in a crouch. They saw nothing.

Hadwyn was the next to feel the bite of the Cassibellanaus. When he regained his feet, blood flowed from a deep gash in his cheek. He shouted curses and swung his hammer at the darkness. His brother held his axe ready, but there was nothing to fight. It had vanished once more.

A sudden realization dawned on Elac. This was how the Cassibellanaus was able to kill large numbers of well-armed soldiers. Darting, hit-and-fade attacks, coupled with frustration, fear, and eventually, panic, led the creature's prey to make bad decisions. They could stare at the terrain around them all night, but at best they would only catch occasional, brief glimpses of it as it circled them. Since he was unable to see it, he closed his eyes. Perhaps by focusing on his hearing, he might find it.

At first, he could only hear the sibilant whisper of Noria's breathing. But then he caught a different sound. A faint hissing snarl carried to him through the night air. It approached from his left, on a direct approach to him and Noria. Why not, when they could not see it from the front?

"Noria," he whispered. "It comes."

He motioned with his head, eyes still closed, and listened as the sound came closer. Noria brought her shield up just as the creature charged. It clanged into her shield and knocked her over backward.

Elac dove on top of the falling armored form, and his hands told him what his eyes could not: he had it. The slender beast squirmed in his grasp. Its clawed hands tore at his face and neck, leaving bloody trails of torn flesh, but he refused to relinquish his grip. He strained his muscles to their limit. Bit by bit, he managed to rotate it to one side. For the first time, he looked directly at the mystical predator.

Dark, bristly fur covered its skin. The eye he could see from his angle was narrow and almond-shaped. Muscles rippled beneath the covering of fur, mute testimony to the immense strength it possessed. He felt his grip loosen as the Cassibellanaus squirmed its way to freedom.

CHAPTER 8

"Noria! I've got it, but I can't hold on!"

Noria dropped her sword and reached out to place her free hand around one of Elac's. But even the extra help was not enough. The creature slipped free of their grip like a plume of smoke. Elac barely managed to raise his arm in time to deflect the blow as it descended for his head. Razor-sharp teeth locked onto his forearm and punched through his chain mail.

Then Jayrne appeared in the falling snow, sword in hand. She slashed at what she obviously could not see. The blade jumped in her hand, and a flash of blood sprayed across the snow. The pressure on Elac's arm vanished, along with their foe. But this time, it was different. Blood from the wound Jayrne inflicted dripped onto the snow where it stood. Elac grabbed the sword he had cast aside when he came to Noria's aid. The three advanced together.

Three rapid snaps of a bowstring broke the silence. The arrows seemed to become affixed in mid-air. A desperate wail rose from the throat of the Cassibellanaus. Rilen stepped into the circle of light and fired once again.

When the Cassibellanaus tried to flee, it exposed its side to the group. Hadwyn swung the Hammer of Sir Thalitt, and the weapon struck true. The creature fell to the snow, where it struggled to rise. Noria swung a two-handed blow at the creature's neck. The severed head tumbled away. The Cassibellanaus thrashed briefly, then lay still. After a few moments, the body shimmered, then vanished in a puff of smoke.

Elac leaned on his sword, his head sagging. He took several deep breaths and stared at the patch of churned snow where the creature had died. He felt the warm, sticky blood tracking down his arms to drip off his fingers. Jayrne made him hold up his arms, and she examined the lacerations left by the teeth of their attacker.

Hadwyn clapped a sturdy hand on Noria's armored back. "I know your countrymen frown upon having a woman as a warrior. But I can think of no man I would rather have by my side." His gaze darted wildly about his companions' faces. "In a fight, I mean."

"Thank you, Prince Hadwyn. That means a lot."

He shook his head and waved his hand at her. "We're companions at arms. There's no need for ceremony. Call me Hadwyn." He gave an appraising look at her injuries. "Come on. My brother can take care of this for you."

They all returned to the fire. Rilen dropped his pack to the ground and aligned Sir Aleron's longbow beside it.

"Rilen!" Jayrne flopped down at the Elf's side. "You made it back just in time."

"I was lucky. Norseth has his men out looking for us in force. They're scouring the Ranset Plains from about ten leagues north of Firereach to beyond the northern tip of Nightwood Forest. It's good we decided to head south first."

"How did you see that thing?" Gillen asked. "I could never manage more than a fleeting glimpse of it."

"Jayrne helped me there. She marked it with her sword. I just used the blood as a point of aim. It helped that I wasn't directly in front of it."

They tended to their wounds and checked on the horses. Since everyone was wide awake and not too likely to get any further sleep, Silvayn decided they should strike camp and get an early start. Elac and Jayrne dismantled their tent. He carefully wiped away the clinging snow before he packed it away. When the group cantered away from the campsite, the snow had already started falling again.

The sun had dropped to a ruddy glow on the horizon when they reached the entrance to Firereach Pass. Rilen returned at a trot and warned them to stay out of sight.

"If we get much closer, we might be seen. With all the unrest, the size of the garrison in Firereach Pass has been increased, and they are on the alert. They have watch fires built all along the pass. There's no way we can sneak through without being seen."

Rhun squinted into the fading night. "Your Human king has his own army guarding the pass, not the duke's. Would they not let us pass?"

"I think it's too risky," Noria said. "These soldiers know the king is dying. They will want to placate Norseth, in case he becomes the next king. Their commanders would sell their own mothers for a chance at a position in the new government." She spat in the direction of the army encamped somewhere ahead. "Men such as they seek glory in their own name, rather than in the name of their country. They have no honor."

"Can your magic put out the watch fires?" Jayrne asked. "Without them, we could easily get through, especially while their eyes are trying to adjust to the darkness."

Silvayn pursed his lips as he considered her suggestion. "I probably could, but if all the fires go out, they'll put the entire garrison on alert. We need another idea."

Rhun walked several paces away from the group and stared at the hillside. Elac followed his gaze, but darkness cloaked the rocky slope. Despite his sharp Elven eyesight, he could see nothing out of the ordinary.

Rilen grabbed the Kobold by the shoulder and spun him around. "Rhun, if you know of a way for us to slip past the sentries, now would be the time to tell us."

Rhun slapped the hand away with a snarl. "I'm not so anxious to betray my people that I would give away military secrets." He snarled. "Secrets you could use against my people in battle."

Rilen's hand dipped to his sword hilt, and Rhun followed suit. Elac stepped in between the two antagonists and pushed them apart. "That's enough. Rhun, what could we possibly do with any information you give us? If we try to talk to the soldiers, we'll be arrested."

Rhun rubbed a fur-covered finger along the side of his jaw. He stared at Elac for several moments. "Okay. Follow me. Lead the horses, don't talk, and don't light any torches."

Rhun paused to get his bearings. He led the group up the craggy slope. Their feet slipped and slid as they ascended, unable to find secure footholds among the jagged, sharp rocks. More than once, Rhun turned and placed a solitary finger to his lips, scowling at those behind him. After several minutes, they reached the shelter of scattered boulders and narrow crevices. Their Kobold guide slowed his pace.

Rhun held up one hand and motioned everyone closer. Although they were still some distance from the encamped army, he kept his voice to a harsh whisper. "You are aware that the Kobold people have an extensive series of tunnels that crisscross the Paheny Mountains. During the decades leading up to the last war, Overlord Hamedon's father ordered the digging of a new tunnel. This one was to lead from the eastern edge of the Desert of Malator to the western end of the Ranset Plains. By going under the mountain instead of over it, we could sneak large numbers of troops past the Human army guarding Firereach Pass. Hamedon hoped to have it ready by the outset of the war. We could have hit the defenders from both sides simultaneously.

"The war started before we completed the tunnel. However, it was finished not six months ago. The opening at this end is just ahead." He took a step toward a boulder, then stopped. "You see now why I was hesitant to tell you."

"If our troops know about it, they could ambush your people as they emerge," Noria said. "I won't lie to you. Upon my return, I will be duty-bound to report this matter. But you have shown great courage in doing so. Even though you believe it is in the name of the greater good, it cannot be an easy thing."

Rilen snorted. "He just sold out his own people, and you call it courage?"

Rhun's entire body tensed, but before he could offer a retort, Adalyn grabbed Rilen by the arm and pulled him aside.

Elac offered his hand to the Kobold. "Don't listen to him. You made a very difficult decision just now."

Rhun folded his arms. He stared at Elac, at his outstretched hand, and then at Rilen. Without another word, he yanked on his horse's reins and walked him behind the boulder. Elac stayed where he was a few moments longer, shrugged at his discomfort, and followed closely. The area behind the massive stone opened into a smooth-floored tunnel. Shiny pockmarks checkered the walls, evidence of the recent mining activities the Kobolds used to finish the passage. They paused just inside the opening while Silvayn cast a spell to create a source of light.

The horses balked at the opening to the tunnel. Elac and his friends had to drag them inside by their reins. Even after they were inside, they snorted and shuffled, sometimes even rearing up on their hind legs, at least as far as the low ceiling would allow. Elac could not blame them. Try as he might, he could not force his mind away from the thought of how much rock hung suspended over his head. All it would take was one area where the Kobolds' construction was faulty, and the whole mountain could come crashing down on their heads.

They walked for several hours before Rilen called a halt. They herded the animals together to keep them from straying. Elac had assumed, with the death of the Cassibellanaus, they would return to having guard duty limited to one person at a time. To his surprise, Rilen established the order for a two-person watch while they slept. His explanation for having two people awake was sensible. Their camp could be accessed from either direction, which meant two people could more effectively watch for trouble. But Elac knew the real reason. Rilen feared that if Rhun was left alone, he might run away. Or worse, he could kill them all before he returned to his people.

Elac ate a little food and sipped from his waterskin. With a nod to the two Dwarves, who had the first shift, he slipped beneath the blankets next to his sleeping wife.

#

They had been marching for untold hours. Elac's feet ached from the effort, but he refused to complain. He wondered if they might have to sleep in the tunnel again. He hesitated to think of it as "spending the night." Indeed, he had lost all sense of time in the seemingly endless passage. More than anything, he just wanted the tunnel to end.

A red glow appeared in the distance. Adalyn, who had taken over the task of providing light, allowed her spell to dissipate. They stopped and waited for several minutes while their eyes adjusted to the dimmer lighting. Rilen motioned to the others to stay where they were, then he crept forward. Without a sound, he disappeared around a bend in the passage.

He was gone only briefly. He stepped back into view and waved them to his side. As they drew closer, Elac realized the glow he was seeing came from the sun, low in the eastern sky. They gathered around Rilen.

"Silvayn," Rilen said, "I recommend we get some rest inside the tunnel. Even though it's late in the year, I think the desert will still be hot during the day. It would be best to remain inside until an hour or two before sundown."

Silvayn squinted into the morning sun. "Probably not a bad idea. Rhun?"

The Kobold shrugged and sat against the wall. "Your call. Stay or go. I really don't care."

They waited for several hours just inside the entrance. Elac ventured out once in search of water, accompanied by Gillen. The sun beat down upon them, a brutal hammer pounding them against the anvil of the desert.

"Hot work," Gillen said as they filled their water containers from a rippling stream that ran down the mountainside a half-mile from their camp. "I feel like dipping my head in the water."

Elac chuckled. "What do you think of Rhun?"

Gillen squinted into the sun. "He's a hard one to figure. Someone or something convinced him to go along with us, but I'm not sure how deeply his loyalty to us will run. If we encounter a group of Kobolds, he'd be just as like to betray us as help us."

"I think he's on our side. It took a lot for him to give up the secret of this tunnel. What I worry about is Rilen. I'm afraid the two of them will fight."

"Are you worried about Rilen getting hurt?"

"Rilen would kill him. I'm worried because we need Rhun in order to succeed in this. If he and Rilen come to blows, we could be in trouble."

Gillen hefted his waterskins. "It's up to us to be the peacemakers. The ladies, too. I don't think my brother would be much help. He's too much like Rilen. I'll keep an eye on him, if you can keep Rilen under control."

Elac grinned broadly. "I think your brother is busy keeping an eye on Noria."

Gillen gave a heavy sigh. "Aren't we all. But you're right. I just hope he doesn't cause any trouble with her before this is over."

The group set out once more with the onset of evening. Although the sun was still up, the Paheny Mountains cast their shadow well out onto the floor of the desert, and the temperature plummeted. Since they were able to ride the horses again, they made good time. The group spoke little during the journey. Elac felt relieved to see Rilen leading the group, while Rhun stayed at the rear with Gillen. At least for a time, their internal war was put to rest.

It was nearly dark when Elac heard the sound. It resembled an enormous flag fluttering in a summer breeze. He twisted about in his saddle but could not find the source. The others heard it, too, and they all rode with their hands on their weapons. Elac strapped his shield tightly against his left arm and loosened his sword in its sheath.

A thunderous roar shattered the night as a roiling cloud dropped out of the night sky. It swept closer to them and twisted into shape before their eyes. Elac spotted a pair of broad wings sprouting off the back. Four clawed limbs dangled beneath its nebulous body. The elongated, narrow head ended in a hooked beak. The mouth gaped wide as it dropped in for the attack.

Rilen dove from his saddle and rose to his feet, sword in hand. The others were less graceful in their preparations and were not ready when it made its first pass. Rilen swung his sword in an overhead arc, but it passed harmlessly through the diaphanous figure. A leg crashed into Rilen's shield and threw the Elf several feet away.

"Mist dragon!" Adalyn warned.

Silvayn chanted in the language of magic, but Elac knew he would not have the spell ready before the dragon returned. He deliberately placed himself between the banking dragon and the old wizard. The dragon righted its path and attacked once more. This time, the group stood ready. Gillen and Hadwyn struck simultaneous blows with their enchanted weapons. The dragon shrieked in response. It swiped one leg at Gillen, and the claws drew red streaks along the side of his face. Rhun struck with his own weapon, but it was no more effective than Rilen's.

"Stand back," Elac said. "Normal weapons won't hurt it."

As it swerved higher to come about once more, Silvayn released his spell. A cone of fire erupted from his hands and enveloped the dragon. Its cry of pain shook rocks loose from the hillside and sent the horses into a panic. Jayrne, Noria, and Rhun, who had no enchanted weapons, grabbed the reins in a desperate bid to keep their animals from running off.

Rilen knelt to Elac's right, with the Longbow of Sir Aleron in hand, ready to fire. Adalyn stood to Elac's left with held her sword ready. The two Dwarves moved into position on the other side of Silvayn. The group formed a protective arc as the mage readied another spell. The dragon rose higher into the sky and disappeared.

An eerie silence descended. Silvayn finished his chant and stood waiting. All eyes remained fixed on the sky. Elac stood motionless as his heartbeat pounded in his ears. He tightened his grip on his sword and maintained his vigil.

Adalyn shouted a warning and pointed east. Elac squinted into the distance where a dim figure took shape. It was low, almost to the ground, and it raced toward them at breakneck speed. As soon as it entered his range, Rilen opened fire with his enchanted longbow. The dragon roared its fury and bore down on them.

Adalyn's sword flashed with an eerie light when it struck the dragon's flank. It pulled up short and thrust out at Elac with its front legs. The dagger-sized talons wrapped around his struggling form and lifted him off the ground, even as he chopped at the wispy appendages. Silvayn let loose another fire blast. The dragon staggered but hopped on its hind legs and flapped its wings to take flight. Elac knew if he left the ground in its grasp, he would die.

The Dwarves pounded furiously at the beast. Their magic weapons rebounded from the dragon's skin with brilliant flashes of light. Rilen dashed around to the front of the dragon and stood beneath its head. He fired directly into the underside of the massive jaw. The dragon staggered under the onslaught, dropping one of the clawed legs holding Elac in order to regain its balance.

Elac drove Sir Draygen's sword into the shimmering neck. The dragon gave a howl of pain that echoed off the mountainside and left Elac's ears ringing. All around him, he saw his friends shouting, but he could not hear. He tumbled from the creature's grasp and rolled to his feet. His only thought was to finish the fight. He swung at the neck, then swung again.

A wide swipe of the dragon's tail sent the two Dwarves tumbling to the side. It spun and retreated through the hole it had opened. Rilen fired shot after shot until the arrows protruded from the dragon in all directions. It stumbled and fell. Elac and Adalyn were upon it instantly, weapons slashing, the Dwarves not far behind. Silvayn sent another cone of fire into the undulating body. The dragon exploded in a great outrush of wind that knocked the group from their feet.

Adalyn and Silvayn stepped in to help with the wild-eyed horses. Gillen checked on the battered warriors to see if anyone had a serious injury. Elac, Hadwyn, and Rilen studied the ground where the dragon had fallen. The beast's death throes had scorched the ground all around.

Elac glanced at his blood-soaked sleeve, which dribbled small droplets onto the rocky turf. "It's almost like it was never here."

Hadwyn rubbed his bruised ribs. "I think it left its mark on the world."

They remounted their horses. As they resumed their journey, Elac guided his horse next to Silvayn. "That was a mist dragon? I thought demons were the only indigenous creatures on the Plane of Mist."

Silvayn smiled, although the sagging of his shoulders betrayed his exhaustion. "There are all manner of unnatural creatures living on Ardea, what you call the Plane of Mist. During our previous sojourn there, you visited an area overrun by the mist demons. That's why you saw nothing else. Had Tracker's Peak been located elsewhere, those trapped inside might well have been banished to a region of Ardea dominated by the dragons. Or worse. But the dragon was bad enough, being incorporeal. With the demon, our normal weapons might not have been much of a threat, but they could at least cause injury. In the case of the dragon, it was like fighting smoke."

"Let's hope we don't see anything like that again."

They rode for several hours in a northeasterly direction. Rhun guided them among the foothills of the Paheny Mountains. It lengthened their journey, since their path was a circuitous one rather than a straight line. But Elac knew it was necessary. It kept them away from the sand dunes of the desert floor, and it probably made finding the next tunnel entrance much easier. The Kobold led them, moving through the night. When at last he angled up higher into the rolling hills, the sun was already staining the eastern sky a ruddy haze.

A chill, bitter wind blew out of the north, and a heavy cloud cover soon followed. Occasional bursts of snow fell from the gray winter sky. At first, the flurries came several minutes apart. By the time the sun had cleared the horizon, the snow fell at a steady pace. Before long, the ground had been covered. Rilen frowned as he stared at the trail their horses were leaving in the snow behind them.

"If someone is looking for us, they won't have trouble tracking us down."

"We should be fine once we reached the tunnels," Elac said.

"Sure, except that they will be fairly certain where we entered."

At Noria's suggestion, they lined up single file. It would hide their numbers until the falling snow buried their tracks. They rode for another hour. With the snow more than ankle deep, Rhun called a halt.

"I need to check the area. The entrance is nearby, but I'll have to find it."

"You're not going anywhere alone, Kobold," Rilen said.

"Why don't you come with me? I'd let you walk right in front of me."

Elac and Gillen exchanged a glance. The Dwarf priest climbed down from his saddle. "I'll go with him." He slipped his axe from its place on his saddle and followed the Kobold into the swirling snow.

Elac dismounted. "Rilen, we need to trust Rhun sometime. We may end up in a situation where we don't have time for suspicion. He has helped us this far."

"You trust him. I can't."

"Because he's a Kobold?"

"Yeah, that's part of it. Elac, you have a great heart. You always want to see the best in people. That's a wonderful gift, but it can make you lose your perspective. Remember, just three weeks ago he was leading raids into Palindom. His soldiers murdered innocent people and burned villages and caravans."

Rilen snatched several waterskins from the horses and stormed away, kicking at snow drifts and muttering under his breath. Elac watched him go.

He felt a light touch on his shoulder. He knew without looking that it was Jayrne. "Elac, you're not going to change him. He has been through too much at the hands of Kobolds for him to be any other way."

"Six years ago, Kobolds massacred my caravan and killed my friends. Yet I hold no rancor for Kobolds. The entire race is not responsible for the actions of a few, especially when those few were only acting under the orders of their leader."

"I agree with you, Elac," Noria said, who had dismounted and stood beside him, "but remember this. The same Overlord who ordered the raids six years ago is in charge still. He's been ordering raids yet again. Rilen is a military man. He feels most keenly the frustration of not being allowed to take the fight to the enemy. The Unity Council is afraid to act, so they relegate their forces to a defensive posture. Rilen has grown to despise his enemy, and in his mind, all Kobolds are the enemy."

"Your father died in that war." Elac hesitated. "Yet you don't seem to have a grudge against the Kobolds."

Noria sighed. "My father was killed by the undead. Thralls pulled him and his knights from their saddles and slaughtered them. He died as a result of his own foolish pride. Now I must live with his legacy. The Kobolds played no major part in his death, so I do not concern myself with them."

Gillen and Rhun emerged from the concealing snowfall like wraiths. Rhun grabbed his horse's reins from Jayrne. "Follow me. It isn't far."

This time, they blindfolded the horses until they were several dozen yards into the tunnel, which made it much easier to move them inside. As before, the height of the tunnel forced them to walk and lead their mounts. Silvayn lit the way with a spell. Rhun guided them deeper into the passage. The tunnel branched, and he took path on the left.

"This way is longer," he said. "But the other tunnel leads through the city of Nightreach. We need to bypass the cities if you expect to reach Hrcac alive."

Elac noticed immediately how much older the tunnel was than the one at Firereach Pass. The ground had been worn smooth by the passage of countless feet. A closer look at the shape of the tunnel revealed a startling mystery. It was almost completely rounded. How could someone dig a tunnel in a near-perfect circular shape? Perhaps the Kobolds had used magic in the forming of their subterranean roads.

They stopped for lunch. Elac deliberately chose a place next to where Rhun ate in stoic silence. "Rhun, can you answer a question for me?"

The Kobold grunted but did not look up from his food.

"How did your people make these tunnels?"

Rhun glanced up at him, then reached for his water. "We didn't. We're near where Tracker's Peak stood. Where it stands once more. This area used to have an active volcano. Before the volcano erupted, the molten rock had to work its way up to the surface. It cut these tunnels out. When the volcano went dormant, we claimed the passages as our own."

Elac opened his mouth to ask another question, but Rhun turned his back on him and shoved another bite into his mouth. He did not say another word, even when Silvayn announced it was time to move on. Elac contemplated their Kobold guide. Something about him seemed familiar. With a sudden chill, he knew what it was. Rhun reminded him of the reticent bodyguard, Morfal, who had accompanied them at the suggestion of Falstoff. Rilen had not trusted Morfal, either. In the end, both Falstoff and Morfal had betrayed them all. Would it be the same with Rhun?

From somewhere to their front, the sound of rough kobold voices echoed back to them. They froze in place.

"Silvayn," Elac asked, "do we run?"

"No," Rhun hissed. "If they're close enough for us to hear them, they'll have heard us and seen our light. Let me talk to them first."

"So you can turn us over to them?" Rilen asked.

"You'll just have to trust me. If I wanted to betray you, I'd have taken us to Nightreach. You'd all be dead by now."

"That's enough, both of you," Silvayn said. "Rhun, if you think you can talk our way through this, then do so. Going back does us no good. We can't go around them, and we would never make it overland."

Elac knew Silvayn was right. In all likelihood, this would not be their only encounter before they reached Hrcac. With all the Kobold activity in the lands of the West, he was surprised they had not already bumped into a squad of Kobolds. Rhun glared at Rilen, hand on his sword hilt, then walked forward once more.

They rounded a bend in the passage and entered a wide, open chamber. The ceiling was at least fifteen feet high, while the cavern itself was about forty feet across. Torches hung in brackets on the wall. The red flame cast a flickering light on the rounded walls. Fifteen Kobolds stood in a group on the far side of the room. Their conversation broke off when the travelers entered the room.

Their leader stepped forward. "What is this? Rhun, is that you?"

Rhun strode forward with an eager step. "Khalas! It is good to see you!"

Khalas stopped in the center of the room. "Who are these people, and where do you think you are taking them?"

"We travel to Hrcac on a mission vital to the survival of the Kobold nation."

Khalas shook his head and drew his sword. "You know as well as I do, Rhun. Any foreigner caught in our tunnels forfeits his life. The law is inviolate."

The other Kobolds brought forth their own weapons. Rilen's sword leapt into his hand, and he rushed to the front of their ranks. Elac stood with Noria on Rilen's left flank. The Dwarves held the right. Jayrne had wrapped herself in Sir Draygen's cloak and disappeared from view. Adalyn placed herself beside Rilen. In the middle of the room, Rhun and Khalas faced each other.

"This isn't necessary, Khalas. You and I have spoken of the problems we face. You know there is something going on in the capital. Solone has some kind of supernatural hold over Overlord Hamedon. These people travel to Hrcac to expose him and free our leader from his thrall."

Khalas growled. "Why would they help us? More importantly, why do you help them now? I heard your company was destroyed by Elves. Why do you yet live? Why have you brought these foreigners into our land? Have you betrayed us?"

The two groups closed with each other. Khalas slashed at Rhun, who deflected the blow with his shield. He countered with a stroke aimed at his opponent's hilt. With a flick of his wrist, he sent Khalas's sword flying.

"I don't want to hurt you, my friend. We can still end this! We can—"

A Kobold shrieked in agony. At the rear of the formation, a shadowy form held the Kobold aloft, then smashed him to the ground. The other Kobolds backed away, their eyes wide. Their trembling hands lowered their weapons as they eyed the tunnels for a way out. Elac knew the silhouetted creature all too well.

"Khalas!" shouted Silvayn. "That thing is a Mist Demon!"

"We know what it is. These creatures have been killing our people for months in this tunnel." Khalas backed away from the encroaching demon.

Elac slipped to Khalas's side. "Your weapons might injure it. But some of us have weapons that can kill it. Let us help you."

The demon charged.

CHAPTER 9

The demon roared, and the Kobolds fell back. The mists within its body swirled as if driven by some unseen wind. It grabbed the nearest Kobold in a two-handed grip and ripped him from the floor. While the other Kobolds flailed at the translucent figure in a vain attempt to save their companion, the demon slowly crushed the life from its victim. It slammed him to the ground, raised a massive foot, and stomped the Kobold's helmeted head. Blood and brain matter gushed across the floor.

Rilen's longbow hummed, and several arrows drove deep into the demon's shoulder and head. The nearest Kobold launched his own counterattack. The demon took a step backward as it turned its gaze on the Kobold. It recoiled from the sword blows but showed no signs of injury. The Kobold thrust his sword directly at the demon's chest. It grabbed his blade and wrenched it from his hands. One hand seized the Kobold by the throat, and the other drove the point of the sword through his head.

Elac shouldered his way free of the panicked Kobolds. The demon tore several of Rilen's arrows loose and threw them to the side. Elac sidestepped to his right, eyes fixed on the demon. To his left, Adalyn ran to the other side of the cavern. He thrust at the demon, a feint designed to get the creature's attention. It worked.

The demon gave a bellow that echoed around the confines of the stone chamber. With its arms outstretched, it reached for Elac. Two more of Rilen's arrows buried themselves in the diaphanous chest. When it reached for him, Elac swung his blade at the appendage. The demon leapt away.

Adalyn swung a two-handed blow at the demon's broad, unprotected back. The creature's shriek reverberated off the cavern walls and drove Elac to his knees. The demon whirled to face Adalyn, who had lowered her guard to cover her ears. She dropped into a crouch. Her eyes looked unfocused as she raised her sword once more. The demon stalked closer and emitted a low growl. It swung a blow at Adalyn's trembling sword arm.

At the last moment, Noria was there, covering Adalyn with the Shield of Omonis. She staggered under the force of the blow, but she did not yield. Her intervention gave Adalyn precious seconds to catch her breath.

The Dwarves managed to push free of the tangled knot of Kobolds and confront their attacker. They charged together, alternating blows between Hadwyn's hammer and Gillen's axe. The demon pounded its fists on the floor and howled in impotent rage.

Jayrne appeared off to the demon's right. Her short sword drove deep into the torso. It spun and swiped at her with a massive arm, but she had already danced out of reach. She pulled her cloak tighter and began to fade from view.

It was all the distraction Elac needed. He ducked low and charged as more of Rilen's arrows struck true. He dropped to one knee and struck at the back of a tree-trunk-sized leg. The blow hamstrung the demon, which fell to its back. Elac and his friends rushed in for the kill. Their weapons battered the supine, misty form. The demon shrunk in upon itself, then flashed a brilliant light. With an earsplitting detonation that threw the combatants about the room, it vanished.

For long moments, no one moved. The Kobolds gathered together in a tight knot. They could only stare in absolute silence. Khalas sheathed his sword and checked on his fallen men. Somehow, none of Elac's friends were seriously injured in the melee.

Hands on his hips, Rhun stood before Khalas. "Now do you see? There is more involved here than an incursion by foreigners. There are powers involved far beyond our comprehension. These creatures are only the beginning. Mark my words. Solone is involved in this somehow."

Khalas stared at the body of one of his fallen soldiers. "Ghelas was my friend for ten years. Now he is dead in some random fight in our own land." He let out a long breath. "What is the point of this, Rhun? Tell me he died for a reason."

Elac knew the time had come to intervene. "Your friend gave his life for an important cause. It's up to you to make certain his sacrifice isn't wasted. To make sure the lives of none of your fallen soldiers are wasted."

Khalas was strangely subdued. The harsh, tense attitude from their earlier discussion was gone. He spoke in a quiet voice. "What do you mean?"

"You didn't trust us before. I can't say I blame you. If an Elf came into my village leading a group of Kobolds and telling me to trust them, I would have reacted as you did. But you've been given a chance to see things from a new perspective."

Khalas nodded. "Had you and your friends not intervened, I would have lost many more of my soldiers. You could have fled and escaped, but instead you stayed and fought." He sat in the center of the floor and crossed his legs. "I will listen."

Elac and Rhun joined him on the ground. "This Elf and I have shared a vision," Rhun said. "There is a great evil abroad in the land. It reaches its hand into all four of the nations. In Palindom, the agents of this evil tried to sow discord and civil war. In our own country, Solone uses foul magic to dominate the mind of Overlord Hamedon. He sends our people off to die in senseless battles. Something must be done!"

"A vision told you this? How can you trust it?"

"A human prince, who was killed in the last war, came to me in my dream, along with my father. They told me of this Elf's vision, even before he spoke to me about it. They told me I must help him and his friends. In my vision, I saw what will come to pass if they fail.

"And there is more. This is the Elf, Elac, who slew Volnor. I believe Hamedon will at least let him speak."

Khalas stroked the fur on his jaw. "Long have I had my doubts about the sudden change in Overlord Hamedon's attitude toward the West. I have also wondered at the rapid elevation of a foreigner like Solone, who walked into the palace out of nowhere to become the Overlord's new advisor." He turned his attention to Elac. "Can you do this? Can you expose Solone as the traitor he is and free my people?"

"If you will help us get to Hrcac, I will certainly try."

Khalas and Rhun clasped forearms and pulled each other to their feet. Khalas looked past Rhun to Elac, who was still on the floor. "Then we will help you." He motioned his soldiers to his side and faced them. "What I say now, I say not as your commander, but as your friend. Not as a military leader, but as your countryman. If this Elf and his friends fail in what they do, Solone will have all who helped him executed. I will order no one to help us. If you do not wish to be a part of this mission, you may leave now."

When none of the Kobolds moved, Rhun bowed and gestured to the darkened tunnel across the cavern. "Lead on, Khalas."

#

They spent several days in the tunnels of the Kobolds. Although the direct distance between them and Hrcac was about forty leagues, they were obliged to travel further in order to avoid the more frequently traveled passages, as well as the subterranean Kobold cities. Fortunately, their escort knew where to find supply points in the tunnels, so they were able to replenish their stores of food and water.

As best as Elac could tell, it was the seventh day of their journey when they encountered a company of armed Kobolds. This other group had stopped for a meal break, so Khalas's soldiers had not heard them. By the time they spotted the new force, it was too late to turn back.

One Kobold, whose gold-trimmed uniform designated him as the leader, held out his hand in greeting. He froze in place when he saw who the Kobolds were escorting. His hand went to his sword hilt, and his eyes narrowed. "Who are you, and where do you think you're taking them?"

"My name is Khalas. My unit is escorting these people to Hrcac."

"To what end? You know they are not allowed to enter the city, on pain of death."

"We found them just outside the tunnels near Ranset. They have information they will sell to our people, information we can use against the Humans." His eyes narrowed, and he whispered in the harsh Kobold tongue. Elac's knowledge of the Kobold language was rudimentary, at best. He could not understand what was said in the hushed conversation. Elac gave Jayrne's hand a squeeze, as much to reassure himself as her. The two Kobolds spoke quietly for several minutes. The other Kobold laughed uproariously.

When he spoke again, it was in the language spoken in the West. "You may pass. Rest assured, if you try any trickery, you will die."

Khalas led them past the other Kobolds. One leered at Jayrne as she passed. Elac met the lecherous gaze with a piercing gaze of his own, until the Kobold looked away. Raucous laughter echoed down the corridor as they made their tenuous escape.

Elac waited until they were well away from the other Kobolds before he asked the question. "Khalas. If you don't mind my asking, what did you say to him?"

"I told him when you arrive in Hrcac, you would be arrested and tortured for the information you carry."

#

Blisters covered Elac's feet by the time they emerged from the tunnels. After so many days in the endless darkness, the moonlit night sky seemed as bright as a sunrise. Snow blanketed the landscape, and the air was chill. They stood on a wide shelf, high above the port city of Hrcac. Elac breathed deeply of the fresh mountain air, and his spirits soared. To their left, a wide path wound down the mountainside. To his chagrin, the snow on the path was heavily trampled. Their chances of an encounter were high. They pulled their hoods over their heads, mounted their horses, and followed Khalas's footsoldiers down the steep incline.

Since the other Kobolds had no horses, the descent was slow. Elac felt the bite of the stiff wind blowing off the Gulf of Hrcac, but he decided being in the open on horseback was definitely better than walking underground, no matter how cold. Overhead, the stars shone down upon the landscape. In another setting, Elac would have found the scenery breathtaking. Although it was at least two leagues to the bay, he could still see the lanterns burning brightly on the sides of the ships standing at anchor. Hrcac itself was also well-lit. The edge of the city lights marked the beginning of the bay. Further out to sea, an occasional whitecap gleamed against the dark backdrop of the Hrcac Sea.

The sunrise was particularly beautiful. They finished their descent just as the brilliant red disk seemed to rise out of the sea. Elac was grateful; the gradual brightening gave their eyes time to adjust after living in perpetual darkness for so many days. Khalas guided the group onto a broad avenue. The snow had been cleared away. The unpaved turf beneath was frozen solid, with ruts cut in the roadway that would last until spring thawed the land. An occasional Kobold passed by, but none paid attention to the armed and hooded group as it ambled along.

They reached the gates, which were flung wide open. A contingent of Kobolds, dressed in burnished breastplate armor and carrying long pikes, stood to either side. Atop the battlements, smaller groups of Kobolds patrolled the tops of the city's walls. Overhead, a portcullis dangled from a system of chains and pulleys, ready to be dropped in the event of an emergency.

Kobold travelers entered and exited the city with total impunity, but Elac's entourage contained more than Kobolds. Despite having their hoods up and their cloaks drawn about their bodies, they were accosted at the gate. A sentry on their right shouted something unintelligible in the Kobold tongue, and the twin formations of soldiers converged to form a phalanx, barring entrance to the city. Khalas and Rhun dismounted and approached the line of guards.

An especially tall Kobold with a golden crest on his helmet slipped between two of his soldiers. He held up one hand, and Khalas and Rhun stopped. "I am Captain Dolas. Who are you that you would seek to bring foreigners before our walls?" He pointed, and one of his guards stepped forward to yank back the hoods concealing Hadwyn and Gillen. "Dwarves?"

"Captain, if you give me but a moment, I can explain," Rhun said.

Other Kobolds came forward and pulled down the other travelers' hoods. Dolas gave a tremendous roar, and he ripped his sword from his sheath. "Elves! You have brought Elves to the very heart of our nation! You shall die a thousand deaths for this!"

"Captain! I am Lieutenant Khalas. I have taken these people under my protection. They are . . . a special deputation, here to discuss diverse matters with Overlord Hamedon and his Excellency, Solone. They seek to help us overthrow the Unity Council and the three nations of the West. You cannot harm them. I have given my word."

Dolas snorted and stood quietly for several moments, hands on hips. "So be it. While you yet live, these people shall not be harmed." He pointed to his archers on the battlements. Several bowstrings snapped in unison, and Khalas stumbled to the frozen turf, pierced by a dozen arrows. His dying breaths rattled in his chest as he fought to draw air into his lungs. He pushed up to his hands and knees, head sagging, and finally dropped to the cobblestones.

Dolas folded his arms across his armored chest. "Would anyone else care to argue with me? No?" He gestured once more, and at least two dozen Kobolds rushed forward to snatch Elac and his companions from their saddles. The Kobolds who escorted them were left on their horses. One soldier held Elac's arms firmly behind his back, while two others disarmed him. One of them grabbed the neck of Elac's cloak and yanked it open. Between being yanked from his saddle and having his cloak almost torn open, his Knight of the Council medallion had emerged from his tunic. It hung in full view.

Dolas ground his teeth together, spittle dripping from his fangs. He stepped directly in front of Elac. He felt the Kobold captain's hot, fetid breath on his face. Dolas's hand shot out to grasp Elac by the throat.

"Who are you? What are you doing here? No lies this time!"

Elac returned the captain's harsh gaze. He refused to give Dolas the satisfaction of seeing his prisoner quake with fear. He knew lies would be wasted, so he said nothing.

Dolas flung him to the ground and placed the tip of his sword against the tender skin of Elac's neck, just above his armor. The sharp tip of the blade bit into his flesh. He felt his hot, sticky blood trickle away from the wound. The pressure eased off.

"I have a better idea." He looked up at his soldiers. "Search the others. See how many of them are with the Unity Council."

Elac tried to see what was happening, but Dolas applied pressure to the sword once more. He heard shouted protests from his friends. Dolas grinned.

"Excellent. Overlord Hamedon will be pleased. I will escort these prisoners to see him. You see, outlanders, today is the great Feast of Rolados. It is customary for our leader to execute prisoners on this day. His Imperial Majesty will be very happy to see you. As for your escort, they shall share your fate."

Dolas barked his orders, and the Kobolds jumped to do his bidding. Elac, his friends, and the Kobolds who had brought them to Hrcac were bound, blindfolded, and thrown across the saddles of their horses. He tensed the muscles in his stomach, but the constant bouncing still nearly made him physically ill. It took every ounce of his willpower to keep his stomach under control. He would not give his captors the satisfaction.

At length, the horse stopped. A hand grabbed the end of his cloak and hauled him to the ground. He had no way to break his fall. The back of his head slammed into the ground, eliciting a bright flash of light before his eyes. He lay for a few moments on the frozen turf, gasping and panting. Someone grabbed his hair and hauled him to his feet. Unseen hands ripped the blindfold from his head. He squinted until his eyes adjusted to the sunlight.

Before him, on a raised dais, sat a Kobold who could only be Overlord Hamedon. His fur had turned a silvery gray hue. He wore a golden crown, inset with precious jewels. His neck was hidden behind a chainmail hood. A black cloak lay flung out behind his throne, and it billowed in the stiff wind blowing in from the Bay of Hrcac. Beside him stood a Human in thick banded armor. An estok sword hung at his waist, and daggers protruded from the tops of his boots. He held his helmet under one arm. The narrow, slanted eye holes and the broad wings protruding from the sides were impressive-looking, but Elac believed the features rendered the helmet ineffective. Despite the extent of his armament, he carried no shield.

Jayrne leaned heavily against Elac. "That has to be Solone," she whispered.

"I agree."

"Elac, be careful. I think he's a mage."

"How do you know?"

"Look at what he's wearing. He has entirely too many weapons. His armor is too heavy for a man his size. And that sword of his isn't very effective without a shield. I think he's just trying to convince people he's a warrior."

"Silence!" shouted the man beside Overlord Hamedon. "Do not speak unless his Imperial Majesty gives you leave."

Hamedon held up one hand, his eyes on the party before him. The man to his side fell silent. He took a deep, slow breath. "So. What brings you to my city? What mischief has the Unity Council sent you to perform?"

Elac gave a deep bow, a movement hindered with his hands still tightly bound in front of him. "Greetings, Overlord Hamedon, from the Unity Council. We are here on a mission of peace. I assure you, we mean no mischief."

"It is as I told you, your Imperial Majesty," said the man to Hamedon's left. "They will never tell you their true intent. Perhaps I can persuade them to be more open."

"Your point is well-taken, Solone. I shall give them but one more chance, before I turn them over to your gentle ministrations." Hamedon leaned back on his throne. "Care to try again, Elf?"

"We are Knights of the Council. My name is Elac."

Hamedon raised an eyebrow. "The Elf who slew Volnor? You freed my people from the vile yoke of the Necromancers. I will hear you out."

Elac's mind worked quickly. "I come from the Council to bring a message of friendship. I also bring you a gift." He tried to reach the pouch at the small of his back, but his hands were too tightly confined. At a motion from Hamedon, a Kobold wrenched Elac's hands into the air. He flung him around and reached into the pouch. The soldier brought out the Orion Stone.

"Will you accept this gift?"

The Kobold approached the dais, prostrated himself, then handed the Orion Stone to Hamedon. He backed away, bowing low with every step.

"Your Imperial Majesty, the Council hopes to put an end to the border disputes we are seeing. There is a great evil at work in the land, one which threatens all four of the nations of Pelacia. Only together can we hope to defeat this threat."

"Lies!" Solone said. "I'll have them taken to my dungeon immediately. They won't bother you again."

"Not just yet, Solone. I would hear his words."

This time, Elac saw the tiny gestures as Solone used his magic to subvert the mind of the Overlord of the Kobolds. "Are you certain, your Imperial Majesty? I do not wish to stand here and let them insult you with their mendacity."

Hamedon's gaze never left Elac's face. "I have not yet determined their words to be untrue. You would do well to remember your place."

Solone's jaw dropped open, and his face paled. Silvayn approached the throne with a brief bow.

"Hello, Solone. Confused? Perhaps you don't know exactly what Elac so cleverly handed to Overlord Hamedon. It's the Orion Stone. A wonderful artifact, actually. Although it allows enchanted items to retain their magical properties, all other magic fails in its presence." Solone took a hesitant step backward. "Apparently, you can include mind-control spells in that list."

Solone took another step away from the throne as the Kobold Overlord slowly turned to face him. Hamedon rose from his seat. His face twisted into a mask of rage. Solone leapt from the dais and ran for a picket of horses, but Rilen was quicker. He slid feet-first between Solone's legs, and the two went down in a tangle. With his hands still secured by ropes, Rilen ripped a dagger from Solone's nearest boot. He sliced his bonds away as he rolled to his feet. Solone drew his sword and swung at Rilen's head. Rilen ducked the strike. He dropped to one knee and thrust his dagger just below Solone's armor. The blade angled upward, drawing a bright gush of blood.

Solone staggered against the horses, one hand pressed to his side, blood spurting between his fingers. He reached for the reins, but it was too late. Kobolds swarmed him and hauled him to the ground. Their weapons rose and fell in a sickening cadence.

"No!" shouted Rilen. "We need him alive!"

In their rage, the Kobolds either did not hear him, or they chose to ignore him. When they were finished, Solone's armor had been peeled back in several places. The blood no longer flowed from his countless injuries. His head hung at a crazy angle from the deep gash in his neck.

One Kobold spat on the corpse. "Justice is done."

#

Elac sat to Overlord Hamedon's right. The enormous banquet table lay covered with steaming plates of food. Along one wall, several barrels of ale stood in piles of snow. Hadwyn, of course, wasted no time. Before Elac finished his first serving, Hadwyn was on his third. Elac lost count of how many mugs of ale the Dwarf had drunk. Gillen sat beside his brother and refused to look at him. Elac decided Gillen had changed tactics. Previously, he would badger his brother about eating and drinking too much. Now he simply ignored him. Somehow, Hadwyn managed to devote some of his attention to a conversation with Princess Noria. She laughed frequently, but to Elac it seemed she was less amused by his words than his antics.

Elac looked to the Overlord's left. Rilen kept his face down, concentrating on his dinner. Elac knew how Rilen felt about Kobolds. Under normal circumstances, Rilen would attack any Kobold on sight. His self-control had been strained by the extended trip with Rhun. And there he was, three feet from the leader of the Kobold nation. Elac almost laughed when he thought about what must be going through his friend's head.

"Elac," said Hamedon, "you have done the Kobold nation a favor this day, one that can never be fully repaid. Yet I find that I must ask another boon of you."

"You need but ask."

"Solone sought to dominate me, and by extension, all of the Kobold nation. He cost us the lives of countless loyal soldiers. He nearly started another war between our peoples. I must know who is behind this foul plot. Tell me who, and I will wreak my vengeance upon them."

Silvayn raised his glass. "Perhaps this is the beginning of a new era. In trying to sow the seeds of war, our invisible foe has laid the foundation for a new peace. If the four nations can work together to combat this evil, it would usher in a time of cooperation and reconciliation like this continent has never seen.

"Before we can deduce who is behind this whole mess, we need to capture one of the conspirators alive. Two of them escaped from duchies in Palindom and were likely heading this way. By chance, did Solone make you privy to the identities of his cohorts?"

"He did. In fact, I know where one of them is. Penallo, who beguiled Duke Lonn into the war with his neighbor, has taken up residence at Fort Julan. He has Duke Maich under his thrall."

Silvayn winced. "That could be trouble. He may be stirring up another war. We need to get to him as soon as possible. To do that, we need your help."

"It shall be even as you have said, good Silvayn. To that end, I find I must make the first offer toward that sense of cooperation."

Hamedon rose to his feet. Elac sneaked a glance at Rilen. The Elf's grip on his fork was so tight, his knuckles were white.

"It is my command that these people be outfitted with whatever supplies they need. They will be given an honor guard escort to whatever part of the kingdom they wish. I shall return the Orion Stone to Elac. And to represent our nation, it is my decree that Rhun shall accompany them, until the quest is completed."

Rhun and Rilen bore expressions so similar, Elac almost laughed. Both sat slack-jawed. Veins bulged in Rilen's neck, and Rhun's eyes were so red they almost glowed. Despite their almost comical reactions, Elac felt his heart beat faster. These two had not had their last argument. It would be a difficult journey.

#

It took ten days to reach the Kobold border city of Narlam. They emerged from the tunnels to find the sun had dropped below the horizon. While it was not dark yet, it would not be long. Silvayn announced they would set up camp for the night. Their escort erected the new tents they had been provided, then disappeared back into the tunnel. The company gathered around the campfire.

"Let's ride at first light. We'll stop outside the walls of Fort Julan and work on our disguises. Jayrne, I think we'll send you in first. Find out where the aide to Duke Maich is hiding. We'll sneak into the city, grab our target, and get out as quietly as possible."

"You make it sound easy," Rhun said, poking a stick at the embers of the fire.

"It wouldn't be necessary," Rilen said, "if your fellow Kobolds had allowed me to take Solone alive."

"You stabbed him in the gut. He would have died anyway."

Rilen raised his voice. "A knife wound to the belly won't kill a man, and least not right away. We would've had plenty of time to interrogate him before he died. I'd be more than happy to demonstrate on you."

Noria tossed the last of her dried beef into the fire. "Your bickering isn't helping us. It doesn't matter why Solone is dead. What matters is that Maich's aide is our last link to whomever is behind this conspiracy. You do yourselves no honor with this ceaseless quarrel."

Adalyn put a gentle hand on Rilen's shoulder. "Come on. Let's get some sleep."

Elac grabbed another chunk of firewood. As he stood, he saw something move in the growing darkness. He froze in place.

Jayrne was instantly at his side. "What is it?"

"Something's out there."

Silvayn gave a low chant and slapped his hands together. The globe of light he summoned rose higher into the night sky and grew brighter. Three silhouetted figures, each carrying colossal, two-edged battle axes, approached their camp. As the light intensified, they came into focus. Their grotesquely muscled Human bodies were covered with hardened leather armor. But what Elac had thought to be helmets was something terrifying. Their large, scale-covered heads ended in rounded snouts and were topped by curved horns. Long, skinny tongues flickered in and out of their mouths.

Silvayn gestured, and his light became brighter yet. Two more of the creatures appeared off to the right. Elac and his friends stood their ground and waited.

"Silvayn, what are they?" Elac asked.

"They're called zelendril. They're strong and incredibly fast. Take nothing for granted." He hesitated. "They're also carnivorous."

One of the zelendril hissed, and the five creatures attacked.

CHAPTER 10

Elac and the Dwarves fought alongside Rhun. They met the trio of charging zelendril with a clash of weapons. To their left, Rilen, Adalyn, and Noria fought against the remaining two attackers. Silvayn maintained the globe of light while he readied another spell.

Gillen struck first. His axe descended in a deadly arc toward one zelendril's head. Somehow, the creature raised its own axe at the last moment and deflected the blow. It thrust at Gillen with the end of the axe. The blow knocked him several feet away, but he rolled to his feet and engaged another zelendril. Hadwyn's hammer blow had better results. Even the speedy zelendril was not able to ready its axe in time to parry the attack. The hammer struck it on the left shoulder. Te crack of breaking bone echoed off the hillside.

Rhun delivered a furious series of blows, ending with a solid thrust. He buried his sword in the zelendril's thick hide. The creature swung a clumsy axe stroke at Rhun's head. He had to release his weapon to avoid the blow. Elac's sword left a scarlet trail down the zelendril's right side. Unhampered by the blade protruding from its stomach, it swung a backhanded strike. Elac's armor deflected the keen edge of the axe, but the force of the blow knocked him on his back. The zelendril took a step toward him, but had to turn its attention to Rhun, who fought with a dagger. Elac drew a few painful breaths before he regained his feet.

Rilen engaged a solitary foe, while Adalyn and Noria fought side-by-side against the other. Rilen was hard-pressed to block the lightning-fast blows from his opponent. He had to give ground, and the zelendril pressed its advantage. It closed the gap between them and swung an overhand blow. Rilen dodged back, then leapt forward, just over the descending axe. His shortsword flickered back and forth like a whip, leaving several profusely bleeding wounds. Another swing nearly severed its wrist. His final blow disemboweled the zelendril, and it dropped to its knees, arms wrapped around its abdomen as it shrieked its pain and rage.

Noria and Adalyn alternated blows against their foe. They slowly battered the zelendril into a defensive crouch. Jayrne appeared from the darkness, and her shortsword bit deeply on the zelendril's thigh. It dropped its axe as it pitched backward. She rushed in and stabbed her sword through the creature's throat. It gurgled and spat blood, then thrashed and lay still.

The zelendril Hadwyn had wounded picked up its axe with its uninjured arm. The creature raised the axe over its head, but the weapon tumbled from its grasp as Noria's longsword emerged from the armored chest, buried to the hilt in its back. Noria twisted the sword around, then allowed the zelendril to slide limply off the blade.

Elac and Rhun closed with one of the remaining attackers. It had wrenched Rhun's sword loose, and bore it in one hand and its axe in the other. Rhun's dagger was completely impotent against the zelendril. Between the impossible speed and the two weapons it wielded, he could not get close enough to strike. Elac prodded and slashed, but the zelendril easily blocked his every attack. Elac was bleeding from several small wounds on his chest, arms, and shoulders. His hands trembled with fatigue as he raised his sword one more time.

An arrow hissed over Rhun's shoulder to strike the zelendril's chest. The beast staggered back, and Rilen fired once more. Elac drove his sword home in the zelendril's side. It grasped his hand and held it tightly against the wound. After a few seconds, the zelendril fell. Beside it, the remaining attacker succumbed to simultaneous strikes from Hadwyn and Gillen.

Elac leaned on his sword and gulped deep breaths of the freezing night air. The pain of his wounds worked its way through the fog of fatigue. His blood stained the light dusting of snow covering the ground. Jayrne came to his side and helped him to a log. A look around the group told him how lucky they were to have everyone still alive. With the exception of Silvayn and Jayrne, everyone had injuries of some kind. Gillen would be busy.

Silvayn knelt beside one of the fallen creatures to examine it more closely. Elac tried to rise, but changed his mind and decided to ask his question from where he sat. "Do you think they were alone? Or are there possibly more of them out there?"

Silvayn gave a gentle smile. "These creatures don't have enough comprehension of tactics to be surreptitious. All they understand is killing. If there were any other zelendril in the area, they would have been part of this group. We'll still camp here, if that's what you were asking."

"I need to tend to our injuries, anyhow," Gillen said. "Elac, I think you should be first."

#

When the others emerged from a long, winding draw, Elac and Jayrne were waiting for them. In the distance, the stone walls of Fort Julan towered above the Ranset Plains. From this distance, the soldiers manning the walls appeared as ants to Elac. They stopped at the mouth of the draw. The first feathery flakes of snow drifted out of the sky. Within a few minutes, a heavy snowfall was upon them.

"Silvayn, this is perfect," Jayrne said. "Soldiers guarding the gates won't pay much attention to anyone with this weather. They'll stay by their fires and keep their hoods pulled up. I think we need to step up the timetable. Let's break up into three or four groups, slip in through the gate, and meet inside."

"Why split up?" Noria asked. "Isn't it safer if we all stay together?"

Jayrne closed her eyes and shook her head. "Larger groups draw too much attention. Besides, half of us have facial injuries. If nine people walk through at the same time, looking like they were just in a fight, the guards will be suspicious."

"All right," Silvayn said. "Jayrne, Elac, and Rhun in the first group. I'll go next with Adalyn and Noria. Rilen, you are with Hadwyn and Gillen."

"Where will we find you?"

"I have a suggestion," Hadwyn said. "Follow the main street about halfway across town and turn left on Fairwind. There's a tavern two blocks up on the right called The Walking Dead. It has an inn upstairs as well."

Gillen groaned and walked away.

Jayrne laughed. "Who came up with that name?"

"It seemed appropriate, considering how many cities were burned by undead forces in the last war."

"And by Kobold raiding parties," Rilen said as he poured a cup of water from a skin.

"That was war," Rhun said. He stepped around the fire to stand before Rilen. "What about the ten thousand Kobolds who were slaughtered on the Ranset Plains? The war was over. We were beaten. Yet you pursued a defeated, routing army and massacred it. What was the point of that?"

Rilen threw his cup to the ground. "The point was to make certain it would be more difficult for a large force of murderous Kobolds to invade our lands in the near future."

The others moved to separate them before they resorted to blows. Rhun allowed Elac to pull him away from Rilen, but he thrust a furry finger at his antagonist. "Remember my promise, Elf. When this is over, I will kill you."

"Silvayn," said Adalyn, "I think it would be best if we started now. We need to keep these two apart for the time being."

"I agree. Each group will wait an hour to give the others a head start. We'll see you at the tavern."

Elac, Jayrne, and Rhun rode into the gray afternoon. Between the deep cloud cover and the heavy snowfall, they cast no shadows. The whole milieu had an eerie, otherworldly feel to it. The accumulated snow muffled their horses' hooves, and the rest of nature had fallen silent. Elac kept a nervous eye on the surrounding groves of trees, but nothing emerged to attack them. They fell in behind a group of thirty or forty travelers, leaving about a half mile buffer to show they were not part of the caravan.

As Jayrne had predicted, the caravan received scrutinizing looks from the guards at the gate. They paid virtually no attention to Elac's tiny group. Rhun had his hood drawn tightly about his head to hide his race, but with the frigid weather, even that surreptitious gesture drew no attention. Jayrne pointed in the direction of the tavern. The trio led their horses by the reins. They tied their horses to the rail outside the tavern and went through the doors.

The wooden floor was hazardously slick. Water, mixed with half-melted slush, made the trek across the room a tricky one. Elac shuffled his feet and held his arms out to his sides for balance. They dropped into a booth. He kicked the snow from his boots and blew on his hands for warmth.

Elac and Jayrne chatted while waiting on the others, but Rhun refused to join their conversation. After the appointed hour had passed, Silvayn, Adalyn, and Noria joined them. By the time the rest of the group arrived, Elac's head was feeling stuffy from the ale he had drunk. Hadwyn spotted the telltale signs of too much drink and saluted him with his tankard before resuming his conversation with Noria.

Elac hiccupped. "What do you think we should do first, Silvayn?"

The mage's voice dropped to a whisper. "First, we rent rooms for the night. A taproom is not the place for such talk."

Rilen counted out a few silver coins to rent three rooms on the top floor. They all gathered in the room farthest from the staircase. Elac and Hadwyn carried a small keg and several tankards with them. For a reason Elac could not explain, he found the frown on Gillen's face to be hilarious. He giggled all the way down the hall.

"Jayrne," Silvayn said, "do you know where Duke Maich's estate house is?"

"I have a general idea."

"Okay. I need you to reconnoiter the area tonight. See if you can figure out which part of the estate the duke's advisor calls home. Once you've located him and a way to get to inside, come back here. We'll go a few hours after midnight tomorrow night."

Elac placed an arm around his wife's shoulders. "I can go with her."

She removed the arm and stood up. "Elac, right now, I think you would have trouble not spilling your drink. I'll be fine. In fact, I think I'd like Rilen to go with me."

She gave Elac a kiss and tousled his hair. "Have another drink, dear. And don't wait up for me."

#

Elac's headache had not completely faded. He had found that, as he grew older, his hangovers tended to last longer. But despite the inconvenience, he still had an occasional extended bout with the ale barrel. He scooped a handful of snow from a nearby drift and held it to his forehead.

Hadwyn gave him a crooked smile. "Me too, my friend."

Although it had quit snowing sometime during the previous night, the swirling wind picked up tiny bits of ice and snow and filled the air with stinging whiteness. Elac squinted into the wind while he watched for his wife's return.

Certain the others would not overhear, he moved closer to Hadwyn. "How are things going with you and Noria?"

"Me and Noria?"

Elac laughed softly. "Come on, Hadwyn. We've known each other for too long to be coy about it. I've never seen you focus your attention on one woman for this long."

Hadwyn sighed. "There's something about her, isn't there? She's a magnificent warrior. I wonder if she likes short men?"

"You haven't asked her?"

The Dwarf was silent for several moments. "I really don't know what's gotten into me. With every other woman I've known, if I wanted something from her, I just told her. With Noria, it's different. All we do is talk, and I'm as happy as an Elf in a forest."

Elac was about to answer when a figure appeared in the haze, gradually growing sharper until he was certain it was Jayrne. She kept her hands buried in her cloak. Her hood was pulled up over her head, and she kept her eyes on the ground. Several steps behind her and off to one side, Rilen also approached the group.

"Luck is with us," she said. "My greatest fear was that the duke's troops could follow our footprints in the snow. But

Duke Maich held a military parade today, all around the estate house. The snow is completely churned for about a half-mile in all directions. There's no way anyone can follow us." She raised her eyes to Elac. "Are you ready?"

He nodded. Silvayn accepted the reins to his horse. Jayrne, Elac, and Rilen left the others behind and approached the house on foot. Elac decided it was at least an hour past midnight, so the guards on duty should be fairly tired. The late hour and the inclement weather would work well for them.

Jayrne led them to the southwest corner of Duke Maich's compound. A wall, eight feet high and made of small stones held together by mortar, surrounded the estate house. Jayrne scampered up a tree and spent the next several minutes silently watching over the wall. She slid down the trunk and pulled her companions close.

"The cold weather has driven most of the guards inside. The others just broke off their perimeter check and gathered around a fire."

Elac dropped the bundle he had carried. He undid the ties and pulled out a burlap tarp. He hid it against the fence under a snowdrift.

"Let's go in," Rilen said.

He tossed a rope over the wall and secured one end to the truck of a tree. Jayrne climbed onto Elac's shoulders, grasped the top of the wall, and pulled herself over. Rilen helped Elac scale the wall, then he managed the climb alone. They dropped over the wall and hid in the deep shadows, but nothing moved.

Jayrne pressed a finger to her lips, then pointed to a window on the nearest wall of the estate house. Elac checked left and right, but none of the guards were walking their patrols. As it had been outside the walls, the snow had been disturbed by the passing of countless booted feet.

They stayed low, darting from bush to bush as they worked their way closer to the house. Jayrne was the first to reach the window. She pulled a pair of metal rods from her boot, selected the one she wanted, and slid it between the window and the frame. With a muffled *click*, the latch released. She eased the window open and climbed inside, the others right behind her.

It was much warmer inside the house. Elac peeled his gloves from his hands. His fingers were so cold, the inside air actually felt as if it was searing his skin. Torches burned in the hallway outside their room. The door was slightly ajar, which allowed some of the flickering light to reach them. Jayrne wrapped Sir Draygen's cloak firmly about her body and sidestepped through the doorway.

Elac stood in the semi-darkness and listened to his heartbeat. Gradually, his hands adjusted to the new temperature, and the fiery sensation subsided. When the feeling in his toes also returned to him, he eased closer to the door to get a look into the hallway. All he could see was a decorative wooden table supporting a vase, with a painting of a lake hanging directly above it.

The door quivered, and suddenly Jayrne was there, dropping her hood and flashing him her smile. "Surprised?"

He nodded. "Never saw you."

"Did you find him?" Rilen asked.

"Yes. He's still in the same room, only three doors down from here. There's a guard outside his door, but he's going to be sleeping for a while."

"What did you do?" Elac asked.

"Nothing, actually. I think it has something to do with the empty bottle of rum at his side."

Elac gave a grand, sweeping gesture. "Lead on, my dear."

The trio slipped into the hallway. A red, shaggy carpet covered the floor. The walls were made of stone with exquisitely carved edges. Jayrne skipped ahead of them, but Sir Draygen's boots masked her every sound. Just around the corner, Elac saw a pair of feet sticking out from the wall beside a discarded spear. The soft sound of snoring reached his ears. An overweight man wearing a leather jerkin sat just outside the door, his helmet on the floor beside him. A ceramic rum bottle lay on its side beneath his chair, with an oblong puddle next to it.

The door was on the far side of the slumbering sentry. Elac turned the latch and eased the door open. After his companions were inside, he gently closed the door. Jayrne positioned herself by the door, in case someone should come in before they were finished.

The room was dark, except for the faint glow of the cooling embers in the fire pit. The duke's advisor slept quietly in his bed, covered with heavy blankets to ward off the chill.

Rilen pulled a heavy cudgel from a pouch and stood ready beside the slumbering Penallo. Elac withdrew a thick cloth and a small, brown bottle. He took a deep breath, removed the cork, and liberally poured the contents of the bottle onto the cloth. He lowered the cloth over Penallo's mouth and nose. The sleeping man awoke immediately. Rilen helped Elac hold him down, but he kept his cudgel ready. Eventually, Penallo's struggles weakened, then his body went limp. Elac held the cloth in place for another minute before he tossed it aside.

Rilen bound their captive's hands, and Elac his feet, while Jayrne checked the hallway. Rilen tossed the rangy Penallo over his shoulder and held him in place with his left hand. He hefted the cudgel in his right and nodded. Jayrne opened the door. She checked once more, then waved them forward.

This time, they had to open the door all the way to allow Rilen to carry their prisoner into the hall. At the furthest limit of its range, the door's hinges gave a piercing creak. The slumbering, intoxicated guard snorted twice and opened his eyes.

Elac held his hand over the man's mouth, muffling his outcry. Rilen's cudgel descended with a sharp thud, and the sentry was asleep once more. The Elf shrugged his shoulders to set Penallo back in place.

"Quickly, now," whispered Jayrne. "If we had made our escape cleanly, they would not have missed Penallo. But when they find him gone and this guard assaulted, the search will be on."

They trotted back the way they came in. Jayrne slipped out through the window first, checked the area outside the house, and whistled softly. Elac climbed through the window, then helped Rilen pass Penallo through the opening. Rilen followed and picked up their captive. They allowed Rilen to set the pace as they ran to the barrier fence. Elac marveled at the luck of having the military parade that day. The only thing that could hinder their clean escape at that point was a fresh snowfall.

They were passing the inert form over the wall when the first flakes fell. By the time they had him wrapped in the burlap tarp, snow was falling in earnest. Even though Penallo was concealed within the folds of the tarp, they stuck to the backstreets and alleys. If they encountered one of the night patrols, an overenthusiastic young officer might demand to see what was in the tarp.

"Can you two take it from here?" Jayrne asked. "I want to go back to the estate house. If Maich's people are on to us yet, we need to know."

Elac squeezed her hand. "Good luck. Come back to the inn as soon as you can. If we have to leave before you return, we'll meet you at the same draw where we stopped on our way here."

She flashed him a dazzling smile before she disappeared into the swirling snow. It took the two Elves another fifteen minutes to reach the inn. They found a darkened alley nearby.

Rilen waited there with Penallo while Elac went inside to alert the others.

They were all gathered in the same room. Silvayn and Noria were awake, but the others were resting. Elac closed and latched the door behind him.

"We have to hurry, Silvayn. We had to knock out one of the guards, so it won't be long before the duke's soldiers are looking for Penallo."

Rhun grunted and rolled to his feet. "Why knock him out? You should have killed him."

"What good would that do? If they find Penallo missing and his guard murdered, you don't think they would start looking for him?"

"Of course they would. But when that guard comes around, he'll not only tell everyone that Penallo was kidnapped, but he can tell them what you look like."

Elac gathered his and Rilen's gear. "Sorry, Rhun. I'm not a murderer. Besides, as drunk as he was, he'll have a hard time describing us."

The Kobold snarled. "Suit yourself."

"Where are the others?" Gillen asked.

"Rilen has Penallo in an alley nearby. Jayrne went back to check on pursuit. She'll come back here when she can, but if we're gone, she knows where to meet us outside the city. We can't wait too long, though. The herbs I used to knock out Penallo probably won't last another hour."

Silvayn tapped a finger lightly against his lips. "Okay. I don't see any need to bring Penallo inside the inn. Let's just gather our stuff and give Jayrne a few minutes. If she isn't here by the time we're ready, we'll have to go on without her."

Fifteen minutes later, Silvayn told them it was time to leave. Elac worried about Jayrne, but he knew she could take care of herself. He shouldered his pack and hefted Rilen's in his arms. Elac took them down the back stairs, into the street, and back to the alley where Rilen waited.

The first thing he noticed was that Jayrne had returned. While Rilen was checking their captive's bonds, she was securing a gag in his mouth. He was awake, but the gag kept him from crying out. Penallo lashed out with both of his feet, which were still tied together. Rilen dodged the kick, then grabbed Penallo by the front of his cloak and pulled him close.

"You listen to me, because I'm only going to say this once. We plan to take you out of the city. We would like to keep you alive and intact, if we can. But rest assured, your days of stirring up trouble in the West are over. If it comes down to either killing you or allowing you to escape us, you will die. Do you understand?" Penallo's eyes narrowed, but he refused to answer. Rilen slapped him across the face. "Do we understand each other?" Penallo stared past his captors, but he finally nodded.

Adalyn, Noria, and the Dwarves brought the horses into the alley. Jayrne tied her equipment to her horse and climbed into the saddle. "We're in luck, Silvayn. The guard was still asleep when I checked on him. I positioned him on the floor with his bottle in his hand. Maybe they will think he passed out and hit his head when he fell. It could buy us some extra time."

Elac drew in a sharp breath. "You went back over the wall?"

She rolled her eyes. "Of course not. I have Sir Draygen's cloak, remember? I just walked right in through the gate."

With Rilen and Hadwyn leading the way, they rode toward the city gates. Penallo was concealed within the tarp once more and slung across the extra horse. Rilen had secured him to the saddle to minimize his movements. Elac and Jayrne rode together at the rear of the formation. Noria dropped back to ride beside them.

"Jayrne, I'd like to ask you something. Just what can your cloak do?" She held up the Shield of Omonis. "I know what my father's artifact does." She gestured to Elac's sword. "And everyone knows what the Sword of Sir Draygen is capable of. But your cloak is something of an enigma. Does it render you invisible?"

"Not exactly. If I wrap it tightly about my body right now, you will still be able to see me, because you know where I am. It . . . it alters my appearance. It definitely works better outside the cities. But even in town, at night I can walk right past all but the most alert sentry without being seen. Sir Draygen's boots muffle the sound I make when I walk, but that effect isn't as pronounced. I'm pretty quiet anyway."

Noria wiped snow from her hair. "You have all proved yourselves worthy of your legacy. Your struggle against the Necromancers is the stuff of legends." She stared down at her shield. "I only hope I can do likewise and prove myself worthy of this divine gift."

Jayrne placed a hand lightly on her arm. "You're a better warrior, a better knight, than you give yourself credit for, Noria. Human noblemen are too blinded by your gender to realize that. At least, until you unhorse them on the jousting field."

When they reached the gate, the changing of the guard shift had just been completed. Elac was about to suggest they wait, allow the new soldiers time to become bored with their duties, but one of the soldiers had already spotted them. They kept their deliberate pace, but he waved them to a stop.

The guard yawned and shivered. "I need to search your belongings."

"What is this?" Silvayn asked, his face assuming a haughty expression. "Do you have any idea who I am?"

"Sorry, sir. Orders for the night. Someone stole several valuable pieces of art from the museum."

Elac's first thought was to use their status as Knights of the Council to bluff their way past the checkpoint. But they had already considered that option and decided it was too risky. Even if it succeeded, the guards would certainly remember encountering them, and theirs would be the first names thrown out as suspects in Penallo's disappearance. They needed another option.

Jayrne was the first to react. "I can't believe they're making you stand out here in the weather like this. It's positively freezing."

The guard stepped closer to Jayrne's packs. "I know. But I have the lowest seniority. *I* get to search the travelers." He jerked a thumb at the guard house. "And *they* get to enjoy the fire."

"I wish we could convince you we haven't stolen anything." Jayrne pulled a jingling pouch from under her belt. "Wait. What if we left you this as collateral?"

He accepted the pouch and bounced it on one hand. "So, if we don't find the missing artwork tonight, I get to keep this as compensation?"

"Absolutely."

He grinned, glancing back to make sure no one in the guard house had seen the transaction. "On your way, then."

They kept the horses at an easy walk. Elac's mind told him to drive his heels into the horse's flanks and flee, but to do so would draw unwanted attention. They kept to their southerly heading. Once they were far enough from the walls of Fort Julan, the group would turn southwest and make for Unity.

Jayrne gasped. Elac followed her startled gaze back to the distant walls of Fort Julan. Several flaming arrows arced up from the center of town to fall outside the walls.

"I'd say they have found out he's missing," Jayrne said. "A little more speed would be prudent."

"Agreed," Silvayn said.

Rilen nudged his mount, and it trotted away at a rolling canter. Great clumps of sod and snow flew up behind their horses' hooves. The frozen ground was uneven. Elac worried that a horse might injure a leg in the dark, but he knew they had to take the chance. It was only a matter of time before a pursuit would be mounted.

They reached the Unity River an hour later. Rilen guided them southwest along the banks. They would ride until fatigue slowed their horses, then find a defensible place to spend the night. Elac's fingers were numb with the cold. He clenched and unclenched his fists, trying to force warmth back into the frozen digits. If the soldiers caught up to them, he would need his hands to grip his weapon.

A single torch flared up in front of them, and they reined in. A second came alight behind them. Then several more, and within moments, they were surrounded by flaming torches. The soldiers from Fort Julan rode cautiously forward, armor jingling, weapons held ready. There were at least thirty of them. A group of archers, with arrows nocked, waited behind the men-at-arms. The group stopped about twenty yards away. Elac and his friends were trapped. The leader dismounted and came closer.

"I am Sergeant Talic with the garrison at Fort Julan. What have we here?" He smiled as he eyed the extra horse, with its bulky cargo wrapped in a tarp. "Is he breathing okay? I'd hate to recover Penallo for Duke Maich, only to find out he died in your custody."

"He's fine," Rilen said. "But he's not going anywhere."

Noria moved her horse to stand beside Rilen. Talic threw back his head and laughed. "A woman? Am I supposed to feel intimidated?" He shook his head. "You must be awfully foolish. I have a platoon of my finest soldiers, backed by a line of archers. If I give the word, you will die."

Noria drew her sword and pointed the tip at their antagonist. "And if you give that word, you will die first."

Ten bowstrings snapped in unison. A volley of arrows streaked ahead but veered away at the last moment to strike Noria's enchanted shield. Talic stood dumbfounded.

Noria raised her blade into a warrior's salute. "I would suggest you call off your soldiers, Talic. I don't think you know what you are up against. I'll make this simple. Back off, or die."

But Talic never had the chance to answer. A cry went up from the archers. Elac spun around in time to see the swarm of imps bounding over the fallen soldiers to attack the next line.

CHAPTER 11

Elac drew his sword, but Rhun waved him back. "Let's ride, you fool! This is our chance to get out of here!"

"And leave these men to die?" Rilen asked.

"If we save them, we still have to fight them." Rhun gave Rilen a cold stare. "If we leave now, they won't follow. I'm sure some of them will survive."

Rilen swore and started for Rhun, but Adalyn grabbed his shoulder. "I hate to say it, Rilen, but Rhun is correct. These soldiers will defeat the imps. But this fight is the distraction we need."

Silvayn frowned but wheeled his horse about. Elac felt a sharp pang of guilt in his stomach as they charged away from the field of battle. The howls of the imps mingled with the cries of the wounded and dying soldiers and echoed across the snow-covered hills. He refused to look back.

They rode hard for several hours. It was after midnight before Silvayn allowed them to stop and rest. Elac climbed down from his saddle. His muscles were stiff from the cold and the long ride. He paced back and forth, slapping his arms and stomping his feet to restore the circulation. Jayrne and Hadwyn dug a fire pit and banked snow around the edge to hide the light. By the time they had a warm blaze going, he was exhausted. His exertions had served a purpose, however. He no longer felt paralyzed with guilt over the decision to leave the soldiers to fight the imps alone.

The group gathered around the fire to hold their hands close to the life-giving heat. They rubbed their horses' legs and made sure they were fed. Silvayn allowed them to stay long enough to have a hot dinner. With sunrise still some time away, he announced it was time to leave.

They traveled south along the banks of the Unity River for another hour. Elac could not lose the feeling of déjà vu. Something about their journey seemed familiar to him. In his fatigue, the answer did not come to him until Rilen motioned them to silence with a finger to his lips. Elac and the others followed him down a steep slope to a waiting ferry. Elac recognized the Temel Ferry, where he and Rilen had evaded their undead pursuers six years prior. He managed to give Rilen a lopsided grin as they led the horses onboard.

The ferry was in much better shape than he remembered. The owner had conducted extensive repairs. This time, Elac did not fear the rickety craft would capsize or sink. With more people pulling on the ropes, the journey across the river was much quicker than before. They reached the other side and disembarked. Rilen swung one foot into his saddle, then stopped. His shoulders drooping, he returned almost reluctantly to the ferry. He used the mooring lines to secure the ferry to the bank. Elac grabbed the rope leading back across the river and severed it with his knife.

He gave Rilen a wink. "This time, it was my turn."

The mood in the group was lighter, and they talked among themselves as they continued their journey to Unity.

#

The horses turned onto the long, cobblestone street that was home to Silvayn's house. Elac almost prodded his horse into a dead run, just to escape the cold. It had stopped snowing, but the driving wind had piled the snow into drifts along the sides of the street. He brushed away a few flakes that clung to his cloak. They entered Silvayn's courtyard, and the grooms came out to take their mounts. Elac noticed a number of queer looks from the servants who saw Penallo riding side-saddle, with his arms and legs tightly bound.

Rilen and Gillen carried their captive into Silvayn's study. They sat him on a bench in the rear of the hall. While a grim-faced Hadwyn stood guard over him, the others moved to the far side of the room to discuss their next step.

"Let me talk to him," Elac said. "I think I can convince him to tell us who he is working for."

"Elac," Rilen said, "after all this time, I thought I had squeezed the naiveté out of you. This man was involved in a plot to start an insurrection, cause a civil war, maybe even overthrow a king or two. People usually call that sort of thing treasonous. And charges of treason are typically rewarded by the hangman's noose. I don't think he's going to be very forthcoming."

"Silvayn," Gillen asked, "can you use any kind of magic on him, to convince him to help us? Sort of like Solone, with the magic he used to overwhelm Overlord Hamedon's mind."

Rhun grunted and crossed his arms. "Overwhelm the Overlord? That's not too hard. He isn't the brightest torch on the wall."

"Sorry, Gillen," Silvayn said, "but that is beyond my abilities. I've heard of some mages besides Solone who were able to do this, but I think they were drawing their power from something besides Life magic."

Gillen sighed. "I was afraid of that. We could always get my brother drunk and turn him loose. After he broke Penallo's knees with his hammer, Penallo might be more talkative."

"Only as a last resort, and only with Council sanction. I don't want this to come back to haunt us later. Any other ideas?"

"I have something," Jayrne said. "It's less forceful, but more devious. Is that what you had in mind?"

Silvayn raised one eyebrow. "What is it?"

"I think you'll like this."

#

Elac had to admit, his wife's plan definitely had merit. He had married a very devious, albeit attractive, young woman. Elac grabbed a tankard of ale, flopped onto a wooden bench next to Jayrne, and watched her plan unfold.

Rilen and Hadwyn entered the study, carrying several metal implements in their hands. Rilen laid out a collection of knives and small axes, while Hadwyn made a great show of placing the tips of three iron bars into the fireplace. He stoked the fire, then brought a pair of foaming tankards, drank from one, and handed the other to Rilen.

Rilen took a long drink, then set his mug on the table. "Hello, Penallo. I'm Rilen. This is Hadwyn. We're here to have a nice little chat about what has been going on in the eastern Human duchies. In fact, we'd also like to know about the trouble being stirred up in the Kobold lands."

Penallo broke into a cold sweat. "What do you mean? I know nothing. I was sleeping in my bed when you kidnapped me." He sat up straighter. "In fact, I'm going to see to it the Human ambassador to the Unity Council hears about this."

Rilen chuckled softly. "Aren't you in the least bit curious about how we found you? After all, you made a clean escape from Nightwood after Duke Lonn found out what you were doing. You made it all the way to Hrcac, in fact."

Hadwyn picked up a long knife with a serrated blade and checked the edge with his thumb. "And that's where we come in. Your friend Solone made a sudden departure from this world. He's currently entertaining the sharks at the bottom of the Bay of Hrcac."

Rilen spread his hands as far apart as he could. "*Big* sharks. Sharp teeth."

Penallo went pale at the mention of Solone's demise. "What does this have to do with me?"

Hadwyn took a few steps closer to Penallo. The knife was still in his hand. "Overlord Hamedon was very grateful to us after we freed him from Solone's mind control. So grateful, in fact, that he told us about Solone's plans to sow discord in the West. A plan, he told us, which was aided by a few cohorts. You are one of them."

Rilen placed the tip of a long dagger beneath Penallo's chin and brought him around. "He told us what you were doing, and he told us where to find you. What Hamedon didn't know, however, was who you, and ultimately Solone, were working for. This is where you save your hide by helping us out."

Hadwyn grabbed Penallo's hair and yanked his head back. "Who are you working for?"

With wide eyes, Penallo looked back and forth between his interrogators, but said nothing.

Rilen smiled. He pried one of Penallo's fingers loose and held the edge of his dagger against it. "Hadwyn, may I have the first cut?"

Hadwyn bowed low. "By all means. I prefer the red-hot iron, anyway."

The Dwarf drew one of the rods forth. The tip glowed bright red. A trail of wispy smoke drifted off the end. Penallo screamed his terror and tried to break free of Rilen's grip.

The door at the far side of the room slammed open, and Noria stormed into the room. "What are you doing? We don't torture prisoners!"

Penallo was actually shaking. "You . . . you have to stop them! They're insane!"

Noria leveled a finger at them. "I'm getting Silvayn. If you touch this man before I return, you will feel my wrath." She spun on her heel and left the room, slamming the door behind her. Rilen and Hadwyn spent the next several minutes entertaining themselves by holding up the various instruments displayed on the table in front of them.

The door opened once more to admit Noria, Silvayn, and Rhun. Silvayn crossed the room with long strides to stand before Rilen and Hadwyn. "I cannot believe this. You would torture a man . . . in my house, no less! This is outrageous!"

Rilen folded his arms across his chest. "We need to know what he knows, Silvayn. What do you suggest I do, buy him a drink?"

"Have you tried just asking him?"

"Yes. He says he knows nothing about it."

"Then that's all we can do." Silvayn stepped back. "Rhun? He's all yours."

Rhun walked slowly across the floor to stand directly in front of the captive. "Well, Penallo. It seems you and I have a lot to talk about." Penallo opened his mouth, but Rhun motioned him to silence. "No, don't talk, just listen. I just came from the Unity Council. They decreed that you are to be given the Council's protection for so long as you prove useful. Once you decide not to help any longer, you are to be extradited, by me, to the Kobold city of Hrcac. Overlord Hamedon is really interested in having an extended conversation with you."

Penallo squirmed in his chair, looking from one face to another. "You can't do this. Do you know what the Kobolds do to their prisoners? You can't!"

"They can, and they have. You are mine, Penallo." Rhun turned his back on Penallo and moved away. "My wagon is on the courtyard, Silvayn. I expect him to be loaded onto it immediately."

"*WAIT*!" Penallo's breaths came in short, rapid gasps. Even from where he sat, Elac could read his heartbeat by the veins in his neck. "As long as I help you, the Kobolds don't get me, right?"

Silvayn gave a slow nod. "That's correct. But you had better talk fast. Rhun is ready to leave. And one other thing, Penallo. Lie to me, and I'll hand you over to Overlord Hamedon myself. He's very anxious to meet you."

Penallo exhaled sharply and looked down at his feet. When he spoke, it was in a quiet voice. "It started about five years ago. I was living in the city of Thorbin."

"Wait," Hadwyn said. "Thorbin? Where is that?"

Sylvain pulled a chair closer and sat down. "It's on the island of Wyborn, about ninety leagues south of the Pelacian continent."

"I was called to the capital at Wyborn for a meeting with Emperor Azorok's top advisors. The Emperor and Dalnoq, the High Priest of Voldaz, had come up with a plan to expand their power by conquering this continent. My first duty was simple. I guided a thief and an artist to Unity. While I waited outside, they went into the museum, where the artist made a detailed drawing of an artifact called the Temira. That was about two months before the thief stole it from the museum."

"Impossible," Noria said. "I just saw the Temira not two months ago."

Penallo finally looked up from the floor. "What you saw was a reproduction. We brought the drawings back to Wyborn, where an expert jeweler created a replica so perfect, there was no way to tell the difference, even when they were side-by-side.

The thief and I returned to Unity, and she switched our Temira for the real one."

"Names," Gillen said, slapping his hand on the table. "We need names."

"Her name is Coliac. She lives in the city of Vols, along the southern coast of Brynolf Bay. As for the artist . . ."

"Don't worry about the artist," Rilen said. "Continue."

"I really don't know why they wanted the Temira. They didn't say, and I didn't ask. It's safer that way.

"A few years later, I was sent back to Pelacia. You know the rest. There were several of us, all on the continent with orders to disrupt your governments. We concentrated on the Humans, because there was already so much turmoil within the governmental hierarchy. Setting duchy against duchy was fairly simple, really. As for the Kobolds, they proved more difficult. Our first two messengers were executed. I guess the Kobolds became isolationists following their defeat . . ." He froze, casting a quick glance at Rhun. "I . . . uh . . . after the end of the war, the Kobolds kept to themselves and wanted nothing to do with outsiders. That was why they sent Eigil."

"Who?" Silvayn asked.

"Eigil. You probably knew him as Solone. He took a Pelacian name, in order to hide his origins. He was a skilled wizard. You must have powerful magic yourselves, if you defeated an agent of Chaos so easily."

Elac saw Silvayn flinch. Something Penallo had just said did not sit well with the old mage. But the middle of an interrogation was not the time or place to ask him about it.

"What else?" Noria asked.

"That's all I know, I swear!"

"Then it's time for you to answer some of our questions," Adalyn said. "You told us Dalnoq is the High Priest of Voldaz. Who is Voldaz?"

Penallo bowed his head and made a complicated symbol with the fingers of his right hand. "Mighty Voldaz is the god of Chaos. He brings us power, he brings us wealth, and he grants us victory. Dalnoq is his right hand. When Dalnoq speaks, he does so with the voice of Voldaz. His power, combined with Emperor Azorok's might, shall guide Wyborn to victory."

It seemed to Elac that Penallo was reciting a formula, rather than voicing an opinion. He decided it was probably part of their worship services. But something seemed missing from the picture. "Was Eigil working for Dalnoq or Azorok?"

"Neither," Penallo said. "Well, I suppose in a way, he was working for the Emperor. But all of the wizards serve under Agalia. She is the most powerful wizard in the world."

Silvayn rubbed his chin. "Agalia. I know of an Elf named Agalia. She was a pupil at the Aleria School of Magic. She had already been there over a century when I started. She became a very powerful user of Life magic. Then one day, she vanished. I always thought she was dead."

"She is over a thousand years old," Penallo said.

"If what you know of her is true," Silvayn said, "then it might be the same woman."

"Do you need him for anything else, Silvayn?" Rhun asked.

Penallo gave a shriek, and his voice rose an octave. "You promised!"

"Sadly," Silvayn said, "I did. Rilen, can you bring in the officers from the Unity prison?"

After Rilen left, Rhun grabbed Penallo by the front of his tunic. "If I find out you lied tonight, or even withheld anything, you'll wish my people had gotten to you before me."

Penallo was trembling visibly when the guards led him away in shackles. The clamor of the slamming door echoed in the wide hall. For long moments, no one spoke. Elac was the first to offer a suggestion. "Should we check on the Temira?"

"I'll send one of my apprentices," Silvayn said, "but I have no doubts about what we'll learn. The Temira has been taken to Wyborn. The question now is, why did they need it?"

Adalyn rubbed her eyes and stretched, barely suppressing a yawn. "The power of the Temira is the ability to bridge the gap between two planes of existence. It has to have something to do with the creatures from Archon, which have been attacking all over Palindom. All over Pelacia, for that matter."

Silvayn's eyes were distant. "This is all starting to make sense. Either Dalnoq, the High Priest, or Agalia, the wizard, is using the Temira to facilitate the transfer of the creatures from the plane of Chaos to this world. Without it, bringing even one creature over would be difficult at best, deadly at worst. They would have to open a new Gate for each summoning. But the Temira might have allowed them to create a permanent Gate from Archon to Pelacia."

"Simple enough, then," Rilen said. "We go to Wyborn and recover the Temira."

"Easier said than done," Noria said. "I have heard of this island of Wyborn. The sailors who search for other ports to ply their wares speak of it. The island is large, probably thirty or forty leagues across. Reefs, barely submerged in the ocean waters, surround the island, making it impossible to sail a ship up to the shores. The only way for a ship to reach the island is through the Narrows, at Brynolf Bay."

"The Narrows?" Elac asked.

"Two arms of land encircle the bay. They almost touch at their tips, but there is an area about one hundred yards wide where a ship can safely pass through. The trip is still incredibly dangerous. It must be made as the waters in the bay are approaching high tide. Go in too soon, and the hull will strike the reefs. Go in too late, and when the waters reverse and head out to sea for the low tide, the ship will be dragged down."

"Can't we just sail in through the Narrows, then?"

"No. The Wyborn navy patrols the area just outside the Narrows. Any ship not sailing under their banner is searched from top to bottom." She gave Jayrne a wink. "And any ship flying their banner under false pretenses is immediately sunk."

"We'll work on it," Silvayn said. "Assuming we make it to the island, our next task will be to locate, then recover, the Temira. That won't be easy, either. It's a big island."

"My area," Jayrne said. "If I understood you correctly, the summoning of these creatures has to be done by a priest?"

"Yes. Agalia is a wizard, but to work with these creatures of Chaos, she would have to have some standing within the church of Voldaz."

"Then shouldn't we find the Temira in a temple? Probably the main temple?"

Silvayn squinted and scratched the side of his head. "Sometimes, you are so clever, you make me sick."

#

They made the journey from Unity to the Human city of Palim, and from there to Wyborn, aboard the relative comfort of transport ships. Normally, the vessels were reserved for members of the Unity Council and their entourages, but Silvayn prevailed upon the Council to let him requisition two of them. Elac stayed belowdecks as much as possible. Outside, winter had arrived in full force. The temperature dropped to well below freezing. A near-constant wind blew out of the north, bringing with it occasional snow flurries. But the passenger cabin was warm and dry, and they had plenty to eat and drink. Hadwyn and Gillen, who were not accustomed to sailing, spent most of their time on deck. They came inside only to eat or sleep. For those who suffered from seasickness, watching the horizon slide by tended to help calm an anxious stomach.

Late that evening, Silvayn gathered everyone around the dinner table. Elac held a half-full tankard of ale in a firm grasp. He had learned early in the voyage not to fill his mug any higher. The South Sea was rough, and since he was not an experienced seaman, he had problems with the constant rolling of the ship. For once, Hadwyn was drinking water. Elac hid his smile behind his tankard. The Dwarf's stomach probably could not handle anything else.

"We'll be dropping anchor in a few hours," Silvayn said. "We won't be following the normal route into Wyborn. Instead of sailing the ship through the Narrows, we'll take a longboat over the reefs, at high tide. We're going to land on a secluded beach on the southwest corner of the island. There's an old smuggler's path leading from the beach, up the side of a cliff, and onto the Hafgren Plateau."

"A path?" Rilen asked. "How could there be a path on a cliff?"

"There is a series of rock shelves, connected by wooden walkways. There are ropes along the sides of the paths, but I wouldn't trust them too much. If you fall, it's a long way down. The climb should only take us about an hour. From there, it's eight leagues to Hafgren. There are no roads, and we'll be on foot, so this will be a long journey. Unless something changes, we can count on spending two days getting there.

"The island has two main temples to Voldaz. One is at the ruins of Thurlow, which is at the foot of an active volcano. The other is located in the city of Hafgren. We'll try Hafgren first, then move on to Thurlow."

"Which one is more likely to have the Temira?" Adalyn asked.

Silvayn closed his eyes. "I really don't know. We have very little information about the current society of Wyborn. What we have on them comes from scrolls I found tonight in the library at Unity. We know the island was settled about twelve centuries ago. The people were a mix of Humans, Dwarves, and Elves. They were led by a Human named Wyborn."

"Of course they were," Jayrne said. "How many cities were named after him?"

Silvayn smiled. "Just one. The capital, of course. They lost quite a lot of people the first few times they passed through the Narrows, until they learned the secret of navigating the riptides and eddy currents. On the south side of Brynolf Bay, they established the cities of Wyborn and Vols. The king ruled from a palace with the assistance of the original Solone, our troublemaker's namesake. Solone was killed when his ship went down while navigating the Narrows.

"For a time, they traded extensively with Pelacia. Eventually, all travel to the mainland was banned, except with expressed royal permission. When King Wyborn died, his twin sons both claimed the crown. Their followers took up arms. The cities of Vols and Wyborn went to war. After three years, they declared a truce, with each city gaining total autonomy.

"Hafgren was settled a few centuries later. A volcano in the southeast corner of the island erupted, covering most of the island in ash. Some of the residents of both Vols and Wyborn moved to the Hafgren Plateau to stay above the lava flows. Not only is the lake on the plateau excellent for fishing, but they discovered a deposit of very high quality iron near where they founded the city.

"Fort Brynolf and the city of Thorbin were the next to be founded. Darton was last. Hopefully, we'll be able to stay clear of that city. Anarchy is their only rule of law. They have no king, no governor, no militia. It's a foul cesspool of the worst the island has to offer.

"About five hundred years ago, the king of Wyborn made a pact with the Queen of Hafgren. She would provide the iron, and his engineers would turn it into steel. The king's blacksmiths had devised a better way of forging steel, so their weapons and armor were second-to-none. His army conquered the rest of the island, with two exceptions. The soldiers at Fort Brynolf capitulated, as their only task was to defend Brynolf Bay, regardless of who held the throne. The city of Darton was deemed too dangerous and of too little value to bother with.

"The king of Wyborn married the queen of Hafgren. They left the existing governments in place and set themselves up as co-rulers of their new empire. About that time, the worship of Voldaz emerged. The self-appointed High Priest of Voldaz built the first temple at the feet of the volcano, which was renamed the Hammer of Voldaz. The temple was later destroyed during an eruption, but the ruins are still there. The temple has been rebuilt and is still active.

"The major cities consist mostly of Humans, but they still have a mix of Dwarves and Elves. Smugglers and wealthy businessmen have taken to hiring Kobolds as mercenaries, so Rhun won't stand out too badly."

"If they are such isolationists, how did you come by all this information?" Rhun asked with a growl.

"Occasionally, someone from Wyborn will be granted permission to travel to Pelacia to study at the School of Magic. Although most are turned away, those who are deemed serious students are allowed to begin their studies. They provided us with information about the history of their homeland."

Silvayn pushed away from the table and stood. "Let's all get some sleep. The next two days will be rough. We drop anchor at dawn."

CHAPTER 12

Elac had never manned an oar on a boat before. The narrow, flat-bottomed vessel plowed slowly but steadily closer to shore. His arms and chest burned like fire. When he craned his neck to stare at the distant shoreline, it seemed no closer. He forced himself to watch his paddle dip into the water, pull to the rear of the longboat, and race forward to dip into the water once more. He hoped that if he looked up less often, he would notice some progress. He raised his oar and drove it into the roiling sea.

The saltwater sea surrounding Wyborn had a bright turquoise hue. It rose and fell in a steady, rhythmic cadence. Luck was with them; the unusually light winds had led to calmer seas. Off to their right, several dolphins leapt from the water in an incredible, athletic display. He leaned over the side and saw submerged coral reefs shimmering in the depths. While the reefs were several feet underwater, they were beautiful. When they were close to the surface, they became extremely dangerous. Even at high tide, the reefs closer to the shore were high enough to sink their longboat.

As a safety measure, Jayrne had been selected to sit in the bow of the flat-bottomed boat. She leaned out like a bowsprit, watching ahead for signs of imminent danger. When she saw a rock formation or a reef that she thought was a hazard, she pointed to her left or right. *Of course, we're on a ship, so it would be port or starboard.* Adalyn, steering their vessel from the aft, would adjust the rudder to avoid the collision.

They drew into shallower water. The rise and fall of the waves became more pronounced, leaving Elac feeling slightly nauseated. He leaned over the edge of the boat and immediately wished he had not. One moment, the rocky bottom of the crystal clear sea looked far away. Then the boat dropped, nearly smashing atop a reef that had been several feet underwater moments earlier.

"Silvayn," Jayrne said without taking her eyes off the water, "this is impossible. The boat is moving so much, I can't tell where it's safe and where it isn't."

"Do what you can."

"How?"

Rilen never broke his cycle of paddle – reach – paddle. "Best guess."

Silvayn stowed his oar next to his feet and chanted softly. He gestured with one hand, and Elac felt the rolling and pitching of the boat lessen. The sea still rose and fell around them, and waves broke over the bow. Although they were soaked, Silvayn's magic somehow kept the boat from becoming swamped. The shore drew closer, less than fifty yards away.

Jayrne leaned forward, then gestured sharply to port. "Hang on!"

Elac grabbed the railing with a white-knuckled grip. Despite Silvayn's magic, the boat dropped precipitously. The descent ended with a sharp jolt and a deafening crash. The impact slammed everyone forward. Elac's head struck the oarlock. The longboat shattered and dumped them all into the South Sea.

They came up sputtering and coughing. The water was shallow enough to stand, except when the waves rolled past. They secured their equipment and what supply packs were still at hand and waded ashore. The group staggered up the sandy beach but only made it as far as a shady outcropping of rock before they dropped to their knees.

Elac sucked in several gasping breaths. "What did we hit?"

Jayrne coughed. "A rock. I didn't see it until it was too late."

"Not your fault," Adalyn said. "With the size of the waves, I can't believe we made it as far as we did. At least you got us into the shallows."

"Yeah, great," Rhun said. "We're shipwrecked on an island none of us has ever visited. We lost some of our food, we're exhausted, and we're soaking wet. And if we make it through this part of the little adventure, we have no way to return to the ship that brought us here."

"What do you suggest we do, Kobold?" Rilen asked. "Swim? Instead of whining about this, why don't you do something constructive?"

Rhun rose to his feet and drew his sword. "I could teach you some manners, Elf."

Rilen also drew his weapon and faced his adversary. "Whenever you want to try."

They closed on each other with a clash of steel and a shower of sparks. Elac reached for the Sword of Sir Draygen, but he stopped. What would he do? Join Rilen and kill their companion? Fight Rilen?

A forceful blast from Silvayn saved him from making a decision. The spell ripped the combatants apart. Each landed several feet from where they stood. Silvayn jammed his weathered oaken staff into the earth and faced the two warriors.

"I don't have time for this foolishness! I don't care if you two like each other or not. But I do care about our task, and I can't complete it without both of you. Stop this foolishness at once!"

Rilen regained his feet and stood motionless, nostrils flaring. For a moment, Elac thought Rilen would ignore the command. Rilen faced Rhun for a few moments more, then sheathed his sword and turned away. Elac let out the breath he had not even realized he was holding. Adalyn placed an arm about Rilen's shoulders and guided him off to one side, while Rhun sat alone.

Elac and Jayrne exchanged a worried look. He thought to say something to Rhun, but Noria took the initiative.

"We are here with a noble purpose. The fate of the world hangs in the balance, and all you can think about is your own petty hatred for each other. When this is ended, I don't care if you find someplace quiet and cut each other to pieces. But for now, I need you, Silvayn needs you, and the world needs you. Show some respect and maturity, and let's do what we came here to do."

Rilen snatched his pack off the ground, slung it over one shoulder, and walked north along the rocky face of the cliff. He kept his face expressionless as he passed among the others. They fell in behind him, Rhun with Noria at the rear, and began their trek to Hafgren.

Although they were drenched, the air was warm enough to keep Elac's discomfort to a minimum. He found it disconcerting to have left winter behind on Pelacia, only to find summer on this island.

The smuggler's path was smooth in some areas, precipitous in others. It did not take many areas with a narrow foot path and a sheer drop to one side to convince Elac that the trail was mainly used for smuggling gold, silver, and precious stones. Nothing else of value would be small enough to be safely carried up the side of the plateau under such conditions. Once, a long, brightly colored snake slithered out from a crack in the cliff face. Rilen stopped the group and allowed it to pass.

By the time they reached the top, they were physically exhausted. A layer of grime and dirt covered Elac's still-damp trousers. Abrasions from the precipitous ascent dotted his hands and knees. He firmed his lips and studied the path before them.

The terrain was dotted here and there with groves of aspen trees. They limped to the nearest group of trees and took a much-needed rest.

Since the sun was already low in the sky, Silvayn announced they would spend the night there and get an early start the next morning. Most of their rations had gone to the bottom of the South Sea, but Hadwyn and Gillen cooked a thick stew for dinner to help the group recover. Rilen disappeared with his bow right after dinner. He returned during Elac's watch, carrying a deer he had shot. With the fire crackling behind them, they set about the task of dressing out the meat.

#

Late on the afternoon of their second day of travel on the plateau, the city of Hafgren came into view. It was still many leagues distant, but Elac's spirits lifted. In just a few hours, they would be able to buy food, horses, and find a comfortable place to spend the night. In the morning, their real task would begin.

The ruddy haze of sunset had filled the sky when they entered the city by the main gates. While more than one guard cast an appraising glance at Rhun, no one tried to stop them. Silvayn asked a passerby for directions to a decent inn.

Elac walked closer to Jayrne, where she could hear his whispered voice. "Are we being followed?"

"No. I wondered the same thing. I've been watching since we entered the city, but I haven't seen anything."

He felt reassured, but his hand never strayed far from the hilt of his sword. The city of Hafgren was filthy. The cottage industry was the forging of steel. Steel weapons, steel armor, anything made of metal could be found in Hafgren. As a result, the soot from dozens of forges clung like ivy to the walls of the buildings. The entire city looked on the verge of burning to the ground.

Although most of the buildings were wooden, the smithies were built from stone. The reason for the difference was obvious. With the extreme temperatures used in the forging of steel, it made no sense to make a smithy out of easily combustible wood. The doorways and windows of the smithies were stained black with the smoke that roiled out of the forges.

They found the inn and went inside. While Noria secured rooms, the others gathered in the dining hall. Over dinner, they kept their conversation innocuous. Jayrne assured them they had not been followed, but there was still no cause for recklessness. Hadwyn and Noria sat together with their heads bent low over their drinks, talking and laughing together. Elac wondered if he really wanted to know what they were saying to each other.

After the meal, Jayrne told Silvayn she and Elac were going for a walk. She took him by the hand and led him outside.

His curiosity got the best of him. "Where are we going?"

She flashed him a brilliant smile. "To the temple, of course."

"How do you know where it is?"

"I made a few inquiries. Silvayn filled me in on the basic dogma they follow in the worship of Voldaz. Don't worry. I won't let you make any mistakes."

He gave a half-smile. As they strolled along the cobblestone streets, Elac kept a disinterested, blank stare on his face while he studied every building, every street, every corner, in case they needed to return to the inn with haste. By his estimate, smithies occupied at least one of every ten buildings. Some were small operations, where one or two blacksmiths pumped the bellows while hammering out a few swords and shields. Others were enormous, some taking up an entire block.

These mammoth smithies belched towering columns of black smoke into the murky sky. Platoons of blacksmiths wandered their halls, turning out enough weapons and armor to outfit entire armies. Since the entire island was already unified, Elac did not like the implications.

The reek of soot was thick in his nostrils by the time Jayrne squeezed his hand and nodded to the temple. The walls were made of shimmering white stone. Since this building was not coated with soot, Elac assumed the clerics put the acolytes to work each day scrubbing the outside of the temple. The main doorway was a double set of steel portals with polished brass handles. An ornate medallion hung over the doors. Two feet in diameter, the circular talisman consisted of a steel spear, tip downward, encircled by a jumbled web of ropy copper. Jayrne paused and bowed her head as they approached the temple, so Elac did likewise. They mounted the steps and pushed their way inside.

They waited in the antechamber while their eyes adjusted to the dim lighting. The cloying scent of incense hung in the air like a miasma. Elac had to stifle a sneeze. On the wall across from them, someone had painted a mural depicting Voldaz, god of Chaos. He wore a steel breastplate covered with protruding spikes. A medallion, which Elac assumed was the symbol of Chaos, covered his heart. In one hand, he held a broad, black longsword; in the other, a round shield. A demonic mask concealed his face, with eye slots that glowed red, and protruding horns. Jayrne removed her boots. She arched her eyebrows, so he kicked off his boots as well.

Two dark-robed Human priests, a man and a woman, passed through the room. Each wore smaller versions of the Chaos symbol on amulets about their necks. They nodded to Elac and Jayrne but said nothing. Jayrne beckoned to them as they walked by.

"Good priests, might we request a moment of your time?"

"Certainly," the woman said. She looked back to her companion. "We will speak of the matter later, Jaron. I must tend to the flock." He nodded and left by another door.

The priestess extended a hand in greeting. "My name is Ehala."

"My name is Jana," Jayrne said, "and this is Dalor. We have recently come to the city for the first time, and we keenly feel the need to explore the Temple of Voldaz, the Powerful."

Ehala bowed her head slightly. "I will show you this humble place of worship. Come."

The tour lasted half an hour. Ehala guided them through the temple. She showed them the main hall, where meals were taken and banquets were held. The priests' quarters were in the basement. Dark, dank chambers smelling of mildew housed the servants of Voldaz. Elac peeked into one of the rooms. The only adornments in the room were a chamber pot and a straw mat. A young Elf woman lay sleeping on the makeshift bed, with her only garment, the black robe, balled up as a pillow. Elac blushed and moved on.

At the rear of the main floor, a great hall lay before a towering wooden altar. The Chaos emblem hung above the altar in a rune ten feet high. A smaller altar stood to one side. Black stains ran down the sides, which Elac feared might be blood. Did they practice human sacrifice? Or was it some form of execution, as punishment for a crime? He chose not to ask.

They returned to the entryway. Ehala smiled, her hands clasped together in front of her chest. "And now, your faith to all-powerful Voldaz shall be rewarded. High-Priest Dalnoq himself has come here from the Temple of Thurlow. Allow me to speak to him. If it pleases him, he may grant you an audience."

Before either of them could object, Ehala led them through the doorway and into a room that stood in sharp contrast to the rest of the temple. Fine carpets covered the floor. Marble busts lined one wall, the inscriptions below them indicating they were former high priests. A mahogany desk stood near the far wall, with a high-backed, padded chair behind it. In the corner beside the desk, a shimmering golden object caught Elac's eye. *The Temira!*

It stood on a dark-stained wooden pedestal. The golden chain was carefully arranged around the medallion. A glass cover kept dust away and likely served as a ward to thieving hands. Elac allowed his shock to register in his wide eyes and slack-jawed expression. The priestess would assume he was transfixed by its beauty, unaware he was thinking of a way to recover the very object he had come to find.

Jayrne found her voice first. "It's beautiful!"

"The Pelacians call it the Temira. You see the various jewels around the edge. Each represents one of the gods worshipped by the Humans, Dwarves, and Elves. But its true value lies not in the intrinsic monetary value, but in its power. With it, our armies will be unbeatable."

"Isn't it dangerous, leaving it unguarded like this? Someone might try to steal it."

"Appearances are deceiving. I don't know where High Priest Dalnoq is, but whenever he leaves the Temira behind, he places a powerful ward over it. Watch."

She reached out with her hand. With a brilliant flash of light, her outstretched arm an unseen barrier flung her hand away. She rubbed her hand and rolled her eyes. "I always swear I'll never do that again. Then someone like you comes along, and I can't resist."

She straightened and looked around. "I'm sorry. I promised you would see the High Priest, but he's not here."

Elac shrugged. "You did what you could, good priestess. Might we stay a while and worship before the altar of the All-Powerful Voldaz?"

Ehala bowed her head once more and gestured toward the door with a wide sweep of her arm. "Stay as long as you like."

Jayrne and Elac approached the altar, bowed, and slipped into a pew. Elac feared they would be overheard, so he said nothing. Minutes passed. The door at the rear of the hall opened, and two young men entered. Both were Human and bore the medallion of Chaos. However, instead of the black robes worn by the priests, these two wore brown. Elac decided it was an indicator of rank within the church. They were likely either acolytes or priests in training. They passed Elac and Jayrne without noticing them, talking quietly with each other.

"I tell you, Zarel, if you get the chance, you absolutely must travel to the Temple of Thurlow and see what Dalnoq has created."

Zarel's face went pale. "Pelan! That's *High Priest* Dalnoq!"

Pelan waved the distinction aside. "I only caught a brief glimpse of what he and Agalia made, and I will never forget it. The scintillating colors. The wavering image of the lands beyond. By the might of Voldaz, you have to see it!"

The two men reached the door leading to the priests' quarters. "The Temple of Thurlow is a terrifying place," Zarel said. "I will go there only if ordered. I know the creatures they have summoned are supposed to help us. But such beasts were spawned in Hell, and Hell is where they should stay."

Elac and Jayrne exchanged a look. Jayrne sneaked a glance at the departing men. "Wait here and cover my back. I won't be long."

"What are you going to do?" Elac whispered.

"That young man may have seen the Gate Silvayn mentioned. We need to know for sure."

"And you think he'll just tell you about it?"

She flashed him her most dazzling smile and gave a slow, sensual wink. Her fingers lightly traced the line of his jaw. "I can be very persuasive, my dear."

Jayrne followed the two priests. She made enough noise with her bare feet to catch their attention just as the door was about to close behind them. Elac could not hear what was said, but Pelan placed a familiar arm about her shoulders and led her downstairs. The minutes dragged by. He knew Jayrne could handle herself, but the thought of her closeted with the filthy priest-to-be made his blood boil.

When he could stand it no longer, he rose from the pew and walked on tiptoes to the door. His fingertips rested on the pommel of his dagger. Just as he reached for the latch, it opened from the other side, and Jayrne stood before him. She pointed to the front of the temple, and they left without further delay.

When they were outside, she slapped him playfully on the arm. "You were jealous!" she said with a laugh.

"Was not. I was worried."

"Call it what you want." She kissed him on the cheek. "It was still sweet, either way."

"What did you find out?"

She crinkled her nose. "Priests aren't too concerned with bathing."

"Besides that."

"Let's wait until we're with the others and away from prying ears."

They left the temple and returned to the inn. The entire group gathered in Silvayn's room, where Elac and Jayrne recounted what they had learned. Jayrne used a charred stick from the fireplace to draw a crude map of the temple and show the location of the Temira. Elac described the conversation they overheard near the altar. He expressed their suspicion that the priests were discussing the Gate being used to bring creatures from the world of chaos.

Rilen looked askance at Elac. "That's pretty thin. Did you get any verification?"

Elac gestured to Jayrne. She smiled and blushed slightly, the added color on her cheeks accenting the dimples. "I followed one of them to his chambers. He thought I had other intentions, so he really opened up, at least until I rapped him on the head with the hilt of my dagger. He was in the Temple of Thurlow a month ago, and he saw the Gate."

Adalyn's eyes opened wide. "Dalnoq summons these things right into the temple? How does he get them from there to Pelacia?"

"I asked the same question. Dalnoq can't really control where they arrive. At first, a lot of them ended up arriving on this island. It took some time, but Dalnoq learned to focus the summoning on a certain region. In fact, the Gate is now permanently locked open. Even Dalnoq's more powerful underlings can perform the rite of summoning, as long as they have the Temira."

Silvayn clasped his fingers behind his head and chewed on his lip. "That priest's information is helpful but inaccurate. If there is a Gate at Thurlow, it would lead to Archon, not from it. Thurlow's Gate is merely a means to an end. It's Archon's Gate we need to be concerned with. That is the Gate bringing creatures to Pelacia. As far as the rest of his information, he's probably right."

Noria folded her arms across her chest and frowned. "Sounds like we need to be wary of attack by these foul creatures even here."

"None of this matters." Rhun slammed his mug on the table. "We came here to get the Temira. Let's get it over with so I can go home."

"Don't forget," Rilen said. "You have to kill me first."

Rhun's eyes narrowed. "Believe me, Elf. I won't forget."

"That's enough," Silvayn said, almost shouting. "Yes, our primary focus is the recovery of the Temira. But if this information is true, we must shut down the Gate. I don't know how, but it can't be allowed to stay open."

"It doesn't make sense, Silvayn," Adalyn said. "How could they keep the Gate open without continuous casting? It should be impossible, without some type of anchor based in Archon."

Silvayn stared at the ceiling for several long moments. "Perhaps they have obtained another artifact, one of sufficient power to hold the Gate open from the other end."

"Can't the artifact be here, at the temple?" Elac asked.

"No. As I said before, the Gates only allow travel in one direction. Since this Gate goes from Archon to our world, the anchor magic would have to be in Archon. The Temira would help control the Gate, but keeping it locked open would require something more powerful."

Gillen glared at his brother, who was sipping noisily from his tankard. "So how do we close it, Silvayn? Can you do it?"

"I don't know. We need more information. If the only thing holding the Gate open is an artifact in Archon, I'm afraid we'll have to travel there and destroy whatever is channeling the artifact's power.

"But first things, first. Let's see about recovering the Temira. Elac, you said the display was warded by magic. Can you tell what the magic does?"

"There was some type of glowing field around it. When the priestess tried to reach through it, her arm was pushed back."

Silvayn smiled. "I can't use my own magic to break the spell, because such a clash of power would alert every user of magic within five leagues. I think we have another way to defeat it."

#

The night air, while cool, was nowhere near as frigid as the winter chill back on Pelacia. Elac wore a black tunic and black pants, with a hood pulled over his head. The clothing was warm enough to make him perspire. He dabbed at his face with his sleeve, trying not to disturb the soot he had used to color his skin. Ahead, the darkened temple sat in stony silence. The moon had not yet risen, but the dim stars shone in the night sky.

They tethered their newly-purchased horse a few blocks away. They kept the animals hidden from sight, but close enough to be ready if they were needed in a hurry. To Elac's right, Jayrne kept watch on the upper floors of the buildings. Rilen skulked along just ahead, watching for night patrols. The rest of the group followed behind. Rilen had suggested sending a smaller team into the temple, relying on stealth. Silvayn was concerned about the possibility of a fight, so he insisted everyone go.

Jayrne led the way along an alley taking them behind the temple. She slipped the lockpick from her boot and jammed it into the sill of a window. In moments, the lock clicked, and she eased the window ajar. She held up one finger, then slithered through the opening and disappeared. Elac edged closer to the window, sword in hand.

She returned moments later. "It's clear. Come through, but be careful. The floor is wet."

The opened window led to a storage room. Boxes stacked in disarray lined two walls, some of them ready to topple onto the floor. She tested the door and found it unlocked. Silvayn inclined his head toward the door. The hinges creaked softly as she edged it open. Elac cringed, but no temple guards emerged to investigate the source of the noise.

Jayrne took them directly to the entry chamber they had seen earlier that night. The room with the Temira lay just beyond, in the next hallway. She glided over to the door and frowned.

Elac moved closer and whispered into her ear. "What is it?"

"This door is unlocked. It's probably either a trap, or they've moved the Temira. Or both."

"We still have to try."

She licked her lips, drew her shortsword, and pushed the door open. A glowing brazier in the corner provided a soft light. Across the room, he saw the Temira, still perched on its wooden pedestal. Other than the artifact, the room was empty. Jayrne waved Elac forward.

He reached into his tunic and pulled forth the Orion Stone. He took a few tentative steps forward, cringing with each footfall as he awaited some unforeseen trap about to spring forth and claim his life. When he was within an arm's length of the Temira he reached out his hand, his eyes pressed tightly shut. His fears were unfounded. The wall of magic did not appear to repel him. He unlatched the cover for the glass case and reached inside. His hand wrapped around the Temira and drew it forth.

Jayrne smiled and held open the bag tied at her waist. Elac dropped the Temira inside. They stepped back into the hallway and rejoined the others.

"It worked, Silvayn," Elac said. "You were right."

"Then let's get moving."

They returned to the entry room. The subdued light, provided by a few sparsely-spaced candles, suddenly flared up.

Torches along the wall spontaneously lit, and the two fireplaces roared to life. Six men dressed in burnished steel banded mail and carrying longswords blocked their path. Their helmets were featureless, exposing only the eyes and mouth. Behind them, a towering man in gold-trimmed priest's robes, who could only be Dalnoq, chanted and weaved his hands as he began another spell.

CHAPTER 13

Four of the soldiers rushed forward immediately, heedless of the party's advantage in numbers. Hadwyn and Gillen flanked them to attack Dalnoq, but the two who stayed behind intervened. The two sides came together with the ring of steel on steel. Elac deflected a thrust with his shield, then countered with a stroke of his own. He heard the snap of Jayrne's bowstring and the hiss of an arrow. The wooden shaft struck his opponent's armor and shattered.

Both Adalyn and Silvayn chanted in the language of magic as they readied their spells. Rilen hacked and slashed, dancing about in the tight quarters, but he failed to find an opening. His sword struck true more than once, but the superior armor of their foes turned the blows aside. Elac was forced to retreat, step by step. The man he fought was by far the superior swordsman. To his left, Noria cursed as her opponent's sword tip opened a gash on her face. Rhun hissed and growled, unable to get past his foe's sword.

Dalnoq roared his fury as Silvayn let loose with a thunderclap. The deafening noise broke Dalnoq's concentration, and his magic failed. He chanted again and gestured with one hand. Gillen grunted as a sudden, sharply focused gust of wind threw him against the wall. Hadwyn thrust the end of his enchanted hammer into his opponent's face, staggering him. Hadwyn followed with a two-handed blow that shattered helmet and bone with equal facility. He kicked the thrashing body aside and closed with the guard menacing his fallen brother.

Dalnoq raised one hand. He gripped an incandescent ball of fire in his fingers. Adalyn gestured to Dalnoq and summoned a brilliant point of light directly in front of his eyes. He staggered and lost his spell. Blinking back his pain, he extinguished her light with a wave of his hand.

Elac dodged blow after blow, unable to find an opening to retaliate. He blocked a powerful strike with his shield, and another. The last attack knocked him to one knee. His attacker ignored three successive arrows Jayrne fired into his armor. The longsword rose and fell, and Elac blocked the stroke once again. Another swing, and Elac's shield tumbled away.

Adalyn charged to Elac's side. She swung the Sword of Salenas at the man's shield. He braced for the impact, but the enchanted blade bit through the layer of steel and tore into his arm. He howled and dropped into a crouch. Elac thrust upward from where he knelt. The blade drove deep below the armor and drew a bright flood of crimson. The soldier dropped to his knees, coughed up blood, and toppled to his side.

Shouting her battle cry, Noria charged recklessly at her opponent. She dropped her shield and took her sword in both hands. Swing after swing drove her foe into a corner. Noria threw her body forward. Both tumbled against the wall and to the floor. She used her body weight to trap the man's sword arm. With her free hand, Noria drew her dagger, slipped the razor-sharp blade beneath the man's steel helmet, and ripped it across the exposed throat. A gush of blood rushed out to spill upon the floor in a widening pool.

Gillen shook his head and looked groggy as he rejoined the fight. Repeated strikes from Hadwyn's hammer had left deep rents on the polished surface of their foe's armor. Gillen feinted a high strike, but changed it mid-stroke and drove his axe into a deep crease along the lower abdomen. The axe ripped through the weakened metal and spilled the soldier's entrails across the floor.

Elac regained his feet and joined Rhun. They alternated attacks, forcing their single opponent to back away. Rhun struck low. His blade dipped beneath the shield to impact the thinner steel warding the man's leg. He staggered back and dropped his guard. Elac lunged forward and drove Sir Draygen's sword through the visor. The man gurgled through his dying breaths as he toppled backward. Adalyn, fighting at Rilen's side, swept her own enchanted blade in a tight arc. It cut through her foe's armor as easily as the other man's shield. He gasped and placed his hands to his side. Rilen seized him about the neck, ripped off the helmet, and drove his sword into the man's brain.

Dalnoq ignored a second thunderclap from Silvayn and conjured another fist-sized ball of fire. He threw it into the chest of the onrushing Hadwyn. The ball erupted into sparks as it struck his breastplate, and the impact knocked the stalwart Dwarf onto his back. Dalnoq raised his hand again. He summoned a third burning globe as Noria slipped between the priest and the fallen Dwarf, shield raised. Before Dalnoq struck, an arrow hissed across the room to sink up to its feathers in his chest. His spell dissipated. He stared with wide eyes at the wooden shaft protruding from his sternum. A second arrow followed the first, and he dropped to his knees, then fell onto his side. Jayrne slowly lowered her bow, a third arrow already nocked but not fired. Dalnoq's last breath hissed slowly from his lungs.

The battered warriors cleaned and sheathed their weapons. Most had sustained injuries that needed tending, but there was no time. Jayrne ensured the Temira was securely tucked away inside her pouch as the group headed to the doors.

"Quickly, now," Silvayn said. "The fight may have made enough noise to raise an alarm. Even if it didn't, they'll seal the city as soon as they find Dalnoq's body. Either way, we need to get out of town as quickly as possible."

"That could be a problem, Silvayn," Noria said. "This is a fortified city. Usually, the soldiers manning the walls of any fortifications prevent egress after dark. If we wait until dawn, it might be too late."

"Then we need another option." Rilen scowled. "We can't sit here for a month waiting for them to give up the search.

They probably have archers overseeing the gate area, so we can't fight our way out."

"I have an idea," Jayrne said. "I need Rilen and Elac with me. The rest of you bring up the horses."

"What will you be doing?" Adalyn asked.

"Picking up some robes and a body. We're going to bring Dalnoq with us."

#

The line of horses trotted to the city gates. The riders all wore hooded cloaks from the Temple of Voldaz. The black garments enveloped the riders in a shroud of mystique, emphasized by the Chaos emblem embroidered over their hearts. As expected, the gates were shut and the locks thrown, barring exit. A dozen armored men holding pikes stood watch before the portal, and at least twenty archers stood atop the wall. Two of the pikemen stepped forward to confront the new arrivals.

"Hold. None can leave the city until first light."

Jayrne threw back the hood of her new cloak and nudged her horse forward. "Under normal circumstances, I would agree, good sir knight."

"I'm not a knight, young lady. I'm just a sergeant-at-arms."

Jayrne waved the distinction aside. She motioned to Rilen, who rode on the horse beside her, holding a second figure in place in front of him. Rilen lowered the second man's hood to reveal the pale, battered face of Dalnoq.

"As you can see, Sergeant, our High Priest has fallen ill with the plague. Curing him is beyond the abilities of those incompetent fools at the temple. We are taking him to Wyborn, where a priest of sufficient power can be found. We must leave at once."

The soldier stood frozen in place, mouth ajar, his gaze shifting between Jayrne, Rilen, and the slumping form of Dalnoq. "I . . . I'm sorry, but our orders are explicit. No one is to leave—"

"You will open this gate at once!" Noria shouted. "If the High Priest dies because of your dawdling, I swear you will not live to see another day."

The sergeant bit his lip and rubbed his eyes. "I hate this." He turned and motioned to the guards stationed in the gatehouse. They turned several cranks, releasing the locks and setting the gates ajar. Several of the soldiers pushed on the heavy wooden barrier and it swung slowly aside. Jayrne pulled her hood over her face and led the way out of the city.

They stuck to the road until they could no longer see the torches burning atop the walls of Hafgren. Before they reached the road to Wyborn, they turned southeast toward Thurlow, traveling only about two leagues before they set up camp. Rilen rode off alone and took the cloaks and Dalnoq's body several miles closer to Wyborn. He discarded them where they would likely be found, then returned to where the others waited, making sure they had left no tracks. Jayrne dug a fire pit, and Adalyn and Silvayn prepared a hot meal while Gillen tended to the assorted wounds suffered in the battle with the temple guards. The sun climbed higher across the eastern sky. Elac leaned back against his packs and closed his eyes. Following the melee with Dalnoq, they had ridden half the night. He definitely needed some sleep.

"Someone's coming." Rilen kicked dirt onto the fire. The others rolled to their feet and drew their weapons, facing out into the fading darkness. Elac heard it, too: the pounding of a distant horse's hooves. He was able to discern the silhouette of a single rider who approached from the southeast. He sheathed his sword but did not sit down.

The rider slowed the horse to a walk, then stopped and dismounted. She was Human, dressed in a tattered cloak over disheveled tunic and pants. Her hair hung in tangled clumps about her shoulders, and her face looked as if she had not bathed recently. She opened her cloak to show she was unarmed. When Rilen motioned for her to come closer, she limped forward, favoring her right leg.

"What do you want?" Rilen asked, his shortsword still held loosely in one hand.

"I'm sorry," she said in a raspy voice. "I was hoping you might spare me some food."

"What are you doing out here?"

"I was attacked just outside Thurlow. They took everything I had. Money, food, everything."

"Then how is it that you still have a horse? I hardly believe bandits would leave you a horse."

She flushed red and looked down at her feet. "I stole it," she whispered. "I'm sorry. There was no other way. I just had to get as far from them as I could. The things they did to me . . ." She covered her face with her hands. When she looked up again, tears ran down her cheeks.

Rilen shrugged and looked to Silvayn for guidance. Adalyn had already grabbed some bread, cheese, and a piece of salted ham. She handed them to the woman, who tore into the food as if she had not eaten in weeks. She washed it down with water provided by Elac.

"What's your name?" Elac asked.

"Ejana," she mumbled, her mouth full of food.

When she had eaten her fill, Gillen handed her a leather bag containing a little more food. She thanked them through her tears as she climbed back on her horse. "Thank you, all. I won't forget this."

She rode east, back toward the road from Thurlow to Wyborn. Silvayn suggested everyone get some sleep, because they would be on the move again in a few hours. Elac lay back with a sigh, took his wife in his arms, and closed his eyes.

#

Four hours later, they were saddling their horses when Jayrne let loose with a string of curses that would have made any fisherman proud. Elac rushed to her side.

"What's wrong?"

"It's gone! She took it! I'll kill her!"

"What's gone? Who took it?"

She turned her furious gaze on Elac, brow furrowed and lips pursed. "Ejana took the Temira."

The others stopped what they were doing and gathered closer. Silvayn ran a hand through his silver hair. "Are you sure?"

"Absolutely. Not ten minutes before she showed up, I tied the bag with the Temira to my saddle. Now it's gone. She's the only one who could have taken it."

"But why would she do that?" Hadwyn asked. "How could she even know we had it?"

"What does that matter?" Rhun complained. "We track her down, and we kill her."

Rilen folded his arms across his chest. "For once, Kobold, you won't get any argument from me."

Rhun flared his nostrils but said nothing. Elac knelt next to Jayrne's horse. "How do we find her?"

"I can track her," Rilen said.

Jayrne's eyes narrowed, and her hands quivered with barely suppressed rage. "Ejana is mine."

#

Elac squinted into the morning sun. With one hand aloft to shield his eyes, he peered at the grass-covered ground beneath his horse's hooves. Here and there, he found a mark left by Ejana's passage. He wondered how many more signs Rilen found. Elac glanced up at the Elven warrior, who rode at the front of the pack. Where would they be without him? His unmatched fighting skills aside, none of them could have tracked the fleeing thief as readily.

Behind them, Rhun plodded along at the rear. He rode alone, an island to himself. The Kobold, too, had proved helpful. He was not Rilen's equal with a sword, but he had managed to get them into Hrcac to see the Kobold overlord. Without his help, they would never have made it. Why couldn't Rilen understand? For some reason, he refused to look past his overwhelming hatred of Kobolds. Elac hoped the rift between them would not cripple their efforts at some crucial moment.

His contemplation of their inner strife was interrupted when Rilen reined in his horse. While his mount pranced from side to side, Rilen studied the ground around him. "She camped here. I'd say we're only about an hour behind her."

They moved out again, faster this time, heading north. Elac felt his pulse quicken with the thought of what was to come. Was she alone? Or would there be a battle for the Temira? Regardless, the talisman had to be recovered. Without it, Silvayn would not be able to close the Gate from Archon, and the creatures from the other side would overrun Pelacia.

"Silvayn," Rilen said without slowing, "there are several other horses with her now. They rode in single file, so it's hard to say, but I would guess she has at least six people with her."

Silvayn grunted. "All right, everyone, be alert for trouble. Noria, I need you up front behind Rilen. If they hit us with archers, I want Sir Omonis's shield up there to protect us."

Noria kicked her heels into her horse's flanks and moved up behind Rilen. Elac studied the trail once again. Where Ejana had been trying to hide her tracks before, the group she rode with was making no effort at concealment. Elac tried to watch for signs that someone had left the group, in case Ejana had chosen to set up an ambush.

Before them, the ground fell away into a broad canyon with a waterway at its base. According to a map he had found in Hafgren, this would be the Red River. True to its name, the waters flowed past them in a dull red hue, the color of the clay lining the riverbanks. Sparse weeds grew along the steeply sloped incline leading to the canyon floor. The soft clay clung to their horses' hooves as they descended. Ahead, near the river, Elac saw several large black lumps spread around a small sand bar.

Rilen brought them to a halt. Elac swung down from his horse and knelt beside the water. What he had seen was, in fact, corpses. He counted seven of them, all cloaked in black and sprawled across the sand bar.

Rhun rolled one over with his foot. "This one was Human." He lifted the bloody, frayed cloak and studied what lay beneath. "These aren't sword wounds. They were attacked by animals."

Elac used the tip of his sword to pull back the hood from the body at his feet. He felt a cold shock of recognition electrify his body. "Silvayn! This is Ejana!" Despite his revulsion, he felt through the pockets and pouches of the blood-soaked clothing but found nothing. The others spread out to search the remaining bodies and the surrounding area, but the results were the same. The Temira was gone.

"Were these friends of yours?" The gravely voice came from the brush on the hillside behind them. They all whirled about, weapons in hand, to face an old Dwarf. He limped down to the river bank. The old man leaned heavily on his walking stick.

"Actually, no," Elac said. "One of them stole something from us."

The old man spat. "Thieves." He inclined his head to the northeast. "Probably came from Darton. I wish the army would burn the entire city to the ground. Nothing but a bunch of murdering cutthroats up there."

"My name is Elac." He held out his hand.

The old Dwarf stared at the outstretched hand and if he was afraid Elac meant him harm, but finally took it in his own. "Calorn. Did you find what they took from you?"

"No, sir."

"Musta been something gold or silver, then. Them namics do love anything shiny."

Elac raised one eyebrow. "Namics?"

"Yep. About four feet tall, gray leathery skin, wings, and fangs. Heads kinda look like bats. There's some of them over there."

He pointed upriver about twenty yards, where two namics lay on the sand. Deep gashes in their sides gave mute testimony to the savage struggle.

"If'n they took what yer lookin' for, forget it. They have it back at their nest, by now."

"And where would that be?"

Calorn cackled. "You must be a bunch of suicidal fools. You'll find them on top of the bluff overlooking Darton. There's an old fort up there somewhere. The army abandoned it long ago, and them namics took up residence. Anything they gather ends up there."

Hadwyn inclined his head. "Thanks for you help, old man. Don't worry about us. We'll do all right."

"Yer a bunch of fools, but I guess free advice doesn't cost me nothin'. Stay away from the jungle. You can make your way up the river, sure enough, but there be some dangerous monsters in the water, too. Yer best bet is to stick to the roads. But by the look of ya, I'd say yer hidin' from something."

Calorn cocked his head to the side and examined the position of the sun. "I got to be goin'. Luck to ya."

For the next hour, they searched the area for the Temira. But as the old Dwarf had predicted, the artifact was nowhere to be found. They rode hard for the rest of the afternoon, following the northeasterly flow of the Red River. At the shallows, they crossed to the north bank. They skirted the city of Wyborn and followed the river north toward Vols.

The sun had settled low in the sky and twilight was upon them when Rilen stopped to wait on the others. "We might as well make camp here, Silvayn."

Silvayn nodded and looked to the west. "Let's move into the trees a bit. I'd rather not be seen if we can avoid it."

They set up their camp and ate a quiet dinner. Elac and Jayrne set up their tent and crawled inside. He pulled her close, content to lie in the dark with his arms wrapped around her.

"Elac?" she whispered. "Are you awake?"

"Yes."

She sighed. "I feel like this is my fault. I shouldn't have left the Temira out like that."

"You can't blame yourself. She stole it right in front of all of us."

She was quiet for a few moments. "I just feel like I'm dragging this out. We could have gone straight to Thurlow and found Archon's Gate. Now we have to go chasing across the island to find the Temira again."

"We'll be fine, Jayrne. It's just going to take a little longer. At least Rilen and Rhun have stopped their bickering."

"Don't be so sure about that, Elac. I get the feeling their feud is just getting started. There will be trouble between those two before this is over."

#

They had been traveling for three days. When they reached the outskirts of Vols, they had tried to save time by going overland through the jungle. After less than an hour, they had been thwarted by the thick foliage. They had returned to the road and shadowed the river the rest of their journey. There had been a couple of encounters with soldiers of Wyborn, but when they stood aside to allow the columns to pass, they were not accosted. Other travelers had passed by but ignored them.

The narrow, weed-choked road through the jungle bent sharply to the left, and the city of Darton hovered into view. Another leg of the adventure was at an end. After days of sweltering heat and suffocating humidity, Elac decided he was definitely ready for a bath. Unlike the other cities of the island-nation of Wyborn, Darton had no walls. No soldiers patrolled the perimeter of the town. No one kept watch over who came and who left. The citizens kept their distance from each other, with sidelong glances at all who walked past. A few merchants hawked their wares from rickety wooden carts, but they had armed guards behind them, alert for trouble.

Elac gripped the pommel of his sword. The air reeked of mildew. The buildings of Darton were rickety wooden structures, many of them in advanced states of disrepair. Some had collapsed, and many others did not appear to be far behind. For the most part, the businesses consisted of inns and taverns. The streets were heavily rutted, marked here and there by puddles of standing water.

They found an inn that looked like a stiff breeze would topple the walls. Silvayn announced they would meet in the taproom in one hour, so they all headed to their rooms to bathe and change clothes. Rhun would remain upstairs in an effort to avoid drawing attention. Elac and Jayrne, distracted by a few moments of privacy, were the last to come downstairs. Hadwyn saluted them with a raised tankard, which he slurped down. Elac flushed with embarrassment, but Jayrne gave a wicked laugh. Noria looked at the Dwarf and chuckled, covering her grin with one hand.

Rilen sat in a corner with an old Elf in a tattered gray cloak. After several minutes, the two crossed the room to join them at their table. Rilen sat down as the others fell silent.

"Everyone, this is Felsoth. He has lived in Darton for the last twenty years. He knows what we're looking for and how to find it."

Felsoth's breaths came in wheezing gasps. Elac worried he might collapse between heartbeats. "Please, don't bother telling me your names," the old man said. "In a place like this, it's better if I don't know." He broke off as he was seized by a series of wracking coughs. Hadwyn grabbed a full tankard of ale from a passing barmaid and offered it to Felsoth. He gave a grateful nod and took a long pull.

"As I was saying, Darton is not safe, especially for outsiders. You had best get what you came here for and get out of town as quickly as you can."

Noria clasped her hands together on the table in front of her. "We can handle a bunch of cutthroats, old man."

Felsoth smiled. "I'm sure you could, at that. Probably a dozen of them, just you, milady. But what if fifty of them came after you? Sixty? It's been known to happen. Not only that, the army out of Wyborn has been making sweeps through town. They round up anyone who looks like they don't belong here and haul them off to Vols."

Gillen wiped his beard with the back of his hand. "Why would they do that?"

"To get ready for the war, of course. Haven't you heard? The Emperor is going to invade Pelacia."

Elac choked on a bite of steak, and Jayrne pounded on his back until he could breathe again. The others sat in absolute silence as the announcement slowly sank in. *An invasion? Is that what this has all been leading up to?* The more Elac thought about it, the more it made sense. First, the Kobold raids started, with the intent of stirring up trouble in the West. To accentuate the discord, the Emperor sent spies into the Human duchies to try and start a civil war. Adding to the confusion, creatures from Archon were crossing over and attacking randomly. All of this was just a distraction, setting up the people of Pelacia for an invasion. The continent was facing a war, one that would make the last Necromancer war look like a street brawl.

CHAPTER 14

Rilen leaned forward in his seat and put one hand on the old Elf's arm. "Are you certain of this?"

Felsoth gave a somber nod. "Without any doubt. My own son, and his two boys, were 'recruited' not two weeks ago in this very bar."

"I thought they were just grabbing outsiders," Adalyn said.

"We operate a smithy out of our home. With the recent financial success we've had, they went out and bought new clothes. Had them on when the Wyborn soldiers came calling." He spat on the floor. "Now they are housed in barracks near the harbor at Vols, waiting on the invasion fleet to be ready."

Hadwyn muttered several curses under his breath and stroked his beard. "Do you know when the fleet will leave?"

"Not for certain. It sounds like they will be gone in less than two weeks."

"We have to do something," Noria whispered. "The nations must be warned, so their armies can stand ready."

"Not now." Silvayn cut off Noria's silent tirade with a glare. He drew a deep breath, then turned back to Felsoth. "We will be out of here soon. But first, we need information."

"Yes. You seek the nest of the namics. Your friend here told me those creatures have stolen a family heirloom, and that you are on a quest to retrieve it. I'd advise against it. The namics are not to be trifled with, especially when they are defending their home."

"Where is their home, old man?" Noria asked.

"Northwest of town, there is a bluff overlooking Black Lake and Darton. Along the edge of the cliff, you'll find an old lookout tower. When the namics first appeared about a year ago, they took over the entire site and made it their home."

Adalyn looked to the ceiling. "We should have known they weren't indigenous to the island. They almost had to be from Archon."

Felsoth raised one slender eyebrow. "From where?"

"Never mind," she said. "You were saying?"

"You'll have some difficulty sneaking up on them from this side of the bluff. You would have to scale the slope right under their noses. I don't see how you could fight them and keep from falling. If you aren't careful, you'll end up floating in the Brynolf River."

Felsoth tapped a solitary finger against the side of his nose. "But I know a little something about the namics, something most folks don't. I was fishing Black Lake one evening, and they came after me. I saw them in the distance and hid. Once the sun went down, I made a run for it. They could hear me crashing around, but it seems their eyes don't work so well in the darkness.

"If you're dead set on going, I recommend you circle the bluff and wait for nightfall. If you're quiet enough, you might even be able to get in and out with the namics none the wiser. But be warned, even if you do succeed in this mad venture, you still won't be out of trouble. Folks around here tend to be a little rough with anyone they think might have been poking through the namics hideaway. They'll want all the treasure you pilfered from the little beasties."

Rilen shook the old Elf's hand. "Felsoth, you've been a tremendous help to us." He dropped several coins into the man's hand. "I wish you and your family the best of luck."

Felsoth bowed his head, then headed to the bar with his new money. The others gathered close about Silvayn.

"What now?" Hadwyn asked.

"We came to Darton for supplies and information," Silvayn said. "Felsoth gave us the news we needed. Let's get the supplies and leave town as soon as possible. I'd like to cross the Brynolf River and be on the north side of that bluff at least an hour before sunset."

"Why don't you take the others and find us a ferry," Jayrne suggested. "Rilen and I can get the supplies we need and meet you at the docks in thirty minutes." She kissed Elac on the cheek. "Be careful while I'm gone."

#

The ferry master was a short, fat Human who reeked of stale sweat and old ale. He had four teenage boys, whom Elac assumed were the man's sons, pulling the ropes to drag the ferry across the river. The passage had been expensive: two silver coins to take the group and their horses across. Elac hoped Rilen didn't plan on cutting any ferry ropes this time.

The ferry itself seemed sturdy enough. The planks were thick and coated with tar, and the rope showed no signs of fraying. The Brynolf River lapped at the sides of the ferry as they inched their way across. Elac looked west at the sun. He judged they still had two hours before sunset. The dock on the far side loomed closer. The ferry lurched under a sudden wave, and Elac grabbed the handrail to steady himself. The ride stabilized, and he edged away from the railing.

With a deep thump, the ferry met the dock on the north side of the river. One by one, they led their horses down the gangplank. Rilen and Jayrne disembarked last.

The placid waters of the Brynolf River erupted with a spray of black water, and a horror arose from the depths. A long, scaly neck weaved about and lifted the elongated head twenty feet above the water. A jutting lower jaw with curved tusks protruded from the face. It had sunken, almost cadaverous eyes, and it lacked a visible nose. It hovered over them for long seconds before it descended in a sudden move toward the ferry.

Rilen and Jayrne slapped at their horses and bolted for the end of the barge. They threw themselves clear just as the roaring maw slammed into the ferry, shattering it into splinters. The ferry master and his sons dove from the sides at the last moment. The head rose from the water once more, the broken body of the old man dangling from one of the tusks. The horses reared and pawed at the air. Some of them broke free and galloped for the jungle.

Jayrne and Elac regained their feet as the creature turned on them. A bowstring snapped three times in rapid succession, and arrows raced over their heads to strike the slavering jaw. Rhun rushed in and grabbed the reins of two horses.

"Run!" Silvayn shouted.

In a sprint, they all ran for the cover of the trees. The sounds of the creature's fury faded behind them, then fell silent. While the others caught their breath, Rilen went in search of the horses that had run away.

"What was that?" Elac asked between gasping breaths.

"Shadoc," Adalyn said. "That would be a good reason not to travel by boat right now."

Elac bent over, hands on his knees. "You'll get no argument from me."

Rilen's tracking skills allowed him to recover all of the horses. When he returned, they checked on the animals' welfare, then took up the reins. They stayed within the concealing canopy of the jungle. Because of the nearly-impenetrable plant life, they had to walk and lead the horses. The stifling humidity and complete lack of a breeze added to their misery. Mosquitoes bit at every inch of uncovered skin.

The incident with the shadoc had cost them time, so it was dark before they had worked their way around to the north side of the bluff. The vegetation changed to a deep yellow grass, almost head high to the Humans, with few trees to obstruct their view. A full moon hung in the sky, providing enough light to silhouette the watch tower. At Rilen's suggestion, they settled into the long grass to wait for an hour or so. The encounter with the shadoc might have set the namics on alert, so a little delay would be helpful.

"I have a suggestion," Jayrne said. "There's no need for all of us to go stomping around the tower. If just a couple of us go inside, we might be able to find the Temira, grab it, and sneak out without them knowing we were ever there."

Elac took her hand in his own. "That's a pretty good idea. I bet we could do it."

She laughed softly. "Don't worry, dear. I had you in mind for the job already. Rilen, too. He's as quiet as I am. I'd like his sword there in case we're discovered."

"I'll go, too," Adalyn said. "If there's trouble, you might need a bit of magic to slow them down until the others can help out."

They tethered their horses to one of the few trees in the area and proceeded on foot. When they were within bowshot of the tower walls, they hid in the tall, waving grass. While the others waited behind, Rilen, Adalyn, Elac, and Jayrne slipped ahead and moved closer to the arched entryway.

Weeds grew in abundance through the cracks between the stones of the floor. The door had long since rotted off its hinges. It lay to the side with rusty hardware dangling from one edge. It was noticeably cooler inside, although it reeked of rotten flesh. Jayrne pulled her cloak about her frame and led them deeper into the tower. Elac nearly lost sight of her completely as the cloak's concealing magic took hold.

In the center of the tower, they came upon a stone staircase winding up into the darkness. Off to their left, Elac's sharp Elven eyes could barely make out another set of stairs, this one leading down. He tapped Rilen on the shoulder, pointed to both stairs, then raised his palms in a question. Rilen pursed his lips, looked between the two staircases, and pointed to both. He and Adalyn took the set descending below ground, while Elac and Jayrne went up.

The darkness pressed tightly about them. Elac's heart pounded so hard he could actually hear it. The fear he felt was irrational, but he could not dispel it. With Jayrne nearly invisible in front of him, he felt isolated, alone, with enemies all about. He squeezed the hilt of his sword until his hand hurt. They climbed the winding staircase to the top of the tower.

The doorway at the top opened onto a round, flat platform. Overhead, the night sky was clear, and the moon shone brightly. Along the far wall, a mound of treasure had been piled high against the stones. Gold, silver, precious gems, all were jumbled together in a hoard. Elac froze in place. He knew such a prize would not be unguarded. Jayrne, too, had stopped, her silhouette barely visible.

Elac finally saw the four namics. A broad shelf ran along the wall to their right, and the namics sat upon it. Three of them had their backs turned to the raiders, looking across the battlements to the lands below. The other faced the pile of treasure.

He felt Jayrne's hand upon his arm, then heard her words lightly whispered into his ear. "I've got the cloak. I'll go find the Temira, and you watch the namics."

He wanted to object, but he knew she was right. He could not cross that floor without being seen. He kept his hand on his sword and his eyes on the creatures that sat barely twenty feet away.

He licked his parched lips and ignored the beads of sweat running down his face. Somewhere to his left, Jayrne hunted for the Temira under the very noses of the namics. If they spotted her, they would be on her before she could regain the stairs. It would fall to Elac to rescue her.

One of the namics muttered something in their growling, guttural tongue. Another shouted back. The two namics stood face to face, growling and spitting, while Elac held his breath. He risked a glance to where Jayrne searched for the Temira, but he could no longer see her. One namic sunk its teeth into the other's shoulder. They fell to the floor in a violent melee while the other two stood by and watched. Elac gripped the wall in front of him with white knuckled hands. *Just a few more minutes . . .*

"Elac."

The whispered voice came out of the darkness, so faint he thought he might have been mistaken. He looked to the source and found Jayrne, the Temira held in her left hand. He returned the smile, kissed her on the cheek, and eased onto the staircase. They had done it. All that was left to them was to find their way out. Behind them, the sounds of the struggle continued unabated. Elac wondered how he could let Rilen know they had been successful.

That was when they heard the sounds of several namics as the creatures ascended the staircase below them.

\#

Adalyn followed Rilen as he descended into the bowels of the cellar beneath the watchtower. Although the building itself was only about thirty yards in diameter, the cellar was much larger. The halls carried a powerful odor of mildew, which cut through the reek of long-dead bodies. Slick, dark slime coated the floors. Absolute darkness blanketed everything around them. Adalyn chanted softly and brought her hands together, creating a dim globe of light. It was enough to see by, but not much more.

They placed their feet carefully for fear of falling and alerting the namics to their presence. The narrow hallway opened into side rooms. Adalyn glanced inside and saw several piles of straw and scattered bones. She changed the color of her light to red, in the hope that it would make it harder for the namics to see her spell glowing around corners. Ahead of her, Rilen left his sword in its scabbard, but his hand never strayed from the hilt. The passage bent sharply to the left. She heard several voices ahead, but could not understand what was being said.

Rilen held up his hand for her to stay where she was. He eased his sword from its scabbard. The Elf stayed close to the lefthand wall and edged forward until he could peer around the corner. His free hand came up sharply in a fist. He extended five fingers, then pointed ahead. *Five namics, just around the corner.* He waved his hand to their rear, and stepped lightly backward. She allowed the light to fade ever dimmer, to the point Rilen was only a dim silhouette. They would try another area of the cellar, provided they managed to get away from these namics without being heard.

#

Hadwyn heard the commotion from the top of the tower. His Dwarven eyesight was not as sharp as that of the Elves, and he could not find the source of the disturbance. The others came to their feet and drew their weapons. Silvayn studied the top of the tower.

"There's someone fighting up there," the old mage said. "I can't see who or what, but I expect the worst. Bring up the horses and be ready to ride."

Rhun and Gillen brought their mounts closer to the tower. Noria found a length of rope in one of the packs and tied one end to a fist-sized stone. The tower was about forty feet high, so the rope would be long enough to reach the top.

Silvayn drew everyone closer. "If they recover the Temira, the time is upon us where we will have to separate. I want Noria with me. We'll take whoever has the Temira with us and try to find Archon's Gate. The rest of you must return to Pelacia and warn them about the impending invasion. The armies have to be ready to meet the forces of Wyborn. And make sure they know about the threat of the creatures crossing over from Archon.

"Rhun, upon you will fall the longest journey. I need you to rally your people to the cause and bring the Kobold army to the fight. It won't be easy. They won't see an invasion of the western kingdoms as a threat. You have to convince them there is a clear and present danger to the entire continent if this invasion isn't stopped."

Rhun nodded curtly. Noria stepped in front of Hadwyn and took his hands in her own. "I guess we won't be seeing each other for a while, Prince Hadwyn."

He nodded somberly. "You take care of yourself, Princess." She discarded her dignity and wrapped her arms around the sturdy Dwarf. It was a long time before he let her go.

Silvayn turned his gaze back to the top of the tower, just as the bloodcurdling shriek broke the stillness of the night.

#

Elac froze in place. The sounds from below grew louder. He turned back to Jayrne, who motioned him away from the stairs. She pulled Sir Draygen's cloak tighter about her shoulders. Elac followed her away from the stairs, painfully aware that the four namics were still there, with nothing to keep him from being seen. He took his time and eased each foot to the stones. A low bench across the floor from the staircase lay only a few steps away.

A guttural hiss broke the silence. The namics gathered in a tight group, their internal scuffle forgotten. Elac drew Sir Draygen's sword and held it in front of him. Jayrne hopped onto the bench and nocked an arrow to her bow. Her first shot sunk into the chest of the nearest of the stocky creatures. It sat down hard and tugged at the shaft. The others came at them in a rush. A second namic fell to Jayrne's bow before they reached Elac, howling their rage into the night.

#

From somewhere in the depths of the tower, shouts rang out. Adalyn and Rilen exchanged a quick look, then turned and ran for the stairs. Two namics bounded off the steps to block their path. Rilen jumped ahead to meet them, his shortsword a blur as he cut and thrust. The hall was too narrow for Adalyn to help. She increased the light from her spell and kept watch behind them. Her fears were realized moments later when several more namics appeared from the end of the hallway.

One namic loomed too close, and Rilen's blade sliced through the outstretched arm. As it fell away, howling, the other threw itself on Rilen. He brought his weapon to bear but was a fraction of a second too late. It bore him to the ground in a blur of teeth and claws. With one arm raised to fend off the deadly jaws, Rilen reached down and pulled his dagger free. He stabbed it into the namic's side and ripped it upward. The namic fell back, and Rilen slashed it from hip to shoulder. A wave of blood and gore spilled out and splashed upon his armor.

Adalyn feinted with her weapon. A namic launched itself at her. The enchanted Sword of Sir Salenas flashed in a deadly arc and completely sheared the creature in half. The others howled their rage but fell back a few steps.

"Rilen? You still with me?"

His answer came in the form of his longbow. Several arrows whizzed past her head to strike the encroaching namics. The first two fell motionless, pierced through with several arrows. She raised her sword and took a few steps forward. The remaining namics broke and fled.

"Quickly, now," Rilen said. "Let's go. They'll be back with help."

They raced up the stairs and gained the ground floor. Namics seemed to materialize from the air. Rilen continued to fire arrows as they ran, but the creatures came on. Their fury made them heedless of the danger from his longbow. Adalyn shouted a warning. A dozen namics had emerged from the dark recesses of the tower to block the doorway. They were trapped.

#

Elac stared at the blood streaming down his arm. The namics lay dead at his feet, but he had not emerged from the melee unscathed. Jayrne kept her bow trained on the steps, in case more of the beasts emerged to attack.

"What now?" she asked. "We can't fly, and we can't leave by the stairs."

"I don't know. Can we climb down the outside?"

"No. I checked that before we came in. The building is old, but they built it well. There is nowhere we can get a grip."

"Then we're in trouble."

Three more namics appeared at the top of the stairs. Jayrne fired, and the first stumbled and fell. The other two came on, but only one reached them. Elac met the rush with tight sweeps of his sword. The disemboweled namic fell motionless to the stones. He placed the tip of his sword on the ground, leaned on the pommel, and tried to catch his breath.

From below, a sharp whistle pierced the night. Elac leaned out over the parapets. A rock flew up out of the darkness and almost hit him in the face. Jayrne caught the rope attached to it. She wrapped it around the bench and secured it with two quick knots.

She gestured to the rope. "After you."

"Jayrne, I—"

"No arguing. I have Draygen's cloak, remember? If they come out while you're climbing down, I can fend them off because they won't know I'm even here. Move."

Elac knew she was right. He tugged on the rope to test her knots, then swung his legs over the side. He shimmied down the rope, hand under hand. Near the bottom, a pair of gauntleted hands reached up to ease him to the ground. It was Noria. Elac tugged sharply on the rope, and Jayrne's slender form flipped over the wall. She slid downward, coming to a graceful stop a few feet from the ground. Just as she let go, the rope tumbled free from above.

Silvayn stood nearby, the reins of their horses in his hands. "Did you find it?"

Jayrne nodded. "In my pouch."

"Then let's go."

"But Silvayn! Rilen and Adalyn are still in there!"

"The others will save them. Our paths lie apart. We must hurry."

#

Rhun led the charge through the open doorway. Hadwyn was next, but by the time he was inside, Rhun had already slain two of the namics. Hadwyn's hammer crushed the chest of one, and Gillen's axe severed the legs of another. Ten feet away, Rilen and Adalyn stood back to back, swords drawn, fighting against an impossible crush of foes. Hadwyn battled his way to Rhun's left side, and Gillen guarded his right. Adalyn shouted to them. They hacked and slashed their way closer together.

Hadwyn shook the gore from his weapon. He risked a glance at his companions.

Adalyn lost her footing on the treacherous floor and went down. Her sword tumbled away. Immediately, a namic leaped upon her. Without regard for his own safety, Rhun pushed his way forward. He stabbed the namic through the side, and it fell away. Another fastened itself to his back and sank its teeth into his neck. Hadwyn redoubled his efforts to reach them, but his push was repulsed in the face of the namics' superior numbers.

A downward slash of Rilen's sword ripped the creature free from Rhun's back. The two warriors flailed about them with their swords in a macabre dance. The namics hissed and roared, but they had learned to fear the duo's deadly skills. They fell back, and Adalyn regained her weapon.

Rilen raised his bloody sword. "Now, while they're hesitating. Head for the door."

It was the longest walk of Hadwyn's life. Namics stood all around them, bloodlust in their eyes, but for the moment they held back. To turn and run would invite another attack, so they maintained their slow pace. Hadwyn gained the doorway and stepped through. He spun about, but nothing threatened. He and Gillen rushed ahead to the copse of trees where their horses waited and brought them out.

They mounted and rode as fast as prudence would allow. The poor nighttime eyesight of the namics should prevent an immediate pursuit, but they still needed to be well away by first light. Hadwyn gave Rilen and Adalyn the instructions Silvayn had left. Rilen in particular seemed unhappy. Hadwyn agreed. He hated not knowing if the others were okay. For a few hours, they rode hard along the winding jungle road that led east toward Brynolf Bay.

They finally stopped to rest the horses near a bend in the Brynolf River. Hadwyn estimated their distance from the watch tower to be at least five leagues. The sky had grown noticeably brighter, so if there was to be a pursuit, it would start soon. While Adalyn and Hadwyn fed and watered the horses, Gillen filled their water bottles at the riverbank. He used his magic to purify them before he tied them to the saddles.

Rilen stood alone, with his gaze focused back the way they had come. Hadwyn paused in his labors, curious about what the Elf had seen. Adalyn noticed it, too, but she shrugged and went back to work. Rilen plucked a long blade of grass from the ground. He tore small lengths away and cast them into the wind.

Rilen tossed the remainder of the grass aside and took a deep breath. He crossed to the riverbank, where Rhun knelt to wash the blood from his fur. He rose at Rilen's approach.

"Rhun, I know you and I have no use for each other. But I want to thank you for saving Adalyn's life back there."

Rhun nodded slowly. "You saved mine as well."

"Which was in danger only because you acted selflessly to save her. Look. You and I will never like each other." He held out his hand. "But I hope you'll forgive me if I have decided not to fight you when this quest is over."

Rhun stared at his hand for several moments, then clasped forearms with Rilen. "I think I could live with that."

#

Silvayn chose a path that meandered back to the river's edge. They followed the banks of the Brynolf for about a league before they located a ford. They splashed across the shallow, rushing water, then turned east. Shortly after the sun came up, they found an old jungle road. Elac pulled his map from his pack, but the road was not marked. He hoped it led where they wanted.

They ate breakfast and lunch in the saddle. The day wore on without much conversation. For a time, Jayrne rode beside him and bound the wounds he suffered in the battle atop the tower. Although her ministrations helped, the gashes in his arm burned like fire. Gillen could have probably done more, but he had no idea where the sturdy Dwarf priest was. Indeed, he felt no small amount of guilt about the fact that he had no idea if the others had even lived through the fight with the namics.

Jayrne noticed his distraction and leaned across her saddle to give his hand a squeeze. "I'm sure they're fine, Elac. There's nothing we could have done to help them."

He nodded and rode on.

They made camp that night a short distance into the heavy undergrowth. They lit no fires. Noria backtracked to the road to be certain they were hidden, then they settled in for the night.

Silvayn roused them early, and soon they were back on the road. Elac kept a nervous eye on the road behind them and the surrounding jungle, but the namics did not appear. By noon, they had reached a road that branched off to the south to bypass Thorbin. Silvayn selected this route as the most expeditious means of getting them safely to the temple at Thurlow. This road was well-traveled, and the upkeep was noticeably better than the narrow jungle path they had followed. They passed an occasional traveler, but no one paid them any attention.

The sound of trotting horses carried to them over the light breeze. Elac glanced behind and saw a column of soldiers overtaking them. Silvayn guided them to the edge of the roadway, where they stood aside to allow the soldiers to pass.

"Is this a good idea?" Elac asked.

"No. But it's the best we've got. It's too late to hide, and running will only draw attention to us. The other travelers are doing just as we are, so we should have some anonymity."

The soldier at the head of the column studied the faces of the travelers around him as he passed. Elac recognized the set of his jaw and the intensity of his gaze. This man tried to put up a show of nonchalance, but he was actually studying everyone intently. The soldier behaved just as a merchant would - size up an acquisition without an outward display of interest. Elac bit his lip and waited.

When he reached Elac's group, the soldier stopped his column. He removed his leather gauntlets and tucked them into his belt. He dismounted and stood before Silvayn. "I am Captain Begeron, of the Wyborn Imperial Guard. Who are you, and where are you coming from?"

Despite his mental preparation for the encounter, Elac was speechless. He looked to Silvayn, who inclined his head to the newcomer.

"Good sir. We are but simple pilgrims. We travel from Thorbin to see the ruins at Thurlow."

"I think not. You have the look of outlanders about you. I believe you came from Darton. And I don't even think you belong there. I'm afraid you will have to come with us."

"Come with you?" Elac asked. "Where?"

"There was an incident in the temple at Hafgren, and High Priest Dalnoq was foully murdered. Agalia acts as High Priestess from the temple at Thurlow. She has dedicated herself to the search for the foul miscreants who defiled our temple. To that end, the four of you will be taken to her at the ruins of Thurlow, where you will be questioned about the incident. Agalia will decide your fate."

CHAPTER 15

Hadwyn hefted his bottle of wine. "Here comes a group of them now. Let's go."

A dozen sailors, far gone with drink, staggered through the dark alley. Their route led toward Thorbin's harbor on Brynolf Bay. Hadwyn and the others fell in behind them, passing the bottle of wine around and feigning drunkenness. They followed the men across town and descended the long, gently sloping hill that lead down to the docks. The wooden planks echoed beneath their feet, and the reek of dead fish assailed their senses.

The sailors crossed the gangplank to a battered, tar-smeared caravel docked in the harbor. Hadwyn paused to allow the sailors time to go belowdecks. The five warriors followed behind them and climbed onto the deck of the ship.

"Okay, we need to find the captain," he whispered. "The tide is about to go out. If we don't leave soon, we'll be stuck in the bay until the next high tide."

Rilen leaned over the railing and studied the ship from end to end. "Let's go down one deck and try below the sterncastle. I see some ornate windows down there. I'll bet that's the captain's quarters."

Rilen climbed down the ladder first and disappeared into the darkness below. He reappeared moments later and motioned for them to follow. Hadwyn descended the ladder next. From the next deck down, he heard snoring. Forward from where they stood, he heard men arguing over a dice game. He followed Rilen aft to an oaken door. Rilen tried the latch but found it locked. Rilen looked over his shoulder, shrugged, and knocked.

A muffled voice said something unintelligible through the heavy door. A few moments later, the latch turned and the door creaked open. An unshaven, gray-haired man dressed in a greasy tunic stared at them, eyes unfocused, a bottle of rum held loosely in one hand.

"Who are you?"

"We're your cargo," Rilen told him as he pushed past him into the cabin. "And we're leaving right now."

"We're doing no such thing. You will leave this ship immediately."

"Look, Captain," Hadwyn said. "We are prepared to make the trip worth your while." He untied a jingling pouch from his belt and bounced it on the palm of his hand. "On the other hand, we're prepared to chop holes in the ship and let it sink to the bottom, if you don't give us what we want."

The captain belched and swayed slightly. He grabbed the wall for support. "I could have my crew in here with one shout. They would dice you up and feed you to the fish."

Rilen drew his dagger and stalked closer, which caused the captain to take a quick step backward. "Your crew is so drunk they couldn't find their way back here. We could slaughter your entire crew and sail the ship ourselves."

The captain's hands trembled violently. He nodded his acquiescence. They followed him from the room into the sleeping area. He rousted his men with shouts, curses, and the occasional heavy hand to the head. They cast off the lines and slipped away from the dock. On his way to the top of the sterncastle, he paused to lean over the rail and empty the contents of stomach.

"We . . . we have to give a recognition signal to the soldiers at Fort Brynolf. They control all egress and ingress through The Narrows. They sink any ships not giving the recognition signal."

Hadwyn leaned on the handle of his hammer. "I tell you what, captain. My brother is going down into the hold. One shout from us, and he will send this ship to the bottom. Do we understand each other?"

The captain nodded several times in rapid fashion. His eyes were wide and his breathing was rapid, betraying the sense of panic he must be feeling. Hadwyn watched Gillen and Rilen disappear belowdecks. In the distance, the watch fires atop the battlements of Fort Brynolf came into view.

They drew abreast with the fort. Atop the battlements, a light flickered on and off in three evenly measured blinks. The boson stood at the railing and flashed a signal back to the soldiers on the walls. The process was repeated, and the light at the fort disappeared.

The passage through the Narrows was hair-raising, to say the least. Hadwyn had spent a little time on ships, but nothing prepared him for the nightmare he faced. The outward rushing tide, combined with a strong wind out of the south, propelled the ship at breakneck speed through the narrow body of water. To both sides, Hadwyn heard the waves crashing on exposed rocks and reefs. All it would take was a simple mistake by their drunken captain to send them all to a watery grave.

Hadwyn heaved a sigh of relief when the last of the warning fires passed astern of the ship. The captain, too, seemed comforted about their achievement. His shoulders dropped with exhaustion, and he rested his head on the wheel. Hadwyn assumed the old sailor probably did not make the trip while drunk very often. In all likelihood, he would not do so again anytime soon.

Once free of the harbor and the incapacious waters leading to it, the ship heaved with the caress of the waves. Hadwyn leaned against the railing. One of them would be with whoever was steering the ship at all times. Hadwyn had elected to take the first watch.

"How long will it take to reach Pelacia?"

The captain belched. "There's a strong northerly current behind us, and we have the wind at our backs. I'd say two or three days."

Hadwyn nodded and stared up at the stars overhead. It promised to be a long, boring voyage.

#

Elac and his friends spent the first few days of their detainment camped in an army bivouac five leagues south of Thorbin. Messengers came and went, but the detachment of soldiers showed no signs of moving. The captives were secluded in a tent at the center of the encampment. Using her enchanted cloak and boots, and her natural ability, Jayrne occasionally slipped out of their tent and brought them information from the captain's meetings. She reported that Captain Begeron seemed concerned about recent troop movements by soldiers loyal to the hierarchy of the temples of Voldaz. Before he took his company too close to the ruins at Thurlow, he wanted to be certain he was not needed elsewhere. Jayrne read his personal journal, where he confided his suspicions of an attempted coup by the priests of Voldaz. Elac saw the beginnings of an escape plan.

Elac had no idea of the time, but he felt a slender hand on his shoulder, shaking him awake. He sat up and rubbed the sleep from his eyes. Jayrne had already moved on to wake up Silvayn and Noria. They gathered in the center of the tent for a whispered conference.

"A messenger just reported to the captain," she said. "Wyborn's army has completed its mobilization. The entire invasion force is mustered in barracks at Vols. They sail in the morning."

"What does this mean?" Elac asked.

Silvayn scratched his head, frowning. "It means Emperor Azorok isn't as worried about the temple soldiers as our good captain is."

"Then the captain's fears are groundless?"

"I wouldn't say that," Noria said. "I would trust the instincts of a soldier over a politician, anytime. If the priests are planning a revolt, this would be the time for it. Most of the forces loyal to Azorok will be off the continent and out of touch."

"One thing is certain," Silvayn said. "The longer the captain waits to make up his mind, the longer we waste our time sitting here. We need to get moving. Likely, we will have to travel to Archon to destroy this Gate. I have no idea how much time will pass here in the meantime."

Jayrne grabbed his arm. "What do you mean?"

"Time moves at a different pace on different planes of existence. We might think we spent two days looking for the Gate, while on Pelacia, two weeks passed. Or two minutes. There is no way to know."

"Maybe we could convince the captain to move sooner, rather than later," Elac said. "I think he trusts us, to some extent. After all, we're not in shackles."

Noria shook her head. "I wouldn't read too much into that. We're the midst of two hundred of his soldiers. We don't pose much of a threat."

"Let's get some sleep," Silvayn told them. "We'll try to talk to the captain tomorrow."

The next morning, however, they awoke to the soldiers striking the camp. After they finished packing the tents, two soldiers brought the group's horses to them. About an hour later, Captain Begeron approached them, trailed by several aides.

He gave them a forced smile. "I apologize for the delay. There have been some issues of logistics to resolve, but we're ready to move out. With a force this size, I'm sure you understand if the pace seems a bit slow. It'll probably take us two days to reach the temple. We'll get this matter resolved, and if you are innocent, you'll be allowed to go about your business."

They traveled south along the road to Wyborn, reaching the city of Vols just before lunch. The captain sent messengers through the gates, but the main body proceeded south. Elac's thoughts drifted to the situation on Pelacia. Hopefully, his friends escaped the battle with the namics and were safely on their way home. If they were able to leave right away, they would have several days' head start on the invading army. It was not much, given the time it would take to mobilize an army of sufficient size to repel the invaders. But the Human duchies were hovering on the brink of civil war, so their troops were already prepared for battle.

Elac nudged his horse closer to Noria. "How long would it take for the army of Palindom to be ready to march?"

Noria drew a slow, deep breath. "Sadly, there isn't much of an army left. King Aldaris's hold on the dukes is tenuous. With his death looming in the near future, and no clear heir, the dukes called their forces home. I'm afraid the city of Palim is ripe for conquest." She frowned, her knuckles white as she gripped the reins. "I should be there. I should be leading our troops into battle, not chasing the priests of some obscure god. There is no honor in this."

Elac shrugged. "If it helps, your father felt the same way during the last war. But his part in that quest was fated. Without him, we would have failed."

"He threw away his life in a shameful, prideful act. He should never have led that charge. His knights were to act as a relief force, not a spearhead for conquest and glory."

"Granted, he made a very poor decision that day. But his participation in the quest, which seemed a waste at the time, ultimately led to victory. I believe the same will hold true for you."

She nodded, but Elac saw the worried frown creep back over her face. "What else, Noria? Something else is bothering you. Are you worried about the others?" He gave her a disarming smile. "Hadwyn in particular?"

She started, then laughed and shifted nervously in her saddle. "Is it that obvious?"

"Hadwyn made it obvious. He's never been one to hide what he's thinking. Jayrne is right, though. Hadwyn is a survivor. I think he and the others are fine."

They rode in silence after that. The jungle slid past them as they followed the hard packed clay ribbon steadily southward. The heat and humidity returned in full force, and Elac was tempted to remove his armor. He took a long drink from his water skin.

Begeron dropped back to ride with his prisoners. "Do you have enough to drink?" They all nodded. He offered them another of his endless smiles. "Good. I'd be in trouble if—"

The thunderous hooves of a running horse brought the captain up short. A soldier came in at a full gallop. His uniform was ripped, and blood covered one side of his face. Elac noticed the soldier's scabbard was empty. When the man yanked on his reins, he stopped so suddenly the horse almost stumbled. He jumped from the saddle and saluted the captain.

"What do you have, soldier?"

"Sir, I just came from Wyborn. The wizard, Agalia, has betrayed us! The soldiers from the temple have attacked the palace. Emperor Azorok and his children are dead! The emperor's head has been placed on a pike at the city gates!"

Hadwyn frowned as he strolled through King Aldaris's sitting area. Busts of kings long dead lined the walls. The marble floor glowed, reflecting the slanting rays of the sun that passed through the windows. In the distance, Hadwyn saw the placid waters of Palim Bay, dotted with merchant vessels. After a moment's reflection, he turned away from the window. He took several deep breaths as he clenched and unclenched his fists. It would not do for a prince of Verlak to be accused of destroying the king's sitting area. The entire continent was in danger, and every second's delay courted failure. The wait was intolerable.

The fussy man in the ornate blue robes returned to the waiting room. "I'm sorry, but King Aldaris is indisposed. He won't be able to see you today."

Hadwyn stalked forward and grabbed him by the front of his robes. "I think you are mistaken. Do you know who I am? Who we are? We will see the king NOW."

The man turned pale and began to tremble. "I can't help you! Duke Adroc has forbidden any visitors from seeing the king. He is worried about the king's health."

Gillen shook his head slowly. "I think you need to worry about your own health. My brother has a terrible temper when he doesn't get what he wants. I've been trying to break him of it for years, but . . . well, you know how family is."

"But . . . I . . . the door to the king's council chambers is locked, and I don't have a key."

Hadwyn released one hand and patted the hammer at his hip. "Don't worry. I have a key right here. Lead the way."

The pale, trembling chamberlain led them to the heavy, intricately carved oak doors barring entrance to the council chambers. The man blubbered his protest, but Hadwyn knocked him aside. Adalyn knocked on the doors while Rilen covered his eyes and shook his head.

A muffled voice carried through the doors. "Go away. I already told you, no visitors."

Rilen gestured to the doors and smiled at Hadwyn. The Dwarf hefted his hammer and spread his feet.

One of the doors flew completely from its fastenings and tumbled into the room in a shower of splinters. The other dangled at an odd angle from one remaining hinge. Hadwyn stomped his way over the debris, followed by his brother, Adalyn, and Rilen. Kind Aldaris sat on his throne, his head bobbing up and down. His distant look spoke volumes about the condition of his mind. Hadwyn wondered how much of what he would tell the king would be comprehended. Several royal advisors sat on chairs or stood together in corners. All stood with open-mouthed expressions at the intrusion.

Duke Adroc, dressed in a full suit of platemail armor and carrying his helmet under one arm, stepped between them and the king. "What is the meaning of this?"

"Out of the way, Adroc," Rilen said with a snarl. "We will speak with the king."

"Do I have visitors?" King Aldaris asked in a weak voice. "I didn't hear them come in."

Adroc thrust his hands on his hips. "I'll have you thrown in the dungeon for this. You have no right."

"Actually, we do," Gillen said. He pointed to the pendant about his neck. "As Knights of the Council, we will speak to the king. Or shall we throw you in the dungeon, Your Grace?"

"They have a point, Your Grace" said another man in armor. His neatly trimmed hair was touched with gray, but his beard was as black as night. He bowed with a creak of his armor. "I am General Golonis. Speak, sir Knight."

"There is an invasion force on its way to Pelacia. It will have left Wyborn by this morning and will arrive within two days. You have to mobilize the army."

"Wyborn?" asked Adroc. "What kind of lies are you telling? That island is populated by merchants and thieves. They don't have an army."

"Their force numbers twice the combined army of Palindom," Hadwyn said, "even if you could convince your wayward dukes to bring their troops together without fighting. If you don't act, Palim will burn by week's end."

Duke Adroc rolled his eyes. Rilen stepped forward and stood directly in front of him. "If you care to continue doubting what we say, I'd be happy to prove it by trial-at-arms. After they pick up what's left of you, the rest of us can get the army moving."

"Duke Adroc," Golonis said, "you may be the Duke of Palim, but I am still the chief military advisor to the king. Unless he cares to intercede on your behalf, by law I can make military decisions on my own."

Adroc's nostrils flared, but he said nothing.

Golonis nodded. "The fleet will sail on the evening tide. I can't risk sending them into the South Sea to look for the invasion force. But if they set up a picket line west of Iress, we can force the enemy to land in Piaras Swamp. The time it will take them to march overland should allow us to rally our forces."

"That will help," Adalyn said. "Can you send messengers to Unity?"

Adroc crossed his arms. "I will do no such thing,"

Golonis chuckled. "I think I might be able to spare a few scout patrols to carry official military documents to the Council. I'll also send dispatches to the Elves and Dwarves directly.

Sometimes, things move a bit more slowly when the Council is in the middle. What about the Kobolds? Are they a threat?"

"We don't think so," Gillen said. "Overlord Hamedon was being deceived by an advisor, just as some of your dukes were. We have freed him from that influence. In fact, one member of our party is on his way to speak to Hamedon about joining us."

General Golonis held out his hand, ignoring the scowl from Adroc. "Then let us see to the defense of the city, my friends."

#

With the return of his weapons, Elac no longer felt like a prisoner. He and his friends sat together with Captain Begeron and three of his lieutenants. The company of soldiers had left the road and plunged deep into the jungle. The green canopy overhead blocked the sun, but Elac decided it was just as hot under the trees as it had been in the open sunlight. A noisy stream gurgled past. Crystal clear waters tumbled over the rock-covered creek bed. There was no hint of a breeze. Elac used the sleeve of his tunic to mop the sweat from his forehead.

"We have to avoid the cities and the roadways," Begeron said. "With the near-complete depletion of Wyborn's imperial forces for the invasion, we must assume the entire island is in the hands of the priests by now."

"A fair assumption," Noria said. "Agalia wouldn't have moved until she was poised for a complete conquest. Surprise was her best ally, and she would not have wasted it."

"The question now is, where do we go from here? We need to alert the imperial army about the coup, but I don't know where we could secure a ship." He dropped his gaze to the mossy ground at his feet. "There's something else. Emperor Azorok's only surviving son is commanding a brigade of infantry. Azorok wanted to keep the information secret, in order to let his son rise or fall on his own merits. Agalia is probably not aware that an heir yet lives. We need to restore him to power."

"There is a way," Silvayn said. "We haven't been exactly forthcoming about our purpose here."

Begeron looked up sharply, and his eyes went flat. "Let me guess. You know something about the incident at the temple in Hafgren."

Silvayn nodded. "Yes. We were recovering an artifact from the temple when Dalnoq attacked us. But our purpose here has evolved into something much more. Are you aware of what has been happening with the incursions by strange new creatures?"

"Somewhat. A few years ago, we started receiving reports of such activity. Some, like the namics near Darton, have been substantiated. But there have been no reports of new creatures in at least six months."

"Agalia and Dalnoq were responsible," Silvayn said. "They have been summoning them from Archon, the Plane of Chaos. Jayrne spoke to a priest at Hafgren who had actually seen the Gate they created."

Bergeron's mouth dropped wide open as his hands flew to the top of his head. "I was at Thurlow a year ago for a banquet. A priestess took me on a . . . private tour of the temple. She gave me a brief look at Agalia's personal chambers. In one corner, there was a blue, shimmering arch of energy. In the center, I could barely see a rocky, desolate canyon. The priestess would only say that this creation of Agalia's would change the world."

Silvayn leaned forward. "Begeron, we are here to find and destroy the Gate Agalia is using to bring Chaos creatures to our world. They are the true source of her power. If she brings enough of them over, your army on Pelacia won't matter."

"Whatever is left of it," Noria said. "I'm sure she encouraged Azorok to invade. Whether your army wins or loses, both sides will be weakened by the conflict. She will allow us to fight it out, and she will destroy the winner. Agalia will own both continents."

"So you four just need to travel to the temple and destroy that Gate?"

"Unfortunately, no," Silvayn said. "Gates only lead in one direction. The one you saw leads *to* Archon, not *from*. We have to travel through that Gate, find the one leading back here, and destroy it."

"Destroy them both," Jayrne said.

Begeron gave a low whistle. "That sounds next to impossible. Do you even know how to destroy these Gates?"

Silvayn squinted as he scratched his head. "Not exactly. There has to be a powerful artifact providing the magical energy needed to keep the Gates in place. Due to the nature of the relationship between this world and the plane of chaos, the power source would have to be located with Archon's Gate. My theory is that the two Gates form an interdependent circle. The artifact draws matter from this world through one Gate, and sends it back through the other. If we remove or destroy the focal point of its arcane power, the Gates will collapse."

"But you are not certain of this?" Begeron asked.

"No. As I said, it's a theory. For that matter, we might have to pass through several gates to get to Archon."

Begeron chewed his lip for several long moments. "Okay, here's what we'll do. My company will provide an escort to Thurlow. We'll battle our way into the temple, eliminate the guards, and set up a defensive perimeter. Then we can go through the Gate."

"We?"

"Yes. I'm coming with you."

"When do we leave?" Elac asked.

"Now."

#

Hadwyn walked the periphery of the defensive lines. It was not the first time, and probably would not be the last. He had been awake all night. His task was to find defensible ground, set his soldiers in place, and ensure he had not missed anything. His mind was befuddled with fatigue, but he was not ready to rest. The sun would be up soon. If there was to be an attack, it would come at dawn. He rubbed his eyes and walked on.

The boggy expanse of the Piaras Swamp lay only a few miles south of their position. Even if it had not been dark, the dense fog covering the land would have blocked his view of the swamp. His troops had lit a picket line of bonfires out on the flat ground before them, some plainly visible, others barely a dim glow in the fog.

Not for the last time, he contemplated his feelings for Noria. He had known many women in his life, but none had affected him the way she did. He could not pinpoint what it was about her that had him so enthralled. It might have been her beauty, although he doubted it. He had been around beautiful women before, and none had made him feel this way. She was graceful, intelligent, and a formidable warrior. Perhaps it was the taboo of a Dwarf prince being with a Human princess. He licked his lips and walked on. Whatever the reason, he could not push her from his thoughts.

Hadwyn commanded a contingent of the defenders of Palim. Iress, a coastal city more than fifteen leagues south of Palim, had a sufficient army and supplies to hold off a siege for at least a year. With Palim undermanned, it would likely be the invading army's first target. Hadwyn intended to slow that army, buying time for the armies of the Elves, Dwarves, and the other

Human duchies to respond. He could not count on help from the Kobolds. Rhun was good in a fight, but he was no diplomat. He doubted Rhun could convince Hamedon to commit his army to a battle in the West.

He chose a hilly region northeast of Iress, east of the Iress River, for his first defensive position. His soldiers worked hard that day. They cleared small groves of trees in the area to prevent the enemy from using them as cover. They built a low bulwark out of rocks, trees, and dirt. They dug holes, filled them with spikes, and covered them with narrow branches and brush. The archers brought in wagons full of arrows and set their position on high ground. He kept his small cavalry force in reserve, in case his position became overrun and needed to disengage. His infantry soldiers settled in behind the makeshift wall and waited.

Movement in the fog caught his attention. He stared at the glow of the most distant watch fires. Shadows flickered in and out of view. His soldiers muttered and moved about, rattling their equipment, but the sergeants ordered them to stand quiet. The archers behind Hadwyn readied their arrows. He studied the watch fires a few moments longer, then motioned for the archers to stand down. This was likely a scouting force, nothing more. He would only engage them if they found his positions. Obviously, the watch fires told the enemy that Hadwyn's army was in the area, but his exact position would be a mystery. He intended to keep it that way.

The scouts drew closer. With a handful of archers, Hadwyn worked his way up to the point in the defensive lines most likely to make first contact with the enemy. The silhouetted figures became more-pronounced shadows as they passed in front of the fires built closer to their position. As he had expected, the scouts allowed their path to be dictated by the terrain. They stayed within a wide, gently sloping draw, and came directly at Hadwyn's position.

At fifty yards, he saw them, not distinctly, but enough that he could count heads. He made it twenty scouts, all on foot.

Beyond them, in the depths of the fog, nothing disturbed the glow of the distant watch fires. They were alone.

Hadwyn raised his hand, and the archers readied their bows. He waited while the scouts came closer. When they were twenty yards away, they were clearly visible. Human soldiers dressed in leather armor edged up the slope, eyes searching the fog for some sign of Hadwyn's force. He gave a grim smile.

His arm dropped in a chopping motion, and the archers loosed their arrows. The scouts' shouted warnings mixed with the cries of pain from the wounded. The remaining scouts froze in place, looking for the source of the barrage. Hadwyn's archers fired again, and again, and the last of the scouts fell. Ten of his infantrymen dashed into the fog to be certain the scouts were dead, and the waiting began again.

He was certain the screams had alerted the main body of enemy troops to their presence. Even if they were too far to have heard the short, ugly battle, the failure of the scouts to report back would have the same effect. The main battle was not far off.

Deep in the fog, something moved.

CHAPTER 16

Necessity dictated that Begeron lead them through the trackless jungle to reach Thurlow. It would have been much quicker to stay on the roads, but to do so would have risked an encounter with the insurgent forces in control of the island. The journey through the jungle would not have been possible without Silvayn's help. He used his magic to keep them on the right course, bringing them out of the jungle at a point due north of the ruins of Thurlow.

The company lost two dozen soldiers along the way to the virulent fevers infesting the jungle. The sickened men struggled along as best they could, but eventually Begeron was forced to leave the weakened soldiers behind. With the men who fell ill, plus twenty more who stayed behind to watch over them, one hundred-fifty soldiers remained. It would have to be enough. Elac had no idea how many enemy troops would be guarding the temple at the Thurlow Ruins, but regardless, Silvayn would find a way to reach the Gate.

They stayed within the cover of the trees until nightfall. Two leagues of open grasslands separated them from the foot of the volcano. From there, they had to climb up the hardened rock formed by earlier eruptions. It would be another two leagues to the temple. Elac moved closer to the edge of the trees where he could see what lay before them.

An easterly wind blew across the grasslands. In the distance, the Hammer of Voldaz rose upward from the plain. At its summit, wispy smoke boiled from the crater. The volcano, which had lain dormant for years, was coming to life. A low rumble echoed across the flat, open ground. The earth trembled beneath Elac's feet.

He walked deeper into the sheltering trees to sit with his wife and Noria. The two women sharpened their swords in silence, in anticipation of the coming fight for the temple. Elac's enchanted weapon never needed sharpening, but his chainmail shirt had rusted again. He dropped to the ground beside Jayrne to clean his armor.

Darkness settled across the land. Begeron checked the grasslands one last time, then motioned everyone forward. The horses thundered across the plains. They reached the rocky slopes of the volcano in a short time. Begeron left a contingent of ten soldiers at the base of the hill with the horses. These men led the horses back to the jungle to hide and await word from Begeron. If no messenger arrived by the next night, they were to take the horses and try to reach Darton. The lawless city was likely the safest place for anyone loyal to the Emperor.

They began the ascent. Elac was glad he wore thick leather pants and gauntlets. The holes that honeycombed the lava rock tended to break off suddenly. More than once, he stumbled and fell, driving his knees and hands into the sharp rocks. Low curses in the darkness around him provided ample evidence that he was not the only one having trouble with the tricky footing. Jayrne, lithe as an acrobat, scampered up the hillside without a slip. He fell yet again, and she threw him a faint smile. He stuck his tongue out at her and climbed on. He worried about Sylvain's ability to make the climb, but the old man kept pace with the group.

A few hours after midnight, the lights of the temple came into view. Begeron pulled his troops back down the slope a few hundred yards to allow them to rest. He gathered his squad leaders together for a conference. Elac and the others joined them.

"We need to know what we're up against," Begeron said. "We can't just go charging in there if we're outnumbered two-to-one."

"Agreed," said one soldier. "But with the ring of fires surrounding the ruins, we have no way of getting close enough to count noses."

"I can do it." Jayrne blew a lock of hair out of her eyes. "I'll sneak up, see what kind of numbers they have, where they have guards posted, and what we're up against as far as getting inside."

Begeron raised one eyebrow. "How do you plan to do that without getting caught? We can't risk it."

"My cloak and boots are enchanted. With them, I could walk right through the gates of Wyborn with no one seeing or hearing me." She pulled the cloak tightly about her body, all but vanishing before their eyes.

Begeron's eyes opened wide, and he whistled his amazement. "All right, Jayrne. Be quick, but be careful."

"I'll be back before you know it."

"Somehow, I'm sure of that."

#

A howl of fury arose from the fog, as hundreds of voices cried out together. Hadwyn felt the anxiety within him dissipate. The battle was joined. The waiting, the planning, all of it was a thing of the past. He returned to the center of his lines to take command.

Darkness still blanketed the battlefield. He was surprised the attack would come so soon. The strategy of attacking at sunrise or sunset was almost as old as war itself. He shrugged. Daytime, nighttime, it would make no difference. He had prepared for both.

Countless shadows moved passed the watch fires in the distance. Some of the fires winked out as the enemy extinguished the telltale lights. Hadwyn signaled his archers to make ready. They knew when to fire, but he would be certain of every shot. In a battle he could not win, he would kill as many Wyborn soldiers as possible before falling back. He watched the enemy rush closer.

The encroaching army passed the next ring of fires, and Hadwyn raised his arm. The enemy had reached the outer limit of the range of his bowmen. He counted slowly to himself, then dropped his arm. The archers fired the first volley in unison, then nocked arrows and fired them as fast as they could. The shadowy figures in the darkness continued their rush until the arrows fell among them in a deadly rain. Shrieks of agony filled the night. The charge faltered, but more soldiers closed in from behind. The rush began anew.

Hadwyn's archers maintained a steady pace, launching arrow after arrow at an enemy they could not clearly see. He heard snapping branches and the heavy sound of bodies striking the earth, and he knew they had reached the spiked pits. Moments later, the lead elements of the enemy army appeared out of the fog. Wielding a variety of axes and swords, armored in simple leather jerkins, they recklessly charged Hadwyn's positions.

The palisade slowed their assault, and the archers fired point-blank into their midst. Dozens fell writhing, but dozens more took their place. They tore at the wooden structures blocking their way until they finally forced a breach. A stream of soldiers poured through. Hadwyn's infantrymen met them at the bulwarks. The sound of steel on steel rang up and down the lines, as more holes were forced in the palisade.

He signaled his archers to shift their fire beyond where the enemy tried to breach the front lines. Rather than risk hitting his own men, he would make the enemy reinforcements approach through a hail of arrows. At the very least, he would prevent a number of them from ever reaching the fight.

To his right, Hadwyn heard shouts of dismay. The enemy was close to forcing a breach in his inner perimeter. He grabbed a handful of the men he held in reserve and led a charge into the thick of the fight. With his enchanted hammer swinging, Hadwyn smashed foe after foe into the ground. The enemy fell back before him. His soldiers took courage from his display and threw themselves back into the battle. In a matter of minutes, the breach was closed.

In the distance, beyond where he could see, Hadwyn heard the rolling echo of a battle horn. It blew in three long blasts, paused, then gave three more. The enemy soldiers disengaged from the fight and retreated into the fog. A cheer went up from Hadwyn's little army. The battle was theirs.

#

Elac kept his attention focused on the rock-strewn slope, but he could neither see nor hear any sign of Jayrne's return. She had been gone for over an hour. Despite the protection offered by Sir Draygen's cloak and boots, he feared that she had been found. He licked his parched lips and scanned the darkness once more.

"Find her yet?" He nearly jumped out of his skin at the sound of Jayrne's voice whispering in his ear. She peeled the cloak back from her shoulders and stood beside him, grinning.

Elac took a few moments to catch his breath. "You just scared me out of five years of my life."

"Glad I could help. Let's go talk to Begeron."

They gathered once more in the shelter of several boulders. Jayrne used the tip of one of her knives to draw a diagram on the rock beside her. "This is the temple, right here." She indicated a spot on her drawing. "It's near the center of the ruins, but they have watchmen covering the entire area. They are spread a little thin."

"How many sentries?" asked Begeron.

"They look a little overconfident. All of the posts I saw were guarded by only one man, and the posts are fifty yards apart. The rest of them are sleeping in an amphitheater in front of the temple. They're sleeping in their armor, so they'll be ready for battle rather quickly."

Noria raised one finger. "Keep in mind the element of surprise. They are asleep and not expecting trouble this deep in their own territory. There will be some disorientation when they are suddenly awakened to find an army bearing down on them. We'll put a lot of them down before they know what's happening."

Jayrne frowned. "We'd better. I counted two hundred soldiers."

Noria studied Jayrne's drawing. "What about this area to the rear of the temple? Is it just your drawing, or is this really the place where their lines are closest to the temple?"

"It's definitely the closest point."

"Okay. We work our way around to that side of the ruins and attack from there." She looked Jayrne in the eyes. "Can you eliminate a few of the sentries?"

She firmed her lips and inclined her head slightly. "Yes."

"Then that's it. Once we're in position, you sneak in and kill two of the guards. That will open a wide enough hole for us to break through unseen. Once we're spotted, we make a rush for the temple. If we get inside the temple safely, we can set up a defensive perimeter around the entrance. We ought to be able to hold them off for some time. Long enough, anyway, to get a few of us through the Gate. Once we start, we don't stop, no matter who falls. Honor and victory will be ours this night!"

Begeron shook Noria's hand. "Let's do it."

They passed the instructions down through the chain of command. Everyone tied down their equipment to minimize the noise. They climbed higher on the slope, staying well back from the edge of the ruins as they worked their way around. When they were in position, Jayrne wrapped herself in Sir Draygen's cloak and slipped ahead alone.

She was only gone ten minutes. Upon her return, the contingent crept slowly forward. Elac set each foot down gingerly, aware that just ahead, two hundred men lay in wait, men who would kill him without a second thought. He glanced to his right and saw the sun peeking over the eastern horizon.

Ahead, a dark shape lay next to a small wooden outbuilding. When he was closer, Elac realized it was the body of one of the sentries. The dead man's eyes were wide open. He lay in a pool of his own blood. Elac averted his eyes and walked on.

The ruins of Thurlow were ancient stone buildings. At some time in the past, a volcanic eruption had buried the village under ten feet of ash. Scars and stains on the gray walls attested to the ferocity of the eruption. Hundreds of years later, erosion and Human hands had brought the ruined settlement back to the light. The air was thick with the smell of sulfur, and a fine layer of ash covered everything.

They were only a few buildings away from the temple when the cry rang out. The attacking soldiers reacted instantly. They charged into the amphitheater, right into the midst of the men who had just come awake. Bergeron's men cut a bloody swath through the soldiers who, as Noria predicted, were armed but not entirely alert. Blood coated the stone steps of the amphitheater as Elac ascended the far side toward the temple gates.

Two guards armed with long pikes barred the way. Elac and Noria rushed forward, swords ready. The pike, while an impressive weapon on a battlefield, is much less effective in single combat against a skilled swordsman. Elac demonstrated this to one of the pikemen, who lunged at him with his weapon. Elac deflected the thrust with his shield, then closed to within striking distance. The guard had no chance; he carried no shield, and the blade of his pike was several feet beyond Elac. Sir Draygen's sword bit deeply through the soldier's banded armor, and he tumbled to the stones. A swipe of Noria's sword severed the head of her opponent. They gained the doors to the temple.

#

The sun climbed higher in the eastern sky, and the roiling fog slowly burned away. Hadwyn was at a loss. First, his opponent had struck blindly at night against Hadwyn's fortified positions. The next logical step would have been to attack again at dawn, striking out of the east. With the sun at their backs, they would carry a distinct advantage over Hadwyn's troops. But the morning wore on, and the attack never came.

He also wondered why the men who attacked the night before wore simple leather armor. If his army was facing hundreds of men wearing armor like they faced in the temple at Hafgren, they would be in trouble. Perhaps the men sent against them the night before were just shock troops, maybe the Wyborn version of militia. Their purpose could have been to test the defensive strength of Hadwyn's army, regardless of their losses.

The fog lifted a bit more, and the enemy army materialized on the field before them. Still a mile distant, they had drawn up into impressive formations. Hadwyn took a quick count and estimated their strength at five thousand soldiers. He had barely a tenth of that number. He assumed this was just the spearhead of the enemy invasion. Not for a moment did he harbor any illusions about the final outcome of the battle. They would hold their positions until it was no longer possible, and then they would fall back. It was that simple.

From somewhere deep in the enemy ranks, deep, booming war drums sounded their song. The army before them marched forward. Hadwyn moved up and down his lines to offer words of encouragement. All knew they were heavily outnumbered, and it would be easy for someone to lose heart.

Once the first man fled, it could become a rout. He would not let that happen.

The leading edge of the enemy force passed the smoking remains of the tight ring of watch fires, which denoted the limits of bow range. Although the new force was comprised mainly of militia, there was also a scattering of heavy infantry wearing steel armor. At Hadwyn's signal, the archers fired volley after volley. Barely an hour before, a handful of crossbowmen had arrived, and Hadwyn gave them the task of firing at the men wearing the nearly impervious breastplates. While the steel of their armor had deflected sword blows, it was not as effective against the powerful bolts from the crossbows. The ping of the shots that pierced the hardened steel echoed back to them and mingled with the cries of pain.

Although the crossbows took much longer than bows to reload and fire, their demoralizing effect on the men in the hardened steel armor was obvious. Their charge faltered. One by one, they fell back, allowing their brethren in leather armor to take the lead. Hadwyn watched the change in the enemy's tactics with satisfaction. The fewer of those troops his own men had to face in battle, the better.

From some point deep in the enemy ranks, a long, brassy horn note sounded. The men attacking Hadwyn's formation fell back, losing dozens more in their retreat as Hadwyn's archers loosed arrows at their backs. The soldiers of Palim congratulated each other, but Hadwyn was not convinced the battle had been won. There was something about the demeanor of the men as they retreated. They had not run, like a routed foe, but rather in an organized manner, as someone who was falling back to regroup. And why would they march through the arrow storm, only to fall back without having engaged his troops?

His hunch proved prophetic minutes later. A dozen creatures charged from the rear of the enemy formation. Even from this distance, Hadwyn recognized them by Elac's description. *Graemons.* They were more muscular than Elac had led him to believe, with powerful arms that nearly reached the ground. As they closed with Hadwyn's soldiers, he saw the red glow from their eyes, set deep in the leathery faces. They roared with a terrifying hunger and charged Hadwyn's position. The archers released several volleys of arrows, but they could not penetrate the thick hide. The crossbow bolts sunk to the feathers of the shafts, but the creatures ignored them.

Some of Hadwyn's troops in the middle of the line gave ground. Their courage failed them in the face of the monstrosities. Hadwyn feared his entire force might flee. The stout Dwarf hefted his enchanted hammer and charged into the fray. He ran past the bulwarks and was the first to engage a graemon. His first blow struck a beast in the side and knocked it sprawling. A cheer went up from the men, and they rushed forward to aid their leader.

The archers had to stop shooting at the graemons once Hadwyn engaged them. Hadwyn hoped they had enough sense to fire on the Wyborn troops if they tried to rejoin the battle. He cursed himself for not issuing that order before he entered the fight. He raised his hammer and struck the fallen graemon in the leg. The snap of the bone sounded like the breaking of a tree limb. The graemon howled its rage but could not regain its feet to fight back. Hadwyn had to back off when another graemon attacked from the side.

He struck three consecutive blows to the creature's side and legs, and it limped away from him. He took advantage of the brief respite to check on the enemy army. They had reset their formation and were on the move. His archers loosed another volley. While enemy losses were heavy, they did not falter. Further across the field, Hadwyn saw the reason for their courage. Another two legions had emerged from the swamp to join the battle. It was no use. The graemons would distract and exhaust his soldiers, and the superior numbers of the foe would win the day. He had to sound the retreat.

He crushed the skull of the closest graemon, then dropped back from the melee. The sergeant in charge of the archers rushed to his side.

"Sir! We're low on arrows, and another army has joined the battle!"

"I saw. Signal the retreat. Send runners to the infantry lines. As soon as the cavalry charge hits the enemy, I want those men to pull back. We may have to stop and fight every mile or so, but we need to get back to the river with enough time to get across."

The sergeant trotted away to carry out the orders. Hadwyn surveyed the line to see where he was needed most. Only two of the graemons yet lived, but the victory had been costly. Fifty of his soldiers lay in twisted heaps in front of the bulwarks. He started forward, but stopped as the final graemon fell beneath the killing blades of Hadwyn's soldiers.

A deep roar went up from the enemy forces, and they charged across the field. A flaming arrow arced across the field from Hadwyn's archers. At that signal, one hundred armored knights rode forward at a full gallop. They wore full plate mail armor, as did their horses. Steel-tipped lances thrust into the air like a forest, topped with multi-colored flags that announced each knight's lineage. In perfect formation, they charged around the end of the bulwarks and directly into the center of the enemy lines.

Even over the commotion of Hadwyn's infantry retreating from their defensive positions, he heard the crash as the cavalry collided with the leather-clad militia from Wyborn. Hadwyn hesitated, anxious to see the result. It was fairly predictable. The knights cut a wide swath of destruction through the Wyborn soldiers. When their lances broke, the knights discarded the useless wooden shafts and drew their swords. Some of the enemy fell beneath the pounding hooves of the chargers, others died by the blade. The enemy charge faltered, then broke into a panicked retreat.

The knights disengaged and rode back to where Hadwyn's troops had organized into groups for the march to the river. The archers stayed at the rear and on the flanks, where they could harass the men in pursuit when they drew too close. If that failed, the knights would unleash another titanic charge. It would be a long walk to the river. Hadwyn hoped the second phase of the plan was already in place.

#

Neither Noria's respectable strength nor Elac's enchanted blade could penetrate whatever warded the doors to the temple. While the two warriors held off the scattered priests and guards who came to the defense of the Thurlow Ruins, Jayrne tried to pick the lock. She had no more success than they did. Elac crossed swords with the last temple guard, a man clad only in a brief loincloth. The Elf deflected the blow aimed for his head. Before he could retaliate, his wife darted in low and buried her dagger up to the hilt in the man's stomach. She ripped the blade upward and spilled a torrent of blood onto the flagstones.

She turned and kicked the temple doors. "I feel better already."

Silvayn sighed. "Let me try." While the others gave him some room, Silvayn chanted in the language of magic. He gestured toward the doors in what was almost a punch. With an explosion that made Elac's ears ring, the doors burst asunder. The way inside was open.

Begeron ran up the steps. "I have a perimeter set around the center of the ruins. We'll slowly collapse inward until all we have to defend is the temple. There's no sense in trying to spread out too far. They can have the rest of this place, if they want it."

Noria pursed her lips as she surveyed the carnage before them. "You are certain you wish to come with us?"

"I am."

"Then you had better alert your men. As soon as we find the Gate, we'll cross over."

Elac and Jayrne entered the temple first. It was deserted, as far as they could tell. Noria and Silvayn waited at what remained of the doors until Begeron returned, then all three came in together. Two of Begeron's men followed to provide an escort until they reached the Gate. Elac kept his sword drawn. Although he saw no one, his instincts told him there would yet be a guardian to fight.

The interior of the temple was a sharp contrast from what he had seen outside. Where the building looked dilapidated on the exterior, the entrance hall was a monument to expensive tastes. A plush, red carpet covered the floors. Silk tapestries hung from the walls, depicting various images of what could only be Voldaz, the god of Chaos. Sculptures adorned tables and alcoves, each inset with precious stones. Gold and silver sconces hung along the walls.

Jayrne put up a hand, and they all stopped. As silent as smoke, she nocked an arrow and knelt, aiming at the darkened doorway ahead on their left. The seconds passed, and nothing happened. She motioned for Elac to move forward along the right side of the hallway. Before he had taken two steps, three men rushed from hiding, swords raised overhead. The first stumbled and fell, an arrow buried deep in his chest. The second made it a few steps closer, but an arrow ripped through his throat. He dropped his weapon and wrapped his hands around his neck as his breath gurgled out. Elac slashed the remaining guard. The blow drew a bright flow of blood as he fell to his back. Noria finished him with a thrust to the head.

"You have good ears," Begeron said.

Jayrne showed him a dimpled smile. "Comes with the job."

They moved deeper into the temple. Elac ignored several side passages along the way. If Begeron's memory was correct, the Gate would be deep in the temple, a couple of levels underground. The hallway turned to the left. A wide granite staircase dropped away before them, a faint glow visible from somewhere ahead. Two by two, with Silvayn at the rear, they descended the stairs.

At the bottom, a short entryway opened into a vast hall. The hall alone was larger than the entire temple, so it must have been cut into the rock beneath other parts of the ruins. Several blazing fire pits provided light and, in Elac's opinion, excessive warmth. At the far side of the room, a shimmering arched portal stood beside a golden altar. An inscription of a pentagram, with undecipherable runes at each point, surrounded the Gate. Before the altar, row upon row of benches lined the chamber.

They were halfway across the floor when the demon emerged from an alcove behind the altar.

CHAPTER 17

The sun was still high in the winter sky when the Iress River came into view. Fatigue battered Hadwyn with every step. Although it was rare so far south, a light snowfall filled the air. The flakes clung to his beard and mixed with the ice clumps frozen there from his breath. He had brought his horse to the battle but insisted upon walking with the rest of the infantry. Gestures like that helped keep morale high, even in the face of incredible odds.

A single horseman appeared in the falling snow. From the short stature and the way the man clung to the saddle, Hadwyn knew it was his brother. They met ahead of Hadwyn's troops and clasped forearms.

"Glad you could make it, big brother."

"I wouldn't have missed it. I see you managed to bring back most of your army."

"I count around one hundred dead, maybe another hundred injured to the point where they can't fight."

Gillen turned and squinted at the distant river. "Let's get your injured across the river now. We have extra wagons standing by. We could start them back to Palim right away. They would be a burden later, if we're in a hurry."

Hadwyn turned to the sergeant at his side and gave a few orders. He looked back at his brother. "Is everything ready?"

"Mostly. We didn't get the numbers we wanted, but we do have elements of all the various contingents. We may have to alter our plans a bit."

"Good. My cavalry and archers have held them back, but barely. They can't be more than an hour behind us."

"We'll be ready."

Hadwyn's soldiers were relieved to find their next defensive lines already built. There was another earthen wall to offer some protection. An enemy trying to reach the wall would first have to push through a palisade of sharpened sticks in front of the berm. With the archers on high ground nearby and freshly supplied with arrows, a breach of the palisade would prove costly to an attacker.

Their greatest asset was the terrain. Waist deep grasses, browned from the winter cold, covered the broad prairie. Any number of nasty surprises could be hidden in the rolling field, completely undetected until it was too late.

The booming of the Wyborn war drums echoed in the distance. The snowfall grew thicker, but far across the field Hadwyn spotted the lead elements of the army. The opposing general followed the same strategy as in the previous battle. His poorly armored shock troops led the way. The heavy infantry in the brightly burnished breastplates followed behind. Hadwyn assumed there were more creatures summoned from the nether regions hidden somewhere within the force assembled against them.

The outer boundary of the range of his archers' bows had been marked by flags planted on the battlefield. The Wyborn troops marched past the markers, shields raised. They ignored the deadly rain of arrows that fell amid their formation. Hadwyn's archers had been augmented by another hundred bowmen summoned from the militia at Goran. Scores of enemy soldiers fell and stained the snow with their crimson blood, but their approach never wavered. They closed two a distance of one hundred yards. With a throaty yell, they charged.

#

The demon hissed softly. A battered black tunic that hung to his knees covered the red torso. Its face ended in a wolf-like muzzle. Eyes the color of midnight sat deep in the creature's head. It moved with a fluid grace that belied the bulk of its massive arms and legs. At seven feet tall, it nearly hit its head on the ceiling when it stood upright. It hefted a wicked two-edged battle axe and stomped closer.

Elac, Noria, and Begeron spread out, moving into the open and closing with the demon. Begeron's soldiers stepped further around the room to come at the demon from the rear. Behind them, Silvayn worked up a spell, while Jayrne pulled her cloak about her body. Elac brought his shield into a defensive position and held Sir Draygen's sword before him like a talisman.

The demon attacked first. It lunged at Noria, the broad axe head a blur as it struck her hastily raised shield. With a shower of sparks, the weapon rebounded. The blow cast Noria backward. She rolled smoothly to her feet and charged back into the fray. One of Begeron's soldiers thrust his longsword at the demon's unprotected back. The demon's axe came around and parried the blow, even before the demon spun to face him. The next swipe of the axe sent the man's head flying.

Jayrne appeared from the other side and slashed the demon's arm. The blade bit deeply, but the demon thrust her away. The little thief tumbled across the floor. Elac drove Sir Draygen's sword into the demon's side. It howled its rage and swung the axe at Elac's head. He barely managed to dodge the blow and almost lost his sword in the process.

"I need some room!" Silvayn's shout thundered in the broad chamber.

Begeron and Noria slid apart. A bolt of lightning burst forth from Silvayn's fingertips and struck the demon full in the chest. The force of the blast picked the creature up off its feet and threw it against the far wall. The stones cracked where the demonic body struck. It rose to its hands and knees, shook its head, and stood.

Elac kept his eyes on the demon. "Jayrne! The Temira!"

She rushed to his side and withdrew the Temira from a pouch at her narrow waist. The demon launched several blows at Begeron. It drove him steadily backward and finally knocked him from his feet. Noria, heedless of her own safety, charged to Begeron's rescue. With Sir Omonis's shield held before her, she swung a vicious series of strokes at the demon. It finally had to forego its attack against the man on the ground. Begeron's remaining soldier stood at Noria's side. The two alternated blows while Begeron scrambled to his feet.

Elac, the Temira dangling from his neck by its golden chain, rejoined the battle. Silvayn released another lightning bolt, but the demon jumped aside. The spell only caught it a glancing blow. In an amazing display of agility, the demon recovered from the assault, spun, and slashed the other soldier from head to hip. With a sharp groan, he fell backward. Blood gushed between his fingers as he tried vainly to stanch the flow.

Noria and Begeron came at the demon from opposite sides. It blocked most of their blows, but they still drew blood. In a frenzy, it swung its axe in a circle as it howled with unbridled fury. Elac darted in from behind and stabbed his sword through the back of the demon's neck, angling up into the brain.

The Temira flashed a brilliant white light. The demon thrust its arms into the air as it screamed in agony. Elac held onto the hilt, twisting the blade and driving it deeper. The demon fell to its knees. Noria and Begeron stood one to either side and alternated blows. With a final roar, the demon fell onto its face. The massive form wavered like smoke, then vanished.

#

The first wave of Wyborn soldiers weathered the storm of arrows with remarkable tenacity. As gaps opened in their front lines due to mounting casualties, more men pushed forward to fill the holes. They crossed the killing field and reached the palisade. The archers intensified their barrage while the hapless men picked their way through the sharpened stakes. Hadwyn's infantry engaged them from beyond the berm. With their shields locked together to form a solid wall, they slipped their shortswords through to thrust at the enemy.

The leather-clad warriors had finally had enough. First in pairs, then in increasing numbers, they disengaged and fell back. They left hundreds of dead behind. But another wave of Wyborn soldiers, light infantry wearing chainmail, had already marched in behind them. Although many of these men fell victim to the arrow storm, their armor protected them from some of the archers' fire. Hadwyn kept his crossbowmen in reserve. Their bolts would easily pierce the armor of the second wave of raiders, but he wanted to save their ammunition in case the men in the hardened steel breastplates attacked next. Besides, he had a different surprise in store for this wave of the assault.

The new soldiers pushed through the palisade and engaged the army from Palim. The howls of rage and screams of agony echoed across the grassland. Hadwyn stood atop a knoll, where he could better see the fight, and he watched the ebb and flow of battle. His veteran's eye spotted a problem on the left side of his lines.

He cupped his hands and shouted. "Sergeant! Take three squads and reinforce the positions halfway down the left flank. They're starting to buckle."

The sergeant saluted and bellowed his orders. He dashed to the north, fifty men in formation behind him. They reached the embattled unit just as enemy soldiers forced a breach. The reinforcements easily repelled the attackers. The line firmed up once more.

Hadwyn sent two more units of reserves to plug growing gaps in his line, then decided it was time to add other resources. He seized a bow, set fire to the arrow, and launched it high into the cloudy sky. Trailing a thin cloud of black smoke, it reached the apex of its arch, then dropped into the field.

At that signal, a hundred Elven archers rose from their hidden position in the grass. They were well to the north of the actual battle, but still within range of their magnificent longbows. The bowstrings snapped as one, and a black cloud of arrows raced across the field, where it fell like locusts upon the men from Wyborn. Their assault faltered, then dissolved completely under repeated volleys from the newcomers. They turned and fled, harried at every step by the Elven archers.

The army from Palim received a brief respite. Minutes later, the war drums sounded their song anew. As Hadwyn expected, the elite heavy infantry advanced. The sun reflected brightly off their polished breastplates. Greaves covered their legs, and plumed helmets with fierce faceguards warded their heads. With the added armor, the regular archers would have a very difficult time finding a vulnerable area to strike. He would have to depend upon the crossbows.

He had close to one hundred-fifty men in the crossbow unit this time after being reinforced by the garrison at Goran. Only about fifty actually fired the crossbows. The others were required to continually reload the weapons. Hadwyn signaled for them to move up to a series of hastily-built raised platforms, where they could more readily fire over the heads of their own troops. Thick wooden walls at the front of the platforms provided cover in case the enemy brought their own archers forward.

Hadwyn scratched his head as he pondered that point. It was strange that they had not already done so. The enemy's strategy made no sense. They charged recklessly into fortified positions, through heavy archer fire, and fought until they were nearly annihilated. They pulled back and tried it again. Not once did they return fire. Hadwyn knew the enemy had to have archers with them. Perhaps they were saving the arrows for the siege of Palim. On a whim, Hadwyn sent his light-armored mounted scouts north and south to check for other enemy armies. If one of them managed to flank him, his soldiers could be in serious jeopardy.

The third wave of soldiers moved within range. Hadwyn signaled for the crossbows to initiate fire. Staccato pings broke out across the battlefield, punctuated by grunts and screams as the hardened bolts ripped through the steel armor to bite into tender flesh.

Most of his scouts returned and reported only empty countryside. Despite the good news, a sudden cold feeling struck him in the pit of his stomach. Perhaps there was a reason the rest of his scouts did not return. That was why the enemy was being so careless and incompetent. He did not care how this skirmish ended. His real thrust was probably already crossing the river, miles to the north or south of the battlefield. If Wyborn troops successfully crossed to the east side of the Iress River, they could cut off Hadwyn's line of retreat and butcher his army in place.

He rushed down the hillside to find his brother. A sergeant directed him to the south. Almost at the end of the line, he found Gillen directing the rebuilding of the bulwark. Another wave of attackers was almost upon them.

"Gillen! Come with me! There's trouble!"

Gillen took in his brother's face, then turned to the men beside him. "Finish up here. I'll be back shortly."

The two Dwarves walked back a short distance from the berm. Behind them, they heard the clash of steel on steel as the next phase of the battle began.

"Okay, Hadwyn, what's going on?"

"They've flanked us. Or rather, they're in the process of it. I think."

Gillen folded his arms and frowned. "You think? You are about to suggest we give up this position because you think they might've flanked us? Our scouts have reported nothing."

"I checked on the way here. All the scouts to the north have reported in, and they've seen nothing. But only half of the scouts we sent south have come back. I think this battle is only meant to keep us here long enough for them to circle around behind us. They'll grind us up like dog meat."

Gillen blew out a heavy breath. "You're certain?"

"I've got a solid hunch."

He nodded. "All right, then. I'll trust your instincts on this one. Let's pull back the rest of the way to the river."

"You make the preparations up and down the line. I'll take care of the rest."

#

One of Begeron's men yet lived. His breathing came in shallow gasps, and his face was pale. Begeron knelt and took the young man's hand in his own.

"You fought well, Levan. By your bravery, the battle is won."

"The creature . . . is destroyed?" His voice sounded very faint.

"Yes. You have earned your place in the House of the Dead. You will walk with our greatest heroes for all eternity."

Levan managed to smile. He gave a wet, ragged cough, spilling blood down his chin. He took one more breath, then died.

Begeron laced Levan's fingers across his chest and placed his sword and shield at his side, then did the same for his other fallen soldier. Elac watched the ritual wordlessly. Begeron crossed the room to join the others in front of the Gate. Silvayn's brow was creased as he studied the shimmering portal.

"We have a problem. This Gate does not lead to Archon. It leads to Aceros, the Land of the Dead."

Elac looked to the ceiling and took a few steps away. "So, now what do we do?" he asked in a quiet voice.

"We go through," Noria said. "There has to be a way to Archon through this Gate."

"Based on what?" Elac asked.

Noria smiled. "Why else would they have such a powerful creature guarding the gateway? If this Gate led only to Aceros, they might have placed a weaker guardian here just for show, but they would have let us go through. We would no longer be a threat."

"I agree," Silvayn said. "Before we go through, I need to cast a spell to make it possible for us to breathe. A toxic fog covers much of Aceros."

Silvayn chanted softly. He spread his fingers wide and raised them over his head. A thick blanket of darkness settled around them. Elac felt nauseated. The overpowering stench of rotten meat filled his nostrils. By the time his vision returned, dizziness had forced him to his knees.

Noria entered the Gate first. There was no discussion, she simply stepped forward into the flickering barrier and disappeared. Begeron followed right behind her. Elac and Jayrne went through together, followed closely by Silvayn.

Elac felt a wave of vertigo. His stomach fluttered, and he almost fell. He regained his senses and looked around.

He faced a barren landscape. Deep draws cut through the rocky terrain, unbroken by any living plants. Dead scrub brush dotted the hillside, but somehow Elac doubted the plants had ever actually lived. The fog Silvayn warned them about hung in the air off to their right. Overhead, the eternal nighttime sky was colored the deepest black. Although he did not know where the light source was, a dim glow covered the land as far as he could see. The air was cold, and a stiff breeze blew in a constantly shifting direction.

"Where to?" Elac asked.

Silvayn closed his eyes and slowly spun in a circle. "I can sense another Gate. It appears to shift locations randomly. For the time being, it's about a league that way." He pointed into the dark Aceros night.

"Can you tell if it leads to Archon?" Jayrne asked.

"Not until I see it."

"Lead on," Noria said.

They scampered up the precarious, steep sides of a wash. Although there was no water to be found, it was obvious that at some point, there had been a river running through the deep cut behind them. They gained the summit and found flatter ground.

A low moaning sound drifted through the air. Elac looked sharply about but could not find the source.

"Stay alert," Silvayn said. "The dead walk this land. They despise any living creatures they see. Remember, in Aceros, we are the trespassers. Elac, your sword will not destroy the undead so readily as it did back on Pelacia."

Their march continued. If anything, the groaning became louder. Where before, it appeared to come from someplace distant, the sound became more focused and seemed to be coming from behind them. Elac drifted over to the edge of the narrow gorge fifty yards to their right. He looked over the edge.

"Silvayn! There are hundreds of thralls after us! Maybe thousands!"

#

The Elven archers fired several volleys into the trailing elements of the Wyborn army, causing them to back off out of range. The archers secured their equipment and ran east toward the river. Hadwyn raised a red flag on a long pole and waved it back and forth. At that signal, the heavy cavalry thundered ahead. They flanked the north end of the battle lines and fell upon the warriors of Wyborn who were engaged with Hadwyn's infantry. The charge of the knights was devastating, even to the Wyborn heavy infantry. The cavalry disengaged, rode north a short distance, then turned and charged again.

The repeated assaults left the enemy with no choice but to withdraw. Even that decision proved costly, as the crossbowmen and archers found easy targets in the retreating army. The infantry took advantage of the break in the fighting to fall back. Hadwyn's entire force began a calculated retreat to the banks of the Iress River.

Getting across would be the tricky part. Gillen had requisitioned every boat, barge, and ferry he could put his hands on. The boat operators worked against time to shuttle the army safely across to the west bank before the Wyborn soldiers attacked once more. Hadwyn put half of his men into a smaller defensive perimeter, where they would try to hold off the enemy for as long as possible. The Elven archers were stationed behind the infantry, where their longbows could make any assault costly. The heavy cavalry crossed the river first. Their absence could end up costing lives, but it would take a long time to get them across. Doing so while under attack would be impossible.

The assault Hadwyn had expected finally came. With a jumbled mix of the different types of warriors Hadwyn's army had faced, the Wyborn soldiers charged directly at Hadwyn's diminished defensive line. The Elves fired arrow after arrow, and a trail of bodies littered the ground. Yet still the enemy came, trampling their own dead.

The defenses at the river were better constructed. A wide trench had been dug in front of the earthen bulwark. This would force the attackers to fight from lower ground. Hadwyn knew he could not possibly win the battle, but he could try to hold them off long enough to evacuate.

The warriors from Wyborn battled their way through the arrow storm. Although countless numbers of them had fallen beneath the murderous fire of the Elven Longbows, there were simply too many for the Elves to kill them all. They reached the trench, and the battle was joined. Men fell dying on both sides. Although the greatest number of casualties belonged to the attacker, Hadwyn's force dwindled minute by minute.

He ordered a portion of his reserves to ready the next phase of the battle plan. More than half of his army was across, but he needed more time. Soldiers not actively fighting rolled dozens of barrels into place behind the bulwarks. Some stepped up to the earthen wall to relieve the battle-weary men who had somehow managed to hold the enemy at bay.

A knot of men armored with the nearly impregnable breastplate armor attacked the center of Hadwyn's line. Although his soldiers fought bravely, the force of heavy infantrymen overwhelmed them. Hadwyn left his post and called to his brother.

The two Dwarves threw themselves into the thickest of the fighting. A dozen Wyborn soldiers had penetrated the line and fought on Hadwyn's side of the bulwark. The two Dwarf princes joined the melee. Hadwyn's hammer was as deadly as Gillen's axe. The magic weapons pounded through the hard steel of their opponents' armor. The men of Wyborn shrank back from the deadly attack.

Their timidity cost them their lives. A sergeant had sent several men armed with crossbows to help repel the breach.

When the enemy backed off to reassess their tactics, the crossbows cut them down where they stood. Hadwyn called for more infantry, sealing the breach.

A messenger ran up, his face flushed with exhaustion. He gulped air for a few seconds. "Prince Hadwyn! We just received word. Hundreds of imps are coming north along the riverbank. They'll be here within the hour!"

CHAPTER 18

The five from Pelacia ran over the broken terrain, dodging sinkholes, leaping over boulders, and trying not to trip over the hazards scattered across the dead landscape. A mile behind them, the thralls followed with mindless tenacity. The undead moved quicker on Aceros than Elac remembered from Pelacia. He wondered if it was because they were closer to their source of power.

But the thralls were not the worst of their problems. Twice, they had been forced to stop and fight roving bands of ghouls. Luckily, the translucent figures never numbered more than four or five. But the delays allowed the group of thralls to close the distance between them. Elac cursed himself for not suggesting Gillen bless Noria's and Jayrne's weapons, which would allow them to defend themselves against the incorporeal undead.

Ahead, the ground rose sharply to a solitary peak. At the top, a twinkling light beckoned to them. The Gate was there, if they could reach it. A wraith appeared in front of them, but Elac cut it down with three rapid swipes of his sword.

A band of dark shapes clambered out of the ditch ahead of them and lumbered forward. Silvayn shouted a warning, chanted, and sent a blast of fire into the group. Their bodies tumbled over the edge and out of sight.

They gained the base of the hill, but some of the thralls drew too close. Elac and Jayrne climbed over the piles of broken rock while Begeron and Noria stayed at the bottom, swords drawn. Silvayn stood his ground behind them.

"Come one, Silvayn!" Elac shouted. "The Gate is here!"

"We're coming," Noria said. "You two go on ahead. And you as well, Silvayn. We'll deal with these thralls and be up shortly."

Silvayn followed Elac and Jayrne. The old mage paused occasionally to cast a spell and obliterate several thralls. Elac looked back and saw the two warriors battling side by side, slaying their foes with reckless abandon. Elac was halfway up the hill when Noria and Begeron finally began their assent.

Elac and Jayrne reached the summit. The Gate stood before them. The image of the other side shimmered as if underwater. Although there was some plant life, the terrain on the other side didn't look much better than the landscape around them on Aceros. Silvayn reached their side and nodded.

"That's it," he said. "That's Archon." He looked back down the slope. "More thralls are coming. They might reach Noria and Begeron before they can get up here. You two go through. I'm going to help our friends. We'll be joining you in a minute."

Elac and Jayrne stepped through the Gate. Once again, he experienced the sensation of falling. A brilliant bolt of lightning lit the sky, followed by a deafening crack of thunder. He stood and realized that at some point, he had taken Jayrne's hand in his own. He gave her hand a squeeze before he released it.

"We're here. Now we just have to wait on the others to—"

He stared, wide-eyed, as the Gate from Aceros flashed a brilliant light, then opened again on completely different landscape. The Gate had shifted, with the others still on the wrong side.

#

Hadwyn signaled for the next wave of soldiers to pull back from the lines and board the watercraft waiting to take them across the river. When the time came to send another group, he would have to shorten his lines again. It would be the third time he had drawn his defensive perimeter into a tighter circle. Other than a single probing attack, however, the enemy had done nothing. Hadwyn brushed the snow from his beard and stared across the battlefield to the enemy formations.

They had precious little time before the arrival of the imps. Hadwyn assumed the enemy commander waited for the imps to launch their attack before starting his own. To slow the imps' advance, Hadwyn had moved most of his Elven archers to the south, ready to fire on them when they appeared. The rest of his archers, assisted by the crossbowmen, he positioned to fire on the Wyborn army, if it should advance.

"My Lord! Here they come!"

The shout came from one of the Elven archers. Hadwyn jogged to the hillock where the archers stood, arrows nocked. From this distance, the mob of imps was a flowing red stain on the white landscape. Moments later, the Elven longbows sang. Volley after volley streaked across the afternoon sky. Dozens of tiny forms lay motionless in the snow, but the others came on. Hadwyn whistled, and fifty soldiers of his heavy infantry unit formed up in front of the archers.

Although their numbers had been reduced considerably, the charge of the imps never slowed. They swarmed over the final hill and rushed directly at the waiting infantrymen. The extensive armor worn by the men from Goran defeated the claws and teeth of the imps. Swords hacked and chopped, and they repulsed the imps. The diminutive creatures retreated only a short distance before they charged once more, despite the sudden wave of arrows loosed by the Elves.

Hadwyn returned to the center of his lines, where Gillen paced back and forth, fingering the edge of his axe. "What's the story with the imps, Hadwyn?"

"The contingent we stationed down there has them under control. We need to worry more about the Wyborn army."

"We have some news. The boats are on their way back across. And we just received word that several more ships will be here in a few minutes. I think we can get everyone across in three more trips."

"Good. I think I need a drink."

"You might want to wait on that. I ordered scouts to patrol both north and south on the west side of the river. They found the army you predicted. It has almost finished crossing the river. It's as large as this force against us now, but they're not exhausted like we are. We'll leave one fight to begin another."

"Maybe not. Let's overload the boats. I know it's risky, but let's try to get everyone to the other side with only two trips."

"Ordinarily, I'd say you're being reckless, but in this case I think you're right."

Hadwyn returned to the archers' position. Only a handful of imps remained, but they had certainly made an impact. His archers were low on arrows, and he had lost many of his infantrymen. As he watched, the last of the imps was slain. He ordered the infantry to pull back further inside the perimeter. The Elven archers returned to the front of the army's position to fire on Wyborn's forces if necessary.

The next stage of the withdrawal was tricky. Hadwyn and Gillen moved up and down the lines, telling the men to stay low and try to avoid being seen pulling out. They removed over half of the infantry and put them on the boats. The maneuver left them vulnerable to a frontal assault. The archers would come with the last wave.

The minutes ticked away, and still the enemy held back. Hadwyn glanced at the sky but could not judge the time. The heavy, gray skies completely obscured the sun's position. The snow had stopped falling for the moment, but the leaden cloud cover still gave the day an ominous feel.

A company of Wyborn militia marched across the battlefield. Hadwyn frowned. Why send the men in leather armor against Elven longbows? And why send only two hundred men? Even with his depleted forces, Hadwyn could easily hold off this attack. He decided the enemy must be probing his strength. If they thought he was out of arrows, they would probably attack.

Although they were indeed low on arrows, Hadwyn ordered the entire contingent of archers to fire upon the militia. The formation melted, and the men ran back the way they had come. The barrage left many of Hadwyn's archers almost empty-handed, but it accomplished what he wanted. The army across the field stayed where it was.

The darkening skies of late evening had set in when a runner approached to report that the boats were almost back on the east bank. It was time to implement the final stage of his plan. He shouted to a sergeant, who raised a red banner and waved it vigorously. The entire defensive line stood and backed away. In orderly formations, they crossed the snow-covered riverbank to board the waiting craft. A handful of men remained behind. They retrieved the wooden casks deployed earlier within the encampment. Hadwyn and Gillen followed behind them, smashing the containers open and spilling their contents onto the slushy ground.

The scouts for the Wyborn army reported the departure, and within a few minutes, the army marched. Gillen shouted for the men to hurry. The remaining elements of Hadwyn's army boarded their boats and pushed off. The two Dwarves left on the last boat. Hadwyn positioned a contingent of archers at the rear of each craft. When the enemy soldiers approached the riverbank, they fired arrows at the men clustered by the water's edge.

From the somewhere in the gloom on the west bank, Hadwyn heard the deep, thumping report of catapults firing. He grimaced, hoping the siege engineers had figured the range correctly. Three spherical infernos roared overhead. Drops of liquid flame spilled away like the tail of a comet as the burning pots of sulfur and pitch descended toward the enemy. Upon impact, the projectiles exploded across the riverbank. The oil Hadwyn's men dumped on the riverbank erupted into a blazing firestorm. Hundreds of voices cried out in agony as a massive conflagration consumed the entire area. Hadwyn smiled and nodded. The men from that army would not trouble them again this night.

#

A torrential downpour washed over them. Elac followed Jayrne's example and pulled on his leather gauntlets. The sporadic flashes of lightning gave him some insight to where they were going. At first, they had thought to wait for Silvayn. They soon realized the mage might never make it to the Gate. He might not even find where the Gate had jumped on his end. They were on their own.

Jayrne spotted a high ridgeline nearby, so they headed in that direction. The wind tore at them, threatening to blow them off the hillside and send them tumbling down among the rocks. The slope became more precipitous. Elac was forced to climb on all fours to continue the ascent. By the time they reached the top, the rain showed signs of letting up.

In the near darkness, they saw nothing beyond a few hundred yards. They crouched low upon the ridge and waited for the infrequent lightning strikes to show them what lay in the distance. Their persistence paid off. Elac spotted an enormous building off to his left, situated atop another ridge. He and Jayrne faced the building. Another flash of lightning, and they were certain of their destination.

"It won't be easy," Elac said. "That's at least two leagues away."

"Maybe more. It's hard to judge distances in this kind of landscape."

"Let's do it."

"Wait." Elac knelt and gathered several small stones together. He formed them into the shape of an arrow that pointed in the direction they planned to travel. "Just in case Silvayn and the others make it here."

"What if something else comes through the Gate?"

"I don't think one more thing here trying to kill us will make much difference."

They were only halfway down the hillside when Elac heard the sound. At first, he thought it might have been the wind, but it grew louder. He held up a hand to warn Jayrne her to stop, and he listened. It was the unmistakable flap of wings. Something stalked them. Something large. It became loud enough that Jayrne heard it, too. She pointed to a jumble of boulders a short distance back up the slope.

In a rush, they scrambled up the hill. Small rocks fell away beneath their feet in their haste. There was an open space where two boulders leaned against each other, and they both managed to squeeze into the opening. A few minutes later, a shadowy form passed overhead. From their concealed niche, they heard it land. Clawed feet scraped across the rocks. It snorted several times. Elac feared it might have their scent. He edged closer to the opening and peered out.

Sitting fifty yards away, with its back to them, was a massive dragon. The green, scaly hide glistened with rain. It snorted softly, lowered the serpentine neck, and examined the ground. Elac tightened his grip on his sword and waited. Nose to the ground, it edged away from their position.

#

Noria and Begeron fought as one, repelling assault after assault by the thralls. Behind them, Silvayn used his magic to thin the numbers of the undead as the three of them continued to work their way toward the Gate. All they had to do was keep the undead at bay long enough to reach the Gate. Noria climbed a few steps up the slope as they awaited another wave of thralls. Glorious victory was within their grasp.

There was a sudden bright light behind them, and then the land around them went dark. It took a few moments for Noria's eyes to adjust to the darkness again. Her mouth dropped open in shock as she realized the Gate was missing.

"Silvayn! Where is it?"

"It shifted! We have to get out of here!"

"Can you find it again?"

"As long as it isn't too far away. Just keep them off me a bit longer. I'll locate the Gate, and then I'll put a little breathing room between us and the thralls."

Noria raised her sword as the thralls approached. Deep down, there was some part of her that thrilled in the entire adventure. This was what it must have been like for her father: outnumbered, surrounded by undead, but battling to the bitter end. If necessary, she would sacrifice her life for the cause, just as her father had. But she would make her death mean something. At least the fools in Palim would take notice and realize what a woman could accomplish with a sword.

Silvayn whistled to them. "I've found it. It's not far. Give me a moment."

Noria swung her sword and ignored the fatigue in her arms. Several more thralls fell beneath her sword, yet they kept coming. Their black, fetid blood coated the slope below her. Another thrall reached for her, and she severed the outstretched limb.

"Get down!" Silvayn shouted. Noria and Begeron both crouched low and raised their shields in front of their bodies. A fist-sized ball of blue light streaked over their heads and exploded. The violent detonation threw both warriors back several feet. Noria picked up her fallen weapon and shook her head to quiet the ringing in her ears. When she looked back down the slope, all she saw were piles of ash interspersed with grotesquely twisted arms and legs. The thralls were gone.

"'I've given us a chance," Silvayn said, leaning on his staff. "But the use of such a powerful spell will draw creatures from all over Aceros. We have to hurry."

Noria wiped her sword and slid it into its sheath. She drank the last of her water and followed Silvayn into the darkness.

#

The battered army followed the road north to Palim. Hadwyn's plans for further delay tactics had not come to fruition. When he realized the extent of the second army's incursion, he knew he could no longer settle into a static defensive position. His army was forced to fight on the move, with little rest or food, while falling back toward the questionable safety of Palim.

With the various elements of his army spread out along the roadway, he needed to be mobile, and that meant being on horseback. He had to coordinate the rotating responsibility for the defense their rear flank. Every hour, he moved a different unit of archers, infantry, and cavalry to the end of the column, where they would take over responsibility for fighting off the sorties from the Wyborn army.

He relaxed when the eastern sky began to turn from dark black to a deep purple. The sunrise would soon allow him to see the gates of Palim. He sent a messenger on horseback to make certain the city was ready for the coming siege. The enemy at their heels would surround the city, construct their siege engines, and settle in to wait until they reduced the gates or the wall and forced a breach.

To his left, Hadwyn studied the waters of Palim Bay. He gauged the distance to the city at less than an hour. All around him, the soldiers' chatter rose. The men knew as well as he did that there had been no guarantee they would ever reach the walls of Palim, but now it was virtually assured. Another hour and they would be safe.

The muddy track under their feet wound across the snowy landscape. As they crested one hill, Hadwyn had to suppress a shout of elation. Palim lay in the distance, its high, solid walls a comfort to those who had known battle the past few days. The soldiers marched a little faster.

Hadwyn nudged his horse into a canter and rode ahead, Gillen close behind him. They trotted up to the gates and dismounted. No guards stood outside; all were atop the towering walls behind the battlements. Hadwyn looked at his brother, then back to the gates. Raising his hammer over his head, he pounded on the gate three times.

A guard leaned out from his post atop the barbican. "Who goes there?"

"Open the gates!" Gillen shouted. "The army returns! The forces of Wyborn are only an hour behind us!"

"I'm sorry, good Dwarf. But my orders are to open the gates for no one."

"We're the Knights of the Council. You cannot keep us out."

Duke Adroc appeared at the man's side. "They keep the gates closed on my orders, Prince Gillen. I'm sure you understand our predicament. The mechanism securing the gates gave us some trouble earlier. I'm concerned that, should we open it, we would not be able to latch it back once you are inside. I recommend you keep moving. You might be able to reach the city of Goran before they catch you."

Hadwyn raised his hammer. "Or maybe I'll open the damned gates myself and discuss this with you personally."

Adroc gestured, and several archers leaned out over the wall. "That would be a bad idea, Prince Hadwyn. Now, I suggest you move right along. Those Wyborn soldiers you mentioned will be arriving soon."

#

Noria's ears had finally stopped ringing. Begeron stood beside her, a silent shadow, while Silvayn walked in front. The mage bowed his head as he focused his attention on the Gate to Archon. They followed a series of washes and draws in the course of their search and quickly lost their sense of direction. Silvayn had discovered that he was able to keep his magic locked on the Gate and walk at the same time, albeit slowly. Their other option would have forced them to stop frequently so Silvayn could reorient them and keep them on the right path.

It was slow going. Noria wished she had brought more water with her. In truth, she had not realized she would need it. Elac had explained that when he traveled to the Plane of Mist, no one needed to eat, drink, or sleep. Noria had assumed, incorrectly, that this would carry over to Aceros and Archon. She would have to live with the consequences.

A sudden sense of foreboding overcame her. She could not shake the feeling, nor could she explain it. They plodded along, and finally she could stand it no longer.

"Silvayn, I have the feeling we're being followed. You two keep moving. I'll climb to the top of this wadi and have a look. If we reach a split, leave me a marker to tell me which way you went."

The old Elf gave a barely perceptible nod. Noria ascended the first half of the slope with ease. But the incline went from steep to nearly vertical. She dug her gauntleted hands into the sandstone, finding small niches to place her hands and feet. With considerable effort, she reached the top and hauled herself over the edge.

From the new vantage point, she could see for leagues. The problem she encountered was the labyrinthine series of dry riverbeds they had been following. She could not see any distance down into them, and certainly could not see anyone, or anything, along the bottoms. She squinted into the perpetually dim lighting. A section of the winding riverbed they followed trailed off to her right. In the distance, it ran in a straight line for about a half mile. She crossed the rocky ground, crawled up to the edge and peered over the side.

At first, she saw nothing. She blinked and rubbed her eyes. Movement appeared in the distance, faint at first, as if it was only her imagination. It became more pronounced and grew in clarity. She heard the sound of tree limbs rubbing against each other, but there were no trees. Bit by bit, discernible figures emerged from the darkness.

Noria rolled away from the edge. She hopped to her feet and ran across the flat ground. It took her several minutes to locate Silvayn and Begeron. She whistled softly to get their attention. Rather than carefully pick her way down the slope, she relied on her armor for protection and slid down the hill. At the bottom, she climbed to her knees and stood up.

Begeron placed a hand on her shoulder. "What did you find?"

Noria held up a hand and shook her head. "How much farther?"

Silvayn closed his eyes and concentrated. "About a mile."

"Then I suggest we run." Noria cast a nervous look back the way they had come. "There is a legion of skeleton warriors coming up behind us and closing fast."

Water dripped off Elac's hood in a continuous waterfall. He chaffed at the delay; they'd had to wait a half hour until they were certain the dragon had left. In the meantime, the rains had returned with a vengeance, a frigid deluge that soaked them to the bone. Beside him, Jayrne shivered in the darkness. They needed to find shelter soon. The only way to escape the rain was to reach the building, somewhere ahead in the endless Archon night. He hoped it was the temple they sought. What else could it be?

They found an ancient, weather-beaten road. The ancient stones had been fitted together in a regular pattern, but they were pitted with chips and cracks. It led from the base of the hill where the Gate had brought them, directly toward the temple. It curved a few times, following the path of least resistance, but continued to guide them closer to their destination. Unfortunately, with the arrival of the heavy rainfall, it became impossible to tell if they still moved in the right direction. Elac had to trust to their fate.

The road curved to the left and changed to a gradual incline. It wound around a hill and became steeper, then changed to a long flight of steps. The silhouette of the temple appeared in the rain atop the hill. Jayrne grabbed Elac's arm and held him back.

"I don't think this is such a good idea, Elac."

He raised one eyebrow and smiled. "Isn't this why we're here?"

"No, I mean using the main road to take us right to the doors. If we're trying to sneak inside, shouldn't we try another way?"

"Jayrne, you have the soul of a thief."

She laughed softly. "You're right. But I'm right, too. Let's climb the hill over here and work our way around to the back of the temple. There's always another way in."

He followed her nimble form as she scrambled up the hillside. Gravel slid away underfoot, but the sound was lost in the torrent of the storm. The building drew into sharp focus as they reached the top of their climb.

The structure was larger than it appeared to be from a distance. Stones held tightly together by mortar formed the towering walls. On Pelacia, Elac would have expected such an ancient building to be covered with vines, but the sparse plant life on Archon did not lend itself to such growth. Beneath the battlements, golden castings of the emblem of Chaos dangled at thirty-foot intervals. The spear surrounded by a tumultuous web sent a chill down Elac's spine.

"I don't see any other doors," Elac whispered. "The only windows are too small to climb through. Too small for me, anyway. They're probably meant for archers, I would guess."

She covered her eyes with one hand. "Elac, Elac, I thought I taught you better than that. You can't see the way in?"

His eyes darted back and forth along the wall. "No. Nothing."

"What's at the top of the wall?"

"Battlements."

She sighed. "And what are battlements for?"

"They provide cover for defenders during an assault."

"And do you suppose those soldiers would fly up there, or is there possibly a door leading inside from the roof?"

Elac felt a slow flush spread over his face. "I can't believe I missed that one. So how do we get up there?"

She tested the wall, feeling the seams between the bricks. "It's too risky to scale the wall without equipment. Fortunately, I came prepared." She stooped and removed four claw-like devices from a pouch at her waist, which she strapped onto her hands and feet.

"Nice. But how will I get up there?"

"I have a rope. Once I'm on top, I'll make sure we're clear, then I'll tie the rope off and send it down to you."

Elac stepped back and watched her painstaking ascent. She only dared move one hand or foot at a time. Although the aged, crumbling mortar allowed her "claws" to dig in, the wet surface made the climb much more dangerous. If she fell from the full twenty feet, there was nothing Elac could do for her.

He looked into the rain, back the way they had come. Occasionally, the downpour would lessen and allow him to see the faint glow of the Gate from Aceros. At one point, the Gate flared briefly, then dimmed once more. He wondered how many such Gates were scattered around the temple. Or perhaps the others were farther away. Maybe there was something about the power of the Gates that prohibited them from being in close proximity of each other. He shrugged and returned to his nervous contemplation of Jayrne's dangerous task.

But his fears proved groundless. Although the climb took ten minutes, she disappeared safely over the top of the wall. He stood motionless at the bottom, listening to the patter of the rain on his hood. Without a whisper of sound, one end of a rope hurtled down out of the darkness. He tested the rope and found it would hold his weight. With his hands and feet securely squeezing the rope, he started to climb.

CHAPTER 19

Hadwyn divided his growing army into three different units. He commanded one, his brother, a second, and Rilen a third. The veteran Elf warrior had returned from his journey to Caldala. He brought with him three hundred Elven archers, in addition to his own militia from Golen. The entire Elven army had mobilized and should arrive by morning. The Dwarves would only be a day or so behind them.

Hadwyn wondered if it would be enough. The army facing them from Wyborn was enormous. The division they fought at the Battle of Iress River had been without archers, without siege equipment, and almost without tactics. They had openly approached the battle because they were a decoy. The rest of their invasion force had circled around to the south. Unopposed, they were able to bring catapults, supply trains, and archers across the river and make a drive for the heart of Palindom. By standing and fighting against the lesser force, Hadwyn's army had allowed it to happen.

But that was all behind him. The Wyborn army had reached Palim that morning and settled in for a siege. Their catapults hurled boulders at the gates and perceived weak points of the walls in an effort to force a breach. In a surprise move, the enemy constructed extra catapults and placed them on the points of land around Palim Bay. Any ship that attempted to reach or leave the city would face a storm of boulders tumbling out of the sky. Despite the harbor, the city had been effectively cut off from outside help.

Hadwyn had not given up hope. Although outnumbered, he had in Rilen the best tactician on the battlefield. It was Rilen who suggested the army be split apart into semi-autonomous groups. Ostensibly, Hadwyn had made Rilen commander of the combined forces. But in practice, each group operated on its own.

Within hours of the enemy's arrival, Rilen ordered a strike against their rear flank. The heavy cavalry charged the Wyborn lines and decimated the soldiers they encountered. When the enemy finally organized a counterstrike, the cavalry fell back. The men from Wyborn charged after them, only to be met by a hidden contingent of Elven archers. Wave after wave of arrows cut the small force to pieces. Their demoralized foes retreated back to the safety of their defensive lines.

Rilen and Gillen entered the woods where Hadwyn's soldiers made their temporary home. They gathered around a small camping fire.

"Is everything ready?" Rilen asked.

Hadwyn nodded. "I picked the men myself."

"If this works, it should buy enough time for the Elves to arrive, maybe even the Dwarves."

Gillen saw the tankard of ale and dumped it before his brother could grab it. "Let's go."

It was after midnight. The three warriors led a contingent of two hundred men into the gloom. Although it had not snowed for two days, at least four inches already covered the ground, which worked to Hadwyn's advantage. The snow cover would be sufficient to mask the sound of their passage. The men from Wyborn had pillaged the woods for lumber to use in the construction of their siege engines. Their frequent passage churned the snow and made it impossible to use footprints to track Hadwyn's men back to their hidden base.

For an hour, they moved steadily southward. Once, a mounted Wyborn patrol approached, but Hadwyn's men hid and allowed them to pass. Eventually, the glow on the horizon became the watch fires at the edge of the sprawling encampment of the Wyborn army. Tents, wagons, and equipment spread far across the plain for at least two miles. Hadwyn frowned when he thought of how many enemy soldiers were camped right in front of him. They desperately needed help from both the Elves and Dwarves to have any chance of hurting a force this big. What they really needed were the Kobolds. The fourth army could tip the balance of power and send the invaders back where they came from.

Rilen gripped Hadwyn's shoulder by way of farewell. With several handpicked members of his militia, he slipped ahead into the night. His was the first task. The outer sentries had to be eliminated before they could get any closer. Hadwyn sat motionless in the dark, listening to the beating of his heart and waiting for Rilen's return. Time seemed to crawl. He jumped at every noise, certain they had been discovered. But there was no outcry, no sudden pursuit, no sign that the enemy was aware of the raiders who lay in wait just outside the perimeter of their defenses.

Without warning, Rilen materialized out of the night. He beckoned, then led the way back to the enemy lines. Hadwyn and the strike force followed him in. They ignored the torn, bloody bodies of the sentries. Pools of blood stained the snow around them. Rilen stayed fifty yards ahead of the main body, where he would deal with any other sentries the Wyborn army might have in place.

A lone soldier rode out of the main encampment, directly at Hadwyn's team. They hid among the long grasses as best they could, but if the man didn't deviate his course, he would find them. Hadwyn tightened his grip on his hammer. He would have to be quick. As soon as the rider drew even with him, Hadwyn would strike.

A shadowy figure sprang out of the night, seized the man and pulled him from the saddle. They made a soft thump when the two combatants landed in the snow. Before the sentry could cry out, a dagger flashed in the moonlight. Rilen stood and grabbed the horse's reins. Hadwyn nodded; of course, it would be Rilen. The Elf handed the reins to another soldier with instructions to tether the animal to keep it from straying. He cleaned and sheathed his dagger while Hadwyn hid the body in a snowdrift.

They reached the edge of the main camp. Along the periphery farthest from the city, the Wyborn general had stationed the catapults. Rilen guided the assault team around the supply wagons to where the spindly siege engines sat abandoned. The engineers waited for daylight to resume the barrage against the city. They would wait longer than they had planned.

Hadwyn made several sharp gestures, splitting his men into smaller groups and setting them to their various tasks. The catapults were the main target, but they would not be the only facet of the invading army to feel the bite of the night's sneak attack. All along the emplacement, Hadwyn's soldiers split open the small casks of oil they carried. They dumped the contents onto the dry wood of the catapults and wagons. Hadwyn smiled as he watched his soldiers at work. Had the enemy built each of its siege engines here, the wood would be too green to burn. But all the newly constructed catapults warded the waters of Palim Bay.

Rilen left with thirty men on their own special mission. Gillen emplaced hidden sentries to guard the main strike team against chance discovery by a roving patrol. Hadwyn took a deep breath of the crisp night air. Everything was going well, but it would only take one outcry to sabotage the mission.

A sergeant tapped Hadwyn on the shoulder and nodded. The Dwarf sent runners to the different elements of his task force to order the withdrawal. They maintained the stealth that had kept them from discovery and pulled back toward the breach. They had done it. Their midnight assault would delay any attack on the city of Palim. They had managed it without the loss of a single soldier.

A shout broke the stillness of the night. Hadwyn froze and dropped into a crouch. Someone had discovered one of the bodies of the outer sentries. The shout echoed within the camp, which stirred to life. Men poured from their tents, dressed only in tunics and boots but armed with swords. There would be momentary confusion while the main body of the enemy troops tried to discover where the trouble was, but it would not take long for an organized pursuit.

Hadwyn whistled to his team, and the entire group broke into a run. A pack of five Wyborn troops lay ahead of them at the observation post. The enemy soldiers looked up just in time to see Hadwyn and Gillen descend upon them, with more men right behind them. After a brief but bloody scuffle, the Dwarves led their detachment into the night.

But the pursuit began. The raiders, led by the two Dwarves, were weary from the hardships of their surreptitious assault. Those who chased them were fresh. The gap between pursuers and pursued narrowed. Already, Hadwyn heard the dull crunch of the Wyborn soldiers' boots in the hard-packed snow. He knew some of them would have to stand and fight.

He heard a rustle in the winter grasses around them. Rilen and his team of archers appeared out of the gloom. They showered the pursuing men with arrows. Screams filled the night, and the pursuit faltered. Hadwyn shouted to his men to take the battle to the enemy.

Rilen's archers maintained the barrage as long as they could, then set their bows aside to join the melee. It was short and ugly. The unarmored men from Wyborn had been demoralized by the arrow storm, and they were not prepared for Hadwyn's counterattack. In a matter of a few minutes, the remainder retreated howling into the night, chased by the cheers of Hadwyn's men. They were safe, but the night was not finished.

Rilen gave a shrill whistle. At that signal, another group of concealed archers rose from hiding. Someone lit a fire, and a barrage of flaming arrows streaked toward the rear of the Wyborn camp. A massive blaze erupted. Tongues of orange flames and billowing clouds of black smoke roared into the night sky.

The chaos among the enemy troops reached a new height. They abandoned all attempts at an organized pursuit as they rushed to save their supplies and siege engines. Rilen and Hadwyn moved their troops closer to the camp to cover the archers' retreat, but it was unnecessary. No one emerged from the darkness to give chase. They slipped away into the night.

#

Noria swung her blade and shattered the torso of a skeleton warrior. The shield of Sir Omonis deflected a blow aimed at her head. She whipped the sword around in tight arcs, more to keep the undead at bay than destroy them. There were too many for Begeron and her to win this fight. Their only hope was to live long enough to reach the Gate before it jumped.

"This way!" Silvayn's voice carried over the din of battle. Begeron, bleeding from a dozen wounds, stayed by Noria's side as the two retreated step by step. Noria risked a glance behind and saw the shimmering Gate atop another hill, no more than four hundred yards distant. Silvayn blasted a bolt of energy into the assembled undead. With an ear-splitting detonation, the force of the spell shattered the bodies of dozens of skeleton warriors. Noria wiped away the blood seeping into her eyes and drew several panting breaths.

They took advantage of the respite to begin their final ascent to the Gate. They had made it but halfway up when another wave of skeleton warriors swarmed over the rocky, broken terrain. They were surprisingly agile and quick. Noria immediately realized they would have to make a stand. She chose a flat shelf just above them. It was mostly clear of debris and would afford them better footing. Begeron joined her when they reached the shelf. Both turned to face the enemy.

The assault began with an assortment of rocks, spears, and arrows. All swerved to strike against Sir Omonis's shield. The enchantment inherent within the shield reduced the force of the impact and allowed Noria to withstand the repeated blows without faltering. The expected charge of the skeleton warriors followed.

But Silvayn had been given the time he needed to prepare for them. Another bolt of energy blasted out from his outstretched hands. It ripped into the enemy with devastating effect. The remaining undead came at them in smaller groups. Begeron and Noria, fighting side-by-side, dispatched them easily.

Noria shouted her family's battle cry into the perpetual night sky. She was invincible; no foe could stand before her. The ache of her wounds faded from her mind, along with the fatigue in her muscles. When the last skeleton warrior within her reach fell, she cast her gaze fifty yards down the slope to a knotted group of a dozen more. With a senseless roar, she charged down the slope, sword held high overhead. Her momentum carried her deep into the enemy cluster. She swung her sword all about her. The blade cleaved through the ancient armor worn by her foes. Almost before the skirmish began, she had destroyed them all.

Begeron grabbed her from behind and spun her around. "What in the name of all that's holy are you doing? We need to reach the Gate!"

Noria came to her senses in a rush. Exhaustion, which had faded to a distant memory, washed down upon her, and she lowered her sword. Every open cut on her body throbbed with each heartbeat. What had she done? This was how her father met his demise: a senseless charge against an overwhelming enemy force, where victory was not only unlikely, but useless. She could stand her ground for hours, destroy thousands of undead, and still accomplish nothing.

But Noria was not her father. She would not lose her head again. Cassius had thrown his life away in a useless gesture. Noria would not. She rose to her feet and followed Begeron up the slope.

A blow struck her from behind and knocked her to the ground. She rolled over to see Begeron swing his sword at a shadowy figure. The weapon passed through the ash-gray robes as if they were made of smoke. The figure swung a clawed arm and knocked Begeron reeling.

"Wraith!" Noria shouted. "Your weapons can't hurt it!"

Silvayn began to chant, building his power for another spell, but Noria knew the old Elf needed more time. The wraith would be upon him before the spell could be released. Noria climbed to her feet, head awash with vertigo, and rushed upon the wraith from behind. She thrust her blade through the ephemeral back, but with no more effect than Begeron. The wraith turned on her. The gossamer hand drove in a sharp blow toward her face.

Noria reacted instinctively, raising her shield and ducking behind it. The incorporeal arm struck the shield and rebounded. *Magic!* The enchantment in the shield allowed it to defend against the wraith. And if it could defend . . .

She dropped her sword and slid her arm out of the straps that held the shield against her arm. With the shield held in both hands, she battered the wraith. It retaliated, but the enchantment within the shield kept her safe. Silvayn's voice rose to a fevered pitch, and the familiar bolt of energy rushed forth. The blast consumed the wraith in its blue fire until all that remained was a pile of ash. She retrieved her fallen weapon while Begeron regained his feet.

The two warriors ascended the slope to stand at Silvayn's side. The mage stood with slumped shoulders, breathing hard and bathed in sweat.

Noria reached out one hand to offer him support. "Are you okay, Silvayn?"

He nodded. "I need to rest, but not here. Let's get to the Gate."

Together, the three climbed the rest of the way up the hill. Another knot of skeleton warriors gathered below them and clambered over the rocks in their mindless effort to reach the three trespassers. Noria looked back in time to see two more groups, hundreds strong, circling the hill in both directions. They were surrounded. If they failed to reach the Gate before it shifted, the enemy would have them.

#

The sun rose upon the battlefield around the walled city of Palim. Smoke from the previous night's inferno still climbed into the sky. Hadwyn raised his tankard, taking a long drink of ale as he admired their success. Beside him, Rilen raised his mug in salute.

During the nighttime raid, a contingent of Human cavalry had arrived. The knight who led them, Sir Shibo, still wore his suit of armor, although he had removed the helmet. He studied the distant smoke with a veteran's scrutiny.

"Your assault last night wounded them, but are you sure it will be as successful as you think? You caused relatively few casualties among their soldiers, and they bring in more supplies daily."

"It's the loss of the siege engines that will cause the greatest delay," Rilen explained. "They will have to build more. It may give us enough time for the other components of the army to arrive."

Sir Shibo consulted a map, which was spread across the table in front of them. "Why would they not simply bring up some of their catapults arrayed around Palim Bay? It would be much quicker than rebuilding."

"They can't," Hadwyn explained. "They need every one of them in place to maintain the blockade. Otherwise, supplies and reinforcements could be brought into Palim by sea. The siege would fail."

"I think that should be our next target," Rilen said. "Let's destroy those catapults."

Gillen pulled on his long, red beard. "They will be ready for us this time. Those catapults will be more heavily defended."

"True," Rilen said, "but that can change. If we mass some troops out near their supply area again, act like we're trying to hide but allow ourselves to be seen, it will force them to commit at least some of their troops to the defense of that flank. Between our threat, the protection of the catapults, and the siege of the city, I think they will be spread quite thin."

Sir Shibo nodded. "According to our scouts, by midnight we should have two hundred more heavy cavalry from the garrison at Aleria, plus a legion of Dwarves arriving by boat."

"And a contingent from the Elven army," Rilen added. "Five hundred infantry and two hundred archers. If we can break the blockade of Palim Bay by destroying those catapults, we can send supplies and reinforcements directly into the city. The Wyborn army will run out of supplies long before we will."

An unarmed Elf dressed in a woodland cloak, her face flushed with exhaustion, ran up to the gathering. Hadwyn held out his hand and braced the young woman when she stumbled. She handed a leather pouch to Rilen, then knelt to catch her breath. Rilen's eyes darted back and forth as he scanned the parchment found within.

He knelt beside the runner. "Are you certain of this?"

"Yes. I saw it myself, when the colonel gave me the pouch."

Rilen dismissed the messenger with a wave of his hand. "The Wyborn army has brought up a dragon. They've given the city until sunset to surrender, or they will burn Palim to the ground."

#

The temple had a distinct musty odor to it. The building's decrepit condition allowed the frequent rainstorms to saturate the interior. Although they were two floors below the roof, rainwater still dripped from the ceiling. It was better than the floor above, where he and Jayrne had been forced to slosh through ankle-deep puddles, but it was still wet. A single drop of frigid water landed on the back of his neck and trickled down his spine, sending chills through his body.

The stone floor was cracked, and in some places heaving, which made for treacherous footing. He gripped Sir Draygen's sword loosely in his right hand. To prevent cramps, he occasionally wiggled his fingers. Beside him, Jayrne padded softly with both hands free.

Ahead on their left, Elac saw another of the Chaos emblems, a spear enveloped in a spiral of thick copper strands, mounted on the wall above a staircase that descended into darkness. Jayrne slipped ahead and leaned out slightly to see what awaited below. She motioned with her head for him to follow. They edged down the steps, which spiraled into the depths of the temple. The darkness was so absolute that even Elac's superior Elven vision was not much help.

The descent dragged on. By Elac's estimate, they were below ground and still could not see the bottom. They had found three landings with passages out of the stairwell, but they had agreed their best chance to find Archon's Gate was to follow the staircase as deep as it went.

They reached the bottom. He guessed they were three floors below ground level, although he really had no frame of reference on which to base his guess. A hallway lay in front of them. Torches burned at evenly spaced intervals along both walls. Although most were extinguished, those at the far end of the tunnel were lit. The ceiling was about forty feet high and barely visible in the dim light. At the far end, the passage turned to the right. Jayrne pulled Sir Draygen's Cloak tightly about her body as they neared the turn.

A dancing glow emanated from the room beyond. When the room came into view, Elac saw the source of the light: an enormous pit loomed in the center of the room. Flames leaped up from the gaping hole to lick at the ceiling of the grotto. Another shimmering Gate stood along the far wall. Silver bars engraved with fist-sized black runes framed the enchanted portal. Elac studied the Gate as they entered the room. While the faint, blurry images in the previous Gates he had seen continually jumped from one scene to another, this one was steady. It was also significantly larger, at least twenty feet across.

A faint white smoke filled the air. The walls and ceiling in the Gate room were in a much better state of repair than the rest of the temple. Although no ornamentation adorned the walls and ceiling, the stones were sharply cornered and fitted tightly to their neighbors. To the right, a granite altar rose from the rocky floor. Another passage to the far left end of the chamber, thirty feet in height and twice as wide.

A tall, lanky Elven woman with thick, dark hair hanging to her waist arose from the side of the altar, where she had been kneeling. She wore scarlet robes covered with silver runes and tied at the waist with an embossed silver belt. In her right hand she carried a polished steel staff; in her left, a black orb about the size of a man's head. She stopped when she saw Elac, then hissed softly.

She placed the orb gently upon a silver pedestal on the altar. "Hello, Elac. I wondered when you would arrive."

Elac took a few cautious steps forward. "How do you know my name?"

"It doesn't matter. What matters is that you are here, and I shall enjoy your death. Now, on to business. Where is your little thief? In here somewhere, of course. She would never leave your side."

Elac brought his sword in front of his face and lowered into a fighting crouch. "I think you had better worry about me, first, Agalia."

She clasped her hands together with a laugh. "Oh, are you here to kill me?"

"Only if I have to. But either way, I will shut down that Gate."

"Then you should have been here a few minutes sooner. Maybe you could have closed it before I sent the dragon through." Her face tightened and she raised one hand. Sparks of energy crackled at her fingertips. "It is time for you to die."

CHAPTER 20

A runner interrupted Hadwyn's lunch with a critical message. The breathless young man announced the arrival of Adalyn and two dozen mages from the Aleria School of Magic. Hadwyn let out a sigh of relief. Although still badly outnumbered, at least his army would have a means of battling the dragon that waited just outside the range of Palim's siege weapons. Based on the latest dispatches from his scouts, another army would arrive from Unity in two hours. With the newly added contingents of Elves and Dwarves, he believed he had sufficient forces to attempt his latest battle plan.

Ten minutes later, he stood in the commanders' tent, ready to address the leaders of the various factions of his makeshift army. His brother sat off to one side, near Rilen and Adalyn. A scale model of the area surrounding the city dominated the center of the floor. A scattering of colored wooden blocks represented his forces, as well as those of the Wyborn army.

"We'll divide into four groups. One half of the army will be dedicated to the primary thrust, while the other units will form the diversions we discussed."

Sir Shibo harrumphed. "They'll know our first strike is a diversion. They'll commit some of their forces, but not enough for us to attack them anywhere else. Not with our numbers."

"Not necessarily, Sir Shibo," Rilen said. "It's not just their response to the attacks that will prove decisive. Confusion in the enemy ranks will be our greatest ally. Watch and see."

Hadwyn retrieved a long wooden stick and used it to indicate several points on the model of the battlefield. The debate raged back and forth for almost an hour. In the end, they decided to proceed as planned, as Hadwyn knew they would. They had no chance of defeating the entire army, so that was not their intent. They need only prevent the city gates from being breached. Stopping the dragon was the key.

Hadwyn leaned on his massive, enchanted war hammer. "We will provide specific details to each of you concerning your part in this. The army from Unity will be here in a few hours. We'll leave as soon as they are able. We have to hit the enemy before sundown, or that dragon will have them inside the gates."

#

Noria and Begeron stood on opposite sides of Silvayn. Both fought a desperate struggle to keep the undead legions away from Silvayn while he readied another spell. The skeleton warriors seemed to realize what the mage was doing, and they pressed their attack that much harder. Noria snapped her sword around in broad, vicious strokes. Bones from those who had fallen before her lay strewn down the hillside. The sight of her vanquished foes lying before her filled her with a new rush of energy. Even her father could not have fared better!

The Gate loomed closer. Silvayn shouted, and a band of energy roared from his outstretched hands. The blast knocked the two warriors to the ground but shattered the bones of the skeleton warriors around them. Silvayn shouted his encouragement as Noria scrambled back to her feet. They turned and rushed up the hill toward the Gate.

The shimmering portal flashed, a sure sign it was about to shift. Noria reached deep inside herself for a final reserve of energy and surged ahead. The three embattled travelers reached the Gate and plunged through.

Noria staggered to her knees. A wave of exhaustion swept over her, compounded by the vertigo effect of the passage through the Gate. Begeron lay on his side a few feet away, his breath coming in short gasps. Silvayn leaned heavily on his staff. To Noria, he looked nearly as tired as she and Begeron. After a few minutes' rest, Noria rose and faced the others.

"Silvayn," she said between panting breaths, "can you find Archon's Gate from here?"

"Yes. Are you two able to walk?"

She nodded. "I guess we have to be. Elac needs us. Lead on"

#

The sun settled low in the sky. Hadwyn knew less than an hour of daylight remained. The rest of his army had arrived, and everything was in place. With his brother and Rilen, Hadwyn would be a part of the main assault. The enchanted weapons of the two Dwarves might prove invaluable, should a direct physical confrontation with the dragon become necessary. He hoped to stay back and let the mages eliminate it from a distance, but plans had a way of changing in the heat of battle.

The first diversionary force struck their target. Shouts of alarm from the rear of the enemy camp announced the start of the battle, followed by several plumes of smoke. Since they would be unable to get close enough to use oil to start the blazes, most of their incendiary efforts would be extinguished before there was any real damage. Hadwyn would gauge their success by the number of soldiers diverted from the western flank and the confusion among Wyborn's leaders, not by how much food they destroyed or how many siege engines they burned.

Already, the effect was apparent. Several companies of Wyborn soldiers left their carefully drawn formations to reinforce the men who defended the supply train. The sounds of battle reached Hadwyn's ears, carried on the bitterly cold wind. While the detachment's infantry held the enemy at bay, the archers continued their rain of fire.

And then the second phase began. The other two units of Hadwyn's army struck in perfect unison. They hit targets along the bay, one north of the city and one south. Chaos reigned among the enemy commanders. Messengers ran back and forth. Several companies of infantry responded to the new assaults. Conflicting orders redirected those groups more than once as the Wyborn leaders debated how best to respond to the new threat.

A blast from the horn of one of Sir Shibo's knights signaled the start of the true assault. Two hundred knights, lined up in four consecutive waves, left the cover of a forested hillside a half mile west of the Wyborn camp. At three hundred yards, they broke into a full gallop. Their lances lowered as one. Hadwyn led the charge of the footsoldiers, a mix of Human and Dwarf infantry backed by Elven archers. Ahead, the Wyborn army recoiled as the true intent of the attacks became clear. Soldiers rushed to fill in the gaps in their defensive lines. Hadwyn's archers launched several volleys of arrows, further disrupting the enemy camp.

The first wave of the charging cavalry blasted through the front lines of the Wyborn defenses. They met the enemy with a titanic crash that sent bodies hurtling across the field. The next two formations struck seconds later, one to the north of the first group, and one to the south. The last group of knights repeated the center strike, running down two companies of infantry that had tried to close on the other knights from behind. The charge finally bogged down as more soldiers rushed to repel the raiders.

The Elven archers amazed Hadwyn with their unerring accuracy. Even in the midst of the infantry and cavalry charge, the archers fired arrows as they trotted along behind the foot soldiers. The barrage kept the enemy infantry from initiating an organized defense. They reached the outer limits of the Wyborn camp, where the muddy, churned snow mingled with blood and twisted bodies. Hadwyn glanced over his shoulder to reassure himself that his formation was intact: infantry around the edges, archers forming the center, and Adalyn's mages toward the rear.

The Wyborn army recovered from its initial shock. The charge of the cavalry had bogged down completely. Soldiers from deeper in the enemy camp formed up and marched toward the breach in their western flank. Hadwyn's charge met its first resistance, the remnants of the outer guard, which had reformed behind the cavalry. Rilen outraced the others and engaged the enemy. He had three Wyborn soldiers on the ground before Hadwyn reached the battle. The Dwarf's hammer crushed two skulls in succession. The melee was short but ugly. After the rest of the enemy soldiers lay dead and dying, Hadwyn's army pressed on.

Beyond the cavalry, the dragon rose to its full height. Its head rose twenty feet above the snow-covered ground. Wisps of steam roiled from the enormous snout. Red, scaly hide covered the beast from end to end. The massive feet ended in talons a foot long. A pair of leathery wings sprouted from its back, although Hadwyn doubted they were large enough to allow such a creature to fly. The sinewy tail whipped around and struck a Wyborn soldier who ventured to close. The armored form tumbled across the snow-covered field and lay in a crumpled heap.

Adalyn's mages began their chants. They stayed within the circle of protection offered by Hadwyn's soldiers, an island of tranquility amid the chaos of the seething battle. Adalyn was the first to release her spell. A bolt of energy roared over the heads of the combatants to strike the dragon's neck, just below the head. The dragon gave a bellow of rage as it waddled about. With an implacable pace, it stomped its way toward the assembled mages.

Multiple blasts of magical energy ripped into the dragon, but they barely slowed the lumbering beast. Puffs of flame emerged from the gaping maw. It reached the rear of the Wyborn soldiers and pushed through. The clawed feet crushed its allies with indifference as it struggled to reach the spellcasters. Hadwyn deliberately placed himself between the advancing dragon and the group of mages. Gillen and Rilen flanked him.

A blue glow momentarily obscured Hadwyn's vision. When it cleared, Adalyn's voice rose above the din. "I have given the three of you a bit of protection against the dragon's fire. It's the best I can do. I don't have the energy to protect anyone else."

Hadwyn nodded and hefted his hammer. The dragon cleared the enemy lines and attacked.

#

Agalia moved closer to Elac, seemingly indifferent of the sword held in his gauntleted hands. She smiled when she saw the ornate medallion around his neck. "How thoughtful of you. I was very disappointed when Coliac failed to bring the Temira back to me. But I see you have completed her task for her. Whatever happened to her, anyway? Did you kill her?"

"She fell victim to the plague you have brought upon us. Those creatures don't belong on Pelacia. Or Wyborn, for that matter."

The smile melted away, and Agalia raised her hands. "When I take the Temira from your dead body, I will be able to use it to keep the Gate open and permanently fixed. Voldaz will exalt me above all others. I will become queen of the world!"

Elac rushed forward, thrusting with his sword, but she danced aside. She hurled a fist-sized globe of energy at his head. The shimmering globe vanished, absorbed by the Orion Stone. Her eyes fell on the orb. Her brow furrowed, and she took a step back. She clapped her hands together twice, in rapid succession. Two burly guards, armored in steel breastplates and carrying longswords and shields, emerged from the room behind her.

Elac spread his feet into a defensive stance. The two men spread out to come at him from opposite sides. He circled with them in an intricate dance, keeping them both in sight while still monitoring Agalia. He lunged at them when they came too close; one such feint drew blood from a man's leg. He scarcely seemed to notice the injury. Agalia moved farther away and circled behind Elac. He stepped swiftly to his right, but realized too late he had put himself into a corner. While Agalia watched in stoic silence, her minions closed on him.

The man on the left stumbled and pitched forward. A long-bladed dagger protruded from his neck. Jayrne stood behind him with another glittering knife in her hand. Elac took advantage of the distraction to attack the remaining warrior. Elac's enchanted sword was a blur. Showers of sparks cascaded over both combatants each time it struck the other's shield.

Another blow, and the man pushed forward, locking Elac in an embrace. Elac discarded his sword in favor of his dagger. He plunged the knife into the man's thigh. It easily penetrated the leather armor warding the leg. Blood rushed forth, and the man stumbled. Elac raised his dagger to strike again, but his foe was quicker. A knife flashed toward Elac's chest. He stumbled back and narrowly avoided the strike. The blade caught the string holding the Orion Stone and severed it. The orb clattered aside.

Elac tried to stab him again, but the man knocked the blade from his grip. Sir Draygen's Sword lay to Elac's right, the Orion Stone to the left. He dove for the sword and rolled to his feet, weapon in hand. The soldier tried to stand, but his injured leg buckled beneath his weight. Jayrne rushed in and slashed his other leg. Elac finished the battle with a tight swing that slashed across the throat.

A shocking detonation blasted Elac from his feet. His sword tumbled free once more. He lay on the ground, his head swimming. He climbed to his knees but could go no further. Agalia laughed, a cold, heartless sound that echoed in the stone chamber.

"This is it, Elac. No Orion Stone. This is where your tale comes to an end."

Her hands came up, sparks already snapping from her fingertips.

#

The attack of the dragon was terrifying. Many of Hadwyn's troops stood frozen in place. The massive jaws snapped shut on a Dwarf in its path and ripped the body in half. The others took a cautious step backward. Hadwyn and Gillen moved to the fore, weapons raised, ready to face the beast. The mages continued to blast the dragon with magic. Rilen fired arrow after arrow into the bulky form.

Hadwyn's hammer whistled through the air and struck the dragon's flank. A deafening pop announced the cracking of a rib. The long tail whipped around and caught Hadwyn from behind. The impact knocked him to the ground. Gillen's axe bit deeply on a front leg. A flow of dark red blood gushed forth. The dragon engulfed him in a ball of flames, but Gillen emerged unscathed. Another burst of fire, and three soldiers fell aside, screaming as the flames washed over their bodies.

Hadwyn closed with the dragon's head and slammed his hammer against the creature's mouth. One of the dagger-like teeth shattered. The dragon gave a deafening roar of mingled pain and rage. Gillen's axe struck again, and again. The battered dragon bled from a half-dozen wounds. It reared up on its hind legs and snorted fire.

The tail came around again, this time knocking Gillen aside. A swipe of an immense claw tore through his armor and ripped open his side. He tumbled away and sprawled twitching on the ground. Rilen joined the fray, sword in hand. Hadwyn renewed his assault, although he had to leap aside to avoid the tail. Despite the grievous wounds the dragon had suffered, nothing seemed to slow it. With a guttural roar, the dragon unleashed a billowing globe of fire. A blue haze formed around Hadwyn as Adalyn's spell protected him, but the flames incinerated a half-dozen soldiers beside him.

Rilen danced inside the creature's guard, slashed at the belly, then leaped away before it could retaliate. When the dragon extended its neck to attack him, Hadwyn swung a vicious overhand blow, striking at the base of the skull. With the dragon momentarily stunned, Rilen retreated to safety.

"Adalyn!" Rilen shouted. "Go for the eyes!"

The monstrous creature swung its head in a low, swift arc toward its antagonists. The force of the impact knocked Hadwyn and Rilen to the ground. The dragon reared above them, mouth agape. Before it attacked, a blue bolt of energy struck the battered face. The spell shattered bone and blasted one eye from its socket. The dragon gave a bellow of agony that left Hadwyn's ears ringing.

Heedless of those around it, the dragon whirled about and waddled back toward the walled city of Palim. Hadwyn braced himself with the shaft of his hammer to stand up. Before he could order a pursuit of the badly wounded dragon, the soldiers of Wyborn closed ranks and attacked. Hadwyn spat out a sharp oath as he ordered his detachment to form up ranks. They were surrounded on three sides. More enemy troops rushed in from behind, which effectively cut off their escape route.

Despite his exhaustion, Hadwyn fought on. His armor was covered in the blood of his fallen foes, and his arms felt like lead. Sir Thalitt's Hammer was nearly weightless, but he had been fighting for an extended time. The battle with the dragon had nearly killed him. His brother clambered to his feet, still disoriented and bleeding but ready to fight. As Hadwyn's army collapsed into a defensive circle, he looked about for help. His cavalry was hemmed in, unable to mount a charge that could lead them to safety. Adalyn and her mages could not use their magic against the living creatures, at least not those of this world. There was no help to be had.

Moments later, the situation took a turn for the worse. The dragon, momentarily forgotten, shrieked in its death throes. It lurched and stumbled across the battlefield, roaring and spouting flames. At length, it gained the city walls. While the defenders fired arrows and dumped boiling oil on it, the dragon threw itself against the gates. They resounded with a crash. The dragon reared back and struck again, and again. With the fourth blow, the gates split asunder. The dragon staggered back and fell. Roiling puffs of smoke billowed from the mouth of the dying beast.

The sections of the Wyborn army not engaged with Hadwyn's force rushed ahead to take the outer walls. Through the ruined gates, Hadwyn saw the defenders form up ranks, preparing to repel the enemy.

One of the cavalry soldiers nearby shouted to be heard over the clash of steel on steel. "Lord Hadwyn! The Kobold army approaches!"

#

The thick, cloying smoke that hung in the air reeked of incense. Elac tried to regain his feet, but he was still stunned from the blast Agalia had hit them with moments before. He managed to rise but fell back. He turned to his right. The Orion Stone lay at least ten feet away, well beyond his reach. He brought his hands beneath himself and tried again to stand and fight. Agalia laughed, a cold, humorless sound. Elac readied himself for the end.

From Elac's left, a bolt of blue energy lanced across the room and struck Agalia full in the chest. The force threw her against the wall, but she kept her feet. Silvayn, his arms raised in preparation for another spell, rushed into the room. Noria and Begeron raced along at his side. All three looked ragged and battered, but Silvayn's jaw was set with determination. The two warriors crossed the room to place themselves between Agalia and their fallen companions.

"Impossible." Agalia gasped as she shook her head. "You cannot use your magic against me. I'm of your world. You should have been destroyed!"

Silvayn smiled coldly. "You gave your soul to Voldaz. You are his creature now. When that happened, you were no longer of our world. You belong to this one now."

Her eyes narrowed, and her hands snapped up in front of her. "So be it." Twin cones of shimmering red light erupted from her hands, striking Noria and Begeron. The energy hurled both warriors backward with a clatter of armor. Silvayn chanted in the language of magic. His voice reached a crescendo. Before he could release his spell, Agalia cast again. This time, the beam struck Silvayn in the chest. White light flooded over him and protected him from her magic, but he paled from the effort. With a wide-eyed grimace, Agalia raised her hands to strike at him again.

A dagger whistled through the air and struck her upraised right arm. She screamed and staggered back as she tore at the piercing blade. Jayrne's next dagger ripped a gash in Agalia's leg. She yanked the knife from her arm and advanced on Jayrne, who was still on her knees. Flecks of spittle dotted her lips as she growled her rage.

Elac tightened his grip on the pommel of Sir Draygen's ancient sword. He leaped to his feet. Three quick steps put him directly behind the priestess of Voldaz. His blade descended and struck at an angle against the base of her neck. The stroke cut diagonally through her torso and left a foot-long rent in her body. Blood splashed across his chest as she crumpled to the floor.

Elac rushed to Jayrne's side. She was bruised and bleeding from several places, but she assured him she was fine. He insisted on inspecting her wounds before he allowed her to stand.

Their companions gathered around. They stood over the body of the fallen High Priestess of Voldaz.

"We have done it, Silvayn." Noria raised a fist in triumph. "The enemy is defeated."

Silvayn shook his head. "Not yet. We must destroy Archon's Gate. Until then, creatures may still cross over to our side."

"How do we do that?" Elac asked.

"First, we take away the source of its power." He crossed the room and hefted the black orb from the altar. "I thought this was destroyed, long ago."

"What is it?" Jayrne asked.

"The Orb of Malator. Somehow, she recovered it from the ruins of Malaton and turned it to her own dark purpose. Now, only one thing remains. You four must travel through the Gate and return to Pelacia. Once you are through, I will destroy the altar. The Gate will be forever closed."

"Silvayn, no!" Elac took the old mage by the arm. "Pelacia needs you! There must be another way!"

Silvayn smiled and placed a reassuring hand on Elac's shoulder. "No, my friend, this is the only way. I knew it as soon as we entered the temple. The altar must be destroyed. When that happens, the Gate will close. I'll be trapped on this side."

"But what of the other Gates?" Tears stood in Elac's eyes. "Can't we destroy this Gate and use one of the others to travel back?"

"Elac. Your heart is great. But I don't believe anyone could survive the forces that will be unleashed when I destroy this altar. There is no other way to end this."

"Yes there is, Silvayn." Noria stepped forward, her face battered but proud. "This is the moment I have waited for. Let me do it! With this one act, I can vindicate my father's legacy and allow his spirit to complete its journey into the afterlife. This is what I was meant to do!"

For a moment, Elac thought Silvayn would argue. But something passed wordlessly between the warrior and the mage. Silvayn clasped hands with Noria in a warrior's salute. Jayrne sobbed softly, but Elac held her back. Something deep down inside his heart told Elac this was meant to be.

With the Orb of Malator tucked under one arm, Silvayn led the way to the shimmering wall that was Archon's Gate. Through the portal, Elac saw the battle before the walls of Palim. The battered gates stood open, and fighting raged in the streets. Their viewpoint fanned around the site of battle. To the west of the city, a separate fight raged near the edge of the enemy camp. A contingent of soldiers from Pelacia had been surrounded. An army of Kobolds battled their way through the Wyborn lines in an apparent attempt to free the Pelacians from the trap. Armored Human knights rode a short distance away from the battle, turned, and charged back in. The armored horses trampled the enemy beneath their hooves.

Elac looked around his circle of friends. They each clasped hands with Noria, and Jayrne gave her a fierce hug. Then Silvayn, Begeron, Jayrne, and Elac stepped through the Gate.

#

Elac fell to one knee as vertigo assailed him. He surveyed his surroundings. They had returned to Pelacia in the midst of the battle for Palim. Judging by the enormous tents erected nearby, they must have landed in the command center of the enemy camp. Several soldiers bearing pikes shouted at their sudden appearance and surrounded them, weapons lowered. Begeron tried to identify himself but was shouted down.

A tremendous explosion rocked the plains. For several hundred yards in all directions, the force of the blast threw men to the ground. Elac had the wind knocked from his lungs. He rolled to his back and lay gasping for air. The sounds of battle abated. All that broke the silence of the darkening skies was the cries of the wounded. Elac turned his eyes to the Gate that had returned them all to Pelacia, but it was gone. Noria had succeeded.

From the ruins of the decimated commanders' tents, two armored men emerged. With a circle of bodyguards, they approached Elac and the others.

One stopped, eyes open wide. "Captain Begeron? What is the meaning of this?"

Begeron sat up and coughed. He could not stand, so he crashed his fist to his chest in salute where he sat. "General Hosgrow." He rubbed his eyes and looked around. "Sir, I guess we have some explaining to do."

EPILOGUE

The cool, crisp wind whipped across the field. Although spring had arrived, winter had not entirely released its hold on the land. The wind had a bitter chill to it. Three months had passed since the battle before the walls of Palim. To Elac, it seemed like yesterday. He still remembered the sickening carnage of the wounded and slain. Countless thousands had given their lives in a pointless struggle.

Nothing had changed as a result of the brief war between Wyborn and Pelacia. Neither side gained ground. The affair weakened both continents. Wyborn's king had been slain, foully murdered by the forces of the deceptive High Priestess of Voldaz. His son, who had survived the battle, sat on his throne. Despite the fact that the army of Wyborn had been deceived into propagating the war against Pelacia, feelings of distrust and even hatred between Wyborn and Pelacia would run deeply for many years to come. The Orb of Malator had been secured within the vaults of the Aleria School of Magic, but it could not be destroyed. Even with the evil artifact under heavy guard, Elac feared it was still a threat to the lands.

The return of Elac and his friends had come too late to prevent the battle, but at least they had stopped the slaughter. The arrival of the Kobold army had tipped the balance of power and brought the promise of wholesale slaughter on both sides. The destruction of the Gate provided the distraction needed to temporarily halt the war. Once Begeron explained the treasonous actions of Agalia, which had caused the invasion to proceed in the first place, the two sides negotiated a temporary truce. A true peace accord would be agreed upon in the coming months, but at least for the time being, the invaders had left. To date, there had been no reprisals by either side. On the day following the Battle of Palim, soldiers discovered a large quantity of Wyborn coins in the possession of Duke Adroc. The reason for his opposition to mobilization and his refusal to open the gates for Hadwyn became clear. The army hanged him as a traitor the next day.

Elac had come to pay his respects to a fallen friend. *Actually, make that two fallen friends.* Jayrne stood at his side, their hands clasped as one. Hadwyn and Gillen stood together to one side, with Rilen and Adalyn to the other. Silvayn knelt before them. He placed a golden medallion upon a mound of earth surmounted by a granite stone. The winged panther emblem, symbolic of the family of Princess Noria, had been engraved near the top of the stone. To the left, a similar emblem marked the gravesite of Prince Cassius.

"Noria gave her life to see a great evil destroyed," Silvayn said. "She did so willingly, even knowing that her mortal remains would never find their way back to her home. Her body is lost to us, but not her heart. Her memory will walk with us forever.

"It is with great honor that I award Noria the Golden Shield of Valor, the highest award given to a warrior of Palindom. Wherever she is, she can rest easy knowing that the peace we now live is her peace. She has truly brought honor upon her name, her father's name, and that of her family for generations to come."

Hadwyn wept openly. Elac had tears in his eyes as he placed his right hand over his heart. "Sleep well."

Hadwyn placed a hand on Elac's shoulder. "I don't believe she is dead, my friend."

"Hadwyn, I . . . Silvayn said there was no way to survive the destruction of the Gate."

"You managed. And you were as close at your end as she was at hers. I will never give up the search until I find her and bring her home."

"You're serious about this?"

"I am, Elac. I've even given up drinking."

"Really?"

"No." Hadwyn managed to laugh. "But I will find her. And that's a promise."

They turned back to the gravestones, watching as the setting sun bathed the granite markers in crimson fire.

About the author:
Scott Gamboe was born and raised in Peoria, IL. He has been a police officer since 1998, where he currently serves as a crime scene investigator. He spent four years in the Army, where he was a paratrooper in the 82nd Airborne Division, participating in the 1989 parachute invasion of Panama, and Operation Desert Shield / Desert Storm the following year. He currently resides in Edwards, IL, with his wife, Jill, and his daughter, Erica.

Discover other titles by Scott Gamboe at

www.scottgamboe.net

The Killing Frost

The Piaras Legacy

New Dawn Rising

Martyr's Inferno

Titles by Rick Taubold at

www.ricktaubold.com

More Than Magick

Vampires, Inc.

Vampires, Anonymous